I0616030

HEIR OF
AFALLON

HEIR OF AFALLON

*STRANGER MAGICS,
BOOK ELEVEN*

ASH FITZSIMMONS

This is a work of fiction. Names, characters, places, and incidents are products of the author's imagination or are used fictitiously and are not to be construed as real. Any resemblance to actual events, locales, organizations, or persons, living or dead, is entirely coincidental.

HEIR OF AFALLON. Copyright © 2021 by Ash Fitzsimmons.

All rights reserved. No part of this book may be used or reproduced in any manner whatsoever without written permission except in the case of brief quotations embodied in critical articles and reviews.

Print Edition ISBN: 978-1-949861-27-3

Cover design by BespokeBookCovers.com

www.ashfitzsimmons.com

CHAPTER 1

I told myself that there was no reason for me to be nervous. The chocolate bombe couldn't have turned out more perfectly—I'd made two, and Marcus had deemed the spare a triumph between happy groans. The ganache was smooth and almost flawless, the raspberry filling balanced just so between sweet and tart (the Chambord helped), and I'd topped it all with delicate gold leaf, which made for a pretty, if perhaps ostentatious, presentation. Barring a sudden-onset chocolate allergy, there was no reason for the Audleys to be anything less than impressed. They were always complimentary of my attempts, even the carrot cake that had still been a bit runny at the center, and the bombe was a new high from my kitchen.

But no matter how much I tried to reassure myself, my palms continued to sweat as I rode the elevator down to their apartment, and my stomach flopped with anticipation. These visits were never easy.

"Get it together, Kitty," I muttered as the doors opened with a *ding*.

The seven-hour time difference between Arc 1 in rural Montana and Arc 2 in Glastonbury didn't help my appetite, which was a crying shame. Piper Audley, my dad's second cousin, was an excellent cook, the kind who could take a recipe and tweak it into something spectacular. She taught chemistry at the county high school down the road from Arc 1, a wizard who'd run off to get a PhD before returning to the security of Arcanum installation life. "Truth be told," she'd confessed to me during our first dinner, "I was *so* disappointed when I realized that potions weren't actually a common thing. Chemistry helped scratch that itch."

Her husband, Jacob, had taken a more traditional career path, staying in the silo after high school and working his way onto the security team. He was gregarious, a fast talker with a quick smile and ready laugh—and if the reports were accurate, he was even quicker with a wand. But Jacob seldom brought up his work over dinner, instead devoting his energies toward corralling their young daughters, Emilia and Clara, who were far more interested in their dolls than in eating with the boring grownups.

I didn't blame them. No matter how much Jacob tried to keep the conversation going or how often Piper volunteered a story about the latest near-casualty from her clueless students, our monthly dinners were uncomfortable affairs at best.

I would have been willing to give up the exercise as unpleasant and futile, but Piper had insisted as one of their conditions for taking my sister in. "These two hardly know each other," she'd told Grand Magus Pavli, sitting between Beth and me as my sister pretended I didn't exist. "I understand the, uh…*situation*…but I'm not okay with letting them write each other off just yet."

The grand magus had concurred, and dinner at the Audleys' had become a permanent fixture on my calendar—a home-cooked meal from my distant relatives, plus a monthly reminder that I was worse than dead to Beth.

Officially, my little sister lived with me for thirty-two days, but that tally was too high. She slept in my spare bedroom for twenty-eight days, and the remainder of her brief occupancy was chaos.

I tried to make her welcome. It wasn't Beth's fault that

we were hardly more than strangers—our mother had intended to keep us apart, going out of her way to make sure that Beth wanted nothing to do with me. Aside from a few brief weeks when I was ten and Beth was a newborn, we'd never lived together; I'd grown up on our dad's farm in Tennessee until he dropped dead, and then Mom had quickly packed me off to boarding school in Glastonbury. She was a busy magus with a baby, after all, second in command over Arc 1, and I was barely a witch, an untalented embarrassment to the family. I'd only made matters worse during my first year at Arc 2: not only had I failed to develop talent worthy of a magus's daughter, but I'd become best friends with Maria Corelli, an orphaned, new-blooded wizard of exceptional ability who'd stuck up for me when a clique of our schoolmates had decided to drive out the witch in their midst. I hadn't given a damn that Maria was actually witch-blooded, let alone being raised by one of the Three in Faerie. As my situation in Glastonbury had worsened, her guardian, Lord Valerius, had stepped in where my mother should have been, generally seeing to my needs and insisting that I sleep over with Maria for my own safety. That I'd been consorting with faeries was the last straw for Mom, who'd refused to have me back to Montana for a single school holiday. She'd destroyed the letters that I'd sent to Beth in an effort to be *some* part of my baby sister's life, and when I'd finally had a chance to see Beth, Mom had threatened me away. I wasn't good for little Beth—I was the witch who'd made unforgiveable alliances and had the audacity to take an Arcanum job instead of disappearing into the sunset like my less talented peers, and if Beth wanted to make the right connections and someday be a magus like Mom, then I was nothing but an anchor to her.

It stung like hell, but what was I to do? Beth was ten years my junior and still lived with Mom—it wasn't as if I could have popped by the silo to say hi and take her out for coffee and a chat.

But then the bomb had dropped. Mom had been conspiring with the renegade Conclave as they attempted to start their own arcanum, ours having been "polluted" by our witch-blooded grand magus. She'd stolen from the Archives, and in the process, she and former magus Francine Leighton had attacked Maria and left her to die. Maria had recovered—she was far closer to fae now than she had been, but she was alive and intact—and Mom and Leighton had been taken into custody as the Conclave crashed down.

For once, I wasn't our greatest familial embarrassment. My mother was a traitor and accomplice to attempted murder, and though I hadn't seen Maria's injuries, what I'd heard after the fact left me nauseated. But even if I had no great love for Mom, she was still my mother, which made matters tricky. On the one hand, if I started to feel the slightest bit of concern for her, my guilt rose up like a hammer blow—she'd tried to kill *Maria*. On the other, though I loved Maria like a sister, my wavering conscience niggled that I should care more for my actual blood, no matter how little said blood cared for me.

While I tried to sort through my feelings, Beth had a more pressing problem: with Mom incarcerated and awaiting trial, she had no one to look after her. Since a thirteen-year-old couldn't be left to fend for herself, the grand magus had decided to place her with family…and by default, that meant me.

I'm sure that Toula meant well in the placement, but Beth made it clear from the outset that she wanted nothing to do with me. I couldn't entirely blame her—she'd been yanked from the only home she'd known in the silo and plopped into the guest bedroom of a virtual stranger on another continent. The plan was for her to go to school at Arc 2 as well, so she'd be leaving behind her friends from Montana and starting over in a place where news of her mother would almost immediately make the rounds. That alone would have been miserable for Beth, and making her live with *me* only compounded the problem.

But I tried to get to know her. Ted Girard, my avuncular boss on the Away Team, was more than generous when I asked for time off, and I spent Beth's first days in Glastonbury hanging out in the flat, occasionally coaxing her out of her room for quick tours of the castle and the highlights around town. She claimed to hate everything about Arc 2 and Glastonbury in general, though I didn't entirely buy that; windows, at least, must have been a pleasant novelty to someone who had grown up underground. But she picked at her meals in the castle's cavernous dining hall, grumbled when I tried to show her the nearby historical sites, and said little to me. I couldn't even tempt her out to go to the movies.

Truth be told, I could have used some friendly faces that month, but I knew that wouldn't have improved the situation. Beyond helping me move Beth's belongings over—there was no way that I could have made a gate between the installations by myself—Maria kept her distance, giving me occasional glances in the dining hall but otherwise staying out of Beth's line of sight. The rest of the Team made sporadic passes by our table—Frank, a mind reader of the first order, took to sitting across the room and asking for updates while I ate—but they, too, knew to give us space. To my surprise, however, I found that the person whose company I missed the most was Marcus.

I couldn't choose a word to fully describe our relationship. Val's son and Maria's distant ancestor, mentally about my age but technically over twenty-two-hundred years old, a quarter-blooded faerie frozen in stasis and buried alive until I'd stumbled onto him just a few months before...Marcus was, well, *complicated*. For the five months after his rude awakening, he'd made the best of his situation, coming to terms with his power, his newfound position as heir to one of the three faerie courts, and his sudden loss of everyone and everything he'd known and loved. Marcus's world no longer made sense, and he had approximately ten trillion questions. Maria had her own problems to work through at the time, but fortunately, Marcus and I got along just fine.

Once he understood how to use it, he took full advantage of my phone number, shooting me enquiries at all hours of the day (and apologizing once he realized how frequently the realms didn't synchronize watches). Even if I couldn't make gates, he soon picked up the knack, and he found creative excuses to come over to my place. I didn't mind—I knew he had to be lonely, and I enjoyed his company. In July, we borrowed an Arcanum car and set off on a driving tour of England and Scotland, me playing tour guide and him marveling at the world (and occasionally, despite my admonitions, sticking his head out the window to feel the rushing air). On our return, Ted let him come with us to Peru, a test run that eventually earned him a spot on the Team.

Marcus made me laugh. He made me feel clever and appreciated, and even if he seldom mentioned it, the way he watched me made me feel pretty, which hadn't happened to me often. I started to miss him when he wasn't around.

But he understood as well as I did that it wouldn't help matters with my sister if Beth knew I'd been entertaining faerie lords, and so he stayed away—physically, at least. His messages continued, sometimes to pose more of the usual questions, but increasingly to ask how we were surviving each other.

Survival was really the best we could do that month. Young and scared, Beth latched on to me as a convenient focus for her anger, and she lashed out with growing frequency—never with her wand, thank goodness, but her shouting was painful enough. Though I'd had nothing to do with Mom's situation, Beth blamed me for her imprisonment in the Arc 2 dungeon, and my efforts to defend myself fell on deaf ears. I breathed a sigh of relief when Beth started school at the end of August, if for no other reason than the respite it gave me from the accusatory silence of her locked bedroom door. But if I'd expected school to brighten her mood, I was disappointed; Beth stormed in and slammed her door after class, ignoring the snack I'd had waiting for her, and turned up her music when I tried to ask her about her day. I'm sure the Team knew I was a mess when I returned to work— Frank was known for selectively sharing intel, even if my face didn't give it away—and they were kind, leaving me to work in peace in my office aside from periodic offers of tea or food. At one point, Frank simply dropped several pounds of chicken fingers on my desk without explanation, which, coming from our resident obligate carnivore, was a heartfelt offering.

The situation hadn't improved by September, and I was preparing myself for a long standoff with Beth when there came a knock at the flat door one Monday evening. I found Maria and Marcus in the hall, both bearing plastic bags from an Indian place in town. "Chana masala, medium, and loads of extra naan," she said in greeting. "May we come in?"

Within minutes, we'd cleared the kitchen table and begun sharing the bounty—all but Marcus's extra-hot curried goat, which no one else was keen to try. As I was telling the others about Ted's tentative autumn travel plans for the Team, I heard Beth's door squeal open, and she poked her head into the main room, frowning. "Hey," I said, waving her over with a piece of naan. "Do you like curry? The tikka masala is super-mild, if spice isn't your thing."

Beth didn't move. "What's *she* doing here?" she asked, pointing to Maria.

Maria's dark eyebrows rose, and I took a deep breath, praying for patience. "Magus Corelli is my best friend," I told Beth. "Let's not be an asshole, okay?"

"Seriously," Maria added, "there's way too much food

here. Come on, join us. You can keep sulking, if you'd like, but at least eat dinner."

My sister hesitated on the threshold a moment longer, eyeing the takeaway containers while we continued to eat, then marched to the table and sank into the empty chair with a pained sigh. I started to rise to get another plate from the cupboard, but Marcus, not thinking, gestured one into existence on Beth's placemat. She pushed back from the table in alarm, staring at the plate as if it had grown fangs, and Marcus dropped his plastic fork as he realized what he'd done. "Oh…um…sorry," he mumbled. "There are others in the kitchen—"

"Who the hell are you?" she interrupted.

"That's Marcus," I said, trying to keep my tone light. "Remember? He stopped by on your first day here."

But the light of recognition had dawned in Beth's wide eyes, and I knew the night was lost. An Arcanum education included at least enough about the courts to give young wizards a healthy fear of them. My introduction had involved photographs of the Three, and I assumed Beth's had as well—and there was no getting around the fact that Marcus looked *very* much like his father.

Beth jumped from the table, pointing and sputtering. I heard Maria sigh and whisper, "Moon and stars," under her breath, but I tried to initiate damage control. "He's a friend of mine, too," I told Beth, raising my voice and moving between them. "Calm down. He's not going to hurt you—"

She wheeled on me, and I saw then that her sputtering was due more to rage than fear. "You're the damn traitor, not Mom!" she spat, then stormed from the room.

Marcus apologized profusely and departed as soon as the leftovers were packed into my fridge. Maria sat with me for a time while I tried to wait Beth out, but she eventually took her leave, and I went to bed.

When I awoke to make a peace offering breakfast, Beth was gone, as were her backpack, purse, and small electronics—and, I soon discovered, the hundred quid I'd stashed in my rainy-day cookie jar. I ran straight to Toula, who cleared her calendar, pulled Mom's blood sample from the collection in one of the Arcanum's many storage rooms, and spent the morning setting up a trace on Beth with the help of an ensorcelled map. After a few hours, she tracked her to London and sent a security team to retrieve her.

Late that afternoon, reunited with the half of my cash not spent on lunch and bus fare, I sat a few feet away from my sister in the grand magus's office while Beth informed her in furious terms that she would *not* be returning to my flat. "You can't make me," she told Toula. "I'll just keep running away."

I'm sure that Toula would have had her ways of keeping Beth on a leash, but seeing as Beth and I were both miserable, she caved. A search through the family records uncovered the Audleys and a few more farther-flung cousins, and I suggested that it might be for the best if Beth were sent back to the silo.

Piper was all kindness when she and Jacob moved Beth out a few days later. Once again, Maria did the honors with the gate, and she stood by and watched as Beth shoved her things into boxes and carried them into her new room in Montana, never so much as acknowledging my presence. "Let's pick a date for dinner in a couple of weeks, eh?" said Piper as her husband ferried the last of Beth's belongings away. "Give all of this a little while to cool down."

I agreed, and she hugged me when she left. Maria hugged me, too, as she closed the gate and left me alone in my quiet flat. The spare room still smelled like Beth's hairspray, the duvet still bore the wrinkles from her halfhearted attempt to make her bed, but the only sound I could hear was my own heartbeat in my ears.

That night, as I was lying in bed and listening to the silence, a wild urge to make cookies came over me.

This might have been a reasonable reaction for some people, but I'd never attempted anything more challenging than break-and-bake. My dad hadn't been a great cook, and with the Arcanum having provided the majority of my meals since then, I'd never had a real need to learn. Still, like most irrational midnight thoughts, this one was unassailable in the moment: if I could make cookies, everything would be okay.

And so I got up, found a recipe, begged the ingredients from the late-night kitchen staff, and set about my grand baking experiment. The recipe I'd chosen was written by an American—I had to guess at measurements, and my oven didn't offer any indication as to what the temperature might be in Fahrenheit—but I sallied on, confident that I would succeed.

Half an hour later, as I removed the smoking, charcoaled result from the oven, something inside me started to crumble. But before I could poke at the disastrous lumps in a hunt for a less carbonized bit, my phone beeped.

Not an emergency. What does penguin taste like, fish or fowl?

I called Marcus back. "Sorry, did I wake you?" he said on answering. "I thought you'd see that in the morning—"

"I don't know," I told him, my throat tightening. "There's a lot of fat on them, but I don't know about the meat. Might taste fishy. Were you going to get one and find out? Don't do that, they're cute."

Marcus hesitated. "Are you all right, Kitty?"

"Burned my cookies," I mumbled, and burst into tears.

A moment later, as I cried into my hands, I heard the crack of an opening gate, then felt Marcus's arms around me. He held me until my sobs dwindled to the occasional hitching breath, then murmured, "This isn't about the cookies, is it?"

I shook my head.

"Beth?" My sniffle was answer enough, and he tightened his hold as I rested my head against his shoulder. "She's young. You said yourself that she's going through a difficult time—"

"I'm a failure. I can't do anything right, I…I'm such a—"

"Kitty, *no*." He pulled back until I raised my wet face to his. "How are you a failure? Your sister doesn't like you? Fine. Since when is that the ultimate mark of success?"

"But—"

"Why does a stupid thirteen-year-old girl get to decide your worth?" he pressed, his consternation mounting. "What does anyone know at thirteen? Maybe it was different for you," he allowed, "but I don't remember being particularly wise at that age. She's an angry child, not the arbiter of failure."

"I failed *her*," I protested.

"No, you didn't. And let's balance the scales—I owe you everything. *Everything*," he said more slowly. "You could burn the damn castle down with those, uh…"—he flapped one hand toward the smoky kitchen—"attempted cookies, and I still wouldn't think you a failure."

I tried to smile. "You're biased."

"As is everyone. *Especially* Beth. So let her sulk in peace—you're not responsible for her happiness." With that, he released me and nodded to the kitchen. "Do you want help with the disposal?"

"Not even going to try them?" I teased.

Marcus sighed. "I will if it'll make you stop crying." He glanced over his shoulder at the pan of blackened cookies, then grimaced. "Are there any even slightly underdone?"

Finally, I smiled in earnest. As I washed my face, he sent the offending batch off the baking sheet and into the ether—much simpler than my original plan of chiseling them free—and opened a window to clear the air. When I returned from the bathroom, the kitchen was clean, and Marcus was busy angling my standing fan to best vent the smoke. "Go to bed," he urged. "It's under control."

"Nah."

"*Nah?*"

I shook my head and opened the fridge. "Going to try again. I've got enough eggs and milk."

While I bustled around the kitchen, gathering my supplies for the second attempt, Marcus watched warily from the other room, then propped his elbows on the bar counter and waited until I'd retrieved my recipe on my computer before asking, "Do you want company?"

The last thing I wanted was to be alone, but I tried not to let on. "If you're bored."

"I could be."

He observed from a safe distance while I whipped around one stainless steel implement after another, using a spare computer to run the necessary conversions for me. By one that morning, a halfway respectable batch of cookies had emerged from my oven, and he stole a sample for the road as he pushed me toward my bedroom, muttering, "Delicious. A success. *Sleep.*"

And for some strange reason, I did, well and deeply.

Piper gave me periodic updates on my sister's progress. Beth was quiet and moody, obedient to her guardians but withdrawn. Her bedroom door stayed closed, and the Audley girls knew not to bother her. School had resumed in Montana, and she was off to an inauspicious start, forgetting homework assignments and pulling detention in her second week when she and one of the other silo girls got into a hair-pulling shouting match in the hallway. In her hunt for an explanation, Piper had spoken to the other teachers from the silo, anyone familiar with Beth's class, and had come to a disquieting conclusion. By all accounts, Beth had been popular in previous years, especially among the silo kids. Now, the wizards avoided her as if our mother's situation were catching, and the mundanes, perhaps smelling blood in the water, had begun to treat her as persona non grata, too.

At the end of September, I made my first trip to the Audleys' for dinner, bringing a bottle of wine as a token. Piper and Jacob were gracious, Emilia and Clara were wriggly and eager to show off their toys to the stranger in their midst, and Beth pretended I wasn't there. When she spoke at all, it was to one of the Audleys, and as soon as she could, she returned to her room and locked the door.

"It'll get better," Piper assured me, escorting me back to Magus Johansson's office for a gate home. "It's hard enough being her age without piling everything else on top. But don't worry, these things tend to work themselves out."

Still, I fretted—over Beth, over Mom, over my role in the whole mess. I sat at my kitchen bar with a cup of tea in the wee hours until I couldn't take it any longer, and then I trekked to the dining hall.

When Marcus dropped by to check on me the next morning, I had yet to sleep, but my chocolate cake had turned out nicely, and I was trying to pipe flowers onto the top with a plastic sandwich bag. He gave me a once-over—the wild hair, the flour-dusted apron, the streak of dried chocolate frosting on my cheek—then pulled up a seat and conjured forth a cup of coffee. "Company?"

"Please," I said, and returned to my labor.

Food soon became my consolation. Every recipe through which I fumbled and still managed to produce a passable result was proof that I had control over my life. Oh, I knew it was unhealthy—all I was doing was channeling my familial anxieties into pies and roasts—but the exercise was, in some weird way, soothing.

October passed. Beth's grades dropped. The Council's investigation team continued to uncover witnesses against Mom. I turned my hand to meringues, to soufflés, to a quest for the perfect scrambled egg. Every failure was a crushing blow, every success a triumph.

And through it all, Marcus stuck around.

I told myself that he was lured by the prospect of food. At that point, he'd experienced a whopping seven months of the twenty-first century, and he was still marveling over such culinary wonders as pre-sliced bread and tubs of rocky road. When I expressed this to Maria, however, she rolled her eyes. "He's not in it for the pastry," she said, giving me an odd look.

"He *likes* my pastry," I pointed out.

She patted my hand and smirked. "Incidental benefit."

Maria could make whatever innuendos she liked. Marcus never made a move, and I was content with our relationship…whatever sort of friendship it was.

By the end of October, he had become my quasi-flatmate by mutual, tacit agreement. Ted had taken him out in the field again, and when he showed both interest in our work and promise, Ted paired him with Antony, a former Arcanum librarian, to begin the basics of research. The learning curve was steep, and Marcus spent many an evening at my kitchen table, grumbling over the atrocities committed to his mother tongue during the Middle Ages, but he persevered as I made mess after mess at the stove.

Beth still refused to speak to me at that month's dinner, but my prosciutto-wrapped dates were well received by the rest of the table.

The British autumn hurried toward dark winter. Maria's secondhand reports from the Council's investigatory committee suggested that Mom and Leighton would have neighbors in the dungeon before long. Beth slapped a girl upside the head in view of three teachers and got two days' suspension. My ratatouille wasn't bad, but it needed more garlic.

One night, I looked up from the cutting board to find Marcus watching intently as I diced vegetables for a mirepoix. "Want to try?" I offered, wiping away the onion tears with my sleeve. "You'll probably want to come up with a knife in something other than steel if you do."

He stiffened, taken aback. "*Me?*"

"Only if you want. It's kind of cathartic as long as you don't slice your fingers."

As he regarded the half-chopped vegetables with caution, I realized the problem. "You've never cooked, have you?"

"*Slightly* too patrician for that."

"Uh-huh. Watch and learn."

The mirepoix was long finished by the time he felt like he had a handle on it—as was the rest of the dish—but the next evening, he enchanted copies of my knives in ceramic for himself and bravely attacked potatoes.

That was the start of our new routine: work all day, cook in the evening, rest and repeat. Thanks to his age and fae blood, Marcus needed far less sleep than I did, and I began to wake to his own early-morning experiments, eggs and pancakes and other dishes pulled from the stack of splattered printouts on the counter. He was quietly proud of himself, and I was quietly grateful that he'd learned by observation how to avoid smoking up the flat.

I brought a maple-drizzled pecan pie to the Audleys' Thanksgiving dinner, a hit with the girls but predictably ignored by Beth. She barely spent half an hour at the table before returning to her room and blasting her music through the too-thin door, and Piper shrugged at her antics. "She's got a book report due when she gets back. Want to guess how much she's read?" she asked as Jacob served coffee.

In December, the Team took a week to clean and tidy our subterranean office suite and plan the first excursions for the new year. After a perfunctory vote, Marcus was offered a real spot and an office, finally allowing him to take his borrowed computer out of the conference room, and Lakshmi added "MVM" to the swarm of initials covering our trip calendars. We celebrated with a bottle of the cheapest sparkling wine we could find, just as we had when I'd come aboard. Some traditions were, after all, sacred, and getting lightly buzzed on bad hooch was a long-established Away Team ritual.

Just before Christmas, Mom's trial date was scheduled for April. I bawled like a baby that night, then begged Marcus not to tell Maria what I'd done. He hugged me as my cookies baked and swore himself to silence.

We did vary up the routine on occasion. After a few near misses in the mountains, Ted had strenuously encouraged the traveling members of the Team to practice on the climbing wall in the castle's expansive fitness center, so I put in my time in a harness while Marcus, paranoid about hidden steel in the gear, spotted from the floor. Sometimes, we took a long weekend off to drive around; I had a list of places I'd yet to see in the UK, and almost everything was new to him. Once a week or so, Marcus returned to Faerie to see Val, whose surreptitious check-in messages to me grew more frequent the longer his son was away.

And then there were the wine nights.

We never scheduled them. A quick look at each other was usually all it took to scuttle the evening's plans and open a bottle—no questions asked, no complaints made. We'd grab a couple of glasses and sit in front of the silent television, and as needed, we'd talk.

Beth had our mother's hair, but her features were close to Daddy's, and it killed me every time I imagined him looking at me with disgust through her. I told Marcus about the old farm in Tennessee, about running through fields of sunflowers taller than my head, a bobbing forest towering above me. I poured, and drank, and told him of the time I'd made the long walk down our dirt farm road to the paved street, where the mailbox had been planted, and when I'd returned to the house, arms laden with catalogues and flyers for the new grocery store one town over, Daddy had been motionless on the ground, staring blankly at the water stain on the kitchen ceiling. I could still hear the thud of the mail as it fell onto the linoleum. I told him about sputtering an almost incoherent cry for help into the phone, and then about kind old Sheriff Dooley, who looked like a skinnier version of Santa but had strength enough in him to pry me off my father's body as I kicked and howled. I remembered the hard plastic of the chair in his office, rough against the back of my summer-bare legs, and the rattling of the window air conditioner when he called Mom at the number Daddy had stored in his phone: *Is this Eva Connolly? Ma'am, I'm very sorry to have to tell you this, but something's happened to your husband...* And I'd sat there, swinging my legs above the thin brown carpet, staring at the sheriff's metal desk, muttering, "Stanhope. My mom's name is Stanhope."

I told Marcus about having to spend two nights with the Dooleys because Mom couldn't get away from her very important job quickly enough. She'd come eventually, wearing Beth in a purple sling across her torso, and had signed the appropriate papers and made the necessary calls with thin-lipped disapproval. Mrs. Dooley had been the one to assure me that Daddy hadn't suffered. We'd buried him in the Methodist cemetery, and then Mom had impatiently helped me pack my things—mostly my many books—and took us to the silo. She'd made a bed for me on the couch and shoved my cardboard boxes of belongings against the wall in Beth's nursery, and then I'd been left largely to myself for the rest of the summer while she sold off Daddy's farm and made arrangements for me to be sent to Glastonbury and out of her sight.

Sometimes, I remembered the flush of shame during my wand ceremony and the sudden nausea as I'd feared I wouldn't merit even the strongest wand. Other times, it was the shame I felt that first year whenever I packed my bag for a holiday with Mom, only to be told that it wasn't a good time for a visit. I'd cried, abandoned and ashamed that my saving grace had been the kindness of strangers—

that no matter how hard I studied, how many exams I aced, how many times I made top marks in my classes, I couldn't figure out the trick to making Mom want me. And though Val had been wonderful to me, the void remained, the throbbing socket where the rotten tooth had been.

Marcus drank deeply and told me of his wife, Fabia, called Tertia due to her two elder sisters. She'd been the most beautiful of the three, dark-haired, slim-hipped, and with large eyes fringed with long lashes. Her heart had always belonged to his cousin Titus, but Marcus had been their grandfather's favorite, the orphaned child of his supposedly battle-dead son, and the old man had arranged the match.

He spoke of their wedding day, of Fabia's thick hair twisted and woven into a perfect tutulus beneath her yellow veil, of how her demurely downcast eyes had regarded him with resignation that night as he unknotted her belt. She had been a proper wife, the picture of good breeding and high birth in public, but there had been nothing but duty between them in bed.

When he drank enough, sometimes he wondered aloud how she had been with Titus—how different it must have been when there was passion in her touch. They must have met in secret for months, Fabia stealing time, Titus pining for her in continued bachelorhood. Marcus didn't know what they had done to escape the household slaves' notice, but he never heard so much as a rumor of his wife's infidelity.

But Publius *was* his son—Maria's aural signature contained a tiny copy of Marcus's, identifying them as links in a chain. Marcus had hoped that parenthood would improve his marriage, that Fabia would someday grow to love him, at least as the father of her children. Staring into the distance, wine forgotten, he told me of the first time he had laid eyes on the boy, a red and squirming bundle in a blanket, lying on the ground at the foot of the birthing bed. He'd taken the child in his arms, his chest tight and full to bursting, and had smiled to keep himself from crying with joy in front of the midwife. They had officially named him nine days later, though Marcus had already made it clear that the boy would bear his great-grandfather's name, and Marcus had put the baby's new gold bulla around his neck, even though it was still far too large for him. Publius would live and grow to manhood, his father had been sure of it—he'd trusted that the gods wouldn't be so cruel as to take from him both his parents and his firstborn.

And they hadn't. Fabia and Titus had, the very next night. The lovers had sold him out to local wizards, who, rightly fearing that the modest healing gift Marcus freely employed was the mark of fae blood, had put him into ensorcelled sleep and immured him in a stone coffin warning would-be rescuers away from the evil chained within.

Always speaking softly, he told me of those last terrifying moments, unable to move or make a sound, his eyes locked open and staring at the stars. Titus had offered a halfhearted apology. Fabia had said nothing in farewell. Soon enough, the world had gone black as his eyes were closed and he was forced into stasis…and when he saw light again, it had been in Maria's guest bedroom, thousands of miles and more than two millennia from the moment he'd left. He spoke of staggering to the window, the impossibly flawless glass, and seeing spread before him the distant lights of Glastonbury, the sky dusky with light pollution, the blinking flash of an airplane crossing the heavens, the shining wards around the castle. He'd been panicked by the disorientation of his abduction and awakening, which turned into paralyzing terror once he understood his predicament. Sweet Publius, asleep in his bed, was dust. His grandparents, uncles, cousins, friends…dust. And then there had come the pale-haired stranger with the unplaceable accent and the glowing tablet computer in her arms, who'd flipped on the overhead lights without a second thought.

I apologized again for that. He brushed it off, months removed from his fear of the fire exploding to life above him, but I still squirmed at the memory.

Some nights, when his thoughts circled toward their darkest places, he quietly confided that at times, he wished the wizards had just killed him. On those nights, we finished the wine and sat together on the couch, wrapped in afghans against the castle's chill, and I reminded him of everything he had to live for. I begged him to find a reason to keep getting out of bed. Sometimes, on those nights, he'd release the tears he usually kept so well dammed up, and I'd hold him while he wept for a dead world.

And in the morning, we'd peel ourselves off the couch, deal with our headaches, and go about the complicated business of living.

Winter began its slow thaw into a rainy spring. When the Team went to Thailand to look for an allegedly fire-shooting ring, Marcus and I took a side excursion to wander through a rural market and buy spices. We learned to make half a dozen curries. Beth pulled all Cs on her report card before spring break and completed her progress toward becoming a recluse, leaving her bedroom only for class and meals. Piper practically had to beg her to go to her night classes in magical theory and practice.

In late March, I admitted to myself that my feelings toward Marcus were veering dangerously far from friendship, but I never said a word. There was no need to further complicate matters between us. I saw him almost every day and night—what point would there have been in trying to put a label on…whatever this was? Besides—and purely in the hypothetical—even if I'd pressed him for something more definite, I knew that a relationship wasn't in the cards. The heir to a court and the witch with a murderously traitorous mother—yeah, *that* wasn't going to happen.

But I enjoyed his company—in our office suite as he cursed at his computer, in my kitchen as he stepped up his sous chef game—and as Mom's trial neared, I began to crave it. Marcus seemed to understand, and he was never far from me that April, a shield against the strange looks and whispers in the castle's corridors. He was there with wine when I needed it, and when I rose with insomnia at two in the morning to make a pot roast, he was on hand with a peeler for the carrots.

I didn't attend Mom and Leighton's three-day trial. Instead, I went alone to the grand magus's office during the second evening and asked Toula to spare my mother's life—no elaboration, no grand, tearful pleas, just a request. Toula, still wearing her formal robe and chain of office, considered that for a moment as I stood in silence before her desk, then softly said, "You're not being disloyal to Maria."

"Tell *her* that," I muttered.

"No need. I'll consider your input," she replied, and that was that—I did my duty.

The next day, both women were convicted of high treason and attempted murder. Toula sentenced them to life imprisonment in the castle dungeon—a mercy in some respects, though the defendants had, apparently, slumped in despair at the news. Unless the grand magus saw fit to bring them above ground someday, neither would ever again see sunlight.

Maria came straight to my flat, where Marcus had been waiting with me throughout the day, to deliver the news. "Are you disappointed?" I asked her, trying to summon any emotion beyond relief that the ordeal was over.

She shook her head. "Life in a hole would be hell to me. I mean, Eva's a silo native, but still, even *they* surface on occasion. Do you…" She paused, then shared a long look with Marcus.

Mental manipulation via magic comes far more easily to

the fae than it does to wizards—glamours, most obviously, the illusory cousin to the transformation bind, but also the ability to see into another's mind. I was powerless on that front, but my companions had mastered enough of their own talents to carry on a conversation without saying a word. But though I wasn't privy to the discussion, the message from Marcus was obvious that evening.

"You know, with the trial and everything, I've fallen behind in my marking, and Arnold's going to want the data on the second-years before long," said Maria. "Can we get dinner this weekend? Catch up?"

"Sure," I told her, and she saw herself out. Once she'd gone, I curled up against Marcus on the couch and stared at the wall, numb but for the sick feeling in my stomach as I wondered how Beth would take the news.

So there I stood, bombe in hand, and smiled as Piper gushed over my offering. "Is that *gold*?" she asked, peering closer as I took it from the translucent cake carrier. "Oh, gosh, that's so fancy. The girls are going to *die*." She tucked the carrier away in the laundry room and gave me a quick hug. "Happy birthday, by the way. Belated, but—"

"Thanks."

"What'd you do to celebrate?" she asked, returning to the kitchen to watch the fish grilling on the stovetop.

"Just dinner," I lied. I'd done nothing to mark the occasion—my birthday had fallen nine days before the start of Mom's trial, and though I'd baked up a storm all that week, I'd barely been able to eat a bite. Perhaps having received a report from Marcus, Maria had let me be and promised that we'd go out on the town later in May.

"That's nice." Piper added a bit more olive oil to the skillet and motioned Jacob closer as he came down the hall. "Check out dessert! It's too pretty to eat."

"Impressive," he declared, nodding solemnly. "Then I suppose we leave it on the counter until it rots, basking in its glory."

Piper rolled her eyes and swatted at him with a dishtowel. "Be useful and get the girls."

I stayed with her as Jacob summoned the others, delaying my sister's monthly glare for as long as I could. But Piper soon had dinner in bowls and on a platter, and I helped her carry it to the table, where Beth was waiting in silence.

"Hey," I said, forcing a smile as I put the rice down in front of her. "How's it going?"

No response was forthcoming, but then I'd expected nothing more.

We made it through dinner and dessert—as Piper had promised, the Audley girls squealed when they learned that the gold leaf was edible—and once they'd finished, their parents dismissed them. Beth had already taken her leave, as usual refusing to touch anything I'd brought, and so, relieved that the ordeal was wrapping up for another month, I helped Piper and Jacob pack the leftovers and tidy the kitchen.

"She's barely left her room since the trial ended," Piper confided, using the running sink to muffle our conversation. "Kid's taking it hard."

"Could have been worse," I muttered, scrubbing at the skillet.

"Could have been a whole lot better, too. Almost all of those Conclave people have been scheduled for parole checks, right? They're still walking around out here."

"Yeah," Jacob cut in. "I've got two of them reporting to me. It's pretty tightly organized—the GM's not messing around."

His wife snorted. "Considering what happened the *last* time a grand magus put traitors on parole…"

"From what senior security's been saying, I think Pavli's learned from her predecessors' mistakes." He paused, then patted my arm and nudged me out of position at the sink. "Why don't you go have a chat with

Beth, huh?"

"*Me?*" I replied. "She doesn't want to hear from me."

"But maybe she needs to," said Piper. "Go on, honey, we've got this. Ah—don't you *dare* point that wand at my cast iron!" she yelled at her husband as I slunk out of the room.

I dragged myself down the hall to Beth's bedroom, steeled myself, and knocked. "Beth? May I come in?" I called through the door.

"*No,*" she called back.

She'd neglected to flip the lock, however, and I had the door open as her hand was still groping on the duvet for her wand. "Five minutes," I promised, closing the door behind me. "I'm going."

Beth sat up and folded her arms. "*What?*"

"Nice to see you, too." I shoved my hands in my pockets and made myself meet her stare. "Look, I know things have been shitty, okay? I just wanted you to know that now that the trial and all is over, you can see Mom. The grand magus told me so. If you want to visit, they'll arrange it—"

That was as far as I got before her seething anger boiled over. "This is all your fault!" she railed. "You ruined *everything!* My life is over, *Mom's* in a dungeon, and you—"

"I asked that she not be executed," I snapped. "What else could I have done? They had her dead to rights!"

She gritted her teeth and glowered from across the room. "Mom was right, you know," she finally said, flushing with anger. "They should have drowned you like a runt puppy. That's what she's always said. You're nothing but an embarrassment, and now you've got Mom locked away. Happy?"

I took a deep breath, reminding myself that Beth was young and lashing out at a convenient target, but that didn't take the sting out of her words. "If you want to visit Mom, I can take you. Just let me know."

"I *hate* you," she said slowly, dragging each syllable out

for added impact. "Get out of my room."

There was more I could have said, other avenues I could have tried, but I saw her wand hand edging closer to its weapon, and so I left without another word.

I told the Audleys to keep what was left of the bombe, took my cake plate, and returned to Magus Johansson's office to go home. Her gate dropped me outside of Toula's office, and I wound my way through the castle's familiar stone corridors, quiet in the wee hours of the morning, until I reached the safety of my flat.

As usual, Marcus was waiting on the couch with tea. "How was it?" he asked as I latched the door and dropped my cake plate in the sink.

"They liked the bombe."

"And?"

I said nothing, but I heard the couch springs creak and soon found his arms around me. "You are so much more than what she thinks of you," he murmured, holding me close. "Please remember that."

"I want to make cookies."

"Tea first?"

I looked up, saw the strain of worry around his dark eyes, and nodded. "Sure. Tea would be nice."

CHAPTER 2

Three days later, I'd put the worst of that dinner behind me after several rounds of peanut butter blossom cookies and brought the spoils to the office. They'd gone over well with everyone but Bob, an older Brit who couldn't abide peanut butter, and Frank, whose tastes for anything beyond meat were unpredictable, but I wasn't bothered. Baking was therapeutic for me, and as long as someone helped me eat the end product, I was satisfied.

Ordinarily, Marcus would have helped, but he, Daphne, and Antony had gone on a quick jaunt to the Orkney Islands in search of a book cache while the weather was decent. Though I'd been up for the overnighter—even if camping was a pain, northern Scotland was beautiful—Ted had held me back in the office. "Two reasons," he'd explained once he'd sent the others off to pack. "One, I want to see how well Marcus gets along when you're not there for him to lean on. I don't think he'll have a problem playing nicely with those two, but I want to get him used to standing on his own."

I couldn't imagine him having problems with that duo. Antony, who was only a marginally more talented witch than I was, was a middle-aged father and one of the founding members of the Team, generally knowledgeable and reliable in the field. Daphne, a few years his senior, was a respectable wizard and cat mom, though she had a tendency to get overly excited about films and shows on the nerdier side of the pop spectrum, and she was eager to theorize about her favorites if given the slightest encouragement. Neither had been anything but kind as Marcus fumbled his way through his first outings.

"What's the second reason?" I'd asked.

Ted had flashed a guilty smile. "The monthly report is due to Maria, and I'm *swamped* right now, so is there any chance that you could—"

"Send me the data," I'd told him with a sigh. It wasn't the first time that Ted had foisted his homework onto me, and I'd doubted it would be the last.

At least I had a quiet office in which to work. Ted was surrounded by a book fort of his own construction; Lakshmi, our logistics expert, was away at a conference at Arc 7, leaving Bob on standby in case support was needed in the field; Frank was holed up somewhere deep in the library; and Mal had slipped home to Faerie for a few days' vacation. Mal, son of a half-fae father and a shifter mother, had a sprawling family who worried about him, and he took regular jaunts back across the border to reassure them that he was still alive and well. Frank, too, had a family on the other side, a mother and five siblings, but he'd been returning with less frequency the longer I'd known him, which surprised me. He needed to shake off the transformation bind and take wing every once in a while. Compressing more than two hundred feet of dragon into less than seven feet of quasi-human took considerable spellcraft, and he'd described the joy of release from its grip as taking off too-tight trousers after a feast. Still, Frank stayed busy, and I tried not to pry.

Armed with tea and a plate of my cookies, I set about condensing our activities into a manageable form, breaking down our work over the past month into numbers and narrative summaries. We'd had a productive spring already, and Ted had hinted during our last meeting that he had a few surprises in the works for the summer calendar. I was confident that Maria already knew most of what I was preparing for her records—unlike her predecessor, Magus Wold, she was intimately involved with the Team and seemed to enjoy the odd midnight call—but still, I prided myself on submitting quality work and dug in.

Two hours into the morning, I jumped when my phone began to ring and grabbed it, hoping nothing had gone awry up north. To my surprise, however, the caller wasn't Marcus, but rather his father. Frowning, I answered and spun my chair around, giving my eyes a break from the monitor's glare. "Val? Everything all right?"

"Hello, Kitty." Though his voice nearly matched Marcus's in timbre, Val's English was colored by two thousand years of speaking primarily Fae, whereas Marcus retained his accent from Rome. "Busy?"

"Nothing's burning," I replied, leaning back in my chair. "Are you looking for Marcus? He's gone to Orkney with—"

"Yes, I'm aware. Would you mind coming over? There's something I'd rather discuss in person."

"Uh...yes, sir, sure," I said, hastily sliding my shoes back on. "Um...I think the Council's meeting right now, but once Maria's free, I'll ask her to make the gate."

"No need."

A neat, lightning-bordered hole in the fabric of space appeared in midair between my desk and couch, widening until I could step through it without crouching. Through the gate, I saw Val sitting behind his desk, the windows around him too dark to reveal the villa's magnificent gardens or the mountains beyond. He smiled slightly and beckoned me through with two fingers, and I said, "One second, let me tell Ted I'm out."

Val waited while I typed a quick message to my boss, then rose and gestured toward the less formal side of his office, a comfortable couch and a pair of low-backed chairs around a coffee table. "Have a seat. We need to speak."

There are certain invitations that one does not ignore, and I hurried toward the chair he offered.

As the gate closed behind me, I briefly reflected on the

absurdity of the situation. To the average wizard—even a talented wizard—a faerie past his centennial is a frightening prospect. Magical talent increases over time, and so almost any wizard my age would have been outclassed by a decently trained faerie with a few centuries on him. Val was ancient and exceedingly well trained, and to make matters worse, he enjoyed a massive boost of power from the realm itself. Kingship had its perks, after all. But while any sane wizard would have considered a summons into Faerie, let alone into the private office of one of the Three, a cause for pants-wetting terror, I barely batted an eye. I'd lived under Val's roof throughout school—my room in the villa remained untouched, just in case—and he'd been more like a kindly uncle than a being out of a nightmare to me. I still didn't want to *cross* him, of course, but I wasn't overly concerned that I was about to be blasted into atoms.

"What's up?" I began, but I'd barely landed in the chair before I felt his delicate touch inside my mind. I stiffened with surprise—Val had checked up on Maria and me in that fashion when we were young, but he'd backed off in recent years at Maria's insistence. She had nothing to worry about, anyway, as she had the power and knowhow to block his intrusions, but as a witch, I couldn't mount a defense. It didn't *hurt*—the sensation was as soft as a fluttering wing and usually passed in a matter of seconds— but the fact that he'd invaded my privacy without preamble was cause for alarm.

As the sensation ceased, my heart began to race. Had Toula let slip that I'd asked for Mom to be spared? Had Val taken that as a betrayal of Maria? I was under the Arcanum's jurisdiction, sure, but that meant nothing if I was trapped in the heart of Faerie and Val decided to administer a little justice of his own…

Calm down, the realm whispered into my mind. *She hasn't said a word.*

Relief washed over me like a chill. *Hi, Ros*, I thought,

knowing she'd pick up on it.

Hi yourself. And he'd understand.

Let's not risk it, okay?

She laughed as she left me, and I waited in silence as Val sank onto the couch opposite me and steepled his fingers. I met his gaze and quickly glanced away. Older faeries' eyes were always unnerving in that they seemed subtly wrong for their youthful faces, and finding oneself to be their focal point set off deep, primal alarm bells. From a distance, Val and Marcus could have been brothers, but up close, there was no disguising the weight of ages behind Val's stare.

"My apologies," he murmured, having the grace to sound almost abashed. "I needed a question answered, and I knew you wouldn't be frank with me."

"Little warning next time, please," I replied, rubbing my temple. "And, uh…what question?"

He sat back and crossed his legs. "A few weeks ago, Coileán came to me—and this part doesn't leave this room, yes?"

I stared at him incredulously. "I won't say anything, but I can't guarantee that no one's going to peek inside my head—"

"Yes, fine," he said gruffly. "Sorry. Anyway, he said that Marcus had gone to him for advice, and he wanted me to be aware of the situation."

"What situation?"

Val hesitated, then spoke slowly. "It appears that my son has developed certain…*strong*…feelings for you, and he is somewhat conflicted about the matter. I suppose he didn't want to discuss it with me, but he knows that Coileán is a friend of mine and would presumably give him decent advice." His face twitched in a quick grimace. "Personally, not the man *I* would choose to ask questions on this subject, but maybe Coileán's learned something from his mistakes—"

"Wait, wait, hold on," I interrupted. "Marcus *what?*"

Val arched an eyebrow. "This is news to you?"

"Well...I mean..." I slumped in my seat and frowned at the rug, trying to process everything at once, and looked up again when I heard Val softly chuckle.

"Children," he said, shaking his head. "Very well, let me make it plain: the boy's in love. I checked for myself the last time he came over—we still need to work on that block of his, but for now..." He shrugged. "On occasion, it's nice to get a straight answer."

A flush bloomed from my cheeks and down my neck. While the knowledge that I wasn't the only one whose sentiments had progressed beyond camaraderie was deeply thrilling, my excitement was cut short by the fact that Val was aware of...well, the mess. That was why he'd called me over, I realized, to confirm what he suspected and tell me to break it off. Maybe he didn't want to step on his son's toes, but I knew the way of the world, and the notion of a *relationship* between Marcus and me was—

"What I wanted to tell you," said Val, interrupting my racing thoughts, "was that if you intend to act upon these feelings, you will need to make the first move."

My head jerked up. "*Huh?*"

"He's clueless. This is far beyond his experience, and he's terrified that he'll say or do the wrong thing and lose your affection." Val spread his hands. "My father arranged his marriage. It wasn't a matter of love. This is untrod ground for him, and he hasn't the first idea of how to woo you."

"Fair enough," I mumbled. Marcus had come a long way in the last year, but cultural acclimatization wasn't an overnight process. Just making him understand that offhanded references to his family's slaves would result in looks of horror had taken work. "But..."

"But what?"

"But...uh..." I struggled for a moment, then managed, "You're not upset?"

He laughed again softly at my flustered reaction. "This

thing between you hasn't been subtle, Kitty. Had I objected, I would have mentioned it months ago."

"Okay, but—"

"But you're a witch?" I nodded, and he gestured a glass of ice water into existence on the table in front of me. "Cool off, your face is scarlet." He waited while I drank and tried to quash my blushing, then said, "I want you to be happy, I want Marcus to be happy, and if the two of you can find happiness together, then I'm satisfied. He has decent taste, you know," he added with a teasing smirk.

I leaned against the chair and closed my eyes. "Add this to the list of awkward conversations I was hoping never to have…"

Val laughed in earnest. "What, I'm not allowed to play matchmaker? All I've done is point to the obvious. It's up to you whether you sort yourselves out."

Taking a deep breath in my continued futile effort to stop my flush, I looked back at him and said, "Just to be clear: you *really* don't care that I—"

"No, I do not. Kitty…" He paused, choosing his words. "I've known you since you were a child, and I believe I know something of your character by now. You're a fine young woman, and you two seem good for each other. Marcus would be fortunate to have you—and should he forget that, I'd be happy to remind him."

I frowned. "Meaning?"

"Meaning that I've known you longer than I've known him, and if he should break your heart, then I would need to have words with the boy."

"*Val*," I groaned.

"Only if he does something stupid."

"I'm *going*," I said, pushing myself from the chair before I could melt into it.

"Glad we could have this talk."

I turned around, remembered that the gate had closed, and sighed as I flapped one arm toward the empty space. "Would you—"

A new gate opened into my office, and as I slipped through, I swore I could hear him murmur, "Children."

I had plenty of time to revisit that conversation over the next few days—often at the least opportune moments, like the middle of the night—and though my inner cringing didn't let up, I had the rudiments of an idea by the time Marcus returned from the field trip.

He let himself into my flat around five on Friday evening, still a little damp and smelling faintly of brine. I looked up from the couch and smiled as I took him in. The male members of the Team respected the tradition of the field beard, the scruffy result of forgoing shaving for the duration of the trip, but as Marcus was too fae to grow anything, I knew the dark streak along his jawline had to be dirt. His face appeared to be slightly pinker than it had been when he left—when the summer sun came out in the north, it was easy to get a sunburn with the deceptively cool weather, and Marcus, blessed with a complexion that was quick to tan, had yet to fully embrace the concept of sunscreen. His hair had grown shaggy since he'd started hanging around us, and a few brown strands were plastered to his neck. Beyond the smell, I could tell he'd been somewhere dank and messy from the leavings on the cuffs of his long-sleeved T-shirt and the dark stains on his jeans—custom-made by magic with hardware that wouldn't burn him. His hiking boots were crusty, and he tried ineffectively to wipe them on the mat before dropping his backpack in the corner.

"Hey, stranger," I said, hurrying over to hug him. "Good trip? Find the books?"

"Actually, yes—three, but they're in poor condition," he replied, grimacing. "A thousand years old and not well wrapped against the elements. Archives should be busy for a while. But it's beautiful up there, I wish you'd come. I took pictures…"

His voice faded as he reached toward his pocket for his phone, and I realized he was looking at the kitchen table. "Marcus?"

He gently gripped my shoulders and searched my face, photos forgotten. "What happened? Beth again? Did something happen? I would have come back if you needed—"

"Nothing happened, I'm fine," I said, confused by his reaction.

He cut his eyes back toward the table. "Really? Those six pies suggest otherwise."

"Oh. *Oh*, those," I said, trying to laugh it off. "Couldn't sleep, so I thought I'd be productive."

But Marcus refused to give it up. "Why couldn't you sleep? If Beth is failing her classes, it isn't your fault—"

"I promise you, this has nothing to do with Beth," I replied, and patted his dirty cheek. "And at least we have dessert for days. Go on, get cleaned up. Are you hungry?"

Though he gave me a look of lingering doubt, he finally surrendered. "Nearly starving," he muttered, heading for the spare bath. "Camp cuisine was abysmal."

I followed him and leaned against the door frame as he grabbed a wash rag to protect his hand from the steel tap. "No one wanted to grill?"

He plugged the basin and let the streams mix. "Campsite wouldn't allow it. We used a place on Westray. They had an electric hookup, but no one thought to bring equipment, so our meals were largely crackers and things from tins." He tested the temperature, then sloughed off his shirt and began sponging himself clean. "But the scenery is truly beautiful."

In all honesty, I didn't mind my current scenery. A year of field expeditions and the fitness center had done wonders for Marcus's pecs and abs. "I'm sure Ted'll have us back up there eventually," I told him, trying to focus. "He was hoping for more than three books, right?"

Marcus paused to wipe down his face. "Ten or so.

There may be another cache, but that's all we could find this time. Then again, considering the age, they may very well have rotted." As he scrubbed at the grime, he asked, "What's on the menu tonight? Anything thrilling?"

"Haven't checked. Want to go out?" I replied, hoping my voice didn't betray my nerves.

"Sure. Do you have a restaurant in mind?"

"I don't know," I lied—I'd thought of little else all afternoon—"what about that sushi place in the alley? The one with the eel roll you liked."

Sushi was a safe bet. While Marcus had been hesitant at first, he'd cultivated a taste for it, and with a little practice, he'd become competent with chopsticks. Dining experiences that didn't involve explaining to the waiter why he'd brought his own plastic silverware were always preferable.

"Yeah?" He glanced my way and grinned before turning his attention to his neck. "Perfect. I think Antony said that Madison was making dinner, but I don't know if Daphne has plans. Do you want to call her? Or Maria, she may be free."

This was it—*be cool*, I begged myself. "Actually, uh…I kind of just wanted to go…you know…the two of us. If that's okay," I added hastily.

"Oh?" Again, he smiled. "No objection here. More dumplings for me."

"We'll see about that. Make yourself decent," I said, turning to go. "Nice evening—I figure we can walk, right?"

I was surprised when I reached the couch, looked around, and realized that Marcus had followed me—and he was perfectly presentable. "I've been working on the quick cleanup," he explained before I could ask. "Miss anything?"

"Looks good," I said, then cut my eyes toward my yoga pants. "But you're going to have to give me ten minutes."

I threw a skirt on, because why not? It was a flowy purple mid-calf number, impractical for field work but more than adequate for the walk from the hidden castle into Glastonbury. Marcus seemed surprised when he saw me—my typical wardrobe leaned heavily toward trousers—but he didn't tease me for the departure from the norm.

That late in the spring, we had full daylight until well past eight in the evening, and so we forwent the castle's semi-permanent shortcut gate and took the long walk into town, catching up on our time apart. The restaurant wasn't terribly crowded for a Friday night, and we lingered at the table, ordering more rolls to fill the bottomless pit of Marcus's stomach and polishing off a bit more plum wine than usual. By the time we made it back to the street, the shops had closed, leaving us with the option of a bar or home. Ever so slightly tipsy, we staggered back toward the castle in the twilight, laughing at terrible jokes that even we wouldn't find funny under other circumstances.

As we returned to my flat, Marcus eyed his castoff gear in the corner, grunted, and waved it into a neater pile. "Good enough for the night?" he asked.

"Mm. Definitely." I hunted through the fridge and emerged with a bottle of prosecco. "Thirsty? And there *is* pie."

He pulled glasses from the cabinet and waited while I poured. "Are you going to tell me the truth about the pies?"

"Hang on. And cheers," I added, clinking my glass against his before downing it in a long, bubbly shot of liquid courage. When my subsequent coughing fit ceased, I found Marcus watching me with concern, and I poured a refill. "It's not Beth, I swear. Val gave me something to think about, so I did, and then I didn't sleep, and voila, pie."

Marcus's concern deepened. "What did he say?"

"Never mind that," I replied, and took another sip for good luck before I pushed my glass away.

"Marcus...there's, uh...there's something I need to tell you."

He, too, put his glass to the side, then took my hand. "What's wrong?" he said gently. "Whether it's Beth or not, you can tell me, Kitty. What's happened?"

The moment of truth had arrived, and I was feeling *just* lightheaded enough to go through with it. "I...well, I..." I paused, took a deep breath, then blurted, "I like you."

He regarded me bemusedly. "Likewise."

"No, you don't get it..." Collecting my thoughts through the alcohol haze was a bit trickier than usual, but I managed, "I *like* you like you." His expression didn't change, and I gathered that my stunning eloquence hadn't quite pierced his fog. "What I'm trying to say is...we're friends now, right?"

"Yes..."

"Well...I want us to be more than friends. Is that, uh...clearer?" I could feel myself blushing, but I chalked that up to the wine and told myself I was being so suave.

Marcus puzzled over that declaration for a few seconds, and then his eyes widened as the lightbulb flashed. "Oh! *Oh*, that explains..." he began, then asked uncertainly, "So you...want to, um...date?"

"I mean, I think we're a little beyond that," I replied, reaching for my glass as my facial burning intensified. "We're basically cohabitating already."

He nodded. "True. Then what..." He frowned at the refrigerator in consternation. "Antony told me about dating one night after Daphne went to bed. I was wondering why."

The wine only made my flush worse, and I folded my arms across my chest, fearing that I'd miscalculated. "You, um...you aren't interested?"

"Huh? Oh, yes, *very* interested," he said quickly, "but he began discussing it without cause, and I didn't know what brought it up in his mind."

"Apparently," I muttered, "we aren't subtle."

"How so?"

"From what I've gathered—and maybe this is just Val talking—it's been obvious to everyone *but* us that there's, uh…something…" I waved one hand back and forth between us. "You know?"

I realized I'd said too much when I saw Marcus's face begin to color. "Is that what Pater wanted to discuss with you?"

"Hence the pies."

We looked at the laden table, then back at each other, and laughed as we blushed furiously. I put my glass on the counter and wrapped my arms around him, and Marcus held on as tightly as ever. "What now?" he murmured into my hair. "Antony was kind of vague about the process."

"We…well…we try each other out, I guess. See if *this* is what everyone seems to think it is. There's dating, right," I tried to explain, "like when you're trying to get to know someone, and if that clicks, then you're in a relationship…and after a while, if *that* works, then you might think about something more permanent."

"So, this is the relationship phase, then?"

"Mm-hmm. But we don't have to rush anything," I added. "There's no timetable."

He held me in silence as he considered that. "And Pater approves of this?"

"That's what he tells me."

"Hm. Whom else should we consult?" Catching my quizzical expression, he added, "Your father is dead, your mother is"—he started to say something, probably disparaging, then settled for diplomatic—"your mother, so who—"

"No one." I patted his shoulder and grinned at his befuddlement. "Whatever happens is up to you and me, and no one else gets a veto. Welcome to the future."

Marcus sighed—annoyed, as usual, to learn that not only the rules, but the gameboard itself, had changed in his absence. "You're certain?"

"Positive. Trust me."

I rested my head against his chest again and closed my eyes, and as he slowly rubbed my arm, he asked, "Where do we go from here?"

I'd never been one to take the lead. My experimentation at uni had been sporadic, a handful of inebriated one-night hookups instead of a concentrated effort to build something lasting, and my partners had always been willing to set the tempo. But the wine that night had made me just reckless enough to be brave. I twisted in Marcus's grasp, wrapped one hand around the back of his neck, and pulled him toward me as I went in.

The kiss surprised him—I could feel his body stiffen and heard the sudden intake of breath before I pressed my lips against his—but only for an instant. He returned it with gusto, quickly, then deeply. I pivoted, pressing my back against the counter, and he came with me without missing a step, his exploratory kisses trailing down my neck. I arched my back and tilted my head, giving him room, then met his lips again with full reciprocity.

No one in the Arcanum wanted to be with a witch, and I'd had a long three-year drought since leaving Oxford. In his arms, my body woke like a desert in bloom after the flood, my pulse quickened until I heard it in my ears, and the flush that had just begun to subside returned full-force. The look on Marcus's face was reminiscent of a starving man who'd been tossed a steak, and I sensed a new urgency in his touch.

I pushed myself up onto the counter, then wrapped my legs around his waist and let him hold me off the floor. "Bedroom," I managed to get out between kisses.

"Which one?"

"Don't care."

Cautiously avoiding the steel traps all over the kitchen, he carried me into my room and put me down on the duvet. I helped him unbutton his shirt, and as he tossed it against the wall, I pulled mine over my head and flung it after his.

Marcus stared at me, first with undisguised desire, and then with consternation. "Let me do it," I said, reaching around my back. The white lace bra was one of my favorites, but for a guy who'd never observed one in the wild, getting it out of the way could present a challenge. I cast it aside, then fought the irrational urge to cover up again as his eyes drank me in. I'd never been particularly well endowed—enough for a handful, but no more—and finding myself the focus of that much naked hunger was both a little unnerving and strangely empowering.

Perhaps noting the precipice over which we were poised to plunge, he blinked, then ran one hand back through my tangled hair. "Is this...okay?"

"I want to keep going," I told him. "Do you?"

He bent down and kissed me again. "Is that not obvious?"

"Thought so," I said, then pulled him onto the bed beside me.

I woke Saturday to a dry mouth and the sort of dull headache that nags you about your sins from the night before. Grunting, I rolled toward the middle of the bed and squinted against the sunlight, only to see Marcus lying on his side next to me, watching me reluctantly regain consciousness. "Hey," I mumbled, wishing I'd thought to draw the shades.

He reached over to brush a lock of hair out of my eyes. "Hi. Sleep well?"

"Mm."

"Hungover?"

"*Mm.*"

His fingertips landed on my temple, and an instant later, I saw the brief flash in the magical spectrum as the enchantment took effect. Marcus had a long way to go yet in his training, but he was a natural healer, and he had the knack of treating a hangover down pat. Then again, the Team had given him plenty of opportunities to practice.

With my headache dispatched, he kissed me, then rolled out of bed. "I'll see to breakfast. Go back to sleep."

Through drowsily drooping lids, I watched as he padded around the room, rummaging through the detritus of the previous night's clothing for his missing pants. It wasn't a bad view at all—Marcus was well built, hard in all the right places—and he grinned when he looked up and caught me ogling. "Satisfied?" he asked.

"For now."

His eyebrows waggled, and he slipped back into his trousers. "Food first, and then we'll see about other matters, hmm?"

Saturday mornings were glorious things in and of themselves, but rolling back over into the warm hollow I'd left in the mattress was heavenly. We'd worn ourselves out the night before, going too quickly at first in order to satiate the immediate hunger, then slowing and enjoying the experience. Neither of us would have won any prizes for our performance—alcohol, excitement, and nerves made sure of *that*—but when I'd started giving directions, Marcus had proven an eager and apt pupil. For all I knew, it was the first time he'd had a partner who was more than a passive participant in the enterprise, and he'd seemed to enjoy the challenge, even producing condoms from the ether once I explained the need and described them. By the time we passed out, we were both amply satisfied, and I'd fallen into a deep, dreamless sleep.

I pulled the duvet up to my chin and listened to the muffled clanging of pots through the closed door. Surely he'd have put on a shirt and socks, I told myself; he wouldn't have tried to cook without covering as much exposed skin as he could. It was a pity but a necessary precaution when you were dealing with a faerie in the kitchen.

Oh, God, a voice in the back of my head groaned,

interrupting my pleasant reverie. *Now you've done it. You've really done it. Sleeping with a faerie? There's no coming back from this, Katherine. I hope you're proud of yourself, young lady. You've torn your Sunday britches, now and forever.*

That inner voice had a point. If—*when*—Beth found out, that'd be the end of it. She probably wouldn't even leave her room when I came to dinner. Consorting with the enemy was one thing, but getting intimate with him escalated my transgressions to a whole new level. I was the worst kind of traitor—

That voice, I realized, sounded suspiciously like my mother's, and I shut it up. Marcus wasn't the enemy—he was one of the best things to have come my way, certainly my favorite find from my work expeditions, and even if it was too soon to broach the topic with him, I admitted to myself that the complicated knot of my feelings toward him looked suspiciously like love. Yeah, I'd slept with Marcus, and I'd damn well do it again—and if the previous night was any indication as to his thoughts, the feeling was mutual.

Somewhat comforted, I drifted off, buried in blankets, until the smell of bacon lured me from bed. Naked but for the necklace I never removed, I grabbed my robe off the bathroom door and emerged to find the table set, the telltale pies moved onto the counter, and Marcus pulling maple syrup from the microwave. "She's alive!" he teased, and, armed with grill mitts, removed a dish from the oven. "Hungry yet?"

I took him in—the bed-mussed hair, cowlick and all; the red apron with the jagged, blackened corner, victim of a small grease fire; the mitt-swathed hands cradling what appeared to be perfect French toast; and the expectant, hopeful look on his face—and I quite nearly melted into the floor.

"Starving," I told him, and kissed his cheek in passing as I went to collect the plates.

There was no need for a coffeepot—Marcus could

make several respectable brews from memory—and he kept refilling my mug as I inhaled breakfast. Despite his initial hesitation, the boy could *cook*, and he practically beamed when I got up for seconds. Once my stomach felt less like a black hole, I reached over and took his hand. "That was fantastic. Thank you."

"It was only fair. You *did* give me at least half your sushi last night," he replied, and pushed his syrup-streaked plate away. "And speaking of last night..." He let the thought hang, unfinished, until he'd glanced away from me and cleared his throat. "Would you be honest with me?"

"Of course," I said, tightening my grip on his hand even as a vise started to compress my overstuffed stomach.

"Last night, we...um..."

"Yes?" I prompted when he stalled again.

Marcus found his courage and resumed. "We both had a few drinks. Maybe more than a few," he muttered. "If, uh...if there were things said that were just the wine talking..."

I froze, waiting for the blow.

"Would you tell me?" he finished. "You shouldn't pretend for my sake. Last night was wonderful, but if it was the wine—"

"It wasn't the booze," I interrupted, awash with relief. "I swear, I meant what I said. The wine just helped it come out in a more eloquent fashion."

His face broke into a teasing grin. "*That* was eloquent?"

"Bite me."

Laughing, he squeezed my hand in turn. "I'm glad you told me."

"You didn't suspect?"

"I...*thought* I might have seen something, but...you know..."

"Couldn't bear to risk rejection?" I prodded, smirking.

But Marcus had sobered. "Sometimes, it's difficult to know how to proceed," he murmured. "How not to offend. I didn't want to offend you, so…" He shrugged. "I did nothing."

"It'll all make sense someday."

"I keep telling myself that," he said, and sighed. "But this—you, me, *us*—I don't exactly know what I'm meant to be doing."

I scooted my chair closer to his. "It's uncharted territory for me, too. This is the closest thing to a long-term relationship I've ever been in, and that's counting at least part of the last year toward our total."

He smiled. "I think that's a fair assessment."

"So, this is new for us both, okay? I mean, heck, you've already done the marriage thing—"

"Not well! And everything was different then. Fabia…" He stopped himself, then cupped my cheek in his palm. "Fabia was nothing like you."

"She didn't get nervous and make pies, you mean."

"She didn't have your fire."

There was still a trace of maple syrup on his lips, and I didn't mind lingering when he pulled me closer. "There's no need to rush," I whispered. "We have plenty of time. Take it slow, feel it out."

He kissed me again, more urgently. "I've learned one thing already."

"Have you, now?"

"Yes." He sat back ever so slightly and met my gaze. "There is nothing I want more than you."

I kissed him that time, and when I rose and pulled him toward the rumpled bed, he voiced no complaint.

CHAPTER 3

We agreed that there was no need to trumpet from the rafters our change in status. While the Team was, for an Arcanum group, unusually accepting of outsiders, I wasn't sure that the reaction we'd get from all corners would be positive if we let slip that we'd shifted from unofficial roommates to lovers. Marcus had been around the castle long enough to understand the general disfavor for his kind, and he raised no fuss when I suggested that we play it cool. We even worked out a cover story for the weekend's activities before the Monday meeting, just in case it came up.

As we took our seats around the conference room table that morning and passed a platter of doughnuts stolen from the dining hall, I told myself that no one suspected a thing, even though I felt as though there were a flashing neon sign over my head. Sitting beside me, Marcus seemed calm but for the tapping of his pen against his notepad—nothing extraordinary, I decided. I turned on my computer, pulled up my calendar, and was absently checking my messages and trying to keep flecks of chocolate glaze off my keyboard when Frank walked in. He took the chair across the table from mine, started to open his own computer, then paused.

I could feel the weight of his stare on me. Frank wore dark glasses outside of our offices to reduce some of the weird looks he got in public—tall, buff, and albino pale was a striking combination—but down in the subbasement, his red eyes were on full display, and there was something *off* about the way he focused on people. Once you understood that the intelligence behind those eyes wasn't human, you recognized the siren blatting deep in the instinctive part of your brain as a warning that you, despite your fancy tools and whatever skill with magic you might have attained, were in the crosshairs of an apex predator who was one careless sneeze away from turning you into ash.

Glancing up from my screen, I found him regarding me with faint amusement, and then I felt the quick flicker of his thoughts mingling with mine. Before I could protest, he held up a finger to stay me, then stood just enough to pull a small notebook from his back pocket. He flipped through the pages until he found what he was looking for and cleared his throat. "Lakshmi takes the pot."

The others stopped what they were doing, and Lakshmi, looking far more put-together than the rest of us in an embroidered peach sari, clenched her fist in victory and took a bow to a smattering of applause from her end of the table.

"What?" Antony asked, sounding disappointed. "Are you sure?"

"Quite sure." Frank ran his finger down the page, glancing it over a second time, then nodded. "Maria had the fifteenth of January. Lakshmi was the tenth of April. You're not until the first of June. Closest without going over."

"*Fuck*," he muttered, then glared at Marcus and me in exasperation. "You guys couldn't have held off for three weeks?"

Marcus turned to me, confused, and I dropped my doughnut as the realization set in. "Oh, my God, y'all, there's a pool? *Really*?"

Most of the Team had the decency to look slightly ashamed, but Lakshmi gave me a knowing smile. "It was only a matter of time. Last year's pool rolled over, and—"

"*Last* year's pool?" I yelped. "How long—"

"October," said Maria, helping herself to the hot water in the corner of the room. "Honestly, I thought this would have been settled months ago."

"These things take time," Lakshmi told her. "Like Rohan and Kim. My boy's clever, she's clever, and yet, they were both blind for ages. But congratulations," she added, turning to us, "and thank you for the windfall."

By then, Marcus understood what had happened, and he slumped in his chair as my face tried to spontaneously combust.

"Well, now that those two are thoroughly humiliated," said Ted, taking his spot at the head of the table, "let's get down to business, eh? Bob, could you cut the lights, please?"

Bob leaned back and flipped the switch, and Ted turned on the projector. "All right, people, get excited," he said. "It's that time again…"

The screen on the wall flashed an image of an ornate chalice, and the elder members of the Team groaned.

"Oh, come on," said Ted, "you know you want to do this."

"What *is* that?" asked Marcus.

"Ted's white whale," said Lakshmi, looking down at her screen. "It doesn't exist, but don't tell him that."

"*That*," Ted retorted, cutting his eyes to Lakshmi, "is an artist's rendering of the Grail, and if you'll look at the literature, you'll see that there are far too many mentions of a wondrously powered vessel for this to be pure fantasy."

Lakshmi grunted her disbelief, and even Bob quietly sighed at the other end of the table.

"Wait," Marcus cut in, frowning, and pointed to the screen. "Isn't that movie with—"

"*Last Crusade*? Yeah," said Ted. "I think the truth is quite a bit different. Anyway, *people*," he continued, giving the table the sternest glare he could muster—which, coming from a short, chubby wizard with a gray ponytail, transition lenses, and a Hawaiian shirt, wasn't exactly intimidating—"I want to try a different approach this time."

"Anything *but* another Grail quest?" Daphne muttered.

Ted ignored her quip and changed the slide to a picture of the nearby Glastonbury Tor. "Avalon."

At that, Maria lifted a hand to get his attention. "There's nothing on that hill but a gate into Faerie, and that's buried under the tower."

"Yeah, my dad told me about that one," Mal added. "It dumps into a lake in the wilderness, apparently. If you want to see the other side, there's easier ways to get there than moving the stone."

"We're not going up the Tor. This is just a cover picture," Ted explained. "Right, then, what do we know about Avalon?"

We looked around at each other, and then I sighed and cleared my throat. "Legendary site out of Arthurian mythos, possibly an island, strongly associated with the Tor, which is otherwise known as Ynys Wydryn, the Glass Island."

"Island?" Marcus whispered.

"It was an island once. Or maybe part of a peninsula, I forget. This whole area is reclaimed marshland. Anyway, Avalon is supposed to be around here."

Ted nodded. "Bingo. But I think the location in the popular imagining is off by about thirty miles." The picture changed again to a satellite view of Somerset and the Bristol Channel. "Those two islands are Steep Holm and Flat Holm," he continued. "There are other, smaller rocks out in the channel."

"So…we're going out to sea?" Antony ventured.

"Not yet." The picture changed to an inconspicuous leather-wrapped book. "The travelogue of Magus Llewelyn ap Dafydd of Powys, written in the late twelfth century. The guy got around, particularly in Wales and on this side of the channel, and he took notes of anything interesting.

Seems he was the kind of guy who could find drying paint interesting, since there's a whole lot of junk in there, but he *did* record a story he picked up about…here." A red dot appeared on the English side of the coast, southwest of Weston-super-Mare. "That's the best approximation I can give, based on the landmarks he described, but play along," said Ted. "So, the magus overnights in a fishing village, and this innkeeper tells him about the hidden island in the channel. It's cloaked in fog, and you can't find it even if you know the water like your own backyard. But he claimed his son had seen it—a storm came up at twilight, the kid's boat capsized, and he'd have drowned had this stranger not come out of nowhere with another boat and taken him to this island. He said the place was as green as summer, even though autumn was turning cold elsewhere, and there was no one around but the man. So, this stranger put the kid up for the night, took him home in the morning, then rowed away, never to be seen again. But here's the kicker: when the kid asked him what the island was called, the man said, 'Afallon.' Pretty neat, huh?"

Ted waited, but when the table failed to mirror his enthusiasm, he shrugged and went on. "There are other reports about that stretch of coastline in the Archives. It's been making wizards twitchy for centuries, but no one's ever figured out why. Look, I know this is a rabbit trail, but my thought is to go out to the coast, poke around for a few days, and see if we can't find any clues pointing to this Afallon. I'm not saying the Grail will be there if we do find a hidden island, but we could cross it off my list, maybe explain away the twitchiness. Now, who's in?" When the room didn't immediately cheer, he added, "Think of this as a seaside holiday. Come on, guys, we'll get hotel rooms and everything. No tents." He looked to his right. "Lakshmi, how about it? I don't think we're going to need home support this time out."

She took a sip of tea. "That's good, as my holiday with Rodney has been on the calendar for six months."

"Oh…shit," he muttered, peering down at his computer. "Right. Good timing, then. New Delhi again?"

"My niece is getting married. Bob has offered to run support while I'm away…"

"But if you don't need it," Bob interrupted, "then I'm off to France. Sylvester's found a lovely B&B in Provence ahead of the lavender tourists, and we could do with a holiday."

"Suppose that's fair," Ted mumbled. "Anyone else abandoning me?"

Antony raised his hand. "Madison's off to Montana next week, and I'm looking after Allie."

"She's old enough to stay in the dorms for a few days, isn't she?"

"If you'd like to convince her mother of that, then by all means, be my guest."

Ted sighed and looked around the table. "Frank, bud, you've overdue for a holiday if you want to bail, too."

He shook his head and continued to scribble on his notepad. "No, no, the coast sounds, uh…is *lovely* the word we'd use?"

"Not me," Daphne whispered.

In the end, ours would be a party of six, Ted and the five of us who didn't have solid excuses. He'd even asked Maria if she wanted to sub, but she'd declined, citing the pressures of the spring term and her class of second-years, who delighted in learning new ways to maim each other with wands.

As Ted and Maria headed upstairs to meet with the grand magus and Lakshmi retreated to her side of the suite to book lodgings and a van for us, Marcus followed me into my office and flopped onto the couch. "I'm sorry about that," he said, rubbing his eyes with the heels of his hands.

"Well, at least now we won't have to sneak around," I replied, pulling a Coke from my minifridge. "Could have been worse. No one's come after us with torches and pitchforks, right?"

"Yet." He stretched out, taking care to dangle his shoes off the edge of the cushion. "All right, would you mind *actually* telling me what we've agreed to do next week?"

I chuckled. "Where would you like me to begin?"

"Why is everyone but Ted convinced that this is a fool's errand? The Team has found remarkable things—"

"And then there's you."

He tossed a throw pillow toward my desk. "Seriously, what's the issue with this trip?"

"It's not just this trip," I said, stretching out a kink in my back. "Ted's been after the Grail for decades, and every couple of years, he puts together a little excursion to go test one of his hunches. They never pan out."

"Not at all?"

"Nope. The Grail's a myth. There might conceivably be an ensorcelled vessel out there somewhere, but something as powerful as the Grail? Forget it. This is a drawn-out wild goose chase."

"And this Afallon place?"

"Avalon." I sighed and cracked my knuckles. "Ever heard of King Arthur?"

Marcus frowned at the ceiling. "No. English?"

"British, and I mean that in the original sense." He rolled over and regarded me with confusion, and I shrugged. "This goes way back before unification. So yeah, Arthur, *if* he existed, was a British king or a warlord, or maybe just a general with good PR. Assuming he actually lived, he could have been born somewhere in England, Wales, Scotland, or maybe even Ireland, and that's also assuming he wasn't a Roman left behind when the imperial troops withdrew. He probably won a few battles against the Saxons, made a name for himself, and disappeared well before anyone actually started writing about his supposed life."

"Saxons?"

"Hold on," I muttered, and dug through my files until I

pulled up my old notes from a European history seminar. "Right, then. So, you had various groups of ancient Britons, a Celtic group, living in modern England and Wales, and Picts up in Scotland. Then the folks around the Med got curious, Julius Caesar came through in the first century BC, and the Empire was holding territory here by the first century AD."

"*Right.* You're welcome."

I threw the pillow back at him. "Then y'all had the brilliant idea of subsidizing your so-called barbarians in return for military assistance, and we all know how that turned out for you. Anyway, the Saxons were Germanic, and they were eventually allowed to settle on the island as foederati. Imperial troops were withdrawn in the first years of the fifth century because of all the problems at home, leaving Britannia to look after itself. Without Roman governance, petty kingdoms popped up, the Saxons gained a foothold in the east, and suddenly, you've got Britons and Saxons duking it out in a giant turf battle that went on for ages. The Saxons mostly won in the end," I added. "There's a remnant of the Britons in Wales, but there was also a lot of eventual intermingling, and then 1066 rolled around, and it was everyone versus the Normans. And a good time was had by all."

"Sounds like it. So, this Arthur…"

"Again, may be nothing but a story, but if he existed, it was probably right around the time that y'all packed up and went home. Now, guess what's absolutely *not* discussed in any early mention of Arthur?"

Marcus smirked. "The Grail?"

"Exactly. The problem is that the original core of the story was warped over the centuries, particularly by the French. Suddenly, Arthur's this king presiding over a legendary court at Camelot—God knows where *that* might have been—with the knights of the Round Table, and everyone's being chivalrous and wearing shining armor, and Arthur's wife and his best knight are cheating on him together, and his bastard son wants to kill him, and half the court ends up running off on a Grail quest. It gets *complicated*." I closed my notes and shook my head. "Back at uni, I had to slog through Thomas Malory's *Le Morte d'Arthur*, and let me tell you, just keeping the family trees straight takes work. But at the end of that book, Arthur's fatally wounded by his son, his magical sword gets tossed back into the lake from which it came, and he's carried off to Avalon. There's a folk tradition that he didn't actually die, and he'll come back and lead his people again in a time of great need. The once and future king, if you will. But since there's no actual proof that Arthur existed, much less that he went off to a place called Avalon to indefinitely recuperate, it's almost guaranteed that we're going to find squat at the seashore. I'll totally understand if you don't want to go—just tell Ted that Val needs you. He won't pry too deeply."

"And abandon you to Ted's madness? Ha." Marcus sat up and smoothed his mussed hair and shirt. "Maybe I should read some of these legends before we go so I don't continue to look like a complete idiot. What was that book you mentioned?"

"What, the *Morte*?" I stood and searched my bookcase for a moment, then found my battered copy, which had seen me through several of Ted's Grail quests. "You won't like it."

He made a face as he skimmed through the thick paperback. "This is huge…and what language—"

"Middle English, but a late version of it. Predates Shakespeare." Seeing his forlorn expression, I grinned and beckoned for the book. "How about I find you a condensed version online?"

There was precious little to recommend Port Warren to the seaside tourist. The best holiday destination on our side of the channel was Weston-super-Mare, which, if you overlooked the expansive mud flats at low tide, was a pleasant enough getaway with activities designed to appeal to tourists. Port Warren, on the other hand, didn't particularly seem to care about visitors. There was one grungy inn near the sea, a place that had probably been rundown thirty years prior, but it was the best Lakshmi could do for us.

Having seen my room, I'd almost have preferred a tent. The bed was narrow, the mattress unforgiving, and the ancient electric tea kettle had developed a fine ring of rust inside. The brown splotches on the ceiling spoke of hastily patched leaks, and the bed linens, done in a busy floral pattern that would easily hide small stains, carried a certain funk that made me reluctant to crawl beneath them. But Port Warren was at the epicenter of Ted's map of reported weirdness, and as he wouldn't hear of making camp elsewhere, we had no choice but to settle in.

We'd told the bored desk clerk that we were a hiking club when we checked in on Sunday evening, which had earned us a raised eyebrow and a glance at the computer behind the desk. "You haven't looked at the weather, have you?" he'd asked. "Supposed to rain all day tomorrow."

Ted had promised him that a little rain wouldn't stop us, but Daphne and I woke at three the next morning to howling winds and the rapid staccato of rain driven against the window. "Bloody hell," she muttered, lifting the shade to take a look out at the storm-black night. "If Ted thinks I'm going out in *that*, I'm having his head examined."

According to Frank, our fearless leader was up and out just after five, armed with a raincoat and a hand towel in his pocket to mop off his face. With the constant wind, any attempt at raising an umbrella would have been pointless. The rest of us gathered in the lobby, clutched our mugs of tea, and stared glumly out at the pounding rain. "I've got breakfast bars in my bag," Daphne finally announced. "That'll keep me going until this passes. Any takers?"

"You're not even going to pretend?" Mal asked.

"I'm going to sit in my room and work on a paper. No point in wasting a perfectly good writing day," she replied. "You're not thinking of going out there to drown, are you?"

Mal beckoned her into the glass vestibule, then pointed to the warm lights half a block down the street. "The Olde Anchor is open for breakfast, lunch, dinner, and everything in between. We're going to set up camp in there."

"So…the plan is to stay pissed until the rain passes, then?"

"Pleasantly buzzed," he corrected. "This is a working vacation, after all."

Frank and Marcus nodded with faux earnestness, and Daphne sighed, shaking her head so hard that her box braids bounced off her shoulders. "Boys. I'll be in my room if Ted gets swept out to sea. Kitty, are you going carousing?"

"Eh, maybe later," I said, holding my tea closer for warmth. "Think I'll start the day's fun with something marginally less scandalous." Marcus began to protest, but I cut him off. "Go on, have some male bonding time. Drink pints or throw darts or whatever. Trust me, I won't be far."

The unrelenting rain made walking any distance of more than a few feet a miserable, cold experience, but off I trudged, keeping my hood up and my hands in my jacket pockets. The morning desk clerk had been unhelpful when I'd enquired as to points of interest, but she'd recommended a café near the shore for breakfast. "Or there's the pub," she'd offered, thumbing her hand toward the wall behind her. "Not great, but it beats a good soaking."

The café it was. I'd mapped a route and committed the

turns to memory before setting off, and I marched as quickly as I could around the puddles, ducking under the occasional awning for a moment's respite from the deluge. But as unpleasant as the weather was, I was still drawn away from the protection of the line of buildings and down to the sea wall.

Ted was right—there *was* something odd about the area, and like an iron filing to a magnet, I felt it tugging at me from out in the channel. The tide was out, exposing a long stretch of muck and rocks like the bottom of a dredged lake, but beyond that, the sea still flowed, and something—*something*—waited out there in the fog.

I might have stood there all morning, contemplating the disquieting gray scenery, had a delivery truck not driven past, hit a pothole, and soaked the back of my jeans. Swearing in a most unladylike fashion, I squelched in my black Wellingtons across the street and down another two blocks until I found the promised café.

The décor was, at best, utilitarian, a dozen or so mismatched wooden tables between the plate-glass window and a counter with a soda fountain and a basket of silverware rolled in paper napkins. A window behind the counter opened into the kitchen, and the sizzling hiss of the grill and the lingering smell of sausage made my stomach growl. I had no trouble getting a table—only three were occupied, all by weathered old men in oilcloth caps who studied either their tablets or the muted TV mounted in the corner as they ate. The matronly waitress gave me a pitying smile as I dripped my way across the room and shucked off my sopping coat, and then she approached with a laminated menu. "Tea, love?"

"Absolutely," I muttered, and gave the menu a quick perusal. "Two eggs over easy, bacon, and toast?"

"Can do. Tea'll be right up," she promised, and bustled off with my ticket.

Alone, damp, and grateful for the café's noisy heater, I opted to do as the locals did and pulled my tablet from my inner coat pocket. Even inside, my senses continued to insist that something was amiss, but I'd be damned if I was going back into the wet without at least a few bracing cups of strong tea down me, and I planned to distract myself with my notes from the previous week's pre-trip research while I waited for my breakfast.

The tea arrived, blessedly hot, and I propped the tablet in my lap and scrolled while I tried to warm up. Before I could finish my first cup, however, I heard another chair at my table slide across the tile floor, and I looked up to find one of the old men taking a seat. "Morning," he said, putting his mug on the table and scooting closer. "Haven't seen you before, have I?"

"Probably not," I replied, packing the computer away to be polite. "I'm on a hiking trip."

"In *this*? And all the way from the States, too?" He clucked his tongue and lifted his tea. "Lousy luck."

"Not so bad as it could be," I said, shrugging. "I've been UK-based for a while."

"Is that so?" He sounded surprised. "Your accent—"

"Was strong before I left. It's a lost cause."

He chuckled and nodded. "You're down in London, then, I suppose?"

"Glastonbury, actually."

"Glastonbury? *Pff.* Nothing but hippies over there." His dark eyes squinted at me with a hint of suspicion. "You sell crystals or some rubbish like that?"

It was my turn to laugh. "Hardly. I'm an archaeologist," I told him, stretching the truth ever so slightly. "Unless someone's fashioned a piece of quartz into a spear point, I couldn't care less about pretty rocks."

That seemed to reassure him. "Ah," he said, settling back in his appropriated chair, then doffed his cap and smoothed his wispy white hair. "So, an archaeologist on holiday at the mud flats in the monsoon. Did you make an enemy of your travel agent?"

"I don't know, but I'm starting to wonder if I've upset

someone," I replied, and extended my hand across the table. "Kitty."

My new companion's grip was firm, his hand calloused and warmed by his tea mug. "David. Sorry to interrupt—were you waiting for a friend?"

"Just waiting out the rain." I cocked my head toward the window and the carwash sounds from outside. "The rest of my posse's either working or gone to the pub."

His wrinkled face split in a grin, exposing crooked, slightly yellowed teeth. "Maybe you should have followed their lead, girl."

"Or maybe this is my masochistic streak coming through." I glanced up at movement from the corner of my eye and saw the waitress approaching with my breakfast. "Sorry, have you eaten? I don't want to be rude, but—"

"Go on," he urged, and held up his mug in greeting. "Claire, dear, will you top this off? Might be a while."

The waitress put the hot plate in front of me and patted my shoulder. "If he's bothering you, just say the word. And Captain, stop flirting with my customers."

"*Flirting?*" he replied in a tone that suggested he was deeply scandalized by the notion. "I'll have you know that I'm being friendly and welcoming to the one holiday visitor in this godforsaken town—"

"There are six of us, actually," I said.

"One of the six holiday visitors in this godforsaken town," he amended, "and I am *shocked* that you would attribute any other motivation to my actions." He dropped me an exaggerated stage wink, and I chuckled as I reached for the salt and pepper.

Claire's sigh spoke of long suffering. "Seriously, dear, don't let him bother you," she told me, and took his mug to the counter for a refill from the water urn.

When she'd dropped his tea off again, he sobered. "Are you working? I didn't mean to intrude..."

"No, no, this is fine," I said, my mouth half-full of

toast. "Glad for the company." I swallowed and drained my mug. "So—*Captain* David, was it?"

"Indeed. Of the *Nymph*. A little fishing, the occasional fishing charter, and whatever else I want to do." He gave me a sly grin, adding, "There are certain perks to being a pensioner."

"I bet. You know the channel pretty well, I take it."

"As well as one can," he replied, wrapping his bony hands around his mug. "She's unforgiving, especially once you get into the mouth of the Severn. It's the tide, you see—get caught in the wrong place when it goes out, and you're stuck in the mud. But there's decent fishing, if you know where to look." He peered at me over his mug before taking a long sip. "You wouldn't be interested in a fishing trip, would you? You and your hiking friends?"

"I'm not much for fishing," I said apologetically. "But, uh…" I paused, hoping I wasn't about to come off sounding like a nut. "You're from around here?"

"Most of my life. Look, if you really want a nice hike, you'll want to push on to Minehead and the South West Coast Path."

I lowered my voice and leaned toward him over my plate and the short vase of plastic daisies. "Honestly, we're not just here for the trails. Some of us are, uh…amateur anthropologists, I guess you could say."

One bushy eyebrow quirked. "How so?"

"Sort of goes hand in hand with the archaeology, doesn't it? You want to see what was left behind, but you also want to know the people who put it there in the first place."

He nodded as he considered that. "All right, fair, but I can't imagine there's anything here to hold your interest, unless you want to hear stories of the monstrous fish out there that barely got away," he said, and pointed over my shoulder at the other breakfasting codgers. "Plenty of those tales to go around in a town like this."

"And I'm sure you've got your share of them, right?"

"Madam," said David, hand to his breast, "all of mine are *true*. But what's got your interest, hmm?"

I sipped my tea to stall, giving me time to think through my question. "This is a long shot," I finally said, "but have you ever heard of a hidden island out in the channel? Like, if you see it once, you can never find it again?"

The old man pursed his lips and frowned into space, and I thought he was on the verge of coming back with a joking denial until I saw the solemnity in his eyes. "Not since I was boy," he murmured. "Old story, that one. Place is shrouded in fog, and if you get too close, it vanishes. Maybe it moves around the channel, I don't know. But yeah, I've heard tell of it. You want to know what I think?" he continued, meeting me over the middle of the table. "I think it's a tall tale told to cocksure lads who think they're the greatest sailors to ever pilot a dinghy to remind them that they don't know the sea."

I decided to press my luck. "Ever heard anyone call the island Avalon?"

"Avalon?" he echoed. "Isn't that meant to be over in your bit of the county?"

"So I hear, but my friend swears he heard that the disappearing island was supposed to be Avalon."

David snorted and finished his tea. "News to me, but who's to say? Going to go out and hunt for it, are you?"

I shrugged and resumed my attack on my eggs. "Haven't planned that far yet. I think we're just trying to avoid being washed away for now."

He cut his eyes to the window as lightning flashed over the sea. "Good plan for the short term, but this should be gone by nightfall. Tell you what," he said, steepling his fingers, "I haven't got plans for tomorrow, and from the sound of it, neither have you. How'd you feel about skipping the hike and putting out to sea? Pack a lunch, I'll take you around and let you look for your mystery island, and if that gets boring, I'll show you how to fish."

The offer was tempting—I could easily envision myself alone for a second day while Daphne hid in our room and the guys hunted for Avalon in the pub. "How much would you charge?"

"For you?" He glanced at the ceiling and screwed up his face. "Well, now, this would be for research purposes, and there were…six of you?"

"That's right."

"I see. Say twenty quid apiece, and if you should bring beer along, bring some to share with your captain. How would that suit you?"

"*Twenty*? That's it?"

"As I said, I'm a pensioner," he replied. "I do what I like. And besides, this way, I'll get a captive audience for my incredibly true and not at all exaggerated fish stories."

I had to smile at that. "That's very generous of you. Let me get with my people—can I give you a call later today?"

"Sure." He pulled a business card from his wallet and handed it across the table. "The number's my mobile, just leave a message if I don't answer." He rose, wincing as he pushed himself from his chair, then put his cap back on and turned up the collar of his jacket. "One little hiccup. I did mention the tides, yes?"

"Yes, sir."

"Well, you see, the moon's at full tomorrow, and we'll need to leave when the tide's in." He tucked his hands into his pockets and rocked back on his heels. "If you don't want to waste half the day, meet me at the marina at midnight. Remember the beer, now," he said, and took his leave.

I watched him duck out into the storm, head bowed against the blowing rain, and caught Claire's eye. "Any chance of a refill?" I asked, raising my mug. "I think I might just need it."

CHAPTER 4

Ted was almost giddy when he saw the *Nymph* bobbing in its slip shortly before midnight, though some of his exuberance might have been a product of the hour. I'd called everyone shortly after the old captain left me to my breakfast, and though I'd stressed the importance of getting a pre-departure nap, Ted had remained out until after dinner, surreptitiously poking around town and down by the shore with the smallest specimen from our arsenal of magic-detecting devices. Officially, we had no such tools—most of our toys came straight from the Fringe crafters in Faerie, who had no love for the Arcanum but didn't mind helping a mixed group out—but the grand magus, who was all too aware of the arrangement, turned a blind eye. Ted's favorite was roughly the size of a pack of playing cards, easily hidden in a pocket, and came with an earpiece. He'd walked the streets of Port Warren until sundown, listening to the beeping as it increased and decreased in tempo, but he hadn't been able to pinpoint a source.

I didn't know how he planned to explain the earpiece on the boat, but Ted seemed unconcerned as he hurried down the dock to shake the captain's hand. "Hi! Captain Donovan?" he called, jingling like a recycling bin thanks to the bags of beer bottles slung over his arm.

David, who stood near a security lamp in his jacket and cap, cast shadows in that light, the boat's lights, and the bright moonlight above. As Ted neared, he met his grip and smiled. "So says my business card. David. Welcome aboard, watch your step," he cautioned, grabbing Ted's elbow as he wobbled near the side.

Ted dropped his gear on the deck and glanced appraisingly back at him. "Rock climber's gloves?"

The captain lifted one hand and flexed his fingers, which were sheathed to the knuckle with black and gray padding. "Boater's, actually. It gets cold out on the water, and with the arthritis…"

My boss, nearly seventy himself, nodded in commiseration. "Say no more. Here, Daphne, I've got you," he said, holding out his hands to help her aboard.

I passed David a stack of twenty-pound notes and stifled a yawn. "Thank you again. That's Ted," I said, pointing to him as he poked around the boat like an excited child, "and Daphne, and Mal's boarding now…and those two are Frank and Marcus," I concluded. The others lifted fingers to identify themselves, and David's head dipped in greeting.

He gave Marcus a second glance, then smiled. "Clever boy. Spent time on the water, have you?"

Marcus, alone of all of us, had worn gloves for the occasion. One generally didn't need them in late May, after all, unless one was concerned about brushing up against something iron-based and erupting into weeping sores. "Not enough," he replied, "but with the breeze tonight…"

"Oh, you don't need to convince me," the captain said, and clapped Marcus on the shoulder as he climbed aboard. Once we and our bags were safely on deck, David unmoored us and headed for the cabin, as steady on the gently bobbing craft as if he were padding around his bedroom. "Let me take her out of the marina, and then we'll get sorted. Make yourselves at home," he offered, and disappeared inside. A moment later, the engine purred, the boat backed smoothly out of the slip, and we turned for the open sea.

I'd expected the *Nymph* to be somewhat grungy, a utilitarian vessel with traces of fish scales stuck in the paint and maybe a minifridge on board for sodas and bait. Instead, when I entered the cabin, I found myself in a well-appointed entertainment room in shades of cream and brass, complete with a long, plush sofa, a pair of swiveling leather stools, and a television mounted on the wall. A fake tree occupied one corner of the room, a spot of green popping against the neutral background. The sitting area gave way to a respectable kitchen—the quartz countertop and brass fixtures continued the color theme—with a dinette big enough for six tucked in against the wall. An interior staircase led up to the bridge, I assumed, while another disappeared below the deck.

This wasn't at all like the pontoon boats I remembered from the lake outings of my childhood—this was a *yacht*.

I was still goggling when the boat slowed to a stop and David climbed down the stairs. "Oh, good, you found the cabin," he said, and flipped on the recessed lights. "Are the rest still on deck?"

"Unless they've fallen overboard," I replied. "This is gorgeous…"

"Thank you. It's home." He poked his head out the cabin door and called, "Come in out of the wind! You won't spot any islands in the dark."

Soon, the rest of the Team was warming up by the electric heater as David examined the beer offerings. "Newcastle and Guinness? I like your taste, Ted."

"Do what I can," he chirped, glancing at the stocked wine fridge as he passed. "And, uh…a little something extra for taking us out in the middle of the night."

David grinned as Ted pulled a small bottle of scotch from his jacket pocket. "Good man. I'll put it to use," he said, hiding it in a cupboard. "Now," he said, turning back to the mass of us clustered in the sitting area, "we've got time to kill until dawn. Sunup's not until five. I'm happy to introduce you to the joys of night fishing in the meanwhile, but if you'd prefer, there's bedrooms below."

Daphne sagged with relief, and David pointed to the

staircase. "Watch your step and your head. Linens are in each closet. Go on," he urged, "we'll wake you for breakfast. Does anyone need something chilled for now?"

While Daphne and Mal went downstairs to catch a nap, David filled the kettle, left boxes of teabags and sugar on the counter, then shepherded us back onto the deck. Exchanging his arthritis protection for a pair of yellow rubber gloves, he dragged a bucket to the side of the boat, pulled poles from a closet, and set to work baiting hooks with the bucket's odiferous contents. "Sorry about the smell," he said as he worked. "I find that the bits that are *just* about to turn do the trick, but the gunk is hell to get off your hands. Take it from experience," he muttered, holding up his soiled fingers. "Unless you want to smell like the fishmonger's back room all day."

We followed his instructions as well as we were able— Ted, at least, knew which was the business end of a fishing pole, and his enthusiasm almost made up for his lack of skill. Though we'd had little success by dawn, David offered to put our catch on ice for later, then returned to the cabin to see to breakfast. "Nothing fancy, but I've got porridge oats and granola bars," he said, "and more than enough tea. Come warm yourselves."

I took a cup of tea onto the deck to watch the sunrise, and Marcus joined me at the railing. "Having fun?" I asked, leaning against his shoulder.

"At least no one is counting on me to bring in a meal," he replied. "I think the bait may have aged too long."

"It does have a certain bouquet."

He sipped his tea, then wrapped his free arm around me and planted his feet against the light chop. "Do you feel all right?"

"Sure," I said, surprised by the question. "I'll probably crash as soon as we get back to the hotel, but the caffeine is still working. You?"

"Oh, I'm awake, but that's not what I was asking." He leaned closer to my ear and murmured, "Do you get a strange feeling out here?"

"Uh, *yeah*. I've had it since we pulled into town."

"Stronger now?"

I nodded. "There's got to be something in the channel. Maybe not an island, but something's making my senses tingly. Is it driving you nuts?"

"Not exactly, but it's...*there*. Like an itch." He peered out at the water, but all we could see was pink sunlight glinting off the waves. "Lovely morning, though."

"Will be. Better dig out my sunglasses before it gets much brighter," I said, and turned for the cabin. "A pretty day on the water. Will wonders never cease?"

We found the others, even the sleepers, sitting around the dinette and on the sofa when we returned, most clutching mugs of tea. David, who'd taken a stool near the heater, beckoned us into the cabin. "Never realized there were so many archaeologists based in Glastonbury," he said as I shut the door. "Suppose there's enough around here to keep you busy, eh?"

"And then some," said Ted. "Especially once you get up into Scotland. Let me tell about what I found once up on Fair Isle..."

Bless him, Ted could talk to an unfriendly tree, and while he and David swapped stories, Frank walked around the room with the kettle, topping up mugs. He caught me shivering near the door, snorted, and hugged me for a moment, which was just as nice as cozying up to a space heater. While Frank's bind could alter his appearance, it couldn't stop his internal combustion once he was exposed to dark magic, and he always ran warm. Whenever we camped in the cold, there was an unspoken struggle among us to sit beside him—and if Frank minded that we were blatantly taking advantage of the situation, he bore it in stride.

"University contacts, mostly," I heard Ted tell David. "I snagged Daphne once she finished her studies, and that eventually led to Mal, and then the rest of the kids," he fibbed, gesturing around the room. "They still play nicely together, which is all you can ask, right? But hey, tell me about this yacht of yours—these are swanky digs."

David chuckled over his porridge. "I decided that as long as I was going to be spending time out on the water, I might as well make it comfortable. The marina's good for cleanup and pumping," he explained, "and fuel, of course, but aside from the occasional shop, I could stay out here indefinitely. Then again, the walls close in, so I find myself in town every few days. Glad I caught you," he added, grinning at me. "Lucky for us both, eh?"

"Even luckier if we find the island," I replied.

"Patience. Let the sun rise, and I'll take you up and down the channel." He stood and took his dishes to the kitchen. "Just pile everything in the sink. I'll see to it later."

I was following him with my mug when I felt it—the subtle flutter of another mind peering through my thoughts. My shoulders tightened, and I shot a sharp glance over my shoulder at Frank and Marcus, who were talking to Mal on the sofa. The intrusion annoyed me— Marcus knew it was impolite, and Frank typically limited his snooping to moments in which he wanted to carry on a silent conversation, so the fact that one of them had popped in without cause or a word of explanation rankled. Unburdened, I returned to the sitting area, intent on chewing out the guilty party once David was out of earshot, but as I neared them, I saw a flicker of surprise cross Frank's face, which hardened almost instantly into a blank mask. He caught my eye, and when I nodded, I heard him in my head: *Someone tried to look in my mind.*

Mine, too, I thought, forming the words and waiting for him to find them. I couldn't broadcast my thoughts, but Frank was adept at dealing with the untalented.

Wasn't me.

Marcus?

Before Frank could answer me, Marcus jerked, then frowned at him. "Something wrong?" he asked quietly.

When I heard Frank again, I assumed he was speaking to us both. *That wasn't me. There's another mind reader on this boat. Would you like three guesses?*

I looked back at the kitchen, but David was whistling and running water in the basin to soak the porridge bowls.

Someone tugged my sleeve, and I glanced down to see the question on Mal's face. "What's going on?" he whispered.

Frank tapped his forehead, and when Mal nodded agreement, he looped him in. While Mal had inherited his half-fae father's perpetual youthfulness, most of his skills came from his shifter mother—including a shifter's natural imperviousness to mental snooping. Frank could work past almost any mental block, and I suspected that most defenses would prove flimsy if Val really wanted to sniff around, but shifters' mental shields were like twenty-foot walls of reinforced concrete.

Did you feel anything just now? Frank asked.

Mal nodded again, and Frank's lips parted slightly, revealing clenched teeth. *Unless Daphne and Ted have been holding out on us, I think we have a problem. I blocked the intrusion. Marcus?*

Blocked, he replied, the thought carried to the rest of us via Frank's transmission.

Which leaves three, thought Frank, looking down at me. *And you're wide open, Kitty.*

At that moment, I wanted to be anywhere else but on that lovely yacht, bobbing in the middle of the channel. *Maybe it's not him*, I thought. *Maybe this is tied to the other weirdness out here.*

Perhaps, but let's assume that the most probable answer is the correct one.

Gate? Marcus offered.

Yes, that's very subtle, Frank retorted. *I was thinking something more along the lines of playing it cool, pretending that we noticed nothing, and finding an excuse to get back to shore after lunch.* He cut his eyes toward the kitchen, then added, *If he's a wizard, he's probably Minor Arcanum. If he's fae, he's unlikely to fuck with six of us. Be calm. I'm going to go fill Ted and Daphne in.*

The other guys followed Frank onto the deck, but I headed below to the lavatory, where at least I'd have a moment to collect my thoughts. Locking the door, I rested my palms against the cool marble vanity and closed my eyes, then took a deep breath and internally kicked myself. All of this was my fault. If I'd put David's invitation off for a day, if I'd let someone with more than my modicum of talent vet him first, then we wouldn't be out on the water with a stranger who was, in all likelihood, spying on us. And to what end? Best-case scenario, we'd stumbled onto a decently gifted wizard, one of the Minor Arcanum's individualists who had no use for the bureaucracy and oversight that the rest of us in the community endured. The Arcanum was on speaking terms with its renegade cousin, but that was no guarantee of our captain's personal feelings about the matter. Still, I told myself, if he was MA, he wouldn't hurt us. Not with the numbers stacked against him.

I opened my eyes, poked at the dark circles beneath them that the mirror revealed, and ran a hand through my wind-tangled hair. It was going to be okay. We'd cruise around for a bit, call it a day, and put Port Warren behind us. Ted would take care of everything—he had the people skills to finesse our way back to shore—and then I'd return to my room and sleep the whole thing off—

Even muffled, the sudden yelling from the deck reached me below, and I scrambled topside to see what had happened. The cabin was empty, but when I headed for the bow, I found myself on the edge of a standoff.

There was a man standing near the railing, holding Ted's neck in the crook of his arm and aiming a steak knife at his face. Though Ted's assailant wore David's jacket, he looked almost nothing like the captain: young and wiry, with large, deep green eyes set in a thin face that blazed with color on the high apples of his cheeks. I thought his thick shock of hair was as white as Frank's until the sunlight caught the pale blond. He stared with fury around the semicircle gathered at the bow, then snarled in perfect Fae, "Who sent you? Tell me, damn it!"

Great, said my inner voice, *you get the <u>worst</u>-case scenario. Angry faerie trumps hermit wizard any day.*

Marcus, apparently the focal point of his anger, raised his empty hands in placation. "No one sent us," he replied in kind, keeping his voice calm. "Let him go."

The young man—David, I supposed—only tightened his grip on Ted. "If you don't think I'll do it, try me. *Who sent you?*"

Before anyone could start throwing fire, I pushed my way through the line and stood between David and Marcus. "We're not here to hurt you," I said in Fae, hoping he'd understand me through my accent. "We have no idea who you are."

He scowled at me, taken aback. "You're Arcanum. How do you know the—"

"Long story. Let Ted go, and I'll tell you whatever you need to hear." When that didn't sway him, I said, "Yes, I'm Arcanum, but I'm a witch. Not even a good one. Take a look if you don't believe me," I offered, tapping my head. "You obviously didn't stick around in there long enough the first time."

But David didn't jump at the bait. "You should choose your traveling companions more carefully, girl," he said, staring past me at Marcus. "*That* one isn't Arcanum."

"He's on loan."

David grunted his skepticism. "Since when has the Arcanum—"

"Since his aunt became grand magus."

That finally gave him pause. "His aunt?" he echoed, bemused. "What about...*oh.*" His grip on Ted relaxed by a degree. "I suppose Harrison would be rather old by now, wouldn't he?"

"Grand Magus Harrison?" I asked, trying to keep my

tone conversational. "He was killed when I was little. Like, maybe two. Toula Pavli's in charge now."

The knife swung away from Ted only long enough to point toward Marcus. "*His* aunt, you say?"

"She's witch-blooded. One of Mab's two surviving children," I volunteered. "The other one runs that court, so it would be a *very* bad idea for you to attack Marcus. Now, how about you put the knife down and we talk about this like rational adults?"

David's expression shifted toward befuddlement. "*Mab's* court? When did *she* return?"

At that, Ted cleared his throat. "Do you remember back in '13 when Faerie closed off for a few days?"

His assailant's eyes bulged. "Wait, how do *you* speak—"

"Eh, you know, you pick up things along the way in this line of work," he said with a slight shrug. "So, you know what I'm talking about?"

"Of course."

"Well, the way I hear it, that was all due to Mab trying to get back into Faerie, and she didn't last long on the other side."

"Mab's dead?" he asked, still wide-eyed.

"Yes," I told him. "Titania died around the same time, and Oberon only lasted about another two years. There's been complete turnover in the Three, and—"

"Stop, wait," he interrupted, shaking his head. "Titania—*what* did you say?"

"Dead."

"Dead?" he whispered. "Are you sure?"

"Aunt Toula killed her," Marcus offered from behind my left shoulder.

David looked as if he'd been hit in the head with a mallet. He released the knife and let his arm fall away from Ted, then dropped to his knees and stared up at me as Ted hurried away to join Frank and Daphne. "You're certain? You're absolutely certain that she's dead?"

"I mean, I wasn't a witness to it," I replied, "but her

son runs that court now, so I think it's a safe bet."

"Which son?"

"His name's Coileán."

"The Ironhand?" David's disquiet only seemed to grow. "*That* boy got the court?"

Seeing his face work, I took a risk and knelt with him. "If you and Titania were close, I'm sorry. Didn't mean to spring that on you like—"

"Are you kidding?" His face broke into a wide grin. "I've been hiding from the old bitch for sixteen hundred years! This is great news! The son, now, not so much, but Titania..."

I felt him plunge into my thoughts, seeking confirmation of my sincerity, and when he retreated, he shook his head and stood. "Amazing. You lot really are just a bunch of nerds on a spree, aren't you?"

Ted spread his hands. "I've been called worse. Can we take this inside? Maybe without anything bladed?"

As David dried the deck-dampened knees of his trousers, I picked up the knife and pointed to the cabin. "Okay, folks, truce. Come on, no one's killing anyone."

Though Frank in particular appeared to be poised to object, the rest of the Team filed back into the cabin and sat, and David leaned against the door with his arms folded. "So, ehm...explanation, I suppose," he said, glancing at the rug. "Once I realized what he was"—he nodded toward Marcus, who'd positioned himself between David and me—"I assumed you'd been sent to kill me. Hence...well. Sorry about the mix-up," he muttered to Ted. "Nothing personal."

"No harm done," said Ted, who was far more gracious than the situation warranted. "But, uh...how'd we give you that impression?"

David exhaled slowly. "When I was much younger, I did something stupid, and Titania put a bounty on my head."

"What, did you kill someone?" Daphne asked.

"Worse. She had this gala one night, you see. Had them all the time, actually, but I might have drunk more than was wise that evening, and the queen was wearing this hideous dragonskin frock—"

I cut my eyes to Frank, but there was no sign of imminent explosion.

"—and I made the mistake of telling one of her favorites that the dragon had died in vain. Word got around to her, she didn't appreciate my commentary, and I went on the run to save my own hide. I've been in this realm ever since, mostly around here. I assumed she'd given up the chase after a while, but I couldn't be too careful. And then you showed up out of nowhere, and your cover story seemed odd—no one has spoken of the hidden island for generations," he explained. "So I decided to look for myself and see what you were doing in Port Warren, and when I saw *your* mind"—he pointed to me, eyebrows raised—"it set off every alarm bell. I almost thought you were delusional until I started getting blocked and realized what I was up against." He frowned at us and cocked his head. "How the hell does a group like this exist, anyway?"

"Started as an Arcanum initiative," Ted replied. "Everyone else involved wanted a challenge, and the grand magus doesn't mind."

"Seriously, we're the closest thing the Arcanum has to archaeologists," I added. "I mean, *my* degree is in archaeology—so is Ted's. We just go after less traditional finds."

"And you're telling me he's a high lord?" David asked, pointing again to Marcus.

"It was a surprise to me, too," Marcus muttered.

"Look," said Frank, "I'm not best buddies with Coileán or anything, but I know enough to predict with confidence that he won't kill you for insulting his mother. I've yet to hear him utter a kind word about her."

Marcus pulled out his phone and showed it to David.

"I'll make the call, if you like. You can go home."

"Not just yet," he replied, "but, ehm…thank you." He glanced out a window at the steadily brightening sun, then seemed to reach a decision and turned back to the room. "Why are you searching for Afallon?"

As one, we looked to Ted, who shrugged and smiled. "Knowledge. To see if it's there. This stretch of coastline has been pinging on our collective radar for ages, and I dragged the rest of these folks out to see if there might be anything to my disappearing island theory." He paused, then asked hopefully, "Is there?"

David nodded. "What you're feeling is a side effect of the enchantment I built around the island. It's huge, and it practically gobbles magic."

"Glastonbury's wards are huge, too, and they don't feel like this," Ted countered.

"Because a large part of my construction is repellant. It's designed to make anyone sensitive to magic uncomfortable in the area." He drummed his fingers against his arm. "The island doesn't disappear—it doesn't move, it doesn't come and go. I've hidden it with a series of camouflaging wards and disruptions. Unless you know how to see it, you sail right past it, and your equipment shouldn't register anything. I've had to modify the wards over the years," he continued, "especially once air travel and satellites came about, but as far as I can tell, the cartographers still aren't aware of it."

"So why have we never noticed the wards, then?" Ted probed. "Something that size would be pretty obvious, camouflage or no."

"And they were when I first built them," said David, "but that was centuries ago. I've had time to play with them, fine-tune them almost into invisibility. They blend into the background nearly perfectly—I've got a set of camouflaging wards designed to help hide the output from the rest of the system. No small piece of work, that," he added with a touch of pride. "Took ages to figure it out."

Ted nodded. "Okay, I'm suitably impressed. So…any chance that we could see them in person?"

David gave him a long, hard look, and Ted grinned.

"You know what?" our captain finally said. "Very well. You brought me the best news I've had in a while."

"And it would go a long way toward making me feel better about being held hostage," said Ted.

David rolled his eyes. "I'm sure it would. Right, then, I'll take you ashore," he said, and headed for the staircase to the bridge. "But don't expect anything glorious—it's just an island, I promise you. Twenty minutes away, tops."

While the others tried to keep Ted from dancing around like an overstimulated child on a school trip, I slipped upstairs after David and found him at the wheel—which, like every other piece of practical metal on the yacht, was brass. "Thank you," I said once he'd noticed me in the doorway. "It means a lot to Ted."

"I suppose I did threaten his life. Seems fair."

I sidled closer and watched as the horizon dipped and rose with our passage. "I just wanted to tell you that I've known Coileán since I was a kid. He's never been anything but kind to me, and I gather that he's a hell of a lot less homicidal than his mother was."

"You *have* heard why he's called the Ironhand, yes? He has a history of using iron against his own kind."

"Still, he's more likely to pat you on the back than stab you for insulting Titania. You should stop by, explain the situation."

"Perhaps another day," he replied, barely adjusting our heading. "Though it *is* somewhat reassuring to have a half faerie at the helm. Maybe he'll hear me out before striking me dead."

"All three of them are half-blooded," I offered. "Marcus's father—"

"Yes, I saw. Can't believe he's Mab's brat," he muttered. "I knew Valerius when he was one of Titania's guards—good with a sword, but nothing special. Wonder when his mother finally claimed him."

I could only shrug. "So...you're half, I take it?"

"Indeed."

I watched as a sailboat breezed past us, heading west toward the open sea. "Figured, considering your name. I mean, I know there are full-blooded faeries with non-Fae names, but it seems less common."

David turned to me, faintly smiling. "That's correct—or it was when I left the realm. But I'm afraid I have to throw a spanner into the works. I wasn't actually named David Donovan. Been my alias for the last fifty years, but hardly my original name."

"That does complicate matters," I replied with mock gravity.

"Not by much. My mother named me, and she chose one from her own tongue. Father sent her back when I was a boy, but she was always...warm," he murmured, staring out at the water. "My father didn't care what I was called. He was a lord—not a high one, but since he slept with the queen on occasion, he was favored in court. I was just another of his bastards until I upset his girlfriend. Suppose he *had* to remember my name after that," he joked.

"Which is..."

"Myrddin."

"Mm. Your mother was Welsh, then?"

"Not exactly. My mother predated Wales, but her people came from that part of the island, I assume. I left Faerie far too late to find her here."

Though he kept his eyes on the horizon, I heard the note of regret in his voice and tried to pivot. "So," I teased, "you were named for Merlin, the *wizard*? That seems awkward."

He laughed softly. "There was never a wizard called Merlin."

"Oh, I wouldn't be so sure about that. There are some weird old family names in the Arcanum, you know? My poor dad was *Orson*."

"I'm talking about historically. You refer to Merlin the wizard and King Arthur, yes?"

"Yeah…"

"Two problems with that statement," he replied. "First, the name was Artur, nor Arthur. And second," he said, cutting his eyes to mine, "I am not, nor have I ever been, a *wizard*."

Startled, I stepped back from the console. "You—"

"Are the original," he finished, then pointed to an unremarkable patch of empty sea. "And there, if you squint just right, is Afallon."

Even expecting the pushback of the wards, I still fidgeted in the cabin as we neared the hidden island. The enchantment suggested that keeping our current heading was wrong, if not dangerous, and the pit in my stomach warned flight was the safest course of action. But as soon as we broke through, the unease fell away like a wet cloak dropped on the floor, and I stared out the window at the *very* visible inside of the enormous ward bubble, an intricate lattice that pulsed and glowed in the magical spectrum as it rose from the water to arc over our heads.

Daphne whistled in appreciation beside me. "That's gorgeous. Almost as tidy as spellcraft."

It had to be, to work as effectively as it did. Faerie-made magic—enchantment—was by nature big and messy. They could create quickly and blow their enemies to smithereens with ease, but that sort of work was greedy in its consumption of raw magic—not a problem when one was in Faerie, but somewhat more challenging in the mortal realm, where Faerie's outflow competed with the dark magic spillover from the Gray Lands. Spellcraft, on the other hand, was designed to be precise and efficient, making the most of a limited resource, and the process was longer and more demanding. In school, we'd learned the techniques necessary to focus our minds to the task of spell construction, the creation and amplification of channels that would, in theory, take background magic and bend it to our will. As weak as I was, I needed a powerful wand to make magic do more than ignore me, but with the proper focus and coordination, I could cast minimal spells. Marcus, who could enchant, barely had to think of what he wanted before reality shifted around him—and therein lay the problem for faeries in the mortal realm. Accustomed to easy, instantaneous results, faeries generally lacked the discipline to shape their constructions into forms more effective for a lower-magic environment. Faerie-made wards were easy to spot, jumbled hedges of glowing channels that sucked power and fell apart if the background levels dipped too low. The dome around us, however, was nearly as precise as the wards around Arc 2, a complex system of neat amplification channels and reinforcing bands.

"Backup pockets—see?" I said, pointing to a bright nodule in the lattice. "It's reinforced just like—"

"The castle," Daphne finished. "How do you even *do* that with enchantment?"

Marcus, who'd caught us ogling, could only shrug. "Think of how long he's been working at it. Maria said she was able to adapt some of her old techniques—perhaps he learned from a wizard."

"Or hired one," Daphne muttered.

I'd almost have been inclined to believe that a wizard had built the wards but for the fact that this wouldn't have allowed Myrddin to tweak them down the line. Melding spellcraft and enchantment usually resulted in disaster—one or both constructions would overload and catastrophically fail when they were linked, which could lead to impressive craters. Arcanum researchers had theorized about the phenomenon, mostly concluding that there was something fundamentally different in the ways in which faeries and mortal practitioners affected magic, which helped explain the witch-blood phenomenon. The majority of those unlucky enough to have equal parts fae and wizard blood were incapable of wielding magic, and the ones with talent often had only minimal ability. The great exception was Toula, the long-theorized "perfect" witch-blood who could cast and enchant with equal facility, but even she was careful not to get carried away with hybridized constructions when, say, improving the craft-built wards around the castle.

I was still admiring the wards when the yacht made its final approach, slowing and turning as it headed for its slip. Seeing the island itself, I almost forgot the larger construction. We were aimed toward a natural harbor at the foot of a short cliff. A set of stairs had been carved into the stone, and at the top, I could just make out the gray turret of what appeared to be a castle, all but the top of which sank from view as we neared the dock.

When the engine died and Myrddin descended from the bridge, we'd already gathered in the cabin, and Ted was waiting with a wide, boyish grin. "You told them?" Myrddin asked me.

I nodded, and Ted seized his opening. "I have *so* many questions," he began, his eyes gleaming with a manic sparkle.

"I'm sure you do," Myrddin mumbled, and sighed. "Let me tie her off, and I'll show you the place."

We followed him onto the deck and waited as he secured the mooring lines, all of us craning our necks to see the top of the cliff. With the yacht safe, he disembarked, took two steps to steady his legs, then pointed to the staircase. "This way."

Ted practically ran after him, and Daphne, the second-most senior member of our party and more responsible by far than our boss at that moment, just shook her head and shouldered her bag.

The stairs were wide and straight, an easy climb, and as I topped them, I got my first clear glimpse of the island.

Physically, it was a flat outcropping, dominated by the stone tower that rose from the verdant meadow all around it. It was hardly a castle, as I had first assumed, but still amply large for a single inhabitant. Around the tower, almost forming a natural wall, stood a double line of trees, green with the season.

"Afallon," said Myrddin, sweeping one arm to encompass our surroundings. "Not exactly El Dorado, but it suffices. Tea?"

Daphne perked at the offer, and we followed him up a gravel path toward the tower. As we neared, I saw that the barrier trees were heavy with fruit—far too early in the year to be anything but the result of magic. "Apples?" I asked as we passed through the orchard.

"And pears, plums, cherries—there's a lone orange in the back, but it's never really thrived," Myrddin replied. "Had to do something in the way of landscaping, and this seemed practical."

Mal pointed to a tree nearly hidden by the tower. "That's a coconut palm."

"Okay, maybe not *practical*, but it's nice to have more than fish to eat."

Instead of entering the tower, we walked around it and found a sort of patio on the far side, a stone-floored platform over which a large, vine-heavy trellis arched. "Sunshade and an arbor," said Myrddin, and gestured to a pit sunk into the stone. A small fire sprang to life, and a semicircle of wooden chairs appeared around it, pointed out at the sea. "Make yourselves comfortable, and excuse the mess. I haven't entertained in years."

"Dare I ask how many?" I replied.

He smirked. "More than you've seen, girl. Have a seat."

Another flick of Myrddin's fingers brought forth a low table with tea and small cakes, and we tucked in as he pulled his chair closer to the fire pit. "So," he said, stripping off his gloves to warm his hands, "you want to know about Artur, I take it."

"For starters," said Ted.

"Suppose there's no harm in it now," he murmured, and a full pint glass appeared in his hand. "What would you know?"

"He actually existed?" Ted pressed, leaning closer. "There *was* a King Arthur?"

"The stories are all wrong, but yes, Artur was a king." Myrddin sipped his breakfast brew and gazed into the fire. "It's a long story…"

"We're in no rush."

He glanced up at Ted's eager face and smiled sadly. "I thought you'd say that. Very well."

CHAPTER 5

The heavy silence hung over us for a long, pregnant moment before Myrddin spoke again. "By my best estimate, I was three hundred sixty-seven when I fled Faerie. I'd never visited the mortal realm, but I knew there were gates that would bring me here. You see, I'd also never attempted to make an inter-realm gate, which is a problem when one is on the run. A friend told me of a gate deep in the forest, at the bottom of a lake. I don't know how I ever found the way, but I swam to the bottom, saw daylight, and pulled myself out onto the top of a hill."

"The Tor gate," I murmured.

He nodded. "Precisely. And aside from a little settlement, I was in the middle of bloody nowhere. But I wanted to put distance between myself and that gate, so I dried off, descended, and tried to find a road to somewhere more inhabited. But this would have been"— he squinted up at the grapes above us—"oh, about the year 435 or so. The island was a mess of petty kingdoms, and I'd escaped to one of the smallest. The original Afallon."

"The stories are correct, then?" Daphne cut in. "It *was* Glastonbury?"

"Yes and no. What's now Glastonbury was at the heart of the territory, and since the Tor was so close to an island once, perhaps that's where the confusion arose. Anyway, I made it to a road—barely more than a trail by the river— and I stumbled onto a robbery. A young man was trying to fight off half a dozen others, all armed with swords, and he wasn't faring well. I decided to improve his odds."

"You're a decent swordsman?" Mal asked.

"Nothing spectacular, so I just set them all on fire," he replied with a shrug. "They extinguished it, realized what I'd done, and ran, but their victim was too terrified to move. I copied his language from his thoughts, assured him he wasn't about to be crisped, and got the story from him. Poor lad was carrying gold to his king. So, I tidied him up and accompanied him to the lodge where the king was staying—a long hall, really, nothing of permanence— and the boy told his liege what I'd done. The king was intrigued, so I pulled off a few glorified parlor tricks, and he decided that I might be a useful fellow to have around. I got a position, and Uther got a faerie in his back pocket. Didn't exactly give him the truth about why I was wandering around his territory, but it didn't matter in the end. He even took my advice and built a guard tower over the lake in the top of the Tor. It didn't close that gate, but I hoped it would dissuade the curious."

"Wait," Ted interrupted, "you're talking about Uther Pendragon?"

"He was just Uther when we met," said Myrddin. "A boy of twenty, if that. Not until he proved his skill on the field did anyone call him the Pendragon—and he *earned* that sobriquet," he insisted. "Uther was brilliant with a sword, and he had a tactical mind. I helped with the occasional fireworks, but I tried to keep a low profile, you understand. I thought Titania was looking for me, and if word got back to her of a minor king with an all-powerful right-hand man, then surely she'd have known." He drank his beer and glanced out at the horizon as the logs in the fire pit crackled. "Uther didn't have much territory, but he had heart, and he tried to protect his people. I respected that."

"So…he wasn't actually king of the Britons, then?" Ted asked.

"Not all of them. Hell, Dumnonia was several times larger than Afallon—it's a wonder that they didn't annex us in Uther's time. Then again, the Britons had larger problems."

"The Saxons," I murmured.

"Exactly. Once Rome abandoned the island, the petty kingdoms coalesced, then formed alliances and looked for a leader. There was a man called Guothigirn who'd been a well-placed civil servant at the end of the Roman occupation, and even as the government fell apart, he still figured out how to get things done. He was high king when I arrived—had been for a decade or so. I saw him a few times when Uther traveled to meet him. Middle aged, well spoken, a little paunchy. Kept the Picts at bay. He just made one tiny tactical error—"

"Foederati?" I asked.

Myrddin pointed at me and winked. "Someone's studied this, hmm?"

"Took a class at Oxford."

"*Well*, aren't we fancy?"

Mal raised a finger. "Um…the hell are foederati?"

Myrddin gestured to me in invitation, but I shook my head and declined. "Mercenaries, more or less," he explained to Mal. "Saxon mercenaries, in this case. They came over from the mainland and were permitted to settle in the east as long as they helped the Britons out against invaders. Rome had brought them in originally, and Guothigirn followed in their footsteps. But there was a slight problem," he continued, leaning toward us. "Rome could pay, and pay well, and Rome had a highly disciplined army of its own. We had neither the finances nor the might of the empire, and the Saxons gradually realized that they didn't need our permission any longer. And then what happened, Miss Oxford?"

"The foederati revolted in 441," I dutifully replied.

"It was *ugly*," he said. "Whole villages wiped off the map. The Saxons here joined up with their incoming kin and friends, and they started pushing west. Fortunately, there was Ambrosius."

Ted perked up at the name. "He *did* exist?"

"Indeed. Ambrosius Aurelianus," he said as Mal's mouth began to open. "His parents or grandparents were from the old country, and they stayed when the troops pulled out. Boy was educated, well connected, and far more charismatic a leader than Guothigirn could ever dream of being. Men *wanted* to fight for Ambrosius. Anyway, his parents were killed in the foederati revolt, and he never forgave the Saxons or Guothigirn. I heard tales of him as he came of age and started gathering forces about him, and in, oh, 455 or so, he challenged Guothigirn for his throne."

"And won?" Mal guessed.

"He killed Guothigirn, so yes. Uther respected him— everyone did. And Ambrosius respected Uther as a warrior. Uther was some years his senior, but he fought as well as a younger man. I was only there to offer counsel and the occasional bit of magic, you understand—Uther seldom needed my assistance. Until he did."

Myrddin paused to drain his glass, which refilled as he put it aside on the wide arm of his chair. "Uther was a good man, a good king. I counted him as a friend," he said softly. "But he failed in one crucial respect: he couldn't produce an heir. Not for lack of trying," he hastily added. "His wife was much younger, and a stunning beauty. Eigyr, she was called. Both of them were dark-haired, but hers was almost black and fell past her waist, and she would plait it into these complicated..." He seemed to catch himself and shook his head as if to clear a vision. "A lovely girl. And a dutiful wife, from what I gathered. She wanted to give him a son, and he wanted to get one on her, and they did their part. It never worked. So...eventually, Uther knew he was getting along in years, and time was growing short, so he came to me and asked for a magical solution."

I frowned. "Enhanced fertility via enchantment? Birth

control is one thing, but if we try to go the other way…"

"Yeah, we're no better at it than you people are," Myrddin replied. "I couldn't do anything for him, especially if there were no arrows in that quiver. I suspected he was the problem—he'd had his share of bedmates over the years, and not once had he got a bastard on any of them. But Uther was desperate, and I didn't want to see a power vacuum in Afallon after his death, so I…well, I improvised."

"How so?"

Myrddin scowled at the flagstones for a long moment. "I've told this story to one other soul. You've brought me great news, but…do you really want the whole truth? Artur lived—that's more than you came here knowing."

"Here's the thing," Frank replied before anyone could protest. "If you start a story like that in front of him"—he pointed to Ted, who was quite literally on the edge of his seat—"and cut it off halfway through, you'll never get rid of him. Nerds on holiday, remember?"

He cut his eyes to Ted's hopeful face and sighed. "All right, fine. You asked for it," he muttered, then downed half of his refilled beer before he resumed. "I had to do *something* for Uther, so I made him several fertility amulets—mostly variations on the fascinus model, if you know what I mean."

We did, all too well. My incredibly mature classmates at uni had giggled like kids when we'd first seen pictures of the protective charm. Some months before our excursion, Antony had asked Marcus if our understanding of the symbol was accurate, Marcus had been perplexed that anyone *wouldn't* think of wearing a winged penis to ward off the evil eye, and some wag—my money was on Maria—had left a life-sized bronze statuette on Antony's desk the next morning. Like a phallic hot potato, the fascinus had been making the rounds ever since, popping up in unexpected places around the subbasement. Truly, the Team was a bastion of restraint and good taste.

"We get the picture," I told Myrddin, catching Daphne's embarrassment.

"He wore them all, for whatever good it did," he muttered. "Continued to make the attempt with Eigyr. And then, late at night, I'd sneak into their room and put him to sleep on the floor, and she and I did what the amulets couldn't."

Mal looked at Myrddin incredulously. "I thought you said Uther was your *friend*, man."

"He was," Myrddin protested. "He wanted a son more than anything, and that was the kindest thing I could do for him. Eigyr was willing, but only if I glamoured myself to look like him. She did love him, you know."

"Still…"

"Yes, I fucked another man's wife," he snapped. It took another sip of beer before he was ready to resume. "If my calculations are correct, Eigyr gave birth in 465. Mid-spring. I told Uther that because of the magical forces in play, I needed to be alone with her during the delivery to ensure the baby's safety. He bought it, fortunately."

Ted frowned. "Something happened to the baby?"

"There were two things wrong," said Myrddin. "One, the baby had my coloring." He tugged at a lock of his fair hair. "The eyes might have shifted to brown eventually, but the hair was far too light to have come from Uther or Eigyr. Anyone with sense would have made the connection."

"And two?"

"Two," he said slowly, "the baby was a girl."

We stared at him in silence, waiting while he rubbed his forehead.

"The whole damn process had been to give Uther an heir," he murmured. "He needed one. *Afallon* needed one. And so, before Eigyr could see the truth, I transformed the baby. The child I put in her arms was dark-haired and male, and then I called Uther in to meet his son."

My boss's excitement had shifted toward horror.

"You…you made—"

"I thought that if Artur was a boy from the beginning, he'd never need to know the truth," Myrddin said in an almost apologetic rush. "He'd have a future, a kingdom, he could take a wife…I knew he'd never be able to sire a child, but that was a matter for the future. Uther's legacy was secure, and he adored Artur. I don't think he ever suspected, to tell you the truth. And Eigyr died of a fever when Artur was five, so she never said a word."

When he looked at us, I could see the shadow of guilt in his expression. "I thought I was doing the best thing for him. For all of us."

As usual, it was Ted who was first to extend the olive branch. "I'm sure you did," he said, though he still sounded troubled. "And he—she—never found out?"

"Eventually, in part." Myrddin finished his second beer, then waved the glass back into the ether as it tried to refill again. "Like I said, Uther loved his boy. He put Artur on a horse before he could walk, and the lad had a sword in his hand as soon as he could hold it off the ground. At least Artur wasn't fae enough to have my problems," he added with a soft sigh. "On the contrary, he seemed every bit his father's son—tall for his age, quick on his feet, and almost preternaturally gifted in combat. He was an absolute prodigy, leagues beyond the other boys his age. When he wasn't being trained at arms, Uther allowed me to work with him—a king needs at least basic literacy, I've always thought."

"No talent, though?" I asked.

Myrddin snorted. "Oh, it was there. Hiding at first, but he had a touch of it. I couldn't test him or train him as I liked with all of Uther's court around to watch, so when Artur was seven, I brought him here for the summer, where we could be alone. Built the tower—well, the first version of it—and gave him space to try out his abilities. Uther understood," he explained before I could press him. "I said the child had been born through magical means, so it was to be expected that he'd be somewhat unusual. Anyway, Artur's natural inclination was toward combat magic—shields, mostly. He eventually learned to throw fire, but never anything exceptional. Honestly, his true talent was with a blade."

He turned his face back toward the sea. "And then Uther fell."

"Fell?" Frank echoed.

"Died in battle. Some damn Saxon cut through his armor. And suddenly, Afallon had a ten-year-old king." He shook his head at the memory. "I'd expected trouble from the rest of Uther's inner circle, maybe a coup, but his men accepted Artur without a fuss. It was known by then that he was touched by magic, you see, and with his other apparent talents, they anticipated great things from him in a few years' time. In the interim, he had enough loyal men to keep him safe, and they knew I wouldn't allow him to come to harm. I'd given Uther good counsel, and I always tried to do the same for Artur."

"You told Artur the truth, then?" Ted asked.

"*No.* Moon and stars," he muttered in Fae. "He held the throne only because he was Uther's son, and I wasn't going to jeopardize that. Besides, he was very close to his father, and I...I didn't want to complicate matters. He was only ten, remember. But I did what I could to mentor him as he grew, and fortunately for us all, Ambrosius stepped into the gap. He was still high king, and once he heard about Uther's death, he visited to see Artur for himself. Ambrosius knew of the boy's gifts as well as anyone, and he sent weapons masters to further Artur's education. They must have sent back glowing reports because Artur went into battle for the first time at twelve, and he fought at Ambrosius's side."

"But you protected him, right?" Daphne cut in.

"I couldn't stay close enough. In the end, he didn't need me—Artur more than held his own, and Ambrosius honored him that night. The boy was out to avenge his father, you understand, and he fought like a berserker. And he was still tall—you know how girls outgrow boys at first. I tweaked the enchantment to give him a little extra height in the end. His strength, though…that was all him. His men called him Pendragon as well, and he deserved it." He paused long enough to produce a glass of water. "And then the boy began to become a man."

I sneaked a glance at Frank, whose intense stare at Myrddin belied his mask of neutrality. Transformation merely changed the physical form. It did nothing to the mind—the only difference was the shell in which the mind was presented. Frank still had to give conscious thought to his facial expressions, which didn't come naturally and were all too likely to end in a bared-teeth snarl if he was frustrated. The easiest way in the world to fluster him was to put him in proximity to an unsuspecting woman who then tried to flirt with the tall, strong, chocolate-voiced guy. Frank understood human mating behavior from an academic vantage, but the notion of *engaging* in it was profoundly disturbing to him. ("Would you screw an iguana?" he'd once protested after escaping a drunk bachelorette party that wouldn't take no for an answer.) But Frank, at least, had been fully grown when he first underwent transformation. The idea of going through puberty in the wrong body was appalling to me, and I could only imagine his thoughts on the matter.

"I saw to it that he changed at the same rate as his peers," Myrddin continued. "His beard began to grow in, his voice broke…the spots came on their own…and then the rest of it. Artur started to withdraw, grow sullen. I thought it was just moodiness until he came to me in the middle of the night, begging for help. He'd dreamed of some of his men, and it wasn't the first time he'd caught himself fantasizing. He was horrified, humiliated, desperate to fancy girls…he asked me to fix whatever was wrong with him. So I—"

"Told him the truth?" Mal interrupted.

"In part. I told him he'd been born a girl, and that I'd changed him so that he could be king."

"Must have been a relief, huh?"

"Hardly," he muttered. "Artur was aghast—furious with me at first, and then panicked that the truth would get out. I swore that his men would never know, and I kept that promise."

As he drank his water, I saw the faint tremor in his hand.

"I offered to break the enchantment for a moment, just long enough to let Artur see his true form, but he refused. He threw himself into his training, pushing himself until he could best any master Ambrosius sent to teach him. I overheard him with the other young men when they discussed women, and Artur played along beautifully. There was nothing on the surface to indicate that he was anything but what he seemed."

"Still," I murmured, "Artur had to be miserable."

"He was," Myrddin admitted. "And there was nothing I could do about that. But he pressed on, the sun continued to rise, and we held the Saxons at bay. Sometimes, I caught that fear in his eyes, when he thought he might have slipped, given away some hint that he was just a woman beneath it all—"

I bristled at that.

"—but he grew into a fine king. Old before his time, perhaps, but the responsibility on his shoulders molded him into a man wise beyond his years. He continued to fight under Ambrosius and did remarkable things—magic always seemed to come to him most readily in the heat of battle. He earned the other kings' respect. Afallon was small, but we were mighty.

"And then, when Artur was fifteen, Ambrosius invited all of them and their closest men to a banquet after a victory. One of Guothigirn's sons was still around, and no one saw him sneak in and poison Ambrosius's drink until it was too late. But the fool stayed at the back of the hall to watch him die, Artur spotted him in the chaos, and he caught him as he tried to flee. Threw him against a wall with enchantment, then ran him through with a sword." Myrddin shrugged. "So suddenly, the Britons were down one high king, and one of their own had just slain his killer *with magic*. Someone nominated Artur for the throne, and the rest fell in line."

"At *fifteen*?" said Daphne in disbelief.

"Times were different. I helped Artur as I could—gold and jewels to make his men loyal, secret training in magic, and a quiet, effectively vague rumor campaign about the fate that befell his enemies. And I gave him a gift. A sword."

Ted's eyes widened. "As in—"

"He called it Caledfwlch. Created from pure magic, stronger than steel, sharper than a razor, and able to deflect magical attacks when wielded properly. He bore it into battle from then on, and he never lost. Ten years, and he didn't lose one clod of dirt to the Saxons. Artur was unstoppable, and the more he won, the more talk turned to driving the invaders back across the sea. His men started to believe it was possible."

At that, Marcus folded his arms. "Couldn't you have driven them back without risking an army? Seeing what you've done with this island—"

"This was the work of centuries," Myrddin protested. "I was barely four hundred at the time, and whenever I did anything remotely large, I lost sleep worrying that Titania was going to come for me."

"By doing nothing, you risked Artur's life. Every time he rode into battle and you made no effort to scatter the Saxons…"

His eyes narrowed. "I don't need a lecture from a whelp."

"Only stating the obvious, and what makes you think I'm a child?"

Myrddin's lips curled into a smirk. "You're young yet—

I see it in your eyes. And besides, I knew your father when he was nothing but the queen's foot soldier, so you can't be…"

His voice died away as a curtain of blue fire bloomed around the patio, rising to cover the laden trellis and harmlessly flowing around the vines. An ornate chandelier of flame descended from the middle of the ceiling, and Marcus, who hadn't so much as twitched during the proceedings, slowly cocked his head and smiled back at Myrddin. "You assume much."

I recognized a pissing contest when I saw one and pushed myself from my chair to stand between them again. "Put out the fire. He gets it," I ordered, keeping my eyes on Myrddin. The flames died instantly, and I murmured, "It would be best not to provoke him. You've already held one of us hostage today, and Marcus gets tense when situations deteriorate. Clear?"

He held my gaze for a long moment, then barely dipped his chin. "Sit, girl. Would you have me continue, or are we to duel?"

I looked back at Marcus, silently warning him to ignore the bait, then took my seat. "So, Artur spent a decade fighting Saxons?"

"Not just Saxons." Myrddin leaned forward and clasped his hands between his knees. "Shortly after Artur became high king, a gate into the Gray Lands opened just outside of your Glastonbury. Big, stable—it was new but natural, and I didn't have the strength to close it. Anyway, had I made the attempt—"

"Titania, yes," I said.

He nodded. "Not only did he have Saxons at his borders, but now he had nightmares at his front door. All manner of things—trolls, monstrous wolves, a whole battalion of cyclopean ogre things, a damn bloody dragon…"

Frank quietly snorted.

"And then Morgen wandered into this realm," said

Myrddin. "Ran, more accurately."

Daphne straightened in her seat. "Morgan le Fay? *She* existed?"

"Essentially, though there was nothing fae about her. Morgen was cynaeli." Catching our blank looks, he explained, "They're native to the Gray Lands and talented with dark magic."

"Blue?" Ted asked. "Too many eyes?"

"No. They might seem human but for their coloring—they're purple, with black hair and eyes. A bit smaller than average, I'd say, assuming Morgen was honest with me."

Ted nodded in recognition. "Oh, you mean svartálfar. That's what they're called in our files, anyway. You actually spoke to one?"

Myrddin hesitated, then looked out to sea. "More than spoke," he said, but no one pressed the issue. "I had taken a watch by the gate one evening after several nights of raids, and shortly before dawn, she ran across, cloaked and dripping with rain. I stopped her and challenged her, we took each other's language, and she told me she was running for her life. She was high ranking among her people—half human, but still of high birth—and she said that several of the lords had started to war among themselves. Her husband and his fighting force had been slaughtered, and so she'd fled before she could be discovered. I considered her a kindred soul, in a way, what with us both exiled, and I helped her design a glamour sufficient to allow her to pass."

"I didn't know they could use glamour," said Daphne. "There's plenty in the files about the blue ones, now, but the svartálfar—"

"Cynaeli," he corrected. "They're gifted, but their talents run in different directions. The tennuwaya are the blue ones—they have a strong affinity for their physical surroundings. Elemental magic, you might call it. And Morgen said they were unparalleled for combat sorcery. The cynaeli are better at working with the mind—

glamours, illusions, you get the picture. That's not to say that one couldn't work the other's specialty, but their strengths are generally divergent. And since the tennuwaya are the stronger and larger of the two, they chose the best territories. The cynaeli settled deep in the mountains and tried to ward against attack. Or so I was told. I've never been across the border."

"What happened to Morgen, then?" I asked.

"I quietly explained the situation to Artur and requested that she be allowed to remain as my guest. He agreed, and she and I…ehm…became friends, I suppose you could say." He sighed softly and frowned into space. "She was the only other person who knew the truth about Artur. I dropped my defenses one night when we—"

"We get it," Mal interrupted.

Myrddin seemed relieved to be spared the retelling. "She kept my secret, though, since I was keeping hers from the rest of the kingdom. I don't know how long a violet-skinned sorceress would have lasted."

He fell silent for a time, swirling the water in his glass, his face shifting through flashes of subtle emotions as he collected his thoughts.

"As I said, Artur was unstoppable," he finally resumed. "His greatest victory was at Badon—I don't know how many he killed that day, but his face and arms were scarlet with Saxon blood by sunset. The carrion birds feasted in the dark, and Artur's men feasted in their tents alongside the dead." He smiled faintly. "I remember him that night—his beard unkempt, his hair hastily tied back, scratched and bruised but whole. He'd washed before the meal, but he'd missed a streak of blood near his left ear. And he celebrated until the morning—there was feasting and drinking, every manner of song, even dancing when the men were far in their cups. I remember sitting near him, watching him and thinking he was every inch a king, and he was only twenty-four. Still such a child, but a ferocious one."

"What about the Round Table?" Daphne asked. "Any truth to that?"

"No. Artur had his favorites from across the kingdoms, a few talented men who stayed at his side, but nothing like the stories." He began counting off on his fingers. "There was Bedwyr, who'd been born with a withered arm but fought left-handed, which made him difficult to block. Madoc, the son of one of Uther's cousins, I forget which. Kei, yes, and Medraut, both good lads. Medraut's been treated horribly in legend, and I haven't the faintest idea why. He was loyal to a fault."

"Then who killed Artur at Camlann?" Ted interrupted.

"No one. Artur never fought at Camlann, and Medraut certainly didn't kill him." Myrddin's jaws clenched and unclenched as he again paused for thought. "A few months after Badon, Artur was in residence when these...*things*...came through the gate one morning. I don't know what they were, and Morgen never told me, but they were enormous, maybe ten meters high, but that varied. They were like sentient smoke—a gray cloud with a ring of red spots around the midsection. I *think* those were the eyes, but honestly, I've no proof. Two of them came through together, and a third followed, and all hell broke loose.

"The guards on the gate were the first to die. They couldn't fight smoke, and when the clouds enveloped them..." He closed his eyes and grimaced. "What was left after the clouds passed was barely recognizable as human. There was something *in* the smoke, you see. I don't know if it was the clouds themselves or whether they had some sort of symbiotic relationship with a more solid creature, but whatever was swallowed by the smoke died screaming."

"Jesus," Ted muttered.

"The priests prayed, but they found no help there," Myrddin said. "At least the clouds were slow—the common folk had time to run for higher ground. I directed everyone up the Tor and tried to throw wards together, but have you ever tried to ward a mountain under those conditions? Not my best effort. But as the people were fleeing up the mountain, Artur and his men rode out to fight. Artur had that damned sword, after all. Probably thought he was invincible by then."

When Myrddin fell silent, I quietly prodded, "What happened?"

"A massacre," he murmured. "The men on foot went first, running and yelling their war cries, and they were slaughtered. Like they'd run through a meat grinder," he said with a shudder. "Artur sent the next wave. Same end. Arrows had no effect—*flaming* arrows had no effect—and I was too busy trying to ward the mountain to give them more than the occasional firebolt. But Artur wasn't one to surrender. More men went out with swords and horses and bows, and more fell.

"Morgen had been away from me when the attack began," he continued, "tending to a woman in labor in the village. She had a skill for healing. Anyway, as the last of the main forces were being mowed down, Morgen finally made it up the Tor. She told me she'd seen those creatures in the Gray Lands, and she knew how to defeat them."

"How?" Ted whispered, leaning almost out of his chair.

"In short, necromancy. Some of the cynaeli have a talent for working with the dead."

"*Necromancy*?" I yelped. "That's just a theory—"

"Probably impossible when you're working with magic, but Morgen managed quite effectively," said Myrddin. "She stood on the mountaintop, focused, and started chanting, and…well, it was like a mist rose from the field behind the smoke creatures. It started to clump into individual shades, all of them translucent at first, but they solidified to near opacity in moments. And when their swords struck, they struck *hard*."

From the look on his face, I gathered that Mryddin wasn't seeing us in that moment.

"Artur should have stayed back. The recently dead were doing a fine job without his help, and Morgen was giving them every drop of power that she could channel. But Artur had never stayed on the sidelines for long. I watched as he and his closest men rode for the fighting. The creatures were sorely wounded by then—one may have even died—but the living didn't last more than a few moments. I watched them fall, one by one, and then Artur rode at one of the creatures with his sword sparking. His shield was up, he was throwing everything he had into it, just as I'd taught him…" He swallowed, then blinked hard. "It got him. A glancing blow, maybe, but fatal all the same.

"I was on the field before the last creature fell, and I ran to Artur, but his wounds…one deep gash across the stomach, another across the chest. I tried, but I couldn't stop the bleeding, and he lost consciousness…" Myrddin struggled for a few seconds to hold his composure, then muttered, "My apologies, I thought I could get through one damn recitation without coming apart, but as you can see—"

"You lost your child," Marcus softly cut in. "There's no shame in mourning his death, is there?"

"He's not dead," Myrddin replied with a brittle smile. "Morgen followed me just in time. The creatures died, the dead disappeared, and she did what she could for him. Stabilized, I suppose. But we both knew that we couldn't heal him in this realm—not enough power for either of us. I couldn't very well take him into Faerie, but Morgen offered to take him home with her and see what she could do. She'd been gone for years, you know, and she had hope that the fighting had ended in her absence. I didn't have a better idea. She gave me his sword to hold until their return, then took him into the Gray Lands. I watched until they disappeared into the mist."

"They never came back, did they?" I murmured.

Myrddin shook his head. "Not yet. Two days later, the gate closed. I don't know if it happened naturally or if something on the other side saw to it, but it was gone. Afallon fell into chaos almost immediately—the king was missing, most of his men were dead, and all that was left to hold the throne was a handful of old men and me. As far as the common folk were concerned, magic had got their loved ones killed, and I saw the writing on the wall—never mind that I saved their lives," he said bitterly. "So, I fled in the dead of night, went west until I found the sea, and took this island as my own. It's all that's left of Afallon now. I don't know if Dunmonia absorbed Afallon before the Saxons crushed what was left of the Britons, and frankly, I don't care. All I know is that I'm not giving up and returning to Faerie before I learn what happened to my son."

Most of us were sitting in silence on the patio, listening to the sea breeze rustling in the orchard and trying to think of what to say to follow Myrddin's tale, when Daphne stood and tugged down her jacket. "Sorry to ask," she began, turning to Myrddin, "but is there a loo somewhere on this island?"

He cocked one thumb at the tower. "Walk in that door, and there's one to your right."

She hurried off, and I topped up my tea and stood with Marcus at the edge of the patio, taking in the view. When I snaked my arm around his waist, he looked down at me and flashed the sad smile I knew too well from our wine nights. "I'm fine," he said.

"You're a lousy liar."

He didn't protest, and soon, I felt his arm around my shoulders, pulling me close against the cool wind. I drank my tea in silence, and I was trying to work out how the hell I was going to put *this* in the monthly report when Daphne came running out of the tower. When she landed on the patio, she caught her breath, then pointed back at the building and demanded, "Is that what I think it is?"

Myrddin nodded. "I needed to keep it safe. The tower works as well as anywhere."

The excitement on Daphne's face was nearing Ted-ish levels, which was worrisome in almost all circumstances. "Can I show the others?"

Our host sighed and stood. "If it amuses you."

Curious, we followed her inside, and as soon as my eyes adjusted to the dimmer light, I realized what had made her so giddy.

In the middle of the tower was planted a black boulder, as high and wide as a coffee table but substantially sturdier. Protruding from the center of the boulder was a long sword with a gold-colored handle, its blade glittering like well-faceted diamond in the light from the narrow windows.

"Oh, my God," I whispered. "*Excalibur.*"

"Caledfwlch," Myrddin corrected, coming up behind me. "'Excalibur' is a French corruption of the Latin corruption. But yes, that's Artur's sword. Not bad, if I do say so myself."

"It's beautiful. The blade—"

"Crystallized magic. A tight lattice honeycombed with pockets of the stuff. The stone is a security device," he told us. "I tried a few over the years, and once the stories evolved...well, this seemed appropriate."

Ted, who was circling the stone like a hungry shark around a diving cage, paused and looked at Myrddin. "So...only Artur can pull it out?"

"Not exactly." He folded his arms and offered a quick shrug. "Ideally, I'd have keyed it to his blood, but I didn't have any on hand, so I did the next best thing—I keyed it to mine. Only one of my blood can pull it free, so that leaves a class of exactly two. If something should happen to me before Artur returns...you know...it'll be waiting for him."

Ted hesitated for only a few seconds before his excitement got the best of him. "May I touch it?"

"No harm in it," said Myrddin, giving him the same indulgent smile one might show a precocious toddler. "Touch it, give it a yank, take selfies with it. You won't hurt it."

I stood back, shaking my head, as my colleagues swarmed the rock with their phones and cameras ready. One at a time, they grabbed the hilt and pulled, and their failures were eagerly documented by the rest of the Team. Even Marcus, whose familiarity with the stories was barely more than minimal, got in on the sword pictures.

As I checked my messages, I suddenly heard Myrddin's voice in my right ear. "Go on, get your photo. You'll kick yourself tomorrow if you don't."

I glanced up from the screen. "Seems like poor taste," I said quietly. "But thanks for letting us get it out of our collective system."

He considered that, then clapped me on the shoulder. "Thank you, but Artur isn't here to complain. Give me your mobile, I'll do the honors."

Rolling my eyes, I opened the camera and surrendered my phone, and Myrddin got into position as I stood behind the boulder. "Right, this is for your Christmas card," he called, lining up the shot as a few other phones lifted around him. "Ready when you are."

Though slightly embarrassed to have the rest of the group cheering me on to certain defeat, I reached out and curled my hand around the leather-wrapped portion of the hilt. It was warmer than I'd expected, but then my colleagues had just had their mitts all over it. Still, I flexed my fingers around it, getting a good grip, then smiled for the camera and pulled.

Flashes went off once, twice…and then Myrddin dropped my phone onto the stone floor and gaped. "How…" he breathed.

Only when I looked at my right hand did I realize the problem. The sword had come free of its prison, and as I rotated my wrist, it threw jewels of sunlight onto the curving tower walls. The warmth of the hilt seemed stronger, and it radiated from my palm into my forearm, stretching toward my elbow.

"Um…Kitty?" Ted managed as the others gawked. "I could be wrong, but I think you might be queen of the Britons now."

I stared up at Caledfwlch, sword of legend, and tried to square this development with my prior sense of reality. The sword was incredibly light, hardly more burdensome than my wand, though quite a bit longer, and—

Holy shit, my mind shouted, catching up with me, *put that thing back where you found it!*

"Okay…huh," I mumbled, and slid the sword back into the stone. "Sorry about that…"

But my hand wouldn't unclench from around the hilt, which was now growing uncomfortably warm, and the sword came free again when I tried to pull my hand away. "Uh, Myrddin?" I squeaked. "Little help, here?" He just stared, his mouth flapping like a landed fish's, and so I looked to the others for assistance. "I can't drop it! It's stuck to me…*oww*!" Clutching the hilt was now like holding hot charcoal, and my arm and shoulder felt as if they were on fire. "I can't let go, and it's burning me! Someone do something!"

While Frank and Mal tried to pry the sword from my hand, Marcus grabbed his phone and stepped to the side. "This is an emergency," I heard him say in rapid Latin, and I knew he'd called Val. By then, though, the pain had grown severe enough to send me to my knees, and I only heard snippets of his conversation, words that zipped across my consciousness like mosquitos buzzing around my face at a picnic. I lay on my side in the fetal position, letting the cold stone soothe my left arm as the flames inside me spread, and I only realized I was screaming when I recognized the sound of feral howling as my own voice.

Light flooded the tower, red against my scrunched-closed eyelids, and arms lifted me from the floor. "It's going to be all right," Marcus insisted, running awkwardly as he carried me, and I opened my eyes long enough to see Val's office through the gate. There were shapes on the other side, silhouetted and blurred by my tears of agony, but I was too far gone to care about making a scene in front of an audience. I landed on the familiar couch, though the cool leather gave me no comfort that day.

In the middle of my panicked thoughts, I heard Ros's voice: *Shit. I'm sorry, honey. You're going to be okay in a few minutes.*

Help me, I mentally pleaded. *Make it stop.*

The flames flared and engulfed me, burning me to ash until even my voice was no more than smoke.

And then, mercifully, I knew no more.

CHAPTER 6

I floated toward consciousness, bobbing just below the surface and growing ever more aware of the familiar sensory comforts of my bed: the crisp linens, the faintly floral scent of my detergent, the slight depression in the middle of the mattress that had formed to fit the curves of my body as I burrowed on my side. I felt the cotton duvet cover shift against my cheek—truly, I slept best when buried as if against an Arctic winter—and luxuriated in the indolence of an unhurried morning. The sun was well up, and my alarm hadn't gone off, so I reasoned that it must be the weekend.

No. No, that wasn't right.

I flopped onto my back and gazed at the unmoving ceiling fan as I tried to piece together the previous night. Pub outing, maybe? That could explain some of the haziness, but I felt far too good to be hungover. Maybe I'd fallen asleep over my work and been carried off to bed. I glanced under the duvet and saw only a nightshirt and underwear, which dashed that theory. Marcus and I might have been intimate, but he had yet to undress me without my consent, and Maria would have known to pull off my shoes and call it a job well done.

The knot in my stomach told me that *something* had happened, though, and it wouldn't allow me to go back to sleep. Disturbed for reasons I couldn't explain, I dragged myself from bed, threw on my robe, and opened the door. "Marcus?" I called into the quiet flat. "You here?"

"Nah, it's just us girls," said a voice from the sofa, and

I stopped in my tracks when I spotted the speaker.

Faerie's consciousness, the will directing its immense power, was a blonde a couple of inches taller than me with large, dark eyes and a tendency toward loungewear. Like all faeries, she could have been my peer unless you looked too closely. Well, a *close* examination wasn't needed in her case; Ros glowed when she took corporeal form, which had only been disturbing the first few dozen times that she manifested around me. For a woman in her forties, Ros had an eclectic résumé: daughter of a grand magus and a lesser blood, kin to Eleanor and Coileán in equal measure, silo dweller until she went rogue, catalyst of Grand Magus Mulligan's undoing, privately tutored in spellcraft by Toula herself, and now the literal power behind the thrones, a career move she'd made to save the realm and magic as we knew it. Omniscient in Faerie, she'd kept an eye on me during my school years, and I knew I had nothing to fear from her…but…

I glanced around my flat, yet I saw no sign of a gate. "How are you *here*?" I demanded. As far as I knew, Ros was tied to Faerie, able to send part of her consciousness beyond its borders but not manifest in the mortal realm.

She pushed herself off the couch, unkinked her back, and folded her arms across her blue hoodie. "*Here* isn't where you think it is," she replied. "You're not in the castle. This is a projection I pulled from your mind."

"Huh?"

"You're still unconscious. We're having this conversation in your head." She sat again and gestured toward the unoccupied couch cushion, and I sank down as my last memories crashed over me like a wave of fire.

"I got it out of your hand," she said, answering my question before I could ask it. "It's on the dresser. No permanent damage."

"Dresser…"

"You're in your old room at Val's," Ros explained. "It's early evening. I kept you down as long as I did to give you time to recover, but I think the worst has passed. You'll be sore, but that's the damn sword's doing, not mine."

I groped at my scattered memories, searching for coherence among the broken pieces. "What happened?"

Ros sighed, and twin mugs of coffee appeared on the table beside us. I reached out automatically—regardless of whether this was all illusion, my body reacted to the smell of dark roast on instinct—and Ros drank in slow sips, her gaze shifting around the room as she thought. Finally, when she could comfortably stall no longer, she said, "Faeries look down their noses at wizards for a variety of reasons—"

"I hadn't noticed."

"*Right.* The biggest one of all is that wizards have to study to master spellcraft. Faeries can do wonders with a few pointers and a bit of practice, but wizards have to learn focus, discipline…and yeah, I'm preaching to the choir," she said as I nodded along. "But here's the thing: faeries can intuit quite a lot in terms of practical work, but they don't know any damn theory. Well, hang on, that's too broad a brush," she amended, "there are some who've picked up techniques along the way. But in general, because faeries don't need to master the technicalities to use magic, they never learn any of the underpinnings of the system. It's like they're flying supersonic jets and haven't the faintest idea of how they're built or what half the warning indicators mean—you follow?"

"I, uh…sure, I guess…"

"With that in mind, let's talk about the sword," she continued, tucking her knee onto the couch as she turned to better face me. "By all rights, that thing shouldn't exist. It *shouldn't.* That Myrddin actually made it coalesce is just a hair shy of a miracle. Oh, don't get me wrong," she said, holding her coffee close, "he's more talented than he lets on, but even I can barely work out how he made the sword, and that's not Ros talking, that's Faerie. I'd say it's an incredibly technical piece of work, but really, it's dumb luck. Like throwing a deck of cards into the air and having them land in a neat little pile, sorted by suit. Shouldn't happen, but this once…" She whistled low.

"What *is* it? And why couldn't I let it go?"

"Hard to describe in terms you'd understand," she said matter-of-factly. "It's less the product of an enchantment than an enchantment itself, frozen just before it fully activates. Those pockets of magic he built into it have been holding it together for the last…what, sixteen centuries?"

I shrugged and sipped. "Something like that."

"Anyway, it's starting to run low, and I'm not sure exactly how big the explosion will be when it goes off, but it won't be pretty. The slow drain of all those years, plus the '13 closure, plus that little bonus Myrddin grafted onto it—the sword's seen better days. I want someone to give it to Amy Levey. She's the only crafter I'd trust to refill and stabilize it."

"Yeah, but about that, uh, *bonus*—"

"Right." Ros refilled her mug and spent a long moment draining it again before continuing. "Remember what I said about faeries not knowing shit about the technicalities of magic?"

"Yep."

"Exhibit A. Knowing how that sword is held together, what wouldn't you do to it above all else?"

The answer was obvious to anyone with the rudiments of an Arcanum education. "Tinker with it. Adding to the matrix could overwhelm it, and—"

"*Boom*," Ros finished. "Well, Myrddin's a lucky son of a bitch, since that's *exactly* what he did."

I cringed at the notion.

"The good news is that he didn't fully integrate the blood lock with the enchantment holding the sword intact. The bad news is that he gave a shoddily constructed blood lock access to a massive power source, and when you touched it…" Ros hesitated, looking everywhere but at my eyes, then muttered, "Maybe I should have said something sooner. *Probably* should have."

"About what?" I asked, tightening my grip on my mug.

Though the realm didn't need to breathe, Ros took a deep breath and exhaled slowly as I waited, my guts knotting. "The lock on the sword was tied to Myrddin's bloodline," she murmured. "You unlocked it."

I squeezed the mug so hard that my fingers blanched. "What are you saying?"

"I'm saying that I knew the moment you first crossed the border that you're witch-blooded."

My stomach flopped, and I became conscious of a high ringing in my ears as the world began to go gray. With a grunt, Ros reached over and shook my shoulder until the tinnitus and visual effects faded. "We're in your head, remember? You're not actually going to pass out in here. Focus."

"Oh, my God," I mumbled, putting the mug aside to rub my face. "What...but how..." Hitting on a solution, I looked up and found her watching me with a slightly guilty expression. "It's Mom, isn't it? That's why she doesn't like me, she's not really my—"

"Sorry," she murmured, "but no. Eva's your mother."

"Then how—"

My voice snapped off as I answered my own question, but I refused to allow myself to believe it. Still, the quick twitch of Ros's mouth gave me the confirmation I was dreading.

"Please believe me, I didn't want to break it to you like this," she said softly. "I was going to have to tell you sooner rather than later—I wanted you to have the option before you got much older—but when you were a kid, with all the other shit you had on your plate, I didn't want to add *this*. You know how tough it can be when everyone learns you're a mongrel."

She didn't have to elaborate. There were plenty of wizards who weren't afraid to share their opinions as to the propriety of Toula's presence in Glastonbury—hell, even Maria's presence, back before Ros amplified her drop of fae blood into a raging ocean. As a weak witch, I'd had my own detractors—some more murder-happy than others—but if I'd been pegged as…

A thought popped to the fore. *That* was why I was terrible at spellcraft—if I were witch-blooded, of course that would screw up my talent.

But if I were witch-blooded, then…

Ros, who knew my thoughts, let me sort through the maze until I reached the door I refused to open. "Orson Connolly wasn't your biological father." Though her voice was gentle, something within me clenched and shattered as she spoke. "Toula did the aural work this afternoon while you were sleeping. Half wizard, one-quarter fae."

I heard her words, but they couldn't quite penetrate to my core, like rain flung harmlessly against a window. "Quarter?" I echoed.

"By Myrddin." She waited, giving that a second to sink in, then said, "He had no idea. I'm fairly confident that you were an accident. A *happy* accident," she added, putting her hand on my knee. "Anyway, he wants to talk to you, but I'm playing gatekeeper right now, so he can wait until you're good and ready. There's no rush, Kitty."

Ros sat silently as I processed, the word *mongrel* echoing around the deeper, louder caverns of my mind. Mom knew—she had to have known. And she'd never said a word, never explained why she'd wanted no part of me…

As I ruminated, Ros tugged my attention away from the dark place into which it had been drifting. "So, let's get back to the sword."

"Blood lock," I muttered, then laughed once in disbelief. "Shitty piece of enchantment. Opening that thing hurt like hell."

"Oh, it's a far shittier piece of work than you realize," she replied, rubbing her forehead. "Had Myrddin put that particular enchantment on virtually anything else, it would have functioned as he'd intended. Instead, he linked it up with that fucking sword, which had consequences he didn't foresee because—"

"Faeries don't know theory."

"Exactly. Now, that construction was made with blood, but the lock was, technically, keyed to his aural signature. It only opened if it sensed a copy."

"Okay…"

"You have that copy, but only at half strength. The enchantment was…*iffy* to begin with," she pronounced with disdain, "and when he connected it to the sword's matrix…" She shook her head. "Honestly, that thing defies all probability. Long story short, the lock recognized you as a key, but an imperfect one. It tried to *fix* you."

My hand clenched at the memory of the burning pain. "Fix how? Via incineration?"

"No. It was, however crudely, trying to make you match the original key." Her voice sped up as my forehead furrowed. "It was doing to you, albeit much more slowly, what I did to Maria. Amplification and suppression. The process was underway when you got to me, and I couldn't stop it without hurting you, so I stepped in and completed it quickly. Ripped off the bandage, you know? It was either that or let you lie there in agony for hours."

I could feel myself gaping and struggled to maintain control. "You mean…"

Ros smiled weakly. "Magic is about to get much easier for you, but, uh….you might want to invest in new flatware."

"I—"

"Functionally fae. I'm sorry, I really did mean to sit you down and give you the *option*, but the sword made the choice for us both. I've kept you asleep this long to let you heal—it did a number on you. Anyway…" She stood and looked down at me as I stared stupidly at her vacated spot on the couch. "Toula wants to talk to you. Is that okay, or would you rather I barricade the door?"

"It's okay," I heard myself reply, and looked up at the

touch of Ros's hand on my shoulder.

"I know it's a lot. Hang in there, honey," she murmured as my flat began to dissolve around us. "And remember that you're not alone."

I gasped and opened my eyes to flickering light.

Instead of my flat, I was looking up at the familiar ceiling of my old bedroom at Val's. I saw the posts of my bed rising around me, dark wood carved into the likeness of palm trunks and topped with fronds for finials. The blue tint of the world past the garden door suggested twilight, but someone had thought to leave a candelabra on the nightstand. There were few electric lights in Faerie, after all, and our old generator was next door in Ros's room.

I ached. Every muscle throbbed with the deep burn of a week spent on the climbing wall, and my joints protested when I tried to sit up. At least my head wasn't hurting— I'd take whatever small mercies I could get at that moment—but just sitting up in bed took willpower and a healthy dose of hissed profanity. Once I was partially upright, I saw the sword on the dresser, just as Ros had promised. In the candlelight, it glittered rainbows onto the ceiling and wall, taunting me with its presence. I checked my hand, but my palm seemed unburned—nothing was different but for the inescapable pain.

It's much better than it was, Ros whispered into my mind. *You'll be fine by morning. But that's why I let you sleep.*

I silently thanked her and peeled off the covers. Whoever had carted me off to bed had left me fully clothed but for my shoes, which waited by the door. I swung my legs over the side, whimpered when my knees bent, and slid down onto my feet...and then immediately wished I hadn't. The sudden surge of pain was almost enough to send me to the floor, and I gripped the nearest bedpost for support, wondering how much worse off I'd been a few hours before.

And that was how the grand magus found me when she rapped on the door and cracked it open. "*Easy*, Kitty," Toula chided, and I felt myself go weightless as I floated off the ground. Releasing the bedpost, I let her steer me back onto the mattress, though I cried out when my back took the gentle impact of landing. "Be still," she said, rearranging the blankets, and I focused on my breathing until the flare-up had passed.

"This is, apparently, better," I muttered.

"Be that as it may, Bee's on her way with morphine," she replied, waving a chair from across the room over to my bedside. "Can't hurt, right?"

"What about numbing?"

"Look at your arm."

I glanced beneath the sheet and made out the faint traces of enchantment surrounding me, nearly buried in my aura. "That's the best Val can do," Toula explained. "You shouldn't be able to feel it if I ripped off your leg right now, but since that's obviously not the case, we thought we'd supplement with opioids."

"Thanks."

"Don't thank me yet. Ros isn't feeling confident about this working, and neither is Bee, but it seemed like the best option." She took a seat and waited while I slowly rolled over to face her, then murmured, "So. *You've* had a day."

"Yeah."

"And I understand that Ros has had a little chat with you, right?"

I nodded, and she sat back and crossed her legs. She'd forgone her formal robes in favor of well-worn jeans and a thin green sweater that slouched off one shoulder, which brought out the coordinating highlights she'd streaked beneath the top layer of her dark bob. The most powerful wizard in the world could dress any way she damn well pleased.

Witch-blood, I mentally amended. Toula could cast and

enchant with equal facility, though she refrained from doing much of the latter around the castle. While she appeared to be roughly my age, I knew she'd passed her eightieth birthday. She took no pains to hide her years or her true face from the Arcanum—Toula's family tree was no secret, and I gathered that she didn't see a point in glamouring herself with white hair and wrinkles.

"Good," she said. "I'm not going to bother you long— I just wanted to let you know that you don't need to map out the rest of your life tonight."

I tried to grasp at any of the thousand thoughts flitting around my head, but they evaded me like tenacious butterflies. "Um...well, uh...that's—"

"It's okay," she soothed, standing slightly to brush my trailing hair from my face. "Listen to me. The only people who know what's happened are in this realm. Marcus and Maria were informed, and Val finally thought to call me over, but that's it. The Team has been told that you're recovering from your injuries, and I left it at that. What happens next is up to you, but this is not a decision that needs to be made on the spot."

I felt my eyes begin to prick and blinked until the danger passed. "Did you know?"

"About you? No. But damn," she muttered, "that makes sense."

"And you're sure about...about my dad?" I forced myself to ask.

Toula's face softened. "What I'm sure about at the moment is the identity of your biological father. I want to compare you and your sister to see if there are other *irregularities* swept under your mother's rug."

The mention of Beth made my stomach sick. When this little factoid got around, she'd never speak to me again. Not that we were exactly on speaking terms at the moment, but still, I'd hoped for an eventual reconciliation with my sister...*half* sister, I supposed.

Who had always favored Dad. She'd never known him,

but she looked like him. Of course I didn't share that resemblance—I wasn't even Dad's daughter.

"Myrddin's here," Toula said quietly as I struggled. "Coileán can't believe it took this long for him to figure out that Myrddin exists, but given how many centuries that guy's been in hiding, I'm not surprised that he's been overlooked. And you should have seen Val's face," she added with a slight smile. "Stared like he'd seen a ghost. Anyway, Myrddin's staying elsewhere in the villa at the moment. Coileán told him that whatever bounty Titania put on his head has been removed, but he seems eager to get back to England. He does want to talk to you first, though. I could bring him by, if you'd like."

My traitorous throat had started to tighten. "Not yet. Please."

"Say no more. There's no schedule for this, and I'm leaving it up to you to set the pace." She hesitated, then said, "That's another thing that doesn't need to be decided right now. Technically, your affiliation is with the Arcanum, yeah?"

"Yeah…"

"With certain information having come to light, you have options." She began to count off on her fingers. "One, you do nothing. Keep on keeping on with the Arcanum, but that would probably mean staying well out of the spotlight. Witch-bloods are one thing, but you've been, shall we say, augmented. Which brings me to two: you choose a court. If you still want to work on the Team, that's fantastic—I mean, a decent chunk of you guys are on loan, and no one's come to blows yet."

"A court," I mumbled, not quite believing the words coming out of my mouth.

"Yup. Generally, now, these things follow bloodlines. And Myrddin wasn't just affiliated with Titania's court— he's a lord. That's hereditary, incidentally, so if you opt to go that route, you'd be a lady." Seeing my expression as I connected those dots, she chuckled. "Hasn't done much for me, but whatever. All of that said, you aren't *bound* to follow in Myrddin's footsteps, and if you wanted to choose another court…say, the one to which your boyfriend is inextricably entwined…that would be allowed. And for the record, Coileán wanted me to make it clear to you that he wouldn't raise a fuss."

"Decent of him."

"Well, that, and he does *not* want to cross my big brother. Val's no fun when he's pissed. But as I was saying, this isn't anything to worry about tonight…*ah*," she said as the door opened. "Thanks, Bee."

Dr. Powell, Arc 2's only physician, was friendly enough on the few occasions when I didn't catch her at work— she'd been patching me up since I was ten—but when she was in her element, she didn't hesitate to bark orders. That night, she seemed to be in no mood for back-talk. "Of course. Step aside," she told Toula, who complied without protest. Dr. Powell put her bag on my nightstand and frowned down at me in thought, her mass of red curls backlit by the candelabra like a ginger halo. "Conscious, I see."

"Yes, ma'am," I replied, wincing as I shifted in the bed.

"We're in a fair bit of pain?"

"At least."

"Bee," said Ros, materializing at the foot of my bed, "the needle—"

"Ahead of you," she murmured, pulling a syringe kit from her bag. "Titanium set." She turned to Ros and flashed a quick smile. "I *have* been over here a few times, dear."

"Just double-checking."

"Meddling," she replied, not unkindly. "Let me work."

I tried not to whimper when Dr. Powell pulled back the blankets and gave me a shot in the thigh through my leggings. "Wait a moment," she said as she tidied her things. "Let's see if that helps."

To our collective surprise, it did. Five minutes after the

injection, I was feeling closer to numb and slightly drowsy, and Dr. Powell nodded as I began to relax. "That's a start, then," she said, and fished her wand from her bag. A quick, mumbled incantation later, I saw a thin net of magic form above my face and chest, a layer of spellcraft atop the enchantment already wrapped around me, which, aided by the drug, was finally beginning to have a noticeable effect. "Alarm and timer," she told us, and tapped a black band on her wrist. "If your breathing or heart rate slows too much, this will alert me. I'll be back in a few hours to see if we need to adjust your dose. Now, try to sleep."

They left me to my own devices—well, Ros dematerialized, which was as close to privacy as anyone ever had in Faerie—and I stared at the wall as the candle flames bobbed. Freed from the worst of the pain, I felt nothing at first, and then a deep sadness rose from my emotional well and began to flood through me. I clutched the blankets and let the first tears fall, and I'd buried myself in the bedding to hide from the universe when I heard the garden door ease open.

"Kitty?" Marcus whispered. "Are you awake?"

I dried my face on my sleeve, sniffed, and sat up to find him just inside the room, watching with concern as I untangled myself. "Sneaked over the wall?" I asked.

"Came through Maria's room. And…you're not okay."

There was no point in denying the obvious. I bit the inside of my lip and shook my head, and he took a hesitant step closer. "Do you want me to go? I assume I'm not meant to be in here, but…"

Wordlessly, I reached for him, and he kicked off his shoes and slid into bed beside me. I rolled toward him and sobbed against his shirt as he held me, stroking my hair and waiting me out. When my crying jag ebbed into its shuddering conclusion, he murmured, "You don't have to be okay, Kitty. I understand. It's a *lot*."

I shifted closer to him, taking comfort in his familiar scent. "Not what you think."

"Do you want to tell me?" He waited, and when all he got from me was a sniffle, he softly asked, "May I see?"

I nodded, then almost immediately felt his presence in my mind, probing for meaning in my jumbled thoughts. Marcus didn't have his father's finesse or Frank's innate ability to find what he'd come for and retreat, but his touch had grown gentle with practice, and I let him flit through the memories that rose before my mind's eye like soap bubbles, beautiful and fragile and devastating as they seemed to pop, over and over.

I was crying again before Marcus could slip away, but I felt the sudden void when he withdrew, then the pressure of his arm tightening around me. "Your father loved you," he said. "You know that."

"Because he didn't know the truth."

"Kitty…"

"He thought I was his! If he'd known…"

My voice petered out, and Marcus rubbed my shoulder as I tried to hold back the next wave. "Tell me about the flowers."

"Huh?"

"The sunflowers. They're everywhere in your thoughts right now."

He was right. I didn't see them directly, but I sensed them as if in my peripheral vision, more a blur than a true memory. I couldn't help but connect them with my dad— they'd been his primary crop, after all—but after a moment's concentration, I realized which flowers Marcus had noticed and forced myself to explain, revisiting a memory I usually tried to forget. "When I was five, I started playing in the fields. The flowers were taller than me, and I'd get out in the middle of them and hide, play with my dolls and whatnot. It was like I had my own little world under the flowers."

"So you've said."

"Well, I was a little kid, and for whatever stupid reason that summer, I thought the flowers would last forever. But

Daddy had to harvest them in the fall—he sold some flowers, and that was bad enough when those were cut, but the real money was in the seeds, see, and he left most of the crop out in the field until the blooms shriveled and turned brown. I thought they might come back until I watched the combine take them down, and I *cried*. Inconsolable. So that night, Daddy came up to tuck me in, and he had this vase with him. Five of the best flowers, cut short and preserved with a spell earlier in the season. He promised me the fields would grow back, but now I'd always have some with me."

My throat tightened, and I swallowed to press on. "I took them to school once Mom shipped me off to Glastonbury. When the older kids tried to get rid of me, they destroyed my things, you know, and…"

"Your sunflowers."

"I didn't think to hide them in time. Toula was nice about trying to replace everything, but she couldn't bring them back, and…"

"And part of your father was gone," Marcus finished when I couldn't.

I nodded. "With all of this, I just feel like I…like I've lost Daddy all over again."

Marcus didn't need to answer that. He knew the void of loss as well as I did, and he hugged me close beneath the blankets. Though I still hurt beneath the enchantment and the morphine haze, I made no move to shake him off, and he held me until I fell asleep.

Ros was right—I felt infinitely better in the morning, as if all the previous day's excruciating pain had been nothing but a nightmare. As thrilled as I was to wake and be able to move without discomfort, I was less excited to hear a knock at the door before I'd actually put weight on my feet.

Toula, Val, and Coileán let themselves in after that

cursory knock, and if they were surprised to find Marcus with me, no one let on. "Oh, good, you're up," said Toula, her hands tucked into the pocket of a faded orange hoodie that had seen better decades. "So, here's the deal. We worked out the details last night," she said, glancing at the kings, who nodded along. "You're going to stay here for a bit until we're all satisfied that you don't pose a danger to yourself, and then you can come back to Glastonbury if you want. I'll tell Ted that you're in rehab if you don't want the Team to know about this right away."

"You need training," Val cut in as I began to protest. "No arguments. Maria went through this, too."

"It's for everyone's safety," Coileán added. "And she should be here...now," he said, turning as someone else knocked. He opened the door and stepped aside, admitting a well-toned woman with a curly brown ponytail and a face full of freckles.

Marcus groaned behind me, and she smirked. "Good morning to you, too," she said with a taunting wave.

Coileán snorted. "Kitty, have you met Mina? Captain of my guard, general force to be reckoned with, and despite whatever lies Marcus has told you, an excellent tutor."

"Learned from the best," she said, cutting her eyes to Val, who smiled in acknowledgement. "So, child...when do we begin? Before or after breakfast?"

Having heard more than enough horror stories from Marcus's training, I looked to Toula for help, but I found none there. "I know you think you're shit with magic," she told me, "and until, oh, twenty-four hours ago, I'd have agreed. But I've seen your marks, and I know how much you've worked to compensate for your disadvantages. You know every focusing technique Maria knows, and you've seen what she can do."

"But she's *Maria*," I countered.

"Yeah. Who's working off of enchantment now. As are you." She held out her empty hand, and a bright orange fireball bloomed from her palm like an exotic flower.

"Give it a shot."

Fighting the discomfort I felt whenever I was called upon to do magic, the result of failing magnificently on most occasions, I mirrored Toula's pose and stared at my hand. My memory flashed to my awful wand ceremony— once again, I was in front of an expectant crowd, and if I didn't perform, they would think that I—

The flicker of will I sent toward my hand was, perhaps, a tad too focused. A violet flame the size of a basketball burst forth, and I hastily cupped my other hand beneath it before it could fall to the floor. I gaped at the fire, then at Toula, who grinned knowingly at my astonishment.

"Oh," said Mina, folding her arms, "this is going to be *fun*."

But before I subjected myself to the punishment that Mina had in store for me, there was one matter I needed to address.

Myrddin seemed surprised when I cornered him in the dining room, but whether he was caught off guard to see me or to see me holding Caledfwlch with a towel between my hand and the hilt, I couldn't tell. "Kitty," he said, pushing back from the table. "You've healed?"

"Feels like it," I replied, and put the naked sword on the silk table runner. "Ros and Toula want to send this to a crafter for repairs, but since it's yours, you might want to make that call."

"Do with it as you like. You...should keep it," he mumbled. "For your trouble."

"Bad magical cross-reaction. You couldn't have known I'd set off fireworks."

"Besides that," he said, flustered. "Had I known—"

I held up my hands to stop him. "It's okay. Mom never mentioned you, either."

"I'm sure. In all honesty, I haven't thought of her since the night we met," he replied, and finished his tea. When I continued to wait in silence, he put down the cup with a testy sigh. "What can I tell you? I'd docked in Cardiff for a few hours with a fresh face, she was alone at a seaside bar, and we started talking. She said she was working, and then, a few beers in, she told me all about her loveless marriage and the husband who didn't care for her. We had too much to drink, she came back to my boat, and we fucked. She said she was on the pill—maybe that was a lie," he allowed. "She didn't even stay the night—we finished, I gave her a nightcap, and I walked her to her hotel. That was it." He shrugged. "Your Toula showed me photographs, and yes, I do remember Eva, but I had no idea she was *Arcanum*." The word emerged tinged with disgust. "And I'm quite sure she had no idea what I am, so perhaps we're even."

A moment before, I'd been worried about the logistics of working a second father into my life, but hearing Myrddin speak, I got the sinking feeling that my worry was unnecessary. The Arcanum snubbed witch-bloods as mongrels, pitiable but off-putting proof of copulation that should never have occurred. Mongrels born through rape were bad enough, but those that came from consensual relations were the definition of perversity, and all were shunted out into the world as soon as possible—though the grand magus, at least, had returned with a vengeance. While the Fringe took them in, I'd gathered that witch-bloods were still less desirable than their purer-blooded compatriots. Even Slim Matherson, longtime coordinator and proprietor of the Fringe settlement's popular watering hole, remained a permanent bachelor. Slim's mother was the exception to the rule, a wizard who doted on her mongrel son and spent most of her days playing bridge in a corner of the bar with a cup of coffee. Slim's father, one of Mab's court, wasn't in the picture, as Ms. Matherson had killed him when he'd tried to murder their baby.

His reaction, I'd found, was often typical for faeries— particularly ranking faeries—who discovered that they'd accidentally produced a mongrel. Sleeping with mortals was one thing, but bedding a wizard was usually an act of violence or desperation, distasteful but sometimes advantageous. This was why I found it so surprising that Val sanctioned my relationship with Marcus—but then again, Val was deeply fond of his witch-blooded baby sister, and he had more or less given the finger to court society after Maria was snubbed. For his part, Marcus certainly didn't seem concerned about impressing the Right People.

Still, in those silent seconds, my guts began to knot. Maybe Val had been willing to turn a blind eye to a witch, but if word got out that his heir was sleeping with a *mongrel*...

Myrddin's expression was polite, but there was no warmth in it, and I suspected that I could guess what was on his mind. Trying to give him an easy pass, I told him, "Whatever Mom said about her husband...that might have been a lie, too. My dad was wonderful to me. You don't have to worry—"

"Doesn't mean that he and his wife got along," he interrupted. "And correct me if I'm wrong, but they didn't share a home, did they?" As I fumbled for an answer, he pushed in his chair and willed the place setting clean. "No matter. You're here, that's...*unexpected*...but you seem to have done well for yourself. Anyway, we should get acquainted—"

My heart leaped. "Sure—"

"—at some point. You know where to find me."

Deflating, I stepped aside as Myrddin headed past me for the door. "You aren't staying?" I asked, following him into the breezeway. "I can't leave for a while, not until I get some training, but you—"

"I've been away too long as it stands," he interrupted, neither slowing nor looking back as I trailed him like a scared puppy. "I need to be there for Artur."

"Artur..."

"He could return to the realm at any time," he continued, and ripped open a gate to the ground level of his tower on Afallon. I recognized the rock at the center of the room, now missing the sword it had held for so long. "See that you have a care for Caledfwlch," said Myrddin as he crossed. I stood at the edge of the gate as raw magic poured through into the mortal realm, and Myrddin bent, retrieved something from the floor, and turned back to me. "Here, you forgot this. Seems unbroken."

He reached through the gate only long enough to hand me my phone, then gave me a tight smile and waved the hole closed.

Five minutes later, when I slipped into Val's office, I found him and Mina sitting on the couch, laughing with each other. He waved me closer, then frowned bemusedly. "That was quick."

"He had to go," I muttered.

"What do you mean, *go*? Ros?" he asked the ceiling.

I didn't stop him, came the broadcast reply.

Val and Mina traded glances, and she stood and tugged down her shirt. "I'll be in the meadow. Send her when you're finished," she told him, and saw herself out.

When we were alone, Val met me in the middle of the room, where I stood stiffly, trying not to embarrass myself. "I'm so sorry," he murmured, then carefully pulled my gold necklace from beneath my shirt. No matter where I went for work, that was the one piece of jewelry I never left behind: his graduation gift, a delicate sunflower pendant composed of colored diamonds. Slouching slightly to look me in the eye, he said, "*Blood* and *family* are not always synonymous, child. Remember that."

I nodded, and to my surprise, Val hugged me. "Remember, too, that Marcus never had the benefit of an Arcanum education," he added. "Mina's demanding, but she not actually a sadist. Go have fun."

CHAPTER 7

Picture for a moment a cheap plastic squirt gun, the translucent kind you might find in a favor bag at a kid's birthday party. It's never going to do much damage as a weapon, but with well-timed shots, it could still be an annoyance. Now imagine that the gun has a defect—maybe the trigger's faulty, or maybe there's a crack in the plastic, and the water is constantly leaking. But it's your only squirt gun, so you do what you can to work around it: you shore up the housing with duct tape, experiment with the trigger, and hold it a dozen different ways until you have success. Granted, success may mean only a trickle from the nozzle, but you could drip it on your enemy in a pinch.

That was me prior to Afallon. I knew every trick in the book to augment my weak talent—I'd tried *everything* to make myself more than a lousy witch—but even with years of focus and Arcanum-instilled discipline, I never merited more than a dragonscale wand, the tool of last resort for the hopelessly disadvantaged practitioner. At least I'd landed among colleagues who valued me for more than my wand skills, but still, my magical ineptitude was a constant sore spot. What did it matter that I'd taken a first at Oxford if I couldn't produce a reliable shield or shoot a decent bolt? Arcanum life was a marathon, and I had no legs and ineffective prosthetics.

My friends had tried to help me where they could. Daphne had quietly passed along any technique she uncovered that might have given me a boost. Maria, an unnatural prodigy when we were in school together, had been my biggest cheerleader and my lifesaver. Neither of us had known it at the time, but there was a reason that all the nights I spent in Faerie seemed to bolster my faint talent: the realm recognized me as one of its own, and as Ros later confessed, she'd tried to subtly tinker with me from the beginning. Even Frank, who had zero magical ability, had volunteered more core material on his theory that a larger wand might have a greater effect. "Scales shed," he'd explained. "Not as often as hair, but the damaged ones slough off and regrow. Go to the barn, tell Mom I sent you, and take what you need, and if you require something fresher, I've got plenty."

Now, suddenly, the broken plastic squirt gun had been replaced with a pressure washer, and I didn't have the faintest idea what to do with it.

Marcus offered to go with me to meet Mina as moral support, but Val held him back, explaining that this was the sort of task best accomplished without a nervous audience. Still, I could feel Marcus's eyes on the back of my neck as he watched from the villa while I slunk out into the meadow to meet my fate.

Val had chosen a gorgeous setting for his home, a high, wide valley ringed with peaks except for the bit he'd blasted out of existence to clear his view to the sea. But even with the size of the sprawling villa—just accommodating his guards took dozens of rooms—there was ample open space left in the surrounding meadow. I'd often seen the guards taking advantage of the practice field, drilling and honing their skills with offensive magic and physical weapons, though I'd kept a safe distance in the past. Val's guards were scarily *good*…and from everything I'd heard, Coileán's were better. The notion of going out to face their captain made me drag my feet.

To my surprise, Mina wasn't alone when I found her in the middle of the trampled practice field. "Badger!" I called, picking up the pace as she motioned for me to join them. I'd never been so relieved to see my old tutor, a Fringe coordinator who'd shown me a dozen witch-friendly amplification techniques that the Arcanum never bothered teaching.

Though Badger Parsons had opted for her usual training sweats, Mina appeared to be ready for combat, sporting a leather breastplate, matching padding around her forearms, and fingerless leather gloves. She cracked her knuckles as I jogged the last yards, then pointed to a spot on the edge of the practice area. "Drop your things there, out of the way. You won't be needing them for a while."

Reluctantly, I deposited my water bottle and sweat towel as instructed. Having come prepared to run laps and take hits, however, I wasn't sure what to do when Badger and Mina gestured folding chairs into existence, and a third appeared for me.

"Sit," Mina offered.

I slid into the seat, waiting for the first blow.

"I requested that Badger join us because I understand she's worked with you in the past. Correct?" Mina asked.

"Fairly extensively," Badger confirmed. "Kitty takes instruction well."

"That's what I wanted to hear," said Mina, smiling. "Now, I'll be honest with you: I don't know shit about training a wizard. Badger, you've at least seen a bit of both, haven't you? With Seamus?"

"A bit," she replied. "Seamie did most of his basic training without me around, but I used to supervise when he practiced."

"Good enough. If I ask Kitty to do something, and she has no idea what I'm talking about, could you put it in more familiar terms?"

"Oh, probably, but I think you're going to want me more for translations going the other way."

Mina's brow wrinkled. "How so?"

"Observe." She muttered a set of practice cubes into being a few yards away from us, then said, "Kitty, I want you to stack those, pyramid-style."

I hesitated—wandless magic had never been a possibility for me—then stood, stared down the cubes, and stretched out my empty hand as if my old dragonscale had merely become invisible. Moving objects with precision required a delicate balancing of forces, and for witches, any one of a handful of techniques could help keep those forces working simultaneously. I compared my preferred technique to training chopsticks—essentially, I created a ball of energy, then anchored the other forces to and through it so as to prevent them from escaping my control or fizzling out. The trick was placing the anchoring ball, but there was a nice clear patch to the right of the last cube, and I focused my will and whispered…

A brilliant construction erupted, a four-foot sphere of magic that flattened the grass and glowed so brightly that I could almost see it in the mundane spectrum. It held its shape for only a few seconds before igniting and quickly reducing the practice cubes to ash.

As I goggled and tried to mumble an apology, Badger chuckled and pointed to the flames still licking at the barrier Mina had hastily thrown around them. "Buruk's Chain," she told Mina. "A Fringe favorite."

"Moon and stars," Mina muttered, "what *happened?*"

"She doesn't know her own strength. It's all right, love, no harm done," she added, waving me back into my chair. "Plenty of cubes where those came from. But, ehm…probably best if you scratch Buruk from your repertoire, eh?"

It took two days of practice before I grasped the extent of the power at my disposal—an incredible power to someone who had theretofore been forced to beg and plead with magic to do anything at all. Drunk with the thrill of it, I enchanted huge fireballs into being, pulled together solid shields, and, in a moment of giddy joy, fried a set of practice cubes with lightning shot from my fingertips. Badger remained on hand to reel me in, reminding me to maintain my focus and not get sloppy, and Mina set up increasingly more complicated challenges. Some I passed with barely a second thought. One took frustrating hours of effort before Mina was satisfied, and I ended each failed attempt with a muttered apology and a new degree of tension in my shoulders.

After a few such rounds, Mina stopped me. "Why are you apologizing?" she asked. "You've caused no offense."

That took me aback, and I scrambled to attach reason to my instinctive behavior. "Because you told me to do it, and I messed up. *Again*."

She looked at me strangely. "You're learning, child. If you could do everything perfectly, we wouldn't be here. I expect failure."

"But—"

"This isn't Glastonbury," Badger interrupted. "And I know this may be difficult to internalize, but you're not last in your class. There's no shame in imperfection."

"I guess," I mumbled, and pushed up my sleeves. "Okay, so what am I doing wrong?"

Mina shrugged and stepped aside. "I'm not telling you. Figure it out." I glared at her—for some reason I couldn't explain, my temper had been shorter than usual in the last days—but she just smiled. "Frustration is part of life. Deal with it."

That, as it turned out, was the real lesson she'd been teaching me. The exercise she'd shown me was almost impossible for someone my age to pull off, a complex piece of defensive magic nearly indistinguishable in its intricacy from comparable spellcraft. She admitted that I'd done better than most—all of that Arcanum training made my enchantment neater than it had any right to be—but my ultimate failure had been the crux of her plan. "Stop and take stock of your emotional state right now," she told me after my last try. "What do you feel?"

"Angry," I admitted, grinding my teeth as my wards collapsed yet again.

"With whom?"

When I said nothing, I felt her dart into my thoughts. "Interesting," she mused on exit. "You're angry with yourself, more than anything. You're angry at the exercise, and with me for giving it to you. There are other targets in there, less prominent, but that's quite a lot of anger you're holding back."

A few deep breaths later, I felt the worst of the building tension flow out of my chest. "Sorry. I don't know what's wrong—"

Mina's laughter cut me short. "What's wrong? You're *fae*, girl—this is nothing unusual."

I looked to Badger for a second opinion, only to see her nodding emphatically. "You've all got short fuses," she said. "It's manageable, but it's something you need to be aware of."

"Val's never blown up at me," I protested. "Neither have Maria or Marcus."

"Maria is well apprised of the situation and understands control," said Mina. "Marcus understands because I beat it into that stubbornly thick skull of his, and if he's never shown you anger, it's probably because he's too besotted. As for Valerius, he's had ample time to master control, but if you want stories, I have *plenty*. Inexperienced guards can infuriate even the most understanding captain."

"Think that's bad? Try baby police officers," Badger said, and shuddered.

Mina patted her arm in sympathy, then motioned for me to follow her to another part of the field. "I'm going to make you confront your anger," she explained, checking her padding. "This won't be pleasant for either of us, but you need to see what you're capable of doing when you lose control. Don't try to hold it back—let it all out. Are you ready?"

I'd barely nodded before my mother appeared beside

Mina, dressed in her magus's robe and scowling at me. "You ruin everything, Katherine," she began, her voice as sharp and cold as I'd ever heard it. "*Everything*. You're an embarrassment to this family, and if you had the tiniest shred of decency, you'd kill yourself and be done with it."

There.

Finally.

Mom had never given voice to that sentiment, but I'd heard it in the undercurrent of her reprimands over the years, and it rang true. Rage boiled up inside me, a geyser shooting for the surface, and I had to give it somewhere to go. Screaming, I extended my palms and shot twin jets of flame toward her until, shocked and spent, I dropped to my knees and cried.

A moment later, I looked up at the touch to my shoulder and found Mina standing over me. "When Valerius trained me for the guards, he used the same illusion," she said, and took a knee while I wiped my eyes. "He projected my mother as well, and if memory serves, mine said roughly what yours did. She was killed when I was fifty-two, and the last words she spoke to me, just after I expressed interest in the guards, were, 'You're a useless half-breed, and I should have smothered you at birth.' When I had to face the illusion, I blasted a crater into the dirt and threw the captain head over heels." She produced a towel from the ether, licked the corner, and dabbed at a streak on my face. "I can feel myself getting angry even now, just remembering that. I'd love nothing more than to punch her in her smug face. But that's not an option, so I control the anger." She pushed herself up from the grass and extended her hand. "Let me teach you."

When I came in at sundown, drained from facing my mother over and over again, Marcus slipped next door to my room and produced tea from memory. "Long day, eh?" he asked as I slumped at the table.

"Very." I waited until he joined me, then asked, "Why didn't you tell me about the rage?"

Guilt flickered across his face. "I…uh…"

"Because that's what we did today. Mina kept pushing my buttons until I didn't automatically try to lash out. How long did it take you to control it?"

Marcus sighed and raised his cup. "Three days."

"*Three?*"

"I…wasn't in the best frame of mind when I worked with Mina," he mumbled. "She confronted me with two people. You can probably guess who."

One day of constant insults from my mother was bad, but then I'd grown accustomed to her disdain. For Marcus, freshly awakened, with his wife and cousin's betrayal still raw…

I reached across the table for his hand, and he squeezed mine as if clinging to the climbing wall. "So why didn't you tell me?" I asked.

"Didn't want to scare you away."

He seemed fragile in that moment, poised for a blow.

"You haven't," I assured him. "Honestly, I'm more scared of myself. I didn't know I could feel…*that.*"

"Agreed." He slid his chair closer to mine. "I've worked at it, I *keep* working at it, but…I admit, it terrifies me."

"Threat of snapping."

"Right." He hesitated, then said, "You know Seamus, yes? My cousin?"

"Yeah, we've met. Why?"

"Before he mastered control, he burned a man alive."

We sat in silence, contemplating that horror, until Marcus said, "I would never hurt you, Kitty, believe me, but the idea that something like that is *in* me…"

"I know."

He stared at his cup for a moment, then laughed sadly and rose, shaking his head. "Sorry. You're exhausted, the last thing you need is—"

"Marcus?"

"Hmm?"

My throat tightened, but after the hours I'd spent in the field, I was emotionally drained enough to force out the words that had been choking me for three days. "If the whole 'witch-blood' thing is too much, I understand."

His head tilted as he frowned in confusion. "What are you talking about?"

"Well, we all know now that I'm witch-blooded, so if…you know, you'd rather not pursue…*this*…I get it. And that's fine, that's…fair."

He stared at me in disbelief, then whispered, "Kitty, *no*. Why would you think…"

That was as far as he got before I was out of my chair and in his arms, pressed against him with a hunger I barely recognized. We bumped against the furniture, groping in space for the bed until the back of my leg hit the footboard and I pulled him down on top of me. When we landed, Marcus came up for air just long enough to gasp, "Ros! *Privacy!*"

And although I could sense her amusement, we remained undisturbed.

"**Y**ou're doing well," Mina reassured me as she supervised my bone mending two days later. "Don't overload it— you'd need more if you were working on a mortal, but we heal fairly quickly on our own."

"Don't be wasteful," Badger added, mopping her face with a towel.

Mina glanced back at her, then leaned conspiratorially close to me and whispered, "You can be a little wasteful. This isn't casting."

I smiled—the numbing work I'd pulled off made that *much* easier—and continued to repair my broken arm. Once I'd worked my way through basic shielding, Mina had tested my defenses to see how much they could take. It hurt like hell when a bolt snapped the bones of my forearm in half, but at least now we knew my upper threshold.

"I was wondering when we were going to get to the painful part of training," I told Mina once the enchantment had stabilized. "Marcus said—"

"*Oh*, Marcus." She chuckled and tweaked the enchantment ever so slightly, and I felt the deep tingle of knitting bone intensify. "That was a different situation. I had to break him before I could teach him anything." Seeing my bemusement, she explained, "Marcus was a disaster when he came to me, and he was incredibly dangerous. A talent a hundred times older than yours, with no training. At least you came to me with an appreciation of what magic can do. He started with almost nothing. And to make it even more enjoyable for us both, he had certain preconceived notions about taking orders from a woman. I had to make him pliable, willing to listen to me and learn, so I broke him *hard*. You're welcome, by the way."

I grinned at that. "Think Toula might have had a hand in it, too."

"Absolutely. And she's tough—I've had only one fight with her, and that was sufficient."

That surprised me. "I didn't think Toula was the 'recreational sparring' kind."

"Not that sort of fight. We, uh…broke up."

"Wait, you and Toula—"

"Before your time," said Mina. "It was brief. She wanted commitment, I didn't, and she caught me with someone with whom she thought I shouldn't be. There was a lot of shouting, though we didn't actually pummel each other. But we're fine now," she hastened to assure me.

"You…*cheated*?" I asked, slightly aghast.

Mina shrugged off my pearl-clutching. "It's only

cheating if both partners are on the same page, I suppose. As I said, she wanted us to be exclusive. I knew better. We didn't make those positions entirely clear." When I continued to frown at her, she rolled her eyes. "Child, I'm thirteen hundred years old. Had I only had one partner in all that time, I'd be insane. We don't do monogamy well. Get out of the mortal mindset and start thinking in centuries. Now, there are *exceptions*," she added before I could despair. "I'd say the record holders are in Eleanor's court—"

"Rohese and Martin Stowe," said Badger.

I nodded in recognition. "Yeah, their grandson works with me."

"They've been together six hundred years or so, I believe," said Mina. "A rare case. But look," she continued as my face fell, "if you two are happy, be happy. It could last forever. Don't let me dissuade you." She checked my arm, then grunted her approval and produced a bottle of water from the ether. "Marcus told you I was terrible, didn't he?"

"Let's just say he didn't have a good time in training," I replied, copying her movement. My resulting water tasted faintly of orange and mint, but it was a start.

"He wasn't supposed to have fun." Mina leaned back on one elbow and stared up at the passing puffy clouds. "Valerius knew what Marcus needed, and he didn't trust himself to be tough enough on the boy, but he trusted me to do the unpleasant parts. I should have trained Maria, too, but..." She glanced at Badger, who pushed her sunglasses down her nose.

"There were certain other dynamics to consider with Maria," Badger concluded, "and besides, you don't make magus without cultivating extensive control."

"Perhaps." Mina sighed and turned her attention back to me. "Test the arm. Let's see it move."

I obliged, though it felt wobbly, as if someone had replaced pieces of my skeleton with Jell-O.

"Still soft," she decreed. "Ten more minutes, and then we'll see about your shield again."

Mina wasn't satisfied with my progress until we'd spent eleven long days together. By the time she released me, I'd mended most of my major bones (and a few organs), learned the rudiments of mental blocking, and glamoured myself into a spot-on copy of Badger. I could throw a bolt, call forth and control a fireball, and make a shield beyond school-aged me's wildest dreams. My food still left much to be desired, and Mina probably could have spent decades working on my combat skills before I earned her approval, but she agreed with Badger that I was safe enough to release into the wild. Her last lesson had been gates, and I took myself to Toula's office Saturday night and closed the rift behind me as Badger gave me a golf clap.

"Right on time," said the grand magus, looking up from her computer as I counted my limbs. "Come here, I've got something for you."

She rolled her chair to the wall and pulled a leather-sheathed sword from the corner. "I thought a scabbard might be wise, considering how sparkly this damn thing is," she said, freeing a few inches of Caledfwlch from its wrappings. The blade twinkled in the light of her screen and standing lamps, an explosion frozen at the moment of detonation. "Amy touched it up, refilled it, and stabilized it as much as she could. I knocked off the locking enchantment in case Myrddin has any other kids hanging around. Anyway, it's yours," she said, passing it over her desk.

I wasn't sure what to do with the long sword, so I slung the scabbard's strap onto my shoulder like a deadly backpack. "Thanks. I'll try not to gut anyone."

"Much appreciated. So, where do we go from here?" She sat and leaned back, bouncing the chair to an accompaniment of squeaking springs. "Ted still hasn't been informed. You don't have to say anything."

"Until the first time I try to refill my stapler with oven mitts on." I folded my arms, considering my options, then said, "The Team needs to know, for safety if nothing else."

"Mina said that your control—"

"Not that. If we get into an emergency situation—say, on a rock face—I can't be trying to keep up a cover story while I decide what I can and can't grab. Truth's coming out. But first, I want to talk to Mom."

Toula's faint smile spoke volumes. "I think your sister might need to be in on that conversation, don't you?"

Fortunately for Beth, the school year was in its death throes—not that she'd been overly concerned with her studies that year—and Toula had scheduling flexibility on Sunday. Shortly after five that evening, Magus Johansson sent Beth into Toula's office, where she scowled in her Sunday best by the place the gate had been, making no secret of her displeasure with the plan. The grand magus had sent word to the Audleys that Beth needed to speak with her mother, but nothing more.

"What's *she* doing here?" Beth asked, jutting her chin in my direction.

"Eva's her mother, too," Toula replied, and headed into the corridor. "Follow me, girls."

Accessing the castle's prison ward necessitated a trip down one of the few elevators, this one locked against unauthorized use, a descent past another two floors of storage, and finally, a passage through a cordon of armed Arcanum security, who, even with Toula chaperoning us, checked Beth and me for contraband. One of the guards escorted us into a surprisingly comfortable conference room, complete with padded chairs and a pair of large ferns in the corner—magically sustained, I assumed, given the absence of sunlight. The grand magus took up a spot against the wall, Beth and I sat without speaking to each other, and a few moments later, a pair of guards escorted my mother into the room.

The only indication that she was a prisoner was her yellow jumpsuit. She wasn't shackled, but then there was no need. The bind on her was strong and total, preventing her from accomplishing even the simplest casting, and she was locked in a heavily warded facility several stories underground, surrounded by wizards—what would she have gained by resisting? She spared barely a glance for either of her daughters as she entered and took the chair across the table from us, and the guards, at Toula's nod, stepped out and closed the door.

The moment it latched, Beth reached for Mom. "I'm sorry, I'm *sorry*," she babbled, already on the brink of tears. "I've been trying to think of a way to get you out of here—"

"And?" Mom replied, sounding bored. She turned my way, and her lip rose into a snarl of distaste. "Well, now, this is a lovely surprise. Happy? Got what you wanted?" she asked, her voice thick with sarcasm.

I focused on my breathing, as Mina had drilled into me. "Actually, yes. I requested that you not be executed."

"How generous of you."

"I thought so. You *did* betray the Arcanum and tried to murder my best friend, so"—I shrugged—"you know, seemed fair."

Mom sighed and cut her eyes to Toula, ignoring Beth's attempts to take her hand. "Why the reunion?"

Toula didn't answer her—at least, not directly. Instead, she held out her hand, whispered to herself, and smiled coldly as an aural lattice manifested over her palm. "This is yours, Eva," she said, staring Mom down. "I won't bother tracing your generations back. Your Arcanum bona fides aren't at issue."

Mom's mask of bored nonchalance began to slip as her brilliant green orb rotated in Toula's hand. "What's this about?" she asked, just sharply enough to reveal the uncertainty below the surface.

For a second time, Toula ignored her question. With a quick gesture, Mom's lattice flattened into a sheet of interlocking lines and swirls, and Toula pushed it to the side, allowing it to float unassisted. "This won't hurt," she told Beth, and called forth my sister's orb. Again, it was wholly green, albeit dimmer than Mom's. Toula flattened it, then split it, and aligned one half perfectly with our mother's lattice. "As predicted," she said, nodding to my perplexed sister, and nudged the other half of Beth's lattice—Dad's signature—out of the way. "Which leaves only Kitty—"

"*Why?*" Mom interrupted, taut but cringing. Her tone spoke less of ennui than of desperation. "What's the point of this? We know she's a witch, her lattice will be duller than mine. Move on."

The look Toula gave her was that of a chess player about to call mate. She whispered forth my aural signature, and as it solidified from white mist to a colored lattice, Beth gasped and Mom groaned.

Mine was tricolored. Though the hues swirled together, I eyeballed the percentages as half green—Mom—and a quarter each red and blue. As before, Toula flattened and split my lattice, matched the green side to Mom and Kitty's, then pointed to the side that was unmistakably the signature of a half-fae parent. "Eva, is there something you'd like to share?"

I heard Beth scoot her chair away from mine, but I had eyes only for Mom as she glowered at the lattices. "What do you want me to say?" she muttered. "You have what you came for."

"Why didn't you tell me?" I asked, staring at her until she, with visible discomfort, briefly met my gaze. "Don't you think I had a right to know?" When Mom's lips remained pressed together, something in me flared. I thrust one hand out, and the flame that blossomed there finally caught Mom's attention. "Answer me, *damn it!*" I shouted, willing the fire into a tight sphere that I tossed and caught like a tennis ball from hell. "*Why didn't you tell me?*"

Mom stared at the fire, then looked at me, aghast. "You…"

"Met my father. Long story. But I want to know why the *fuck* you didn't tell me about this years ago." Feeling the warning pressure of Toula's hand on my shoulder, I extinguished the fire and leaned back in my chair, putting distance between me and my target. "Jesus, Mom, do you have any concept of how miserable practical magic was for me? I've spent *years* trying to figure out why I wasn't talented like you and Dad. You couldn't have mentioned the mongrel bit?"

With the obvious indicator of my newfound ability gone, Mom recovered her footing. "Whatever misery you had in school was your doing. If you had any decency at all, any respect for what the Arcanum *used* to stand for"— she shot Toula a withering glare—"you'd be gone by now. You'd have accepted your place as a witch and dropped out, and run off to some mundane school."

I laughed in disbelief. "Right. Random American kid, slumming around England, sleeping rough, just marching up to school and trying to enroll? If you didn't want me studying magic, you could have taken me to the silo and just not sent me to night class…but no," I said with mock realization, "that would have meant having me around, wouldn't it? *That* wouldn't do."

"You went to college, did you not? You could have done anything out there, but instead, you had the gall to take an Arcanum job—"

"And I'm damn good at what I do," I snapped.

Mom slapped the table and hunched toward me. "Don't you get it? I've been trying to make you leave since the day I first saw your fucking lattice—"

"So you foisted me off onto Dad? Did you tell him about me? Huh? Guy spends ten years as a single parent to a kid who isn't even his? Is *she* Dad's?" I asked, jabbing my finger toward Beth. "Or did you keep cheating on him?"

"She is," Toula interrupted before Beth's fear could escalate. "Ran a blood trace on his sample last week, and she was the only hit."

Toula had broken my rant before it could ramp up, and I took a moment to breathe and collect myself as Mom watched in sullen silence. "I tried so hard to be worthy of you," I finally murmured. "Studied my ass off. Did the best I could with the talent I had. You have no idea how many hours I spent outside of class with Badger Parsons, trying to get better. Hoping that someday, I'd be good enough for you to like me. And now I understand why that was never going to happen. Doesn't make it hurt any less, but it's nice to have answers."

"Hope you're proud of yourself," she replied, folding her arms. "Airing out every bit of my dirty laundry in front of your sister—"

"Just tell me what happened. What did Dad ever do to you, huh?"

She laughed incredulously. "Orson had no ambition. He wanted to play on that damn farm of his, and I wanted to do work that actually mattered, so we went our own ways. Visited every now and then to keep up appearances, but you know we led separate lives. What was I supposed to do, keep myself in perfect chastity until I visited?"

"You could have just divorced him."

"Oh, of course, how silly of me. A divorced magus—yes, that's the person we want leading an installation. Grow up," she muttered. "Some marriages are more about the mutual benefit than the romance." When I said nothing, she shrugged. "Your father wasn't my only fling, but I was more careful after that. And when you were about three months old and didn't look particularly like either of us, I checked your aura and realized what I'd birthed, and I gave you to Orson to raise. Fresh air and sunshine are good for kids, right?"

"And you wouldn't have to look at me," I replied.

"That, too. I mean, on top of everything else. My job was demanding, and…well, I've never really been the maternal type," she admitted.

I nodded toward Beth, who appeared to be on the verge of tears. "You did all right by her."

Mom glanced at my sister and looked away. "I thought there might be a talent there. Unfortunately, she favors her father. Weak, both of them."

"*Mom*," Beth whispered, crumbling before my eyes.

"But that's not your concern," Mom resumed, once more focused on me. "You figured it out. Gold star for you. So now you can go off to Faerie or wherever it is mongrels hide out these days and—"

"I'm not going anywhere."

My voice was soft, but Mom started as if I'd shouted in her face. "You *know*," she protested. "You're not one of us. There's no place for you here."

Behind me, Toula snorted her disbelief.

"I've got an Arcanum job, which is much more than I can say for you," I replied. "And a flat. Think I'll stick around."

Fear began to show through the cracks in Mom's façade. "You can't. People will find out, especially if you can do…*that*."

"What, this?" I asked, calling forth the purple fireball again. "Yeah, you're probably right. It'll get around eventually. I mean, I'm not planning on shouting it from the rooftops, but I'm going to fill the Team in."

"You have to *go*, Katherine," she insisted, picking up her tempo. "Get out of here. If you had any decency at all, you'd leave before you ruin your poor sister's future—"

"*Beth*?" I interrupted, laughing. "I'm sorry, would that be the sister you've done everything in your power to keep away from me?"

Mom didn't back down. "If you had no attachments, it would be easier for you to move elsewhere—"

"*Attachments?* That's my little sister!" I cried. "Not that you gave a damn about my feelings." My blood pressure began to rise again, and I gritted my teeth and ineffectively willed myself to be calm. "You couldn't even give her the letters I wrote her? *Years* of letters, and she couldn't have a single one? What was I going to do to hurt her from Glastonbury? I only just learned gates this weekend, that wouldn't have been a problem."

"She's living with you now," Mom countered. "If anyone finds out—"

"Beth hasn't lived with me since September. She's staying with Dad's cousin because she hates my guts. What, you didn't know?" I asked, catching her flash of surprise. "No one bothered to tell you she was back in the silo?"

"Didn't you get my letters?" Beth pressed. "I told you about the Audleys and...and school, and..."

Mom's face remained an impassive blank, and my heart broke a little for Beth. "Don't worry," I said with all due sarcasm, "she's being looked after, far away from me. Though if the reports I get are accurate, you've made her life a hell of a lot harder than I ever have."

"And whose fault is that?" Mom snapped. "Who couldn't even stand up for her own mother?"

"I did my duty," I said, forcing myself to be placid as she flushed with anger. "And you're not my mother. You incubated me, that's all." With that, I rose from the table and made a show of straightening my shirt. "We're done, you and me. You're going to rot down here, I'm going to go live my life up there, and I promise you that I will make *no* secret of who and what I am. Thanks, Toula," I told the grand magus, then headed for the door.

Mom's shouts followed me into the corridor: "Katherine! *Katherine!* You can't do this to me! I swear to God, I will *kill* you if you—"

The conference room door slammed, and I nodded to the guards on my way toward the surface.

CHAPTER 8

There were flowers waiting on my desk when I ventured into the subbasement the next morning, a bouquet of brightly colored daisies in a ribbon-tied vase. I was silently grateful that Ted had broken in to leave them for me; my doorknob was made of steel, and my skin, newly sensitive to iron, crawled as I shouldered my way into my office. As I tried to settle down at my desk, I realized that so many of my things were iron-based: the pedestal of the chair, the shelving units, the stapler…even my letter opener was fashioned like a tiny broadsword. Whenever I moved too close to anything with the potential for burns, my internal alarm began to blat, which was less than conducive to work.

While I woke my computer and ran its overdue updates, Maria rapped on the open door and popped her head in. "Ooh, pretty," she said, spotting the flowers. "Got a second?"

I motioned her close, then muttered, "Have you figured out a way to make steel less…obnoxious?"

She laughed softly. "*No*. I recommend replacing everything. But you'll learn to tune it out. It's like being in a room with strong perfume—you grow desensitized to it eventually."

"Not soon enough," I grumped. The headboard and footboard of my bed might have been maple, but the frame and the springs were steel, and I'd sensed them like a pea through the padding of the mattress all night. Showering meant standing exposed in proximity to the unforgiving bathtub hardware, and I'd taken one look at the kitchen and opted to stop with the cup of tea Marcus had made me after seeing my shadowed eyes. He'd known the cause of my exhaustion—he couldn't have missed the squealing of the springs as I'd tossed and turned—and he'd assured me that it would get easier. Until then, though, I had to resist the urge to douse everything around me in kerosene and find a Bic.

"I just wanted to tell you that no one's been informed," said Maria.

"What about Frank?"

"Can you block yet?"

"Getting better at it…"

"Then unless he gets past your defenses, no. You don't have to say a word if you don't want to."

I gave her a weak smile. "Might need to explain myself if I redecorate."

"We'll cover for you." She fluffed the bouquet to maximize the effect and started out. "Ten minutes. Get your caffeine."

My personal equipment wasn't sufficient that morning. I shuffled to the communal breakroom and helped myself to an alarming amount of cheap coffee, then slipped into the conference room with my computer, only to find a banner proclaiming WELCOME BACK! on a string of foil pennants hung over the whiteboard.

"She's alive!" said Bob, and slid a platter of scones down the table toward my spot. "You had us worried, Kitty. Sylvester made these for your homecoming."

"He's a keeper," I replied, barely restraining myself from inhaling half the batch. "How was Provence?"

"Lovely as always, but I'm almost sorry to have missed the excitement."

I bit into a scone and groaned with happiness. "*Almost* sorry?"

"Eh, you know, boats and I don't tend to agree." He feigned vomiting over one shoulder and made a face.

"Spoils the festive outing."

Before Bob could elaborate, Ted and the others filed in and took their seats. "All right, people, good morning, settle down," said Ted, quickly readying his computer. "Glad to see a full complement here again. First order of business…" He grabbed a scone and took an approving bite. "Perfect. And with that out of the way…"

A projection of a photograph appeared on the screen: to the right, me, holding Caledfwlch aloft, looking at it as if it had somehow leapt from the stone and thrown itself into my fist; to the left, Myrddin's face in profile, mouth agape, hands still posed as if holding the phone they'd just dropped. Seeing us together, both stunned, I couldn't miss the resemblance, and I winced. Beyond the pale blond hair and green eyes, he and I were much alike in profile.

"So," said Ted, looking down the table at me, "healed up? And he was right—this would make an *epic* Christmas card."

"I'm intact," I replied, lifting what little remained of my scone as proof of my fitness to resume duty. "And, uh…there's something I need to tell y'all."

Frank, who'd opted for a plate of sausages pilfered fresh from the dining hall, raised his fork to stay me. "You're witch-blooded."

I sighed in frustration. "Whatever happened to asking before you poke around in—"

"I haven't been in your head," he protested. "Deduction, Kitty. You opened a blood lock keyed to a half faerie who looks like your long-lost brother, and then you disappeared for almost two weeks, which either indicated extreme convalescence or training." He shrugged. "That, and Sam might have called."

I should have guessed. Despite her immense power as the realm—or perhaps because of it—Ros could barely make herself heard telephonically. Any attempt sounded like heavy static with a distant whisper that might have been a voice, which soon cut off, as the phone would inevitably fry. Computers were similarly vulnerable around her—she could observe from a distance, but if she tried to type or touch a screen, a meltdown would be imminent. This left her in a lurch as far as Frank was concerned. Having raised him from an egg, Ros adored and missed him. Frank, whose feelings toward her were more difficult to put into human-friendly boxes, once explained their bond in terms we could understand: "I'd go vegetarian for her." As work kept Frank in the mortal realm for longer and longer spans, he and Ros needed someone to pass messages for them, and they'd found a willing volunteer in Sam, Ros's devoted boyfriend, who'd gone into the relationship understanding that he'd always be the third wheel when those two were together. Sure, the *Team* might not have had the official debriefing, but I could well imagine Ros deciding that Frank was a special case.

Most of the others nodded sheepishly, and I cut my eyes to Maria, who appeared to be as irked as I was. "Surprise," I muttered. "Okay if I stick around?"

Lakshmi tutted. "Look at the table, girl. This is already a mixed group."

"Hey, this may be the Island of Misfit Toys," said Ted, "but I love each and every one of you lunatics. And Kitty, we wouldn't have put up the banner if we were planning to kick you out."

"Right," Lakshmi said, and pushed herself from her chair. "We're glad you're back, we're glad you're safe and whole. With that said"—she pushed her bifocals down her nose and glared at me over the lenses—"*what* is the number-one rule concerning unstudied magical objects?"

"No direct contact?" I mumbled.

"Mm-hmm. Did you hear that, *Theodore?*" she asked, turning on our leader.

Ted—and everyone else who'd posed with the sword—looked properly abashed.

"I'm just grateful that you didn't find the damn Grail," said Lakshmi, taking her seat again. "Who knows what you'd have accidentally done with it? Now, Kitty," she continued, "after we go through scheduling, I will meet you and Daphne in your office. I assume you'd like a new doorknob, at the very least, and whatever you two can't make, I'll need to request from storage."

Daphne lifted her mug in salute. "Shouldn't be a problem. Have you thought about repainting?"

In the end, Lakshmi didn't need to make any requisitions. With a little concentration—and ridiculously little effort, my inner witch noted with giddy wonder—I was able to replicate my furniture and desk accessories in any material and color I chose. Hell, I could have stacked my books on a solid gold shelving unit, had I the whim and no sense of taste or restraint. The trick was getting rid of the steel pieces, which was where Daphne did wonders. Mina had warned me that while it was possible to work enchantment on iron and silver, it was a task best left to the experienced and patient. There were no such limitations with spellcraft, however, and so Daphne and I moved in synch around the small office, using my hypersensitive hands as a specialized metal detector.

We were as quick as we could be about it, however. Ted had sent around updated itineraries with tentative travel plans for the next four months, and with pending stints in Iceland, Zaire, and Cambodia, I had my preparation study cut out for me. Still, even with our freshly assigned homework, nearly everyone on the Team stopped by my office at some point that day, either to say hello or to critique my new furniture—all but Marcus, who'd been strangely quiet since my return. Assuming he'd fallen as far behind as I had during our unplanned trip out of the realm, I buckled down and wrote off his silence as concentration.

After work, Daphne and I stopped by her flat to feed Lothario, her ancient, obese cat, who arched his back and hissed when he saw me, then fled to the safety of her bathroom. "Sorry," I mumbled while she opened a tin of wet food. Marcus had griped before about how animals now hated him—"And I love dogs!" he'd complained over the dregs of a bottle of chardonnay one night—but I'd forgotten until that moment that I, too, was now anathema to the mortal realm's non-human fauna.

"No worries," Daphne assured me, wrinkling her nose as she tipped the gelatinous mass into Lothario's bowl. "Most exercise he's had in months, I'm sure."

Leaving the food down for when the coast was clear, we headed to my flat to continue the redecoration. Marcus wasn't home yet—odd for him, but not worrying—and so Daphne and I tackled the place one room at a time, starting with my death-trap bathroom. "Good choice. I *love* copper fixtures," she said as the new sink taps appeared. "Do the basin to match, that'll be lovely. Maybe an oak cabinet. And why didn't you bring me in sooner?" she chided while I created a beaten-copper sink. "Is Marcus's room still standard issue? I could have switched these out months ago!"

"He's never complained," I replied, adjusting the handles and towel rack. "I guess I'll adjust before long, but right now…"

"There's no need to torture yourself." She poked her head into my bedroom and *tsk*ed. "Let me guess, the mattress came with the flat?"

I made a face. "Yes?"

"Oh, *Kitty*," she said, and sighed. "It's high time you were introduced to the wonders of memory foam. Stand back, let me work."

By the time Marcus arrived with enough Indian takeaway for four, Daphne and I had redone both beds and baths, overhauled the living room, and were just finishing up the kitchen. My pots and pans had been rendered in copper, my knives in ceramic, and the old oven had been replaced with a glass-top model. A few bits and pieces couldn't be tweaked, but the flat felt more like home. I invited her to stay for dinner, but she begged off, saying she needed to see to her traumatized cat.

I unpacked the containers while Marcus poked around the place, examining the changes. "You're going to love the mattress," I called from the kitchen. "And if you hate your bathroom, let me know, but it's just like mine."

"Much better," he decreed upon his return.

"And this," I said, opening the cutlery drawer to reveal the new set in gold plate. "Gaudy, yes, but I think it'll do."

He chuckled as he pulled a pair of plates from the cabinet, and we settled in for dinner with curry and wine. Before long, though, I noticed that he seemed preoccupied, quieter than usual and frowning into space as he ate, and I reached for his free hand. "Everything okay? Something on your mind?"

Marcus put his fork down, hesitated for a few seconds, then nodded curtly. "I think it would be best if you stopped doing fieldwork."

Caught off guard, I laughed in surprise and pulled away from him. "What are you talking about? I'm one of the two people on the Team who actually has training for fieldwork. This is my *thing*."

"It's not safe."

"*Life* isn't safe. There could be a meteor headed this way as we speak, and yet, we still order enough food for leftovers."

His jaw tightened with his frustration. "Kitty...when you were in my arms, screaming like you'd been set aflame, I...I thought I was about to lose you. You were dying for *nothing*, and I..." He struggled to give form to his thoughts, then managed, "Fieldwork means taking unnecessary risks. I want you to stay in the office with Bob and Lakshmi."

"You were scared, I get it," I told him, "but that was a freak accident. For the record, I was in pain, not dying. And the photos don't lie—I'm not the only one who grabbed that damned sword barehanded."

"You're the only one who was injured."

"Freak. Accident," I insisted. "This is what I do, and you've known it all along. I'm not going to live in a bubble, Marcus."

"I'm not suggesting—"

My temper began to rise. "Wait, now, let me guess: it's okay for *you* to keep doing fieldwork, right? Because nothing could ever happen to you out there."

"I'm better equipped—"

"*Bullshit.* I've been at this longer than you have, and I got along just fine before you joined up. So don't start that with me." I stabbed at a piece of chicken, splitting it in two with the force of my fork. "I'm sorry to have given you a scare. Certainly wasn't the way I'd planned to end that trip. But if you think I'm going to spend the rest of my life hiding in the basement, then you're delusional."

He fell silent after that pronouncement. Little else was said that evening, even as we packed up the leftovers together, and we slept alone on our fantastic new mattresses.

I woke at five in a cold sweat, grateful for the pale light of early morning through the curtains.

For the last several nights, I'd slept uneasily, waking with a faint but certain sense of dread whose source I couldn't name. Previously, I'd chalked it up to the looming confrontation with my mother, a product of my off-kilter psyche, but I realized I'd been mistaken. The dream had evaded my conscious mind until that morning, and even though I knew it was nothing but a dream, I lay beneath the blankets and stared at the ceiling for a moment while my heartbeat slowed.

Asleep, I'd imagined myself at the bottom of a deep, dimly lit hole, an earthen pit with crumbling sides at least three stories tall. In the way of dreams, I was invisible to the other person in the pit with me, whose face and form shifted as my mind tried to decide on an appearance. But whether the other person was a blond man or a redheaded woman with springy curls like Dr. Powell's, I knew it was Artur. He—she?—wore a long-sleeved white tunic over loose brown trousers, topped with a hauberk. A gray woolen cloak was pinned over the maille on one shoulder with an ornate golden brooch, and dirty leather shoes completed the look. I watched as Artur paced the pit, clutching at a bloody chest wound and calling for help, but none came—and the circle of overcast sky visible from the bottom of the hole grew ever smaller until it was nothing but a pinprick in the darkness. As the last of the light faded, Artur fell to the ground, too hurt and weak to go on, and finally seemed to see me. "Help me," he whispered, then slumped over, dead, as the earthen walls collapsed on us.

Being buried alive was hardly conducive to a restful night's sleep, but with the amount of adrenaline flowing, I knew it was futile to stay in bed and try again. Instead, I pried myself up—Daphne had been absolutely right about the mattress, and I hated to leave it prematurely—threw on my robe, and padded into the kitchen to distract myself from the distressing dream.

Having never had a fight with Marcus—and really, I told myself as I puttered around, mixing batter, that wasn't a true *fight*—I decided that the best way to smooth over our rough dinner was with breakfast. He'd proven to be a sucker for my blueberry pancakes, and as they bubbled in my lovely new skillet, I started a pan of bacon to put him in an even better mood. If the saying about the surest route to a man's affection running through his stomach was true, then I'd boarded an express train.

Sure enough, Marcus emerged just as the food was coming off, and I smiled as he came over to investigate. "Hey, you," I said, smoothing his bedhead. "Hungry? Want to make coffee?"

He did as I requested, but as we settled at the table, I

noticed that he still seemed awfully quiet, even for the early hour. "Rough night?" I asked. "I woke up from this *nasty* nightmare, but other than that, I think I'll go to Daphne for all future decorating needs. Yeah?"

Marcus picked at his food for a moment in silence, then put down his new gold fork and pushed back his plate. "I've reached a decision."

"Oh? About what?"

"What we discussed last night. You will retire from fieldwork."

I frowned quizzically and wiped my fingers clean. "I thought I made my feelings about that clear."

"You did. But this is best, and you—"

"Says *who*? I'm sorry," I said, shaking my head in disbelief, "what gave you the idea that *my* career is *your* decision?"

Though he remained outwardly calm, I saw Marcus's shoulders tense. "If we are to be together, then I need to know that you respect me and my wishes. Fabia didn't. Eva obviously didn't respect Orson. So, when I take a decision, you *will* respect that. My feelings about this matter are firm, and—"

"And what about my feelings?" I shot back, and rose from the table, the better to stare down at him. "Let me put this in terms you'll understand, since you seem to have had some trouble overnight. I'm open to discussion. I'm even open to *some* compromise. But if you think for one second that you get to dictate my life, then you've absolutely lost your senses."

He remained seated, but he was growing fidgety under my glare. "If we marry—"

"That is *so* far in the future right now that there's no point in bringing it up. And let me tell you, bub, if there's going to be any sort of *us*, then it's going to be an equal partnership. If your idea of a relationship is you making all the decisions and me just accepting it, then you don't know me at *all*," I said, my face flushing with sudden anger.

"Kitty—"

"And because we've having this conversation," I continued over his interruption, "then it's clear that you don't consider me an equal. I mean, how dare you give me orders in my own home? Who the hell do you think you are?"

Marcus pounded the table hard enough to rattle the dishes—I noted with alarm that the ones in the cupboard rattled along with them—and stood, taking from me my brief height advantage. "Damn it, Kitty!" he snapped, gripping one of my shoulders hard enough to make me flinch. "You *will* listen!"

I stood my ground, shaking with anger and a touch of fear.

He took a few deep breaths, coming down from his outburst, then released me. "You're emotional, and you're being illogical," he said in the same tone of voice an adult would use to address a tantruming child. "Calm down, and you'll see why this is best. You will resign from the field, and that's final. I'm not losing you over something as stupid as fieldwork."

I met his stare, resisting the sudden urge to throttle him. "You just did."

That shook his footing. "Did what?"

"Lost me over something stupid—you. My work certainly isn't. Pack your things. You're sleeping elsewhere tonight."

I'd almost made it back to my bedroom when Marcus grabbed my shoulder again. "Don't walk away from—"

"Don't *touch* me," I snarled, yanking myself from his grasp. I don't know how I looked when I spun on him, but whatever face I made was sufficiently furious that he took a precautionary step back. "I'm going to get ready for work. When I come out, I expect you to be gone."

A few minutes later, as I stood under the beating stream of my new massaging showerhead, my shocked anger gave way to tears. I'd spent the best part of a year living with Marcus. I'd poured out my heart to him, and he to me. We'd held each other on our roughest nights. He'd been my friend, my colleague, briefly my lover…I'd thought we were on the same page. But this…*this* was what he expected of me? To give up my desires on his whims?

I'd imagined that he considered me an equal. How wrong I'd been. And when he'd shown himself, not only his agitation when I pushed back, but his raw *anger*… Whatever his mental age, Marcus was still ancient, and I knew damn well that I couldn't beat him in a fight. But I'd loved him, or at least the person I'd thought he was. Seeing the truth laid bare like the stinking mud flats of a once-beautiful lake run dry made my chest clench, but I held back the fresh round of tears that threatened to burst forth. He wouldn't see me cry. Never again.

And he wouldn't see me cower.

Part of me expected him to be sitting on the couch when I emerged, trying to understand what had happened and make it better, but the flat was silent but for my footsteps on the wooden floor. His bedroom door was ajar, and when I peeked inside, the place was pristine. Every trace of him had vanished, even his breakfast dishes…which he'd simply willed away instead of putting in the dishwasher, I noted with annoyance as I cleaned up the rest.

Marcus was gone. And though part of me ached at the thought, I shoved that voice deep down and went on with my life.

I'd closed my office door, planning to distract myself with my reading, but I barely made it half an hour before Frank stopped by to check in. "Have you seen Marcus?" he asked as I looked up from my computer. "He and Antony and I were going to start—"

"I have no idea where he is," I replied with what I thought was neutral detachment. "Sorry."

But few things got past Frank's well-tuned radar. "Shit," he muttered, "you're fighting?"

"We've split. And I swear, if there's a breakup pool, I'll *hurt* you."

"Nothing of the kind." He closed the door and folded himself down onto my couch. "Want to tell me what happened?"

I thought of telling Frank to mind his own business for once, but instead, I surrendered and beckoned him closer. In the next instant, as my internal barriers dropped, I felt him in my mind, in and out with the precision of a needle.

Frank sighed, a noise that sounded suspiciously like a sotto voce, "*Humans.*"

"Seen enough?"

"Yeah." He leaned toward me, his red eyes unreadable but intense in their stare. "You're both fundamentally fucked up, you know."

"*What?*"

"Nothing personal. Most of us are, one way or another. But to this point, you two have worked well together. Carried each other's baggage, as it were, or maybe just ignored it. Slid it into a closet. I don't know, extended metaphor isn't my forte," he said, shrugging.

I reached for my tea mug. "Go on."

"Think on it. About, oh, fifteen months ago, Marcus woke to learn that everyone he knew had been dead for two millennia. Shock to the system. And making it worse, he was in that position thanks to his cousin and his mate, two people he'd trusted. Perhaps loved, I don't know. You're *complicated* about your mates," he added with faint reproach. "So now he's stuck here, but he decides that you're the best thing to ever cross his path. And he loves you—don't give me that look, I know what I've witnessed."

I rolled my eyes but drank my tea to dispel the smirk.

"Then Afallon happened. He scooped you off the ground while you were shrieking and got a gate open, and that's the last anyone saw of him until yesterday." Frank's face betrayed the tiniest flash of guilt. "Marcus doesn't guard himself when he's preoccupied, and I took a peek. He may not seem panicked to you, but he's in survival mode. Like, 'the bomb is going off in one minute and I've got to evacuate everyone' mode. And by 'everyone,' I mean you."

"Except I'm *fine*."

"He knows that in the part of his mind that actually thinks. The instinctive bits are on red alert." Frank scowled as he collected his thoughts. "What I'm trying to convey is that his sudden total loss is still very much with him. And when he thought he was going to lose you, too, he fell apart—I assume, I mean, I wasn't with him in those first days after Afallon. But extrapolating from what I saw yesterday…maybe don't hold everything against him, eh?"

My eyes narrowed. "You're taking his side?"

"No. I'm saying he's perhaps not in his most reasonable frame of mind right now. You go into the field, you get hurt, the screwed-up bits of him freak out and associate fieldwork with his desperate need to avoid more loss, and he comes up with a 'solution,' then delivers it in a manner that you find fundamentally insulting."

"Because it *is* insulting!"

"Which he might have realized, were he not prioritizing the bomb above all else." He cocked his head. "Does that make sense?"

"Maybe," I allowed after a long pause.

"But you're not going to have a talk with him, are you?"

I shook my head and clutched my reassuringly warm mug. "He owes me an apology first, and then we'll see. If you'd like to convey that to him, be my guest."

Frank raised his hands and shook his head. "Oh, no. I'm not stepping into this mess. You two work it out."

"Frank…" I wheedled.

"Or don't." He stood and gave me a look of reproach. "Honestly, your mating is so weird. Go about your life, find a mate when the urge strikes, move on."

I sipped my tea. "You're a real romantic, you know?"

"We don't *do* romance, and we're probably saner for it."

As Frank started to leave, I said, "What about me, then? How, in your great estimation, am I fucked up?"

He glanced back and snorted as he opened the door. "You're clever, Kitty. I shouldn't have to spell that out for you."

Frank might not have been willing to play messenger between Marcus and me, but he wasn't above telling the Team to give me space. I worked in peace for the rest of the day, went home alone, ate the oddly tasteless leftovers, ignored my messages from Maria, and went to bed.

Shortly before dawn, I woke screaming from a dream in which Artur and I had been burned alive. I rolled over for the comforting reality of my phone, saw that Maria hadn't let up the barrage overnight, and finally answered her questions—anything to take my mind off the licking flames.

Maria came to my place for breakfast, bearing covered takeaway dishes from the dining hall, and commiserated while I aired my grievances over cinnamon rolls. To my surprise, Marcus hadn't tried to contact her—and when I not-so-casually broached the topic at work, it seemed that he hadn't tried to contact anyone else. For all intents and purposes, Marcus was *gone.*

That night, I decided that I could drink alone like an adult, and so I sat in my too-quiet flat with a bottle of wine and felt progressively sorrier for myself. The man with whom I'd begun to imagine spending the rest of my days had turned out to be a dick who hadn't even tried to convince me to get back together. I hadn't yet heard from the Audleys about scheduling dinner that month, but who could say if they'd ever invite me back? I wasn't their family, after all, and God knew that Beth would never speak to me again. My mother hated me, and the feeling was mutual. My dad had loved me only because he hadn't known better. And as for my biological father...well, he'd made his thoughts crystal clear. No one wanted a mongrel. No one wanted *me*.

At some point, I pity-drank myself to sleep on the couch, then bolted awake before my alarm, gasping and flailing in the unfamiliar space until I remembered where I was and why my mouth tasted like vinegar and regret. Reoriented, I flopped back onto the throw pillow and groaned, trying to purge my mind of the nightmarish images that had been too real for me only moments before. Again, I'd been with Artur, running through an endless forest of gnarled, leafless, black-trunked trees while a pack of vaguely canid beasts pursued us. Their howls had been coming closer, but we had nowhere to hide, and then Artur had collapsed and started to bleed out. Before I could try to help, the beasts were upon us with saber teeth and fetid breath, and I'd woken as one ripped into my stomach.

I gazed up at the ceiling, collecting myself as I realized I wasn't about to be disemboweled.

This nonsense had to stop. And if there was one lesson my dad taught me, it was to do the right thing, no matter how unpleasant.

The grand magus was surprised to find me waiting outside her office when she arrived that morning—perhaps more so because I was still wearing the rumpled clothes from the day before in which I'd slept—but she let me in and gave me a cup of strong coffee. "Well, now, you look like a ray of sunshine," she said, settling in behind her desk. "Something you want to talk about, Kitty? Some*one*?"

I took a bracing sip of sweet, sweet caffeine, then

nodded. "How do I get an audience with Nath?"

Toula blinked. "Come again?"

"I want to talk to Nath," I said. "Artur's still in the Gray Lands somewhere, and I'd like to ask her about it."

Sighing, the grand magus rubbed one temple and gestured her coffee to within easy reach. "I don't mean to be a downer, but you understand that there's a good chance your brother...sister?"

I shrugged.

"That *Artur* is dead. A hell of lot can happen in that many centuries, assuming Artur didn't die on arrival. I got all of this secondhand, but the impression I had was that Artur was shipped off on the brink of death."

"Myrddin wouldn't have agreed if Morgen couldn't have kept Artur safe. You didn't hear him tell it—if there's one person Myrddin cares about, it's Artur."

"I get it, but still, you go a millennium and a half with no word, and that doesn't bode well for recovery. And we're talking about the friggin' *Gray Lands*, here."

"It can't hurt to ask Nath, can it?" I pleaded. "Just a quick conversation, that's all I'm asking for. How do I get to her?"

Toula drank in silence for a moment, her eyes focused on a point in the distance as she considered the puzzle. "Getting into the Gray Lands isn't the problem," she finally told me. "We've mapped the known gates, and I can make a new one if needed. But none of the gates in existence would dump you out at Nath's doorstep, and an unauthorized stroll through the Gray Lands would be a terrible idea." She hesitated, then said, "I know that Badger's been to Nath's citadel. Let me talk to her, see if I can't get enough from her recollection to target a gate, and we'll go from there. I've mentioned that this is a bad idea, yes?"

"Thank you," I replied, and finished my coffee in one long gulp.

As I rose to go, Toula said, "Are you sure there isn't

anything you'd like to talk about? Marcus, maybe? I'm not really prying," she insisted, catching my expression shift, "but word has started to trickle down. If there's anything I can do…"

She let that hang unfinished, and I sighed as I tried in vain to smooth my disheveled clothing. "I'll be fine."

"Okay. If you change your mind, door's open."

I'd almost made it to the corridor when a nagging thought made me turn around. I opened my mouth to ask the question on the tip of my tongue, but quickly bit it back. Though I'd spent enough years in Faerie to be aware of Toula's longtime relationship with Coileán, it wasn't common knowledge in the Arcanum, and it would have been a first-rate scandal had it come out. Taking precautions in case of magical bugs, I asked, "Your person…they don't demand obedience, do they?"

She chuckled softly and beckoned me back to the chair. With a quick fluttering of her hands and a muttered focusing mantra, a bubble of spellcraft coalesced around us, and Toula sat back with satisfaction. "Dome of silence. And to answer your question, I don't take orders well, and he's not stupid."

"He's never tried to pull rank?" I pressed.

"Oh, sure, he's *tried*," she replied with nonchalance. "And I let him do it on occasion. He's got experience in areas that I don't, and vice versa. But day to day, or over…oh, let's just say career choices?" she continued, arching an eyebrow. "No. He knows I'd tell him to go fuck himself. Lord knows I've done it before."

The notion of one of the Three and the Grand Magus in a lovers' quarrel was alarming at best, but I pushed that aside. "Lucky you."

"Luck has nothing to do with it." She propped her elbow on the desk and rested her head in her hand. "He's been around a while, and he's got a good idea of what he can get away with. And we were friends before things got serious. We'd been stuck in Faerie during the Mulligan era for about six years by then, and I'd spent more hours than I care to recall in his library, frantically researching, and after a time…well…we realized we weren't annoying each other much at all anymore. He knew my problems, I knew his, and we figured out how to deal with each other. It wasn't an overnight thing, Kitty."

"Neither was ours," I mumbled. "I thought I knew him."

"I've had a few of those moments, too," she said gently. "They sting. Seriously, if you want to talk about it, I'm here."

"Thanks." I paused, then pressed my luck. "Off-topic question?"

"Shoot."

"Is it weird that you're dating your ex's uncle?"

Caught by surprise, Toula laughed aloud and shook her head. "Nah. He's younger than she is, anyway, and we're all on good terms. Mina mentioned me, huh?"

"Briefly."

Though her expression was inscrutable, I thought I might have detected a hint of wistfulness in her gaze. "She's one of the best at what she does. You could do much worse than studying under her."

"I guess," I replied, "but something tells me I won't be going back to Faerie anytime soon."

"Let me worry about that," said Toula, and popped the bubble around us. "Go on, you look like you slept in a library carrel. Get some rest. I'll have Maria make your excuses to Ted."

While I waited for word from Toula, the dreams didn't stop. If anything, my subconscious came up with more creative ways to die, including the improbable "falling into a monstrous version of an elephant graveyard and sinking into decomposing matter," which was a *real* treat. Alcohol only made my nocturnal imagination come alive, and so I resorted to playing solitaire on my phone until my eyes grew heavy, then trying to think happy thoughts as I drifted off. It didn't work, but I had no better alternative.

Marcus remained silent—sulking, I assumed—and as I wasn't about to be the first to extend the olive branch, I let him pout without me. If he couldn't be man enough to call, I told myself, then I didn't need him. The pang in my chest every time I glanced at his closed bedroom door would dull eventually. Hearts were broken all the time, and I'd persevere…assuming, that is, I could get through one night without running for my life through the Gray Lands of my nightmares.

I'd gone to Toula on a Thursday. Not until Sunday morning did she send me a summons to her office, and when I hurried up, her expression was grim. "Did Badger know how to get there?" I asked even before I reached my chair.

"Yeah," said Toula. "I got enough out of her memory to get you in the neighborhood. Let's just hope that Nath hasn't moved in the last forty years." She steepled her fingers on the blotter and gave me a long, hard stare. "The powers that be across the border have asked me to convey to you, in the strongest possible terms, what a foolish idea it is to mess around with Nath."

"Does that mean I can't go?"

"Nope. This is my circus. I just told them I'd pass the message along. But I'd be remiss in my duty as grand magus if I didn't remind you that that's an *awful* lot of collective wisdom warning you against this, Kitty."

I folded my arms in defense against her implied reproach. "All I want to do is ask her for Artur's whereabouts. How is this such a bad thing?"

"Because this is *Nath*," she replied, leaning into her desk. "This isn't like going to my brother with a request. We don't know much about her people, but every indication suggests that she's not wired for empathy and altruism, you know?"

"Neither are the fae," I pointed out.

"And to this point, you've been around half fae or less, and the inherent psychopathy is somewhat tempered. *Somewhat*," she admitted. "We all have our bad days. But Nath—"

"She's full-blooded, I get it," I said impatiently.

"No, and let me finish. She's half...what did the report say that Myrddin called them?"

"Tennuwaya, I think. Mal did the best he could, but with everything else going on that morning, no one bothered to ask about spelling."

"Understood," she muttered. "Anyway, Nath's half that. Her father is the Gray Lands' version of Ros."

That factoid gave me pause. "That's...*possible*?"

"Nath would seem to be proof. You'd have to ask Ros if you wanted to explore this further—that's her business," she added with a brief grimace. "What I'm saying is that there's no telling exactly how talented Nath is or how she'll take a request like yours. She's one of those monsters on the blank part of the map, and I'm pretty sure she's carrying a grudge."

"Against you?"

"Badger. Nath tried to invade this realm forty years ago, and Badger stopped her through somewhat underhanded means—from what I've heard, basically a combination of subterfuge, duct tape, and prayer. The resultant deal was that Nath wouldn't try again as long as Badger was here to enforce her claim. She knows that Badger's gone now, and I put on a show of force in Alaska to dissuade her from making a fresh attempt, but there's really no telling what her plans are vis-à-vis this realm. Now," she continued, drumming her fingers on the desk, "with all of that in mind, I understand why you might want to do something to find your, uh...sibling...and I'm not going to stop you. I'll create a gate and try to make the introductions. But I can offer no guarantees of your safety or success—"

"Understood."

"And you have to accept that if you get in trouble over there, you're on your own," she finished. "No one will be along to save you. It's not as if we have diplomatic relations with the Gray Lands."

I started to speak, but Toula lifted a finger to silence me. "You haven't been over there. I have, *once*..."—she paused, frowning—"okay, maybe twice. I was probably born there, but I don't remember that part. Anyway, I went back one time, when I was older than you but just as foolish. You've never felt anything like it. A few feet past the gate, there's no magic. *None.* Or what little exists is so diffuse that you can't even sense it. You'll have nothing to draw upon in a crisis."

"I'm used to that."

"Yeah, but you're also used to working with a team that can pick up some of the slack. No magic at all...and no weapons, of course, seeing as this is supposed to be a friendly jaunt, so you'll be unarmed. Not that you have any particular fighting skill, right?"

I shook my head. "A few self-defense moves, and Val's let me hold a sword, but no."

"Let that sink in, then," said Toula. "Take a few hours and really mull this over. And if you're still set on it at after *careful* reflection, call me after dinner. We'd need to get you across under cover of darkness."

I'm sure she was hoping I'd listen to reason, but I stood and nodded. "What time should I plan to meet you, and where?"

CHAPTER 9

There was no ideal hour at which to open the gate. Toula didn't know how far off-synch our local time was with Nath's, and the only way to find out was to punch through and check for daylight. Moreover, as there was no way in hell that Toula was willing to open a Gray Lands gate on the castle grounds and risk damaging the wards, we had to go somewhere out of the way and hope for the best. Having curious mundanes around was a fast way to accrue casualties, after all.

"It's not a perfect location," said Toula as she drove us past the late-night lights of the city center.

The road trip, I surmised, was a last-ditch effort to make me think twice, but I didn't mention it. If the grand magus wanted to take out an Arcanum car at eleven at night, no one was going to question her.

"I assume the birders will be home by now," she continued, adjusting the air conditioning. "There may be some hikers still loitering, but if we go far enough into the marshes, we should have privacy. Got your boots, right?"

Touching the galoshes on the floorboard beside me as reassurance, I said, "I've been out to Shapwick Heath at least half a dozen times. The trails are decent."

"Ever done it in the dark?"

"No, but how hard is it to stay on a trail?"

Toula muttered under her breath but let it go.

Fifteen minutes later, we parked just off a narrow lane barely wide enough for two cars to pass abreast, the kind of paved-over tracks that might comfortably accommodate one American truck, and suited up for the walk. Armed with boots and flashlights, we set off down the road until we reached the trail crossing, then turned west toward the marshes.

I'd been optimistic, but as we plodded on, I began to see Toula's point. Despite all the camping that my job entailed, I'd yet to grow entirely comfortable with the sounds of night wildlife—and in a swampy area, where croaks and cries were amplified, not knowing *what* was screaming *where* put me on alert. I'd worn a thin jacket against the evening breeze, but that soon grew stuffy as we hiked and built up a sweat. Every few steps, I had to swat at the air as some flying insect ventured too close. Sure, I'd had rougher evenings in the jungle, but I'd also had bug spray then.

After an increasingly unpleasant half-hour trudge, with midnight nearing, Toula stepped off the trail and into a soggy copse. We'd had a few dry days that week, sparing us from the worst of the muddy possibilities, but the going was squelchy all the same. I picked my way after her, stepping over roots and startling at rustles in the darkness, until we reached a small clearing. "Hold the light, and give me space," she instructed, then stretched out her palms until she seemed to be bracing herself against an invisible wall. She let slip a long sigh, and then the magic ahead of her burst into brilliant color, fireworks that coalesced into the lightning rip of a gate. Muted daylight flooded out onto the marsh, along with a current of dark magic that swirled and flowed through the magic around us. Working quickly against the spell-killing outflow, Toula shored up her gate, though the hole seemed far less stable than her usual results.

"What now?" I asked, peering through the rift at a grove of black-trunked trees beneath a leaden sky.

"We wait," she replied, taking her flashlight back. "And if you're the praying kind, I'd do that, too."

Just as the local gnats had decided that a stationary

target like my face was too good an opportunity to pass up, I spotted a cloaked figure approaching through the trees and nudged Toula in the arm. "Hey, do you see—"

"Not a word," she ordered, and so we stood in silence before the hole as the figure resolved into something decidedly inhuman.

There were no photographs of the tennuwaya in the Arcanum's system, but the creature nearing us fit the description I'd read. He was tall, maybe six feet, and solidly built, judging by the way his white shirt stretched across his chest. While he received points in the familiarity column for being four-limbed and bipedal, he had far more points on the other side. His skin was the dark bluish-green of deep tropical water, stretched over prominent cheekbones and a brow ridge. His face lacked hair, I distantly noticed as I counted the six solid black eyes that stretched toward his pointed ears and tried to decipher the direction of his stare. Beneath the central, largest pair, where a nose should have been, he had only nasal slits, which flared and contracted as he breathed. When his blue lips parted, I saw that his teeth were pointed as well and fit snugly together, a nasty scissor bite. His dark cloak flapped around his ankles in the current between the realms, and when he stopped before the gate, his head swiveled slightly, taking us both in.

"I am Toula of the Arcanum," she said in slow Fae. "I send greetings to your lady and approach in peace."

The man kept his silence for a moment, but he stiffened as if hearing a distant noise, then turned his attention back to us. "My lady accepts your greeting," he replied, his accent grating to my Faerie-trained ear. "Your purpose?"

Toula declined her head in my direction. "The child requests an audience with your lady concerning a family matter."

Again, he stood silently, and I gathered that he was relaying the message to his queen. "What sort of family matter?" he asked.

"A missing person. I make no accusation against Lady Nath," she assured him. "The girl is simply attempting to follow a potential lead."

The pause was longer that time, but the messenger said, "My lady is amused. She will deign to speak with the girl."

"Please convey to her my thanks," said Toula. "When should the girl return?"

"My lady will see her *now*."

Toula's countenance remained placid, but I heard her urgent instructions in my mind: *Don't speak unless spoken to. When in doubt, err on the side of politeness. And you can still back out.*

I nodded to her in understanding, then showed the messenger my empty hands and approached the gate. "May I cross?"

He stepped aside and curled two fingers, and with a deep breath, I passed into the Gray Lands.

Having spent a considerable chunk of my childhood in Faerie, I wasn't often fazed by the architectural follies of the magically gifted. I'd witnessed whole rooms appear with a moment's thought, stumbled into storage spaces far larger inside than physics would dictate, and seen every flavor of dwelling, from the Fringe settlement's conservative neighborhoods of colonials and ranches to an eccentric lord's sweeping pink fantasy of a castle with almost Seussian flourishes.

Nath's palace—if it could properly be called such—surprised me.

When I first saw its outline through the trees as my escort led me along the wooded path, I thought it might be built of jagged black stone, its blocks left unfinished in the front and its turrets broken. Once we cleared the last copse, however, I stopped in my tracks and gaped at the scene in the valley before us.

My escort paused as well, faintly smirking at my reaction. "Impressed?"

"That's...*wow*," I replied, trying to make sense of what I was seeing.

The palace wasn't made of stone, but rather of wood— *living* wood, a castle formed from the thick trunks and interlaced branches of massive trees, which had formed themselves into firm walls and decorative spires. Another grove of trees grew around the palace—room to expand, I guessed—and an unbroken meadow of short brown grass stretched away on all sides, carpeting the valley. Above hung the eternal, unbroken cloud cover that had inspired the Gray Lands' moniker. In truth, the place gave me the creeps, but I couldn't help marveling at the execution.

"Come," said my companion, and led me onward toward our destination.

A pair of tennuwaya in black armor waited at the end of our invisible path, and one touched the branches behind him as we neared. By the time we reached the palace, the branches had creaked away into a door large enough to admit us, and I heard them shift back into their places once we were through. But I had more pressing matters to consider: the inside of the palace proved to be a maze of corridors and chambers, all formed from the accommodating trees, and to my eyes, one hallway looked much like another. I knew from the familiar burn in my legs that we were climbing, but how far, I couldn't say. Nath seemed to have favored ramps to staircases, and if she'd installed an elevator, she'd hidden it well. All in all, I could have chosen better footwear than galoshes for the trek.

I'd begun to wonder if my escort hadn't taken me on an unnecessarily scenic route through the nightmare treehouse when we reached another guarded section of unbroken wall. It looked like the other hallways I'd seen— windowless, set with glowing yellow orbs for light, and decorated with designs made of the more delicate twigs—

but when one of the guards touched the closest orb, the light darkened to a deep green, and the branches formed a door once again.

The room on the other side of the door was spacious, a domed chamber lined with arched windows. I could see the railing of a balcony beyond them, then the canopy of the ornamental grove and the sweeping brown lawn in the distance. We'd climbed higher than I'd realized, and I resisted the urge to massage my legs. A pair of comfortable-looking burgundy chairs had been positioned by the windows, and another tennuwaya sat in one of them. Though it was difficult for me to say with certainty, the presence of security and the tennuwaya's slighter stature than my escort's led me to believe I'd reached the queen. She looked much like him—same blue complexion, same unsettling half-dozen eyes—but she'd opted for a bright yellow floor-length robe over a brown tunic and leggings, and she wore a circlet of black metal on her brow.

I kept my hands clasped in front of me and stood by the wall as it shut behind my retreating companion, waiting to be acknowledged. Nath either hadn't heard us enter or wanted to make me squirm, but I remembered Toula's warning and held my position, my nerves growing tauter by the moment. Finally, she shifted in her chair, propped her head in her hand, and studied me. "You have my attention," she said in Fae, sounding just slightly better than bored.

"Thank you, um, my lady," I replied, trying to calm my pounding heart. "I'm sorry to bother you…" She waved me on, and I got to the point. "Some years ago, my sister was taken into your realm. I'd like to know what happened to her, and if she's alive, I'd like to bring her home. Please."

Nath rubbed her chin and slowly blinked—a rippling effect, as only one pair of eyes closed at a time. "Brought against her will?"

"My understanding is that she was unconscious, definitely near death. A cynaeli woman carried her across—Morgen?"

At that, the queen's central eyes widened. "Lady Morgen of the cynaeli? She took your sister?"

"So I've been told, my lady."

"Then your sister has been here for many years. Lady Morgen was dead before I was born." She rose from her chair and folded her arms over her thin chest. "I was led to believe that you were of the Arcanum."

"I am, my lady," I replied. "My sister is my half sister."

"*Ah*. Precision matters, child. Now, this half sister of yours—you love her, I suppose?"

I had to think that over before answering the question. "I guess I should," I told Nath, "but honestly, I've never met her."

The queen seemed perplexed. "Yet you've come to me in search of her."

"Yes, my lady."

"*Why*?"

"Because she's missing, and because her father...*our* father...dearly wishes to see her again."

A slight smile of comprehension crossed her face. "Come," she said, and led me through a curtained archway onto the balcony.

I didn't stand too close to the queen or the railing, but if Nath noticed, she didn't seem to mind. "Your father is fae, yes?" she said. "Pure or impure, but fae?"

"Half fae."

"And yet, you claim the Arcanum's protection."

"Through my mother," I replied, hoping she wouldn't press for details.

Nath turned to stare out at the valley as something that sounded suspiciously like a dragon roared in the distance. "Correct me if I am misinformed, but one of your blood is deemed an aberration, are you not?"

"That's correct."

"So, your father…*misplaces* a child. She has no claim to the Arcanum?"

"None, my lady."

"Mm. And though he wishes to locate her, he does not come to me, nor does he ask his…queen? King?"

"Lord Coileán," I offered.

"He does not ask his king to intercede on his behalf," she continued. "Instead, he sends you…the disposable child. Is my analysis accurate?"

Her words stung, but I held my temper. "Not entirely, my lady. He doesn't know I'm here. I came of my own volition."

She squinted into the distance as she fit that into her framework. "But he has told you of your sister, yes? Encouraged you to seek her out? Prepared you for this task?"

I shrugged. "Not exactly. I only met him three weeks ago."

Flummoxed, she turned back to me with a furrowed brow. "Then why are you here?"

"Because my sister is missing, my lady," I said with as much respect as I could muster, "and going after her seemed like the right thing to do."

"Using what metric?"

"I, uh…I don't know," I mumbled, rubbing my arm. "It just…seemed right."

She considered that, then looked away again. "The insanity of your people is remarkable," she said with a frustrated sigh. "But you have come to me for information. What do you offer in return?"

"What would you request, my lady?" I asked carefully.

"Knowledge in kind would seem to be a fair trade. Where is Hannah Parsons?"

The question was loaded like a cannon pointed at my face, and I panicked briefly, wondering what to tell her, before I realized there was no point in dissembling when Nath could always read my mind. "She moved to Faerie. I don't know exactly when, but I would have been very young."

"As my sources suggested," Nath replied with a slight smile. "Then she has forfeited her claim to that realm?"

"She moved away, my lady, and Toula leads the Arcanum now. That's all I know on the subject."

Again, Nath looked back at me, this time with bemusement. "You speak the truth."

"You're obviously talented, and I have no mental defenses in this realm," I replied. "Lying to you seems like a monumentally stupid idea. My lady."

"Perhaps you are not as insane as you seem," she mused, studying me again for the length of a triple blink. "Very well, knowledge in kind. I do not know your sister's whereabouts. Morgen is long dead, and in all likelihood, your sister is dead as well. More than that, I cannot say."

I hesitated, hoping I wasn't about to make the audience go south in a hurry. "Would you grant me permission to seek her out, then? Make enquiries among the cynaeli?"

Nath cocked her head. "Why should I do that?"

It's difficult to tug on the heartstrings of a person who considers altruism to be a sign of mental illness, but I did my best to make my case. "It would cause no harm to you. All I want to do is speak with someone who knew Morgen when my sister was brought over, if anyone like that is still around. I just ask for your permission to go to them and see if someone can give me answers."

The queen considered that, then walked away down the balcony, trailing her fingertips along the living railing. I stood where I was, watching and holding my breath, until she returned to me and smiled—which, on that face, wasn't a comforting expression.

"Do you enjoy games?" she asked.

"That, uh…that depends on the game, my lady," I replied, fearing where this was going.

"My court has been dull of late," said Nath with an exasperated snort. "Perhaps you could entertain me."

"How so?"

Her smile opened, revealing her fanged grin. "My terms, then. I will allow you three days to search my realm for your sister. Use any methods you like. And I will be generous—bring a companion, if you will. You and yours may leave at any time before the end of those days. Should you find your sister, you may take her with you. But if the time expires and you remain in this realm…then you will be mine to do with as I please."

My mind raced as I looked for loopholes in her proposition. "Same goes for my companion, I take it."

"Exactly. Whatever befalls one befalls the other. That seems fair."

There was nothing fair about her terms. I didn't have so much as a map to the Gray Lands, and I'd be limited in my exploration to areas within near distance of a natural gate, since I couldn't make my own without magic. Linger too close to the gate, and I'd never learn anything. Stray too far, keep pushing around the next corner in hopes of the answers I sought, and I'd never make it back in time. And therein, I supposed, was Nath's entertainment: three days of will-she-won't-she, and the prospect of a new plaything at the end.

"May I have some time to think this over at home?" I asked.

"Certainly. Think about it as long as you like—this is about your sister, not mine. If you decide to accept my offer, simply return. I will know, and your time will begin." Once more, she turned away from me to gaze at the land. "Your escort will arrive shortly and return you to your gate. You may leave."

"Thank you, my lady."

"Oh, and child?" she said as I started to go. "Tell your Toula that my agreement with Hannah is well and truly void." She smiled again, and I nodded, hoping the promised escort would hurry up and get me out of there before the queen changed her mind.

Toula was waiting in the dark where I'd left her, standing ankle-deep in muck, though she'd put together a spell to ward off the worst of the night chill. The escort closed the gate behind me, Toula broke down all traces of her craft, and then we started the long, uncomfortable trudge back to civilization. Two minutes into the walk, she muttered, "Forget this," opened a gate to the parking lot, and warned me to clean my boots before getting into her car.

On the drive home, I told her everything, including Nath's friendly threat. Toula said little until we pulled back into the castle's garage, then cut the engine and sighed. "You didn't tell Nath anything she didn't already know, kid. When I sent a lone survivor back from the Conclave attack last year, I said that Badger's claim had passed to the Arcanum. Don't beat yourself up."

"What should I do about her 'game'?" I asked.

"I'm not going to tell you that you can't go," she murmured, "but I think you'd be foolish to go as you are."

"I was planning to read through the Archives' materials—"

"That's secondary. You need to get your butt to the settlement and talk to Kip. If anyone knows the terrain over there, it's him."

When I didn't immediately agree, Toula got out of the car, and I scrambled to follow her. "Time to put on your big-girl pants, Kitty," she said, heading for the elevator. "If you're set on going back to the Gray Lands, then you're damn well going to prepare ahead of time, and that means sitting down with Kip. I don't care if Marcus is pouting over there, and I don't care that you two are fighting. Woman up, get a notepad, and you might want to give my brother a call in the morning."

There were few conversations I wanted to have less than explaining to Val why his son and I weren't speaking, but Toula was right—and if Val was pissed at me, then I wanted to know *before* crossing the border. And so, after a few hours of tossing in bed, I showered, dressed, made coffee to stall, then picked up my phone.

He answered on the second ring. "Kitty! Hello," he said, sounding tenser than I'd anticipated.

"Sorry, is this a bad time?" I hastily asked.

"No, no…Toula warned me to expect your call."

I grimaced in my quiet kitchen. "She told you about last night, huh?"

"In broad strokes. What can I do to dissuade you from this plan?"

"I, uh—"

"Because I cannot convey to you in mere words what a risky undertaking this is," he continued over my mumbling. "If you're to locate Artur, you'll need someone with knowledge of the terrain, and the only person I know who might offer that is Kip. He has no intention of leaving the settlement, which leaves you without a guide. We both know there's no map of the Gray Lands in the Archives, or else someone in the Fringe would have heard rumor of it by now. So how does this end in anything but failure, hmm?"

"I don't know," I muttered. "But I'd like permission to come over and at least talk to Kip."

"Permission?" Val echoed, perplexed. "Since when have you needed that?"

"Well…uh…I mean, with everything that's, uh…"

He let me fumble for a moment, then quietly said, "Kitty, the fact that you and Marcus are feuding doesn't mean that your invitation has been rescinded. I don't care whose team you ultimately claim, girl—as long as I have a say in the matter, you're welcome here. I only ask that you stop for a moment, *think* about what you're doing, and try to see reason."

"You're not going to put your foot down?" I asked, trying not to look at Marcus's empty seat at the table.

"It's not my choice. Toula's given her reluctant permission, and I understand the impetus for this suicidal little jaunt of yours—if Toula had been taken, then I would probably be doing much as you are. But I'm warning you to think long and hard about the risks before you run off a cliff, chasing after ghosts."

"She might not be dead," I protested.

"But she may well be. And even if she lives, her life is no more important than yours, child. Please remember that."

I took a sip of coffee, giving me a moment's pause. "My dad always told me to do the right thing. Even if you're going to lose, you should lose doing what you're supposed to be doing."

"An admirable sentiment," said Val, "and I'm sure he was a good man, if not a military strategist. But Kitty, doing your homework before playing and turning in your cheating classmate are *vastly* different matters than risking your life in the Gray Lands. If your father were here now, what do you think he would say? 'Go for it'?"

"I guess."

"Really? Because if I were your father, I would tell you that you've lost your senses and beg you to reconsider. The choice is yours," he said before I could interrupt, "but at least give it a few days before you dash off to your death, won't you?"

"*Val...*"

"Listen to experience, Kitty. That's all I ask," he said, and pointedly cleared his throat. "Now, if you were planning on visiting Kip in the next few hours, I could keep Marcus occupied elsewhere."

"That...would be nice. Thank you."

Val hesitated before he spoke again. "It's been made clear to me that this is none of my business and I need to keep my nose out of it, but..."

I smiled to myself and drank my coffee. "*But?*"

"But I care about you both," he said softly. "Marcus is in pain, and Toula says you're a mess."

"I'm not—"

"That's only what I've been told," he soothed. "I'm

doing what I can to…well, to address certain issues with my son. Wanda has been most helpful."

"You foisted him off onto Wanda?"

"No. He went of his own will."

Surprised, I put my mug down before it reached my lips. Wanda Fitzgibbon, a psychologist Fringer who'd escaped to Faerie during the Mulligan purge, had counseled Maria and me as kids. While I knew that Marcus had spent a few sessions with her after his arrival, he hadn't spoken about therapy with me, and I wasn't aware that he'd seen the point to it. "Well, uh…good," I told Val. "Hope it's helping."

"Again, I'm not trying to meddle—"

"Ha."

"But as Ros is sometimes rather *free* with information, I have a vague sense of what was said and why. I understand that he hurt you, and he knows he was out of line. What I ask is that you remember how brief his time has been here, and what happened before. That's all."

"I know, I know," I muttered, "but…"

Val waited, and when I left that dangling, he said, "But your temper burns hotter than it used to? But slights that might once have annoyed you now seem like grave insults?"

I sipped my drink. "Didn't think you could get in my head over the phone."

He chuckled on the other end. "I saw this in Aiden and Joey, and even with her training, I've seen flashes of it in Maria. This is hardly unexpected, Kitty."

"It's fucking annoying is what it is," I grumbled.

"As with all else, control will come in time. Think of your psyche as having a fresh wound—tender and easily inflamed, but it will heal eventually. Until then…you might be aware that you're feeling anger more keenly than usual."

I heard what Val was actually saying: *He's trying. Meet him in the middle.* Still, I wasn't ready to surrender. "Understood. It would probably be best if we didn't run into each other while I'm in town."

"Of course," he replied. "I hope Kip's a help to you. And Kitty?"

"Sir?"

"Please try not to get yourself killed," said Val, and hung up.

Fringers were by definition an odd lot, and their settlement near Coileán's palace was the one place in the realm where few cared who or what you were, so long as you didn't cause trouble.

Many of the first-generation settlers had been there forty years or more, having arrived as refugees on the run from murderous Grand Magus Mulligan. Since his preference had been to kidnap witches and kill lesser bloods, a high percentage of the earliest inhabitants could trace their lineage to one court or another, though for some, the fae trace was so negligible that they couldn't pull off the simplest glamour. Most of the other refugees were witches who'd slipped through the Arcanum's net and been evacuated. In the face of genocide, Coileán and Eleanor hadn't been picky about bloodlines. Others had trickled in over the next eleven years, shepherded by the Fringe's ragtag retrieval team and assisted by their contacts in the Minor Arcanum. By the end of the Mulligan era, there were a handful of others in the settlement as well—a few mundane family members and associates caught up in the chaos; many of the half-blooded Stowe brothers, who built houses on the then-edge of town; a handful of witch-bloods; a single wizard, Ms. Matherson; and Poppy Kane, Mal's mom, a shifter who'd settled down with a Stowe. By the time I came along, the settlement was into its third generation, children born to the Faerie-born children of the first arrivals. As the inhabitants grew and paired off and started families of their own, the Stowes continued to add roads and houses and expand the school, even designing a system of self-powered trolleys that ran from the outskirts into the center of town. The population was only going to swell—while the fae reproductive rate was generally low, their lesser-blooded cousins and witch neighbors had proven themselves more than fertile, and few ever left. Sure, most of the teenagers struck out into the mortal realm for a time, either for college or just to see the sights—the Fringer version of Rumspringa—but the vast majority returned to the settlement by their mid-twenties. The mortal realm had its draws, but the promise of eternal youth in Faerie usually won out.

But even with the diversity in the settlement, there was a Fringer who fit into a category of one: Kippit. Tall and muscular, with golden-brown skin and long red hair, Kip stood out in a crowd, and more so than usual in the settlement because he hadn't moved in until he was in his mid-thirties. He'd married Amy Levey, the finest living crafter in either realm, and had happily set up a storefront beside her shop, where he tended to the Fringers' computer needs. Kip wasn't exactly a one-man IT unit—plenty of his neighbors had sufficient technological knowhow to keep everyone online—but having learned from Amy how to build and code, he took pleasure in the enterprise, and he offered instruction to the kids. He and Amy had never managed to have a family of their own, which I suspected came as a relief to some of more *traditional* members of the Fringe. For all her skill, Amy was the child of two witch-bloods, tainted in the extreme, while Kip only seemed human due to a long-lasting transformation bind.

Kip was kadalin—a centaur, in the common parlance—born in the Gray Lands and brought into the mortal realm by a stroke of luck. Kidnapped with his family, he'd been carried along for days as a food source by raiders, who'd had the misfortune of making camp beside a gate that Badger and Seamus intended to close. When they'd found the raiders, they'd killed them and freed Kip, then brought him home with them while he healed. As he'd acclimated, he'd grown friendly with Amy—both had been freshly orphaned and homeless—and in time, and with the transformation bind, they'd set up house together. They made an odd couple—Amy was more than a foot shorter than Kip, blonde, petite, and by blood and the queen's proclamation, a lady of Eleanor's court—but by all accounts, they were deeply in love.

I knew Kip by face and reputation, as I did many of the more prominent Fringers, and when I walked into his shop that morning, he looked up from his laptop at the jingling bell and smiled in recognition. "Kitty, right?" he said, shutting the computer. "Toula said you'd be by."

"Sorry," I began, "am I interrupting anything?"

"Not at all." He waved one hand toward the plate of toast beside him. "As you can see, I'm drowning in clients right now. The missus wanted an early start today, so I figured I could eat here as well as at home."

I glanced to my right, where a window offered a glimpse of Amy's red-lit workshop and the master crafter herself, busily mixing wand cores. Upon second glance, I realized that the window was actually a monitor and stepped closer, frowning.

"Safer that way," Kip explained. "She's just on the other side of the wall, but the work she does is delicate, as is mine in a different fashion. We can't work together, and a real window would be risky, so cameras and microphones it is—both of these areas have to be kept well insulated." He depressed a button on the counter and said, "Amy, dear? Kitty's arrived."

Amy put down her mortar and pestle and gave the camera a look of consternation. "Talk her out of this, will you?" she said, her drawl slightly distorted as it came through a speaker on the wall.

"I'll do my best," he replied, and cut the connection. "So," he said, turning back to me, "you might have guessed that word's getting around."

"Ros?" I muttered.

"She's not thrilled. But since you're here, let me give you what you came for, eh? Pull up a stool."

Kip had placed two long tables down the middle of the shop, set up with workstations for lessons, and I snagged the nearest seat and dragged it to the counter. He pushed his toast aside, pulled four pieces of printer paper from a shelf, and taped them together to make a larger rectangle. "Give me a moment," he said, squinting at the blank page, then sketched a compass rose in the corner and began scribbling a rough map. When he finished, he turned it to face me and began pointing out the features.

"This is Nath's citadel," he said, tapping his pen against an encircled X in the far south. "I'm sorry, this isn't to scale, but I left the Gray Lands forty-three years ago, and I'm working from memory. Bear with me."

"No, no, this is great," I reassured him. "More than I've got now."

"That's not saying much." He ran the tip of his pen over the line of unfinished, overlapping triangles north of Nath. "About a day's run from her, you'll come to a mountain range going east to west. The strangers—Nath's people—surely have their own name for it, but my people call it the Ro Henare…uh, you might say the Dragon's Spine."

"Poetic."

"Not exactly." He made a few marks along the mountains. "There's no need to give you a full course in kadalin mythology, but legend says a great hero around the dawn of time slew a massive dragon, and the Ro Henare is what's left of it. Jagged peaks, few safe passes, and plenty of geothermal activity, just to make it fun. What's a dragon-themed range without a little lava, eh?"

"It's *active*?"

"I remember seeing two minor eruptions, but there could have been more—we stayed well north of the mountains except when the winters were particularly rough. The Gray Lands are far more seasonal than Faerie's ever been, and we had a blizzard or two when I was a kid. But there are hot springs in the foothills, see, so if we couldn't find food in the usual places, we'd pack to camp and head south with everything else."

"Your people are nomadic, then?"

"No. Farmers, mostly, but we'd hunt to bring in meat. If the winter goes on too long, and the stockpiles run out, and there's nothing living for miles around...you get the picture. Nath and her predecessors didn't provide us with a safety net."

I glanced back at the map, which was still mostly white space. "So where are the passes?"

Kip made a face and shrugged. "Couldn't begin to guess. I only crossed once, when I was five, so I wasn't exactly navigating. We tried to avoid the strangers, you see," he explained, and pointed to a series of blobs in the far northeast. "My village was up here, on the longest of these lakes—the Kint Porda. Literally, 'crooked fingers,' but it has more of a sense of being the place where those fingers have been...you know, like dragging your fingertips through sand. The ruts left behind." He laughed softly to himself. "Sorry, the language is strange. And these names, they're just what *we* used. The strangers and the deep dwellers have their own, I'm sure."

"Wait, back up," I said. "These strangers are—"

"Nath's people."

"Tennuwaya? Blue, too many eyes?"

"Sounds right. The deep dwellers are the other major race. I *think* they were all purple, but I never got too close."

"You didn't like each other?"

Kip snorted and began drawing more mountains in the northwest. "They hunted us."

"*Shit*," I muttered.

"Not often, especially not out near my village, but every now and then, you'd see a handful of them in a hunting party. Not like ours—we'd send every available man and half the women out, kill everything we could, and bring it back to preserve. They tended to aim for the largest one of us they could find, and when they'd killed him, they'd stop with the one and go away. Sport hunting, for all I know. Anyway, Ros told me some of what she'd picked up from you and Marcus, and I'm fairly confident that your Morgen was a deep dweller."

"Cynaeli, I think they're called."

"If you say so." He tapped the new mountains. "They live around here, in the Fash Henare—uh, the Dragon's Tail. Maybe if you squint," he suggested. "The mountains are highest in the south, and as they curve toward the northeast, they flatten out. Not active, or at least not as active as the Ro Henare. I was taught that the deep dwellers build their villages in great caves in the mountains, but they may have some surface structures, too. I wouldn't know—I've never seen more of the Fash Henare than a map, and the only time anyone got close was when they had nowhere else to run."

I frowned, and Kip hunched over the counter, his shoulders tightening. "Etalre. Raiders. True nomads. They could strike at any time, and they'd slaughter whole villages in a night. They'd set fires, try to make people panic, then strike them down when they fled. Fucking monsters," he said, glowering at the map. "I can't tell you how to avoid them. The universe would be better off without them, but there's nothing I can do on that count."

Trying to pull him back from the dark place his mind was evidently leading him, I said, "How about gates? Do you know of any?"

"Gates?" he repeated, and studied the upside-down map. "No. I never saw one until I was dragged into the mortal realm. If there's a gate near the Kint Porda, it's hidden well. Maybe you could locate it—you'd sense the outflow of magic, wouldn't you?"

"Not from a great distance," I replied, liking Kip's map

less and less. "You don't know of one near the, uh…deep dwellers?"

"There could be a dozen gates in the Fash Henare, and I wouldn't know about them. Same goes for Nath's base. I only know where those people have their settlements, relatively speaking, because I was taught how to avoid them. But here's what I *can* tell you." Again, he pointed to the encircled X. "From Nath to the southern edge of the Ro Henare is a day's run. Crossing the mountains will take time, especially if you don't find a pass on the first attempt. Once you're north of the range, it's another two days' run to reach the foothills of the Fash Henare. Head west from there, and you'll find the deep dwellers…or more likely, they'll find you."

"So," I mumbled, "even if I crossed the mountains in a day…"

"You're looking at a four-day journey, one way," said Kip. "At *best*. And that's not at 'human out for a stroll' speed—I'm talking about a sustained gallop. A grueling pace."

"What if I started here?" I asked, pointing to the lakes. "Do you remember them well enough that Toula could pull the memories and make a gate?"

"Sure," he replied, shrugging, "but it wouldn't do you any good. Like I said, this isn't to scale. From my village— or what may be left of it—to the Fash Henare is another four days' trip. As you might say, six of one, half-dozen of the other." He put his pen aside, folded his arms on the counter, and looked me in the eye. "You can't win, Kitty. Nath knows that. Even if Artur were giftwrapped and waiting for you outside the deep dwellers' settlement—*one* of their settlements—you'd never make it to her and back in time. Your only hope would be a gate around there, and I can't tell you whether one exists. And there's another thing you should consider." He leaned closer and lowered his voice. "My people aged and died in the Gray Lands. I seem to respond to magic here as well as anyone else in the settlement does—I mean, look at me. I'm almost sixty-two, and the transformation bind has nothing to do with my face."

He had a point—his only wrinkles were faint smile lines.

"Nath may be immortal, and for all I know, the deep dwellers are, too. But I doubt that dark magic alone would be sufficient to keep Artur alive. So, let's say that this Morgen healed Artur. What then? She'd be dead within a century, right?"

"Unless dark magic *does* work on humans."

"Okay, so Artur's still alive and well when you find her, and you manage to locate a gate back into the mortal realm in time, and you take her across. What then? Dark magic isn't strong enough here to sustain the effect, and she drops dead. You *have* heard about what happened to Lady Eleanor's husband, yes?"

I grimaced and nodded.

"And before you get clever, don't tell me that you're going to open a gate from the Gray Lands straight into Faerie—you won't be able to open a gate, period. Kitty, honey, I hate to break it to you like this, but Nath's 'game' is a losing gamble." He reached across the desk and gripped my shoulder, then slowly shook his head. "You're not going to find your sister alive. And even if you did, you'd never make it out of the Gray Lands. Nath is playing to win."

CHAPTER 10

So that was it, then. Finito. My grand plan was DOA.

After leaving Kip, I put in a few useless hours at work, though I could barely focus on my reading. Maria took me into town for drinks that night and murmured sympathetically in the right places as I relayed my findings. "You didn't think that Nath was going to give you a sporting chance, did you?" she said, picking at a plate of garlic fries. "I'm sorry, Kitty. I know you wanted to find...her? Is that what we're going with now?"

"Doesn't matter," I mumbled into my beer. "Never going to get the chance to ask Artur, right?"

"Well, not *tonight*, but I wouldn't say *never*. Look at Myrddin—he's still waiting."

"And maybe he's delusional."

"Hey." She patted my arm and waited until I met her gaze. "We have time. Loads of it. If Artur's still alive somehow, then we'll find a way. Won't be tonight, probably won't be tomorrow. Might be another century. But don't give up yet, okay?"

She hugged me before we parted and offered to let me sleep over, but I declined. Waking up in Maria's flat would only remind me of my missing roommate, who still hadn't so much as sent me a message in the six days since we fought. Then again, I hadn't contacted him, either, but my wounded heart was in no mood to be fair to him that evening. *Nothing* was fair, and I was alone, and maybe I would always be alone—like Myrddin, waiting for someone who would never return.

The next morning, having tossed and turned half the night, I slunk into the office early, intending to make up for my poor performance the day before. As I settled down with my oversized morning mug of tea, Frank rapped on the doorframe and stepped inside. "Have you seen Maria? The new archivist is being fussy about letting me into the controlled stacks, and I need…" He paused, peered at my face, then plopped onto the couch and said, "Talk. You look like shit."

I snorted and opened my computer. "How would you know?"

"I would think that twenty-two years of constantly being around you people has given me a working baseline. What is it? Still sleeping poorly?"

It was sometimes difficult to pinpoint emotion in Frank's voice—verbal communication had been a later-learned skill, and he'd yet to master every nuance—but I could feel the concern rolling off of him deep in my psyche. He was only four years older than me, but as he'd been an adult since he was five, Frank tended to skew parental whenever I was less than content.

"Rough night," I said, which wasn't a lie, but his expression told me he wasn't buying it. "And I got some bad news from Kip, over in the Fringe settlement," I admitted. "Turns out there's no way to even get to where Artur last was in three days, let alone get back to the exit."

He leaned into the cushion and crossed his legs. "Explain."

Obliging him, I unfolded Kip's map from my purse, spread it on the coffee table, and pointed out the distances Kip had written in, I supposed in case I'd had second thoughts.

"So, let me get this straight," said Frank, studying the map. "As the kadalin gallops, it's a day to these first mountains, another day to cross them, if you're lucky, and then a two-day run to reach the *second* mountains, where Artur may or may not be hiding. Yeah?"

"She's probably dead—"

"Put that aside. How far is this trip, really? Do you have any actual numbers?"

I didn't, so we turned to the Internet and a lot of guesswork. "Okay," Frank murmured, looking at my screen over my shoulder, "let's say a kadalin can run forty kilometers an hour, to be conservative, maybe a twelve-hour run per day…"

"Four hundred eighty kilometers a day."

"Times four days is…one thousand, nine hundred, and twenty kilometers."

"Less than that—the mountains will give you altitude to deal with, but surely the pass isn't that long."

"Well, let's not lowball. Say nineteen hundred kilometers."

Automatically, I did the mental calculation, a habit I'd picked up on starting school in England. Just shy of twelve hundred miles…the situation was even worse with numbers.

"And that ends that," I said, looking back at Frank. "There's no way I can cover that distance. Even if I got an off-road vehicle and found a wide enough path through the mountains, just carrying sufficient fuel would be a nightmare."

"I was going to ask," he replied, folding his arms. "How *did* you plan to get around over there?"

"Looks like I didn't plan at all, huh?"

"And Nath's letting you take one other traveler?"

"Generous, I know," I muttered.

He frowned at the far corner of the room for a moment, tapping two fingers against his arm as he thought. "You know, Kitty," he finally said, "if you want to do this, there's a way."

"Buy a jetpack?"

"Nah, you'd burn your feet off. What if I went with you?"

"*You?*"

He chuckled at my shock. "Have you *seen* my wingspan? I can get you to Artur's doorstep in a day, tops."

"Frank," I said, reaching up to clasp his arm, "that's...*amazing* of you, but it's too dangerous to get someone else involved."

"You can't do it on your own," he pointed out. "There's no one in this installation or in Faerie who can do jack with dark magic. But get this bind off of me, and you'll at least have a chance. I'm strong enough to make the trip."

I shook my head. "If I didn't get back to the gate in time, you'd be stuck with Nath, too. No way."

He folded himself until he could sit on the corner of my desk and stare down at me. "Do you want to find your sister?"

"She's probably dead."

"And what if she isn't? In either case, wouldn't you like to have answers?"

"Of course," I replied, "but—"

"But nothing. We'll do it together. One day to the purple people, one day to snoop around, and one day to fly back."

The offer was tempting—something inside me had begun to stir with excitement as I thought through his plan—but caution continued to force its way to the fore. "We'd be defenseless. I won't have any magic to draw on."

"So get a gun and some ammo, and if you don't trust yourself to shoot straight, have I mentioned lately that I'm a *dragon*?" he said impatiently. "Tough scales, big claws, bigger teeth, and—oh, yes—there's that whole 'fire breathing' thing that kicks in when I'm exposed to *dark magic*. Know any place like that?"

"Frank..."

"I'm serious. Let me help you. I can do it."

I floundered for a moment, then managed, "*Why?*"

His answer was immediate and simple: "Because

friends don't let friends traipse off into the Gray Lands alone."

Frank almost fell off his perch on my desk when I jumped up and threw my arms around him, but he recovered and awkwardly rubbed my back. "Easy," he said as I babbled my gratitude. "I need all of those ribs."

Toula wasn't thrilled with this development. Maria was more than a little wary, Ted hated it, and Lakshmi glowered at us both and told us that we were being idiots, but in the end, it was our decision, and Frank never wavered.

There was, however, one tiny hitch: I'd never ridden anything, let alone a dragon.

"It's not complicated," Frank assured me. "Your job is to sit still and hold on. I'll do all the hard work."

"It's the holding on part that's the problem," I replied. "Where, um, exactly, do I…uh…"

He patted my head. "Joey will explain. I've already informed him that we're coming."

"We are?"

"You need gear," he said, tidying his office to leave. "And while you could ride bareback, I've been told that it's less than ideal. You need to figure out what you're doing, *I* need to reacclimate to a rider—"

"Sorry," I mumbled. "I'll eat light."

"Oh, it's not your weight that's the problem." He pulled the cord on his standing lamp and ushered me out. "It's a matter of being conscious that you're back there and not doing something stupid like a barrel roll."

I followed him out of the suite and toward the staircase. "Was that meant to be reassuring?"

He glanced back and smiled, showing far too many teeth. "I get to have a little fun. And you might want an overnight bag."

At dawn, equipped with a backpack, I met Frank and

Toula on the edge of the castle grounds, just inside the camouflaging bubble of spellcraft. She'd thrown on a windbreaker over her apparent pajamas—the grand magus dressed on *her* schedule—but Frank sported only a terry bathrobe against the chill. "We're expected," he told me as I jogged over to join them. "The time's a little ahead of us in Faerie, but Joey said breakfast is waiting. You'll probably want to eat up."

"What about you?" I asked.

Frank snorted. "I've got my own breakfast plans."

As he shuffled his bare feet in the cold, wet grass, Toula, thin-lipped with disapproval, did the honors. While I could open and close a gate with relative confidence, she'd insisted on being there in case something should go wrong with Frank's bind. The hole she made was far larger than usual, a circle perhaps thirty feet in diameter, and opened onto a green meadow. In the near distance stood a barn tall enough to park a cruise ship, and the faint strains of bleating resounded across the pasture. If I squinted, I could just make out the house affixed to the barn, comically dwarfed beside it.

An instant later, a bearded man in an oilcloth duster appeared beside the gate—Joey, occasionally Lord Joseph, Ros's father and Faerie's unofficial dragon wrangler. "Morning!" he said, giving us a once-over. "You two are friggin' nuts, but come on. Kitty first."

I easily slipped between the realms, and Joey directed me to the side, well away from the gate. "Give him room," he cautioned, joining me. "Okay, bud, whenever you're ready."

From my angle, I was just able to catch a glimpse of Frank disrobing, and I quickly averted my eyes. "Prude," he called cheerfully, then ran at the gate and leapt through.

The bind shattered in an explosion that was brilliant red in the magical spectrum, and when the spots cleared from my eyes, there was Frank...*all* of him.

Nose to tail tip, Frank was almost two hundred thirty

feet long and several times my height with his head raised. His milky scales iridesced with a purplish sheen in the sunlight, and he rumbled with pleasure as he stretched, a noise that made the hairs on the back of my neck rise in warning. A Gulfstream could have parked under each of his wings, which cracked like sheets in a gale as he unfolded them.

"Feel better?" I asked as Toula closed the gate.

Much. He took a deep sniff at the air, then broadened his thought to include Joey. *Are they home?*

"Some of them," Joey replied, and gave Frank's foreleg a pat. "Go on, eat up. I've got Kitty in hand."

Frank held his position for a moment longer, however, and I started to ask what was wrong when another voice echoed through my head: *Runt?*

At least, that was the way my mind interpreted the message as it tried to attach words to thought unencumbered by such constraints as language. Frank had once explained to me the difference between how he communicated with us and with his kin. Pure draconic telepathy was like showing the target a picture, albeit with emotional shading and a dozen other layers thrown in. Meaning came in a burst, subtext and all. With the rest of us, mental communication was more like trying to describe the picture and hoping for the best.

The second voice's thought was brief but packed: recognition, surprise, and an acknowledgement of familial connection. As I struggled to process all of the information I was receiving, a third voice chimed in: *Runt? It's Runt!*

In seconds, two dragons had emerged from the barn and were running to intercept Frank. The larger of the pair was red, the smaller black, but both had about twenty feet on him and proportionally more muscle. Joey shoved me out of the way just before the others plowed into Frank, knocking him onto his side in the tall grass. What followed was a flurry of wings, tail swats, and growling roars, but

Joey seemed remarkably calm about the tons of lizard rolling around the meadow. "His brothers," he told me as I watched the dragons snap at each other. "They're just playing, honestly. Here," he offered, and opened a gate into a warm kitchen, revealing a table already set and laden with platters of pancakes and sausage patties. "Let's take the shortcut. Less chance of getting trampled that way."

While I ate breakfast, Joey did his part to remind me once again of what a terrible idea it was to go on walkabout in the Gray Lands. "You know Ros is going to be upset," he added, pushing the last of the hash browns my way. "Frank's her hatchling."

"It was Frank's idea," I pointed out.

"Details." He glanced up at the sound of heavy footsteps in the adjoining barn, which was accessible from the kitchen—*quite* accessible, as an entire wall of the high-ceilinged room was missing. With a grunt, Frank settled down beside the hole and looked in as we finished. *Don't worry about Ros*, he told me. *She and I just had a chat.*

Joey arched an eyebrow. "I didn't see lightning."

Oh, she's <u>unhappy</u>, but I assured her that we have a sound exit strategy. Didn't make her any happier, though I believe she was somewhat reassured to know that we've thought this through. Ooh, sausage?

I grabbed the plate with the last half-dozen patties and carried it to the barn. "Where do you want them?"

In response, Frank opened his mouth, revealing rows of pointed teeth several feet tall. The tufts of wool caught between a few told me he'd already dined on fresh mutton that morning. One by one, I tossed the patties over and into his maw, and he swallowed the lot in a single gulp. "Could you even taste that?" I asked.

Barely. Could do with hot sauce.

"You can critique my cooking later," said Joey. "Let's get you outfitted, Kitty, and then we'll see about flight. Hey, Frank, did the guys let you eat okay?"

Once they climbed off me. His thought carried a cast of

impatience. *You know how it goes. "Squash the Runt" is always a delight.*

"Sorry. I'd keep them away if I could, but—"

Good luck with that. He grunted as something—or someone—heavy slammed into the exterior barn wall. *I thought they'd be out, considering Neve.*

"Georgie's been holding them at bay," said Joey, "but you know how those two are. I'm about to kick them out and tell them to go mate, for all our sakes. Kitty, honey, watch your step," he added as I slid around Frank's snout and almost squashed a mangled rat underfoot. "Ick. My apologies—looks like someone got bored last night." The rat vanished with a touch of enchantment, and Joey, grimacing, steered me past Frank's head and deeper into the barn.

Though impressive from a distance, the barn was positively cavernous from the inside—but then, considering the half-dozen dragons that regularly slept there, it had to be enormous. The floor was covered by a thick layer of straw, though footpaths had been trampled here and there, while nest-like piles marked individual beds. High windows and the open barn door, large enough to fit two dragons abreast, admitted plenty of morning light, and as I peered into the far corner, I noticed a mound of purple scales curled up and watching us.

Neve, Frank told me. *Tending a clutch. She probably won't get up, and I wouldn't get too close.*

"Yeah," said Joey, who'd apparently been privy to his explanation. "Neve's a sweetie, but this is her first, and she's been a *bit* overprotective. Then again, if I had those two knuckleheads roughhousing around me, I might be extra careful with my eggs." He pointed back toward the barn door and the pair of play-fighting blobs out in the yard. "Almost twenty-eight, and they're still big kids when they're together," he said, and led me down one of the paths toward a door in the barn wall. "The girls actually take turns egg-sitting to keep the clutch safe while Neve eats. Obelia and Zafira are out with Georgie," he added, glancing back at Frank. "Early-morning girls' hunting trip. They're due back any minute."

You're going to need a bigger barn.

"Tell me about it," said Joey, though he didn't seem put out. "If all of Neve's hatch, we'll need space for twelve."

I thought she only had five.

"Yeah—those five, Georgie, and the six of you."

Don't worry about me, he replied—a bit too quickly, I mused.

"Eh, it's the principle of the thing," Joey said. "I mean, hell, Ros still has her old bedroom here. We're not crunched for space."

Our destination proved to be a tack room, tiny compared to the barn but still the size of a modest apartment. Joey considered my clothing, then pulled a smaller duster from a wooden wardrobe. "Ros has a couple of inches on you, but this should work for now," he said as I slipped the coat on. "You'll want gloves, too—put them in your pockets until you're set." He passed me a pair from the wardrobe. "Your shoes are okay for the moment, but eventually, you'll want boots. And here." He thrust a black helmet with a smoked visor into my arms. "This won't do you much good outside of Faerie, but we'll use it for training purposes."

I rapped my knuckles against the hard shell. "In case I fall off?"

"No—communication and navigation. Don't fall off. This way," he said before I could fully consider the implications of that warning.

Filling most of the room were odd constructions of leather and brass—saddles, I realized with awe, but unlike any I'd ever seen in pictures. The seat part seemed normal enough, and I recognized stirrups, but each saddle was set atop a mound of padded leather and connected to huge coils of wide straps.

"Val and I designed these to be light," said Joey, "mostly because when I started with them, I couldn't use magic to save my life. You *could* manhandle them, but it's much easier to do it this way."

He gestured, and one of the saddles rose off the ground, trailing its straps like the tentacles of a jellyfish. Joey guided it into the barn and held it in the air as he showed me the various connections on the harness. "Frank knows how it's supposed to go, but you're going to have to be the one to get it hooked on."

No thumbs.

"That, and the buckles are designed for slightly smaller hands," he said, grinning up at Frank. "Okay, shall we?"

Frank lowered his belly to the floor, and Joey floated the saddle into place. "Note where I'm putting this," he instructed. "There's a sweet spot at the base of the neck. Stay north of the wing joints unless you like being airsick—trust me on this one. Now, there's going to be some movement, regardless of where you sit, but the undulation's not bad in this area." He directed the straps into place, one on either side of Frank's neck and a longer pair dangling behind his front legs. "Hook the chest strap first, not too tightly, but not so loosely that the saddle wiggles. The idea is to anchor yourself as much as you can without hurting the dragon, yeah? Make sure the padding faces inward—his scales are tough, but he *can* get rubbed raw if you're not careful."

With the chest strap placed and adjusted, Frank stood, and Joey moved to his belly. "This one goes right behind the shoulder joint. Again, be careful of the padding, and make sure it isn't twisted before you fasten it. Give it a try."

The wide straps gradually tapered toward their buckles, which were small enough for me to manage without magic. Still, the process of fitting the saddle was awkward, and I fumbled as I moved around Frank's legs to check my work. "Uh…let me know if I'm doing something wrong, okay?" I told him.

Feels fine. His head curled around on his serpentine neck to see for himself. *Looks right. What's upsetting you? You're uneasy.*

I tightened one of the straps and pulled it taut. "This just seems weird, you know?"

Frank's response was colored by amusement. *All right, so saddling your colleagues is definitely not contemplated in the Arcanum's HR manual. Ours isn't a normal group.*

"Yeah, but…are you sure about this?"

If I weren't, I wouldn't be standing here. And I won't tell HR if you won't. He shifted his weight into me ever so slightly in conspiracy, almost knocking me off my feet.

When Joey was satisfied with my work, he pointed to the saddle, which rose well above Frank's neck. "What do you notice about this setup?"

I frowned at the arrangement. "Um…the saddle's too thick. Like, those things are normally pretty flat, right? And your legs go over the sides…"

"On a horse, correct. You can help control it by digging your knees in. But Frank's too wide for you to sit comfortably like that. Riding bareback's not a good idea for beginners. That saddle's high enough to give your legs somewhere to go, and then it flares out to fit his neck, see? The bottom of the stirrups should just barely touch him."

It seemed like a precarious perch to me, but I kept my thoughts to myself.

"What I was getting at," Joey continued, "was the halter situation. What do you see?" When I gave him a blank look, he sighed and crossed his arms. "Not a horse girl, huh?"

"Sorry."

"Let me make it easy, then. With a horse, you've got a halter or a bridle—the straps around the head that connect to the reins. That setup lets you direct the horse. Well, you don't get any of that with a dragon. Once you're up there, Frank's calling the shots, and you're along for the ride. If he takes suggestions, great, but you can't *force* him to do anything."

I'm the shark, Frank added. *You're the remora.*

"That's...actually not a bad way of looking at it," said Joey, and swept one arm toward him. "Okay, kid, up you go."

Before I could begin to decide how best to climb Frank, I heard the thump of wings and roaring from outside the barn, and Frank's head lifted. "Right on time," said Joey, and ran out to meet the returning dragons. "Georgie!" he called. "Got one more flight in you? I've got a newbie to school!"

I wish I could say that I was a natural in the saddle, born to fly and calm and collected with the wind in my hair, but that would be a dirty lie.

At least the saddle had a substantial horn, giving me something to cling to as my knees dug into the leather. I hunched up there, rigid as stone, and willed myself to absorb the ways of the barnacle as I desperately prayed not to be shaken loose. For his part, Frank was a gentle tutor, staying low, gliding as much as he could, and speaking reassurance to my mind, but it took me until lunchtime before I began to feel that death wasn't necessarily imminent.

After I hobbled bow-legged back into the house for a bite and Frank picked off another couple of ewes, Joey switched out my helmet for a pair of goggles. Whereas the helmet had a microphone and speaker built in, giving me at least a slim chance of shouting questions at Frank, now I was on my own and silenced.

I can hear you, Frank told me as I gritted my teeth through another running takeoff. *And you won't be able to block in the Gray Lands, so don't worry about that.*

Won't be able to talk back, either, I pointed out. Mina had worked with me on mental communication, but without magic, I would be useless.

As I said, I can hear you. Just think and let me do the work. Hey, ready for those barrel rolls?

Goddamn it…

I could feel his mirth, even without words to explain it.

By the time Joey allowed me to stumble into the house that night, my thighs ached, my hair was snarled into knots, and my face was pink with the sun and wind. Helen—Grand Magus Carver for formal occasions—had emerged from her study while we were out and was putting the finishing touches on a pork loin. The scent of rosemary and roasted meat nearly made me drool, but I held myself together and instead offered to help. "Heavens, no. Sit," she said, nodding to the long kitchen table. "Or stretch. I'm sure you need it."

I tried to work out the kinks before dinner, then cobbled together the best numbing enchantment I could muster to soothe the worst of the ache. Joey was mostly complimentary of my performance, but as I started to take seconds, Ros appeared in the kitchen.

"Hi, honey," said her dad. "Hungry?"

"Technically?"

He rolled his eyes. As the realm, Ros had no need for food, though I'd certainly seen her eat for the fun of it.

"It smells great," she told Joey, "but Sam's grilling for us tonight." She stared at me, long and hard, then murmured, "If anything happens to Frank over there, I will never forgive you. Understood?"

"Yes, ma'am."

"*Never.*"

"We'll be careful."

"Just bring him home safely." She kissed her parents and vanished, and I found that dinner had turned into a lump in my stomach.

With Frank having crashed in the barn, Helen and Joey put me up in their guestroom overnight. At Joey's suggestion, I took advantage of the soaking tub to ease my legs, which, even numbed, were still stiff from a day in the saddle. My whole body was knotted, I realized after sliding into the warm water. I'd spent hours clenched and hunched over, trying not to fall to a messy death, and the steaming bath felt like heaven.

I'd almost drifted off in the tub when Ros manifested in the bathroom. "Busy?"

Startled awake, I shrieked and flailed for a towel, and a layer of modesty-preserving bubbles appeared on the surface of the bath. As I caught my breath, she sat on the edge of the counter and folded her arms.

"Thought you were with Sam," I managed, trying to regain my dignity.

"I am. But he's grill-mastering right now, and his attention's on the meat. Let's talk."

Trapped in the tub, I had no choice but to nod.

"Right. I don't need to tell you how *stupid* you both are for this Gray Lands trip."

"Frank's plan makes sense—"

"Yeah, as long as everything goes right. What happens if you run into another dragon over there? A normal-sized male? You do realize that Frank's small, yeah? And if the fighting I witnessed with his brothers today is any sign, he's out of practice. Have I mentioned that hungry dragons aren't above cannibalism?"

"Frank has." I sank into the water and tried to keep the bubbles concentrated in key areas.

"Something to bear in mind, then."

"Look," I said, "I was going to call the whole thing off, but Frank has a point—we can do this. It was his idea—"

"Because he's trying to help *you*," Ros interrupted, and scowled at the darkened window by the tub. "It's a misconception that dragons are asocial. They can be solitary hunters, but they form bonds as strongly as we do—maybe more so—and they generally do it with their clutchmates. Frank was the late hatch," she explained. "He loves his siblings, but he didn't bond with them in the same way that they bonded with each other. Hell, he bonded with *me* instead of Georgie. And with me over here, and Frank on his own in Glastonbury, he's bonded with you guys. Now, you come in like a broken bird, and his first instinct is to fix the problem."

I chafed at the description, and Ros's mouth twitched toward a smirk. "What? You're a mess, Kitty. I get it, I do, but have you stopped lately and considered that you might not be in the most rational frame of mind? You're mourning your dad once again, you're mourning your mom—*ah*. Stop," she said as I tried to protest. "Kid, I see you better than you see yourself. So yeah, part of you is mourning the loss of this idealized version of your mother that you've made for yourself, the one who will embrace you with open arms once you score highly enough on a test or perform the right spell. She's never existed, and you're coming to terms with that."

I sank to my nose in the bubbles as Ros spoke.

"And then there's Myrddin," she muttered. "Okay, so your mom won't have you, your dad's long dead, and now here's another parental figure who, let's be honest, doesn't give two shits about you. Probably never will. He's fixated on one of his offspring, and it's the one who isn't a mongrel. And let's not forget Beth—you two parted on great terms, didn't you? Tell me, have the Audleys called to schedule dinner this month?"

"No," I mumbled.

"Uh-huh. So, to recap, Orson's out, Eva's out, Beth's out, you and Marcus are on the outs, and you're desperately searching for a family. That's all this is. Rescue Artur, maybe get a sibling who doesn't object to your existence, and maybe then Myrddin will like you." She paused, and her tone was softer when she resumed. "I mean it, Kitty, I get it. I almost got Bee Powell killed trying to find my mom. I just don't want Frank to die because *you* can't see the family you already have. Think about it," she said, and vanished before I could say another word.

Though he looked longingly at me the next afternoon when I announced that I was going home to pack, Frank opted to remain in Faerie. *Less trouble for Toula this way. It's not as if I need to grab a bag—what am I going to bring, socks?* he asked as he grazed his way through the flock outside the barn, eating in peace while his rambunctious brothers were elsewhere on the wing.

I stood on the other side of the fence, well clear of the oblivious sheep. "My stuff's easy enough to get together. What can I throw in for you?"

He looked up, one twitching leg still dangling from his teeth, then tossed his head and swallowed his prey. *Don't worry about me. You'll have enough gear to consider when you factor in food and water. And what about ammo?*

"Joey just gave me a pistol and a lesson, so here's hoping I don't have to use it," I said, patting the canvas bag slung over my chest. "Ammo's not that heavy, and it's iron-free. But what about your meals?"

What about them?

"Well, I'm going to go out on a limb here and assume that a few sticks of jerky aren't going to cut it."

Nope, he agreed, and swallowed another sheep whole. *I'll forage.*

"That sucks," I muttered, adjusting the gun bag against my hip. "I'm sorry—"

For what? You can't possibly carry enough food for me. I've eaten several times your weight since dawn.

There was nothing to be done for it. With magic at my disposal, I could have either compressed the tons of food Frank would require into a portable form or created it as needed. In the Gray Lands, however, I would be just a woman with a backpack full of granola bars...and if we weren't lucky, a *very* hungry companion.

Bidding farewell to Joey, I returned to my flat to lay out my gear, trying to plan for all contingencies. Layers were a necessity when one was traveling on dragonback, as were ponytail elastics. I threw a ski cap in for good measure beside the gloves and coat Joey had tailored for me. Then there was the matter of selecting lightweight food…maybe two liters of water per day…a sleeping bag…a toilet kit…first aid supplies…a toothbrush…

A knock at the door startled me from my contemplation of the mess spread across my bed, and I found Maria waiting in the corridor. "Where's Frank?" she asked as I stepped aside to admit her.

"Stuffing himself, last I saw. Everything all right?"

She gave me a look of incredulity. "*No.* I can't believe you're still doing this. Toula said tomorrow's the big day."

"No sense in waiting, is there?" I asked, heading for the kitchen. "Tea?"

"Sure." Maria followed me and leaned against the counter while I heated water. "Have you mentioned any of this to Beth?"

I stiffened, and the enchantment at my fingertips sputtered. "No."

"Don't you think you should? Before you run off in search of a sister and maybe never return, shouldn't you let the sister who's actually alive and in this realm know where you're going?"

"Why would she care?" I muttered as the water in the mugs started to boil. "We haven't spoken since—"

"Yeah, I know. And stop that before you scald yourself," she ordered, gently pushing me away from the tea fixings. While she hunted through my box of assorted teabags, she said, "Beth may be a brat now, but people change. She's seen what your mother can do—maybe she'll want to connect someday. Don't you want to say goodbye?"

"You make it sound like I'm marching to my death."

Maria turned around and held my gaze, her face solemn. "You may be, Kitty. And I'm fucking terrified that you are."

"Maria…"

"Stop." She held up her palms and curtly shook her

head. "Don't tell me about your foolproof plan, don't tell me about your contingency plan, don't try to reassure me that this is all okay, because we both know that's a lie." She gripped my arms, and I glanced away from her dark eyes. "You're the closest thing to a sister that I've ever had," she murmured. "I'm afraid that I'm going to say goodbye to you tomorrow morning, and that'll be it."

I tried to reassure her, to say anything to calm the fear I heard in her voice, but I couldn't find the words. Instead, I settled for a hug, the duration and strength of which said more than I ever could.

When we parted, Maria swiped at one eye and turned back to the steeping tea. "You need to tell Beth."

"Why? It'd make her day if I never came back. Don't want to get her hopes up prematurely."

She passed me my mug and a couple of sweetener packets. "You know you don't mean that."

I doctored my tea in silence, bringing it to a level of sweetness that Maria found abhorrent, and tossed my bag into the trash. "I don't want to tell her ahead of time," I finally said, "but there's one thing you could do for me, if…you know, if I'm not back by Monday."

"Name it."

Mug in hand, I led Maria to the kitchen table and my computer, wrote down my passwords, and showed her a folder hidden deep among my documents. "I don't have a copy of every letter, but I saved the ones I typed. Only a few from when she was really little, but that's most of the ones from uni—the ones that had to go through you, remember?"

She nodded. "I didn't know you'd saved copies."

"Wanted to be sure I wasn't repeating myself. Since she never got any of them, I guess I worried for nothing. Anyway," I said, closing the folder, "if something goes wrong…do me a favor and give those to Beth. She'll probably junk them right away, but I want her to know that I tried to be her sister. Okay?"

"None of this is okay," Maria replied, putting her tea aside to hug me again, "but she'll have them. I promise."

We held each other for a long moment, until our breathing synchronized and Maria almost felt like an extension of my being. "It's the right thing to do," I mumbled into her hair.

She gave me no answer, but our tea had gone cold by the time we parted.

I ate dinner alone that night, picking at a peanut butter sandwich for which I had little appetite. The Team had stopped by during the day in ones and twos, offering what tips they could and making their last-minute attempts to dissuade me, but their cajoling fell on deaf ears. If Artur was alive, then she'd been trapped for far too long. The right thing was to bring her home, either in the flesh or as an answer for Myrddin. Frank and I had a viable plan, and now all I needed to do was eat a hearty meal, get a few hours of solid sleep, and prepare for the journey ahead.

But my roiling stomach threatened to revolt if I ate more than a few bites, and something told me I wouldn't be sleeping well, if at all, that night.

I double-checked my pack, made sure that my water bottles were tightly sealed, and was about to fall into bed and attempt to nap when I heard a soft rapping at my door. Mentally, I ran through the list of possibilities, but I'd checked off everyone on the Team, and I doubted that Toula would have been so tentative about announcing her presence. "Just a minute," I called, tightening my robe sash, but when I opened the door and saw who was standing on the other side, my prepared remark about the late hour died on my lips.

"May I come in?" asked Marcus, hands in his pockets. He slumped a little, and he sported an impressive set of dark circles beneath his eyes.

I hesitated, then stepped back and held the door open,

and he slipped through the crack, keeping his distance from me. Once I'd latched the door behind him, I took up a spot near the couch, arms folded over my chest, and waited in silence for an explanation for his presence.

It wasn't long in coming. "I'm sorry," he said, simply and with no sign of subterfuge. "I was wrong, and I hurt you, and that's the last thing I wanted to do." He paused, but I kept my face a blank. "I would have said something sooner, but Pater insisted that I not contact you yet. He said it would only make things worse."

"But he let you out?" I asked.

"No. He doesn't know that I'm here. I..." Marcus struggled briefly, then said, "He told me two days ago of what you intend to do in the Gray Lands."

"You've come by to talk me out of this, too, huh?"

To my surprise, he shook his head. "I know you better than that."

My eyebrows rose with my incredulity. "You *want* me to go to the Gray Lands?"

"No, of course not! If I thought it would change your mind, I'd be on my knees begging you this instant. But that would be futile, and I don't want another pointless fight with you. Not now."

It took me a moment to digest what I was hearing. "You...aren't even going to try? *You*? Mister No-Fieldwork-Because-I-Said-So?"

Marcus cringed. "It's been made clear to me in the last days that I am fundamentally not okay. Wanda has had much to say about trauma and interpersonal relationships, and how the few sessions we had last year were nowhere near sufficient. Pater simply told me that if I ever laid hands on you in anger, he wouldn't stop what would come from Maria." He sighed softly and studied the floor. "I love you, Kitty. I want you to be safe—more than anything, I want you safe. But loving you means acknowledging what *you* want, too, what you need, and this...this is you." Glancing up again, he met my eyes.

"You fight harder than anyone I've ever known. Outmatched by everyone around you, you keep fighting. When there's no chance of victory, you fight. You fought for your mother. Admit it or not, you're *still* fighting for Beth. Doing something as foolish as racing the clock in the Gray Lands…I should expect nothing less from you."

"That sounds suspiciously like a compliment," I murmured.

He nodded. "I love your spirit. You burn a million cookies and put on a smile the next morning, and *that*, Kitty…" He hesitated before taking a small step toward me. "You've held me afloat when I've been drowning, and I don't know what I would do without you now. But that's my problem. My…*baggage* shouldn't be your burden," he said bitterly. "Still, if there's something I could say that would keep you here, I wish you'd tell me. If this is so important to you, say the word, and I'll go in your place. I can't be that much heavier to Frank, relatively speaking." Rubbing his neck, Marcus mumbled, "But I assume that you won't be swayed. And I…I do understand. If it were Publius instead of Artur, you wouldn't be able to keep me out of the Gray Lands. But considering the risk, I…I wanted to make things right with you before you go. See if we could be, uh…friends again. Or something like that."

"Okay," I whispered, but I held my ground, and Marcus didn't move any closer.

"Thank you." He tried to smile, but it faltered. "You won't reconsider, will you?" I shook my head, and a look of resignation crossed his face. "Then I suppose this is goodbye. Be careful, Kitty."

As he turned to go, I said, "I'll stop in on Monday, all right? Won't mention this little outing to Val."

When he looked back, his eyes were wet, but he finally managed to smile for me. "I'd appreciate that. Until Monday, then."

"Good night," I said as the door closed behind him, willing my bruised heart not to break.

As I'd expected, I didn't sleep.

Bright and early—well, *early*—Friday morning, just after two a.m., I took a last look around my flat, running through my checklist. My backpack was stuffed to bursting, I'd put Joey's gun safely in a shoulder holster beneath my duster, and I'd strapped Caledfwlch around my waist as a weapon of last resort, or perhaps a good-luck charm. Though I had little skill with a blade, the sword looked intimidatingly glittery.

A few minutes later, I met Toula, Maria, and the rest of the Team in the castle courtyard. There would be no driving necessary; Toula liked her previous gate's location in Shapwick Heath, and she remembered the way well enough to get us there by intra-realm gate. With the portal opened and the coast clear of early-morning birders, Toula led us through into the muck, everyone but me in galoshes for the occasion. I'd opted for sturdy, well-broken-in hiking boots with a thick coat of water repellant, which would give me a heel for the stirrups.

Once we'd mustered in the clearing, Toula checked her watch, then opened a large gate into the pasture beside the dragon barn, where Joey and Frank were waiting—as was Val, I saw with surprise. We made room for Frank to squeeze into the swamp, and Mal and Antony linked hands to give me a boost up his shoulder and into the saddle.

"Come back alive," Toula told us, then whispered open a gate into the grove south of Nath's treehouse. Once she'd taken a moment to stabilize it—working against the outflow of dark magic made her job harder—the others moved aside, and I fought down my sudden nausea.

"It's not too late," said Val, watching from the edge of Faerie.

I looked back and found Ros standing with him and Joey, silent and drawn. "We'll be back by Monday," I said with forced confidence, and gave the rest of the send-off party a tight smile. "I'll try to take pictures for the Archives."

"Man, *fuck* the Archives," said Ted, who, unable to hug us from his position, settled for wrapping one arm as far around Frank's neck as it would reach and patting my toe. "And fuck Myrddin, fuck Afallon, and fuck any and all grails."

Frank reached back to nudge Ted with his snout, and I swallowed the lump in my throat. "Love you, too, boss," I said, looked at the somber faces around us. "Love all y'all."

Toula coughed and tightened her jaw. "This gate's staying open," she told us. "Once you're through, Val and I will camouflage it using the outflow from Faerie. We'll put a mild deterrent into the wards, so hopefully, we won't have any inter-realm hikers over the weekend. And I'm posting a guard, just in case, but…you know, not much we can do from this side. Really, hon, there's no shame in turning back."

The temptation to do so was growing stronger by the second, and I knew that if I lingered much longer, I'd wind up in my flat, kicking myself for my cowardice. "Ready, Frank?" I asked.

Ready. We'll be careful, he assured the rest, and without further ado, he lumbered into the Gray Lands.

"Limber up!" Joey called after us. "You're sitting too stiffly, Kitty!"

As I adjusted my position, I felt my phone vibrate in my pocket—it was to be my backup clock in case my watch failed, and I kept it close. Once Frank had found a wide enough patch to allow him a running start, he thundered skyward, and I fought the urge to scream until he leveled out and headed north. Looking down, I saw the terrain spread out below us in the pale morning light, a patchwork of browns and blacks the colors of scorched earth beneath a gray sky. Satisfied that I wasn't about to fall off, I checked my phone and found a message from Marcus: *I will love you forever.*

I pulled one glove off to respond, but without magic to power it, my phone had no reception…and the battery, for the first time, was at less than a full charge. Stymied, I tucked the phone back into my duster and tried to push thoughts of Marcus from my mind.

Frank, who now had unrestricted access to my head, interrupted my melancholy. *That's Nath's place? The big tree?*

Yes, I thought, feeling him waiting for a response. *Maybe give it a wide berth, huh?*

Read my mind, he replied, banking. *So, what do you say we go find Artur?*

CHAPTER 11

My dad always had a thing for the oldies station—the music popular during his parents' childhood, which, I gathered, had formed a large part of the soundtrack of his own youth. He was never a great singer, but whenever we needed to drive out to another part of the county, he'd pop me unrestrained into the cab of his pickup truck against all safety laws, queue up his favorite tunes, and lead me through a seventies singalong. I couldn't remember them all, but as Frank and I flew toward the ragged, snow-dusted spine of the Ro Henare, one song in particular rose to the surface of my memories and refused every effort I made to take it off of repeat.

Unfortunately, since Frank was plugged into my mind, he soon knew "A Horse with No Name" as well as I did. *Please,* he begged on the tenth time through, *can't you think of something else?*

I got through only the first two lines of "Puff, the Magic Dragon" before he interrupted, *Keep that up, and I <u>will</u> demonstrate a barrel roll. Fair warning.*

Slightly giddy with my lack of sleep, I laughed to myself and adjusted my goggles. *How does it feel to be back in the old country?*

Not bad. I can smell the dark magic everywhere. You can see it, right?

I nodded, remembered that Frank wasn't looking at me, and replied, *Yeah. Unnerving.*

A series of roars off to our left got Frank's attention, and he listened to the distant reverberations until they'd faded to nothing. *Company*, he told me.

How close?

Not particularly. She's nesting, he's hunting, and he's going to get his head bitten off if he doesn't give her space. He's probably not more than a yearling.

You can tell all of that?

Sure. I heard amusement in his reply. *You seem so surprised whenever you're shown that you don't have a monopoly on communication. Human hubris knows no bounds.*

Another long roar echoed from the northeast, and Frank replied in kind, making my whole body vibrate. *What's that about?* I asked.

Another male. We're nearing his turf. He wants to know what I'm about, and I told him I'm passing—not here to mate or pick a fight.

Did he get the memo? I replied as the roaring sounded again.

Frank hesitated. *More or less.*

A few minutes later, I saw a sinuous red blob rise from the hills ahead and come our way. As it neared, it resolved into another dragon—larger than Frank or his brothers, I noted, clinging more tightly to the saddle. Frank slowed and let the other approach, and they flew almost in tandem for a long moment while my heart hammered in my chest. After an excruciating period of silence from my companion, the other dragon flew off, and I released the breath I'd been holding. *Everything okay?*

Yes. He doesn't see many strangers. I told him I'm going over the mountains, and he's satisfied. See, there are three females in the area who are almost in the mood for mating, and he wants the first crack at it.

Big guy, I thought.

Frank emphatically agreed without words. *Which is why we aren't stopping until we cross the range. You picked up on my clutchmates' name for me, I trust.*

I hesitated, trying not to be rude. *Sounded like "Runt."*

That's it exactly. And it's fair—I'm small. Relatively, he added, catching the flash of my disbelief. *So, the game plan is for us to be polite and get through anyone's territory as quickly as possible, understand?*

Got it.

I sensed Frank's laughter again. *He was curious about you.*

Oh?

Yeah. Wanted to know why I was carrying a snack around.

Very funny.

I'm not kidding. But not to worry, you're safe with me...unless your internal playlist becomes unbearable.

That was only mildly reassuring, but I tried not to let on. *Any requests?*

As long as you're doing the old stuff, I like Blue Öyster Cult...

I'd only gotten through the first measure of "Godzilla" before Frank started growling.

Though the Ro Henare weren't Himalayan in scale, they were high enough to make traversing them unpleasant—at least for me. Frank didn't complain, but as he continued to climb, he checked in with his quiet passenger. Could I still feel my face? My fingers? Could I breathe?

The air wasn't too thin, but it was bitterly cold, and the wind from our passage only exacerbated the problem. I hunched as low as I could in the saddle, one hand clinging to the pommel and the other tucked beneath my arm, alternating as my fingers began to cramp. My legs, clad only in jeans, had long lost all sensation, a welcome distraction from the saddle ache. On the other hand, my ski cap did its job well enough, but it left my face bare, and my cheeks burned with the freezing wind. While I'd thrown a scarf in with my gear, I didn't dare to shift my bag off my back and risk losing it, so I hunkered down in silence, trying to think warm thoughts, kicking myself for not rigging saddlebags while I still had access to magic, and wishing I were closer to Frank's hot belly.

A seeming eternity later—it was difficult to track the

time with the thick clouds overhead—we cleared the spine of the mountains and coasted down toward the lower slopes. Spotting a lake in a protected valley, Frank landed for a drink, and I slid off his back, resisting the urge to kiss the solid ground.

As I fumbled with my pack's buckles and zipper, Frank raised his dripping head from the surface of the water. *Tastes fine, if you want to risk it.*

"I've got plenty," I said, forcing the words from between my numb lips.

You're fae, you know. Not like you're going to contract dysentery. And you're frozen. He looked around, then swung his head toward a deadfall. *Grab a few of those. We both need a rest.*

I lugged the smaller logs and branches into a rough campfire on the shore of the lake, and Frank ignited it with a well-aimed breath. The dry wood flared and shot up a rush of sparks, and he snorted in satisfaction as he flopped onto his stomach. *Sit, eat. Thaw.*

I didn't need much encouragement. Soon, with the fire ahead of me and Frank's body at my back, I'd regained enough feeling to knead at my aching thighs in between bites of granola. "I feel bad eating in front of you," I said.

Frank, who'd been resting his eyes, opened one and took in my sad lunch. *I had a big breakfast.*

"And you've been working all morning."

It's easier than you think. I'm built for this. He shifted, moving his head just close enough to the lake to drink without getting up. *Ros and I used to stay out all day.*

I tried to sift through the emotional coloring on that thought, but the components were more complicated than my words could describe. "You miss that?"

Sometimes. I miss her.

"You know, if you want to take a sabbatical—"

No. Besides, Ros doesn't need me.

"She's worried sick that you're out here."

Oh, I'm well aware. He finished his long drink, then curled his head around to watch me with one massive eye.

Whatever she told you, I got it worse.

"Makes sense," I said, leaning against him as I stretched out my legs in the brown grass. "She's kind of like your mom, right?"

Frank didn't immediately reply, and I feared I'd insulted him until I heard his calm, almost wistful thought: *Yes and no. Mom is Mom, Ros is Ros. It's…difficult to convey.*

"I didn't mean to pry—"

It's okay. He glanced up at the clouds, then rumbled and slowly stretched. *Better? We should push on.*

With no latrine in sight, I ducked behind the remains of the deadfall, much to Frank's amusement, and scaled his side on my third attempt. *You're getting better at this,* he thought as he leapt out into space and caught the wind.

Joey makes it look easy.

Joey's been riding for years. You can't expect to be an expert overnight.

And once we're out of here, I hope to never have the opportunity to practice.

Come on, he teased, *this is fun. You, me, and vast, uncharted, possibly dangerous terrain…did you remember to get any pictures in the mountains?*

Hard to work the camera when you can't feel your fingers, I replied. *And the phone's battery is draining. It's our backup clock, so…*

Understood. Frank undulated with his wing beats, taking us higher above the foothills. *I can't see the next ridge yet. Can you?*

I scanned the northern horizon, but all I could make out was the blur where the clouds met the plain. *Nope. Think Kip underestimated it?*

Not yet. If we don't see it by nightfall, I'll start to worry, but not until then.

We flew along in silence, my mind threatening to pick back up with its favorite earworms whenever I let it wander, and I focused on the land below us to keep myself occupied. As I looked over Frank's right shoulder, I noticed a smudge on the prairie ahead, running before what appeared to be a larger, darker smudge. *Frank?*

Hmm?

What's that?

He picked up the direction of my thoughts and took a look. *No idea. Want to get closer?*

Not sure that's a great idea…

Come on, I'm here to protect you, he replied, then tucked his wings and angled into a shallow dive.

When we were perhaps twenty feet off the ground, I realized what we were nearing. *Kadalin!* I thought in surprise. Only five of them, four male and one female, their skin the same bronze as Kip's but their equine ends variously gray and black and bay. They wore their hair tied back, and each carried a long bow and quiver…and they were running hard enough to kick up a dust cloud behind them. Seeing our approach, the leader looked skyward and shouted in alarm, and the others came to a frantic halt, some staring at us, others at the settling dust behind them.

Frank knew as much of the kadalin tongue as I did—nothing—and so he called to them with pure thought, which my brain unscrambled as *Not hunting.*

If that reassured the kadalin pack, they gave no indication. Instead, they took off running again, streaking below us as they passed.

Skittish, aren't they? Frank thought.

You're kind of intimidating, bud.

He started to respond, but his thoughts shifted toward alarm as we closed on the second streak. *Kitty, there.*

I'd already noticed, and my guts clenched at the sight.

For all the extant gates among the realms, neither Faerie nor the Arcanum had much intel about the inhabitants of the Gray Lands. They were like giant squid, occasionally washing up but rarely observed. Kip had done what he could to fill in the gaps in the Fringe's records, augmenting the notes about the creatures who had been caught across the border and adding his own about species unseen in the mortal realm. The entry that received the most ink from him, other than his report on the kadalin, concerned the raiders—etalre to the kadalin, but the translation was close enough. No one knew what they called themselves, as no one had bothered to ask. The only ones recorded in the mortal realm had been the pack that accidentally carried Kip across, and Badger and Seamus had killed them all. This, apparently, was also the practice among the kadalin on the rare occasion that they managed to catch a raider: immediate execution, no quarter given.

The raiders were nomadic hunters—if they had settlements, Kip knew nothing about them. Strong, fast, and skilled with weapons, they terrorized the Gray Lands in packs as small as four and as large as fifty, riding on tamed guronts. Though Kip had described their mounts, Badger had come along and added her own observations: *Take a horse. Mummify it. Give it scales, fangs, and four eyes. Voila.* The riders were no more appealing to human tastes, at least not according to the sketches in the Fringe database. The few observers described them as pale as blood-drained flesh and rail-thin, none taller than two meters, and always dressed in black clothing and cloaks. They were built from a humanoid blueprint—two arms, two legs, two eyes—but they were hairless, instead sporting a low crest running from the base of their spines over their skulls to intersect a heavy brow ridge. They appeared to engage in tattooing, as all of the specimens killed had decorated their faces with patterns in blue and green, but what significance the tattoos had, no one could say. What concerned the kadalin far more were the raiders' well-honed hunting abilities, their clawed, four-fingered hands, and their teeth, a miniaturized version of Frank's unnervingly fanged smile.

And about thirty of them were chasing the kadalin.

I'm not the threat, Frank thought. *They are.*

A few of the raiders looked up as we passed overhead, and one nocked an arrow. Frank banked before the arrow could be loosed, and he rose to safety, circling back toward the fleeing kadalin.

What do we do? I thought. *They're going to kill them, there's too many of them—*

Stop panicking, he replied, and continued his slow turn. *I've got a plan.*

The grass—

Thought of that. Hold on. Get your gun, if it'll make you feel better.

The problem with using a flamethrower in a field is that grass—particularly dry grass—is extremely flammable. If the deadfall I'd seen back at the lake was any indication, there hadn't been rain in the Gray Lands for at least a few days, and though the grass appeared to be alive, it was slightly crunchy. There was no sense in making the kadalin outrun a wildfire, so the trick was to get between the packs and shoot at the raiders head-on.

Maneuvering into the gap was no problem for Frank, who ignored my frantic mind as he dove into position. I felt his lungs expand beneath me, and then, with a focused exhalation, he set the field ablaze.

As weapons go, dragon fire is nothing to sneeze at, and the lead raiders flailed and fell as they and their mounts met the conflagration. A few in the rear of the pack wheeled off in time, however, and as Frank readied for another pass, they regrouped away from the flames. *Kind of like a reverse birthday cake, isn't it?* Frank thought. *I'll get them with the second try.*

I could hear his confidence, and it gave me comfort until we turned around and I saw what three of the raiders had hastily assembled. "Frank!" I screamed, just as the enormous crossbow loosed its bolt.

I should have anticipated that the raiders would have a defense against dragons. The bolt they shot at us was as thick as my thigh, the tip dull black and barbed. Sensing my alarm, Frank tried to move out of the way, but he couldn't bank quickly enough. The bolt whizzed past my left leg and struck him in the second shoulder, where his wing met his body. Frank roared in agony, then dove.

The surviving raiders may have only had one bolt, but they still had plenty of arrows left, which they shot in a volley of black needles. Several ripped through Frank's wings, one hit him in the neck, and he landed hard, bellowing.

And then the raiders made a crucial mistake. Perhaps they were young, kept toward the back so that the experienced members of their pack could be the first to the fight. Perhaps they thought they'd hit Frank harder than they had. But as they hurried closer to finish the kill, I felt Frank's deep inhalation, and with a fiery blast, the last of the raiders were ablaze.

I leapt down and pulled out my gun, ready to join the fight, but Frank stayed me. *Wait,* he ordered, his thought tinged red with pain. *Finish them off.*

I stood beside him as he growled and hissed at the ache of his wounds, and then, when the flames burned low, I flipped off the safety and approached the downed raiders. Only one was still alive, twitching and blackened. My stomach lurched—aside from the odd bug, the only thing I'd ever killed was a small deer when my dad took me hunting the year before he died—but I steeled myself and ended the raider with a close-range shot to the head, telling myself it was the merciful thing to do. None of the others stirred, and as the fire burned away from us, it left nothing but ash and charred corpses.

I thought back to my early days in Glastonbury and my first meeting with Frank, when he'd incinerated two wizards and blown up their car to save Maria and me. As horrible as it been to see them burn, Frank had acted in our defense, and Wanda had been on hand within an hour to console us. Still, I'd had nightmares for a month. I could only imagine what my dreams would look like now that the killing blow had come from my own hand.

But I couldn't afford to dwell on that yet. With the

raiders dispatched, I ran back to Frank to assess the damage and found him still on his belly, his eyes squinted closed. The arrow in his neck appeared to be embedded only superficially—the tip had actually come out, leaving it wobbling like a cheap Halloween prop—but the others had ripped holes through the membranes of both wings, and the bolt was lodged deep in his shoulder. "Lower your head, then hold still," I told him, and pulled a knife from my pack.

He groaned but did as I asked, and the arrow came within range. I sawed off the tip and the back end, then gently worked the shaft out the way it had come. "Sorry, Frank," I murmured, pressing my scarf against the wounds. It was nowhere near long enough to tie around his neck, but it could help stanch the bleeding. By the time the holes clotted, the scarf was soaked, and I tossed it aside as I examined the larger problem. "I can try to work the bolt out," I told him, "but I'm probably going to have to dig in there to get the tip dislodged. Do you want me to attempt it?"

He snorted and eased his neck to the ground. *What choice do we have? I can't pull it myself.*

"Maybe the kadalin—"

Are you kidding? They're not coming back.

"You just saved their lives."

And as you said, I'm kind of intimidating. He scrunched his eyes shut and dug his claws into the dirt. *Try to get it.*

With Frank braced, I scrambled up his side, climbed over the saddle, and carefully scooted along his back until I reached his wing joint. The wound was still oozing, though the area had scabbed around the edges, and I couldn't see the bolt tip. "Shit," I muttered, and pulled my knife from my coat.

That bad?

"Just hold on," I called to him. "This is probably going to hurt."

I felt Frank stiffen as I slid into position, and then I

took a deep breath and began working the tip of the blade—titanium, naturally—down into the wound. He whimpered and growled, then let out a sudden roar when I got too deep. "Sorry, sorry," I mumbled, sticking the knife back in my pocket while I gently wiggled the bolt back and forth, trying to loosen its grip.

Shit shit shit that hurts—

"Doing the best I can." The barbed tip was designed to go only one way, but I couldn't very well push it out through his shoulder. Instead, I put Frank through a long hell as, little by little, I cleared his tissue away from the bolt and started to pull it free.

It was late afternoon by the time I tossed the bloody thing into the burned grass, and Frank groaned as I climbed down. "It's not pretty," I told him, wiping the knife clean. "Big open wound. We should probably pack and cover it."

With what? Those little plasters in your kit aren't going to do the trick.

"Patience."

I pulled all of my spare clothing out of my bag, cut it into pieces, then lugged the rags back up Frank with a fresh bottle of water. "Going to sting," I warned him before I flushed the wound. It wasn't enough—he needed stitches, at the very least—but I didn't have the supplies to do more. Praying that whatever germs were on my clothes wouldn't give Frank gangrene, I filled the weeping hole with rags, then put a shirt over the top and used every bit of my roll of sterile tape to lay it down. "Try not to move that wing too much," I said as I came around to talk to Frank again. "I don't know how well that adhesive works on scales." I tried to read his expression, but Frank's reptilian face was a mystery to me. "How badly does it hurt?"

Bad. He rose, steadied himself, then glanced at the corpses scattered around us. *I'm going to eat dinner. You might want to make camp—we're not going anywhere tonight.*

Sitting alone with my unrolled sleeping bag and a stick of jerky, listening to Frank snort as he rid the plain of dead raiders, I finally accepted what the wiser people in my life had been trying to make me understand.

Sure, the Team took risks—calculated risks, risks understood after study and approached with caution. We planned, we prepped, we worked out backup options in case we'd misjudged the situation, and we never went into the field without an escape strategy in our back pocket. For all of Ted's exuberance and joy in the chase, he would never willingly put any of us in mortal peril. That was why we always had Lakshmi or a substitute on standby during fieldwork, why Maria never slept without her phone within reach—at the end of the day, we cared about each other's safety. We might have been the Arcanum's weirdest side project, but by God, the Team was family.

And what had I done? Ignored every scrap of my training, seized on non-probabilities, poo-pooed the experienced voices warning me of the danger, and dragged a friend along as I chased after shadows. Yes, we had a plan—*a* plan, no backup, no extraction protocol—and now that the plan was kaput and Frank was wounded, we had nothing but a ticking clock.

Badger had walked into the Gray Lands once, when the fate of the mortal realm depended on how well she could convince Nath to stay out. She'd gone alone, unwilling to expose anyone else to the danger. And I…

I was the worst kind of fool. The stupid, blinded, *selfish* kind. And this fool's errand of a mission was the sort of perfect bait that I just had to take.

As much as I hated to admit it, Ros was right. Ever since my dad died, I'd craved a family, reaching out to Mom and Beth and being rebuffed every time. I'd barely met Myrddin, and he'd made his feelings about me plain. That left Artur—a stranger, yes, but kin nonetheless. Maybe my conscious mind had refused to think about it, but my heart clung fast to its truth: *If I rescue Artur, she'll have to like me. Myrddin will have to like me. And I'll have a family again.*

Of course, that wasn't the truth at all. That was a possibility—not even a probability. Maybe Artur would want nothing to do with me. Maybe Myrddin would be just like Mom, unimpressed with my attempts to prove my worth. But the Kitty who had done all her best tricks for an uncaring maternal audience had refused to concede that her vision of a happy family was only one potential of many—*if A, then B; if B, then C*—and she'd refused to consider the myriad of flaws in that plan.

Never mind what a feather in my professional cap it would be if I succeeded in locating Artur. The legendary king of the Britons had been missing for centuries, and *I* could be the one to bring Artur out of captivity. Ted could keep his Grail quests, Maria could keep her magus's chain—I'd have accomplished something massive, something heroic and extraordinary…

…something that even Mom would have to acknowledge.

Little Kitty, still doing her best tricks and hoping for a pat on the head.

And oh, I so wanted to be a hero. I wanted to be more than the witch who tried her best and came away with a shelf of honorable mentions.

Thanks for trying to stop that kid from killing Maria. You almost distracted him for a whole five seconds.

Thanks for helping us all pass theory. We won't attack you in practical class. And here's a trophy for how much theory you know! Clever girl!

You're a terrible excuse for a witch. You spent years hanging out in Faerie and never got off a dragonscale wand. But that's okay, you can go to Oxford. Here's a fancy degree for the wall, since you'll never amount to anything in the Arcanum.

Here's an Arcanum job for weirdos like you. I mean, fieldwork is dangerous, and you can't go anywhere without someone who has actual talent standing there to take care of you, but you can stay in the basement and do research, right? Won't that be enough? You're good with books.

Rescuing Artur—that would be heroic, wouldn't it? That would prove my worth.

I mean, sure, it would probably be a good thing for *Artur*, too—if she was even alive—but in the end, I could rationalize it to myself as Doing the Right Thing as much as I liked, and it would still be all about me.

And I'd pulled Frank into this mess. *Frank*, who'd barely said hello to me for the first time before he saved my life. He'd been a colleague, a mentor, an amateur counselor, a friend…and he'd risked himself to help me once again. Because I'd said it was the Right Thing, and he knew I couldn't do it by myself. Now he was injured, we were alone in the middle of nowhere, and we had two days to find a gate before Nath came to claim us…and I didn't like to think about what would happen if we didn't make it out in time.

As the light faded, I thought about Beth, to whom I hadn't even said goodbye. About Maria, who'd been more of a sister to me than Beth had ever been. About Val and Ted and Toula and the Team, who'd given me a chance and looked out for me when I couldn't manage on my own.

And Marcus.

God, *Marcus*.

I wanted the reassurance of his arms around me, the bulwark against my tides of despair. I wanted to apologize, to tell him that I understood his fears and regretted blowing up at him. I wanted to accept his apology and work to regain what we'd had.

With night falling and Frank groaning as he tried to move his wing, that was as much of a pipe dream as finding Artur alive and well.

I pulled out my phone. Still no bars, and the battery was down to half power.

Kicking myself for my hubris and stupidity, I hunkered

down to wait for dawn.

In the mortal realm, overcast skies sometimes seem bright at night because of lights reflecting off the cloud cover, but there was no such light pollution in the Gray Lands. Half an hour after what I'd assumed to be sunset, the sky above us was a uniform black only slightly paler than the unbroken prairie, and the only way I could see my hand in front of my face was with a flashlight. We couldn't make a campfire—there was nothing but grass to burn—and as the temperature fell, I burrowed into my bag and snuggled against Frank's warm side as he curled around me, a living wall against the darkness. I didn't deserve him or his warmth, but I was grateful not to be alone with my thoughts.

While we listened to the distant scuttling of unknown nocturnal creatures, Frank sighed and tucked his head into the center of the ring he'd made. *I'm sorry, Kitty. I thought I could do it.*

I opened my eyes, futile as that was, and rolled up onto my elbow. "You have nothing to be sorry about. I'm the one who got us into the middle of this mess, and I'm sorry—this was such a bad idea, and I am *so* damn stupid."

I really thought I could do it, he replied, as if he hadn't heard me. *And now we're stuck out here—*

"We're not stuck. Can you walk?"

Yes...

"Then that's what we'll do. Tomorrow, at first light, we'll head back toward Nath."

What about the mountains?

"We'll find a pass," I said, though all the forced optimism in my voice couldn't hide my misgivings from Frank. "Two days left to get to a gate. We can still make it out."

So that's it? We're just giving up on Artur?

I sat up and pressed my hand against his side. "You've

got a hole in your shoulder, two holes in your neck, and a new set of piercings in both wings. We're getting out of here before anything worse happens to you."

Frank groaned as he tested his wounded shoulder. *I'm sorry. I'm really sorry.*

"Nothing to be sorry about. I'm just glad you're alive. If that bolt had hit you in the chest..." I let that hang, unfinished, and shuddered. "We'll head south in the morning. Ros may skin me when she sees what happened to you, but I'd rather face her than Nath. And hey," I added, giving him a pat, "that's five kadalin who are still alive tonight, thanks to you. Not too shabby, Frank."

My pep talk didn't lift his spirits beyond morose. He made no reply for a moment, and I'd settled back into my sleeping bag when he thought, *I really am a failure.*

"Frank, *no*," I insisted, sitting up again. "You took out a whole pack of raiders, we're both still breathing—"

As a dragon. I'm an utter failure. The grass around his head rustled as he shifted closer to me. *And I let us both down. I thought I could get you to your sister, I really did, but...*

"You got me a hell of a lot closer than I'd have gotten on my own!"

Yeah, and now we're stranded in the middle of bloody nowhere because I wasn't fast enough. I'll be honest with you, he continued, *this wasn't just about finding Artur.*

That sounded too familiar. "No?"

No. I wanted to prove to myself that I had it in me...and I don't.

"Whatever you're kicking yourself about, stop," I said, trying to pick his shape out of the darkness. I knew where his head was because of his warm breath, but otherwise, I could just as easily have been in a cave. "You stepped up to do this with me when no one else would, and...and that's really awesome of you, Frank. That means a lot." I felt my eyes prick and wiped my arm across them. "They were right. They were all right about this...about me...*shit*," I muttered, leaning against him. "What was I *thinking?* I can't beat Nath on her own turf. If I hadn't been so stuck on playing the hero, we wouldn't be here."

I still think it's the right thing to have made the attempt.

"And get us both killed? Damn it, I dragged you out here—"

To find your blood.

"Forget that! I don't even know Artur! I barely know Myrddin! And let me tell you something, right now, you mean a hell of a lot more to me than either of them, and I can't begin to say how *sorry* I am that…shit, it took you getting shot before I saw reason…"

He let me stew, then thought, *The right thing for the wrong reason can still be the right thing.*

"Well, the right thing now is getting us out of here intact. And you listen to me, Frank, whatever 'it' is that you think you don't have, you do. You were incredible today."

You're kind to say so. Wrong, but kind.

"You weren't the one with the front-row seat to the flaming carnage."

Frank snorted. *That was nothing. I should have been better…faster. I should have taken them out on the first pass. My brothers probably could have.*

"You're out of practice, that's all."

I'm a runt, he thought, sounding lower than I'd ever heard him. *They're right about me. I'll always be small and slow—*

"Plenty fast from where I was sitting."

I'm weak. He sighed and coiled more tightly. *Tell you a secret?*

"Sure."

I've never even mated. Almost twenty-eight, and I've never tried. I couldn't fight off another male if I wanted to. My brothers, now, they're probably fathers several times over, but me?

I chose my words carefully as I tiptoed through *that* minefield. "How do you know if you haven't tried, huh? When we get back, take that sabbatical you're due. Go hang out in Faerie until you find a nice girl. Size isn't everything, is it?"

Faerie is the last place where I want to take a holiday, and beyond that, I'm not sure if I want to mate.

"Come again?"

Let me try to parse this into words. He sat silently for a time, then thought, *Mating is different with us than it is with you, yes? We meet, we mate, we go our ways. But having been with you as long as I have…having seen what pair bonding looks like for Antony and Bob and Lakshmi…I don't know. Part of me wants that. Part of me still thinks it's a lot of trouble for nothing, but it seems to work for you, and…* He huffed in frustration. *Does that make sense?*

"I think so."

Well, it's __wrong__. I shouldn't want that. But I've always been wrong, and it feels like the longer I live with you, the wronger I become.

Frank had never been so open with me, but then again, there are things said in the wilderness in the middle of the night that can't be expressed in the light of day.

Your mother rejected you, but at least she wasn't always around to remind you of that. By the time I hatched, the others had been out for a week. They bonded with Mom. She went off to raise them and left me to live or die on my own. An ugly cast of dredged-up fear grew over his thoughts. *You can't fully understand, but from the moment I knew __anything__, I knew her voice, and I knew my clutchmates' voices. And suddenly, they were gone. Ros stepped in, and I love her for it, but how do you think that feels? I called out for them for days, and they __never__ answered me. So then I came out and bonded with Ros—weird enough, that—and Mom didn't really care. She had five already, and I was the runty one a week behind the others.*

"I thought you and your mom got along."

We do, but it's not the same with her and me as it is with her and the others. She raised them, but she let Ros look after me. I know __why__, I understand the instinct to focus on the hatchlings most likely to survive, but once I got old enough to see the situation for what it was…it stings. And my brothers—Horus and Rego are close. Always have been. I was the little tagalong who got butted out of the way.

I didn't have comfort for him, so I listened in silence.

They didn't need me. I was the weird one always hanging around Ros, you know, so that was a big strike against me from the beginning. And I've spent the last twenty-two years in Glastonbury while they've done…well, the usual. They're nice enough whenever I go home, but every time I make the trip, it feels less right. They have their lives, I have mine, and it's not like I can tell them about what we do—I tried to explain parchment restoration once, and it was Greek to them. Boring Greek at that. I don't fit.

"You fit just fine with us," I offered.

No, I don't. I've seen the looks you give me, and don't tell me I'm imagining things.

"What looks?"

Frank flashed a series of images through my mind: our faces, all quickly shifting toward caution as we glanced at him. *Instinct, I think. You recognize that what you're seeing is a disguise, and you're afraid. I don't blame you, but I don't know how to fix it. Whoever I'm with, no matter how innocuous the conversation, will eventually tense up and get twitchy. So no, I don't fit at Glastonbury, either.*

Seeing myself in his memory, I felt a fresh pang of guilt and rose, then stumbled through the darkness until I walked into the side of his head. "If I hurt you, I'm sorry," I said, trying for a hug but mostly plastering myself against him. "I didn't mean—"

I know. He leaned slightly into me, pressing back against my touch. *I'm not upset. You can't help it. I just don't fit.*

"We're all square pegs. That's why Ted brought us together, right? Assemble the weird ones and get shit done?"

True, he acknowledged, *but sometimes, I'd love to know what it feels like to be a round peg. They seem to get on happily enough.*

"You know, a wise man once told me that most of us are fundamentally fucked up."

He was speaking of himself, too.

"Yeah, well, he was right about me. And I dragged him

out in the middle of a wasteland on my awful, pointless...*quixotic* quest to locate someone in the universe who both shares my DNA and likes me."

And rescue Artur.

"Because she happens to meet half the aforementioned criteria!"

You're still trying to rescue her. That's a worthy goal. I'm just sorry that you got stuck with the one dragon who couldn't take out a few lousy raiders without ruining everything.

"You're the only one who offered to try. And you don't owe me a damn thing. I'm sorry, Frank. I'll get you home if it's the last thing I do."

He nudged me again, then shifted his injured wing and growled. *Get some rest, Kitty. Long walk tomorrow.*

If I had to sleep in the Gray Lands, lying inside a ring of dragon was about the safest place I could be. After a time, Frank's breathing slowed, and I curled up in my bag, silently berating myself until I fell asleep.

CHAPTER 12

I woke to darkness and the low rumble of Frank's growl, the hackles-raising warning sign just before a roar and a jet of flame. Snatching up my flashlight, I kicked myself free of the sleeping bag and found that he'd shifted position, tightening the loop around me while raising his head to face the threat. "What's going on?" I called, my light hitting nothing but a wall of pale scales. "Frank, what is it?"

Company.

"Let me see."

His tail tip slid away from his body, giving me an outlet. Flashlight in my right hand and sword in my left, I stepped out to confront the nocturnal visitor, hoping that the blade would be intimidating enough to scare him off. "Who's there?" I yelled to the night, hoping the newcomer spoke Fae. "What do you want?"

Coming around toward Frank's head, I shone my light at the sound of snuffling and jingling hardware and found a saddled guront standing nearby, nibbling at something furry in the grass. It looked up at me, snorted, and returned to its snack.

Standing a few feet from the guront was the object of Frank's focus: a cynaeli woman in protective black leathers. She squinted into my flashlight's beam, which was brighter by far than the dim red orb floating above her open hand, and I got a quick look at her. Young—maybe a little younger than me, I estimated—and slightly built, with violet skin and black hair braided up into a coiled bun.

She'd slung a cloth bag over her chest, but I couldn't see a weapon. Then again, as the cynaeli were talented with dark magic, I surmised that she didn't *need* one.

I lowered the flashlight just enough to get it out of her eyes, and as she blinked at me, I hoped I wasn't about to have to try out my rudimentary sword skills.

She seemed to hesitate—wise, as the vibe Frank was giving off stressed that any quick movements would end in flames—then raised her empty hand, smiled timidly, and, to my surprise, said, "Howdy!"

I stared back at her, shocked to hear English in the middle of the Gray Lands, then managed, "I'm…sorry?"

"Howdy?" she repeated with less certainty. "Um…you…it…"—she pointed to Frank—"uh…booboo?"

While I scrambled to put together what I was hearing, she scowled at the ground and muttered, "Think, think, what's the *word*, help, what is help, what is—"

"*Help*?"

Her face brightened when she heard me. "Help! Yes, help! Me you help?"

I turned to Frank, whose broadcast impressions had turned quizzical. "Are you hearing this?" I asked him.

Yes…

"What's she speaking?"

Mangled English and something else. I understand it, but I can't place it.

Feeling warmth in my right hand, I glanced at the lowered sword, which was faintly glowing—not with ordinary light, I recognized, but in the colors of active magic. I'd enchanted without realizing it, and the sword, a blade of crystalized magic, was *fueling* my work.

"Holy *shit*," I whispered, seeing the potential. The damn sword was acting like a shiny battery pack, and if I could draw from it to heal Frank…

The cynaeli watched me with concern. "You…okay?"

"Just talk," I told her. "Normally. Can you understand

me?"

Relief washed across her face. "*Thank you.* I barely remember any of that tongue, and I'd almost exhausted the little I still have. How do you speak—"

"I don't. It's the sword doing it," I said, tapping its point against the ground. "Now, what do you want? I'm warning you, my friend here doesn't like surprises."

"Understood. No tricks." She opened her jacket, pulled out a short knife, and slowly put it in the grass. "Unarmed, yes?"

The polite thing to do was reciprocate, but that wasn't an option. "I, uh…I think the sword might stop working if I drop it. Sorry. Again, what do you want?"

"To help you." She gestured toward Frank, who continued to watch with bared teeth. "Your mount took several hits yesterday. I can heal the injuries, if you'd like."

The name's Frank.

"Oh!" she cried, jumping at the telepathy. "My apologies, uh…I'm Hope."

I frowned in disbelief. "*Hope?*"

She sighed softly. "Lady Imaranta of High Vale, if you prefer. My mother called me Hope." She took a cautious step closer, and in the flashlight's glow, I saw an almost Ted-like gleam in her blue eyes. "Are you from Oklahoma?"

Frank and I exchanged another confused look, and I turned back to find her eagerly awaiting an answer. "Uh…no, sorry. I'm originally from Tennessee."

Her face fell. "Oh."

"But that's close to Oklahoma."

Instantly, she perked again. "Really? You know Oklahoma?"

"Never been, but I know where it is. How the hell do *you?*"

She reached under her shirt and pulled out a silver chain, from which dangled a heart-shaped turquoise pendant. "My mother came from Oklahoma."

I didn't have any baseline for what the cynaeli were supposed to look like, but Hope's face appeared human enough, albeit purple.

"A trader found Mama near a gate and took her to my father," she explained. "They made me. And when I was five, Father sent her back to her people." Her fingers closed around the pendant as she spoke. "Mama is called Hayleigh Lozano," she said, drawling her vowels slightly as she pronounced the name. "Do you know of her?"

She seemed so…well, hopeful…but I had to shake my head. "No, I don't know any Lozanos. But I *do* know people who could find her," I hastened to add to temper her disappointment. "If you could show us to a gate, I could ask someone who might know where she is."

"There are none near here," she replied, almost apologetically. "Just north of my father's lands, there's a gate. It's not the one from which Mama came, but it does lead out of this realm. If I showed you the way, would you take me with you? Help me find my mother?"

I almost balked. The thought of loosing a purple girl in Oklahoma was worrying enough, and to make matters worse, she was highborn. But she knew of a gate that was closer than the one we'd made near Nath, and with limited time remaining, getting out had to be our priority. "Yeah, we could do that," I told her, "but would your father object?"

Hope made a face and shrugged. "Not much, I suspect. I'm a likdenfi."

The word didn't translate, and I frowned, hoping the sword hadn't run out of power. "Come again? Lick-*what*?"

"Likdenfi," she repeated. "My mother was a concubine. I have siblings born to my father and his wife, but we have siblings born to his other concubines as well. Still a lady, but somewhat *tainted*, you might say," she explained, rolling her eyes. "If one of his wife's children tried to leave, he might protest, but a likdenfi? No real loss. And I'm half-blooded on top of that, so I can't imagine him missing me too greatly. I mean, there's a reason why I'm out here and not back at the tower."

Which is?

She twitched less at Frank's voice, but she still gave him space. "Father raises chinols—champion chinols," she said, sweeping one arm toward the guront behind her. "The jinoda steal them. I was following a pack of them, tracking our mounts." She reached into her bag and pulled out a metal disc, which expanded until it was the size of a truck tire. Mountains rose around the edges, and a red dot blinked at the center. "All of our chinols are tagged. I've been tracking the jinoda, looking for an opportunity to take ours back, but you found them first."

Sorry. They didn't suffer.

"I'm sure they didn't." The disc's surface flattened and turned into a screen, which showed our approach from the vantage point of a running guront—chinol—whatever they were. The video showed Frank getting shot in the shoulder and through the wings, and we watched until the feed died in a blast of fire. "Father had hoped to recover the mounts, but he'll be pleased that the band of jinoda is dead. They've been harrying our herd for years. Anyway, I was sent out to follow them. *Definitely* a job for a likdenfi," she muttered. "But I saw, um…Frank…fall, and since you did us a service, I thought I might be able to heal your mount."

"He's not my mount," I said before Frank could protest. "Friend, colleague, not mount."

I mean, technically, only one of us is saddled at the moment.

"You're not helping," I replied, and he flashed his teeth at me in a draconic smile.

Hope took a step back and clasped her hands. "I meant no insult—"

None taken if you can patch me up.

"Gladly. I'll need time," she cautioned. "Perhaps until dawn, perhaps a little after, but I'll do what I can."

"Thank you," I said. "And, uh…I'm Kitty. Kitty

Connolly."

While her chinol lay down in the grass for a nap and I stood guard with Caledfwlch, Hope wove a healing construction around Frank, drawing upon the dark magic surrounding us. Her work seemed akin to enchantment, but very tidy, and she hummed to herself as she cleaned the packing out of his deep puncture and knit his wounds closed. By first light, Frank was well on his way to whole, and Hope joined me for granola. "I just want to find Mama," she quietly explained as Frank dozed. "I miss her so much. If I find her, maybe she'll let me stay. What do you think?"

"I don't know, but I'll do the best I can to track her down," I promised, and cracked open a bottle of water.

"May I ask what you're doing in this realm? Hunting jinoda? They were pursuing a herd of nikots—you missed them, if that was your target."

"Nikots?" I echoed, just as the enchantment provided the translation. "You mean kadalin."

Hope frowned. "Your name for them?"

"*Their* name for themselves. We don't hunt them," I replied, trying not to bristle. "They're intelligent, you know. Not prey."

Her brow wrinkled. "Really? You've studied them? I've only seen them stuffed—Father has a pair, two large males."

"Yeah. One of them told me about this place. Told me y'all hunt them. He lost his family to jinoda, though, so if we make it out of here alive, I'll be sure to tell him about what Frank did. Might make him smile."

"Oh." Hope rubbed her elbow and glanced away. "I didn't know that they, um…that they weren't—"

"Mounts? The one I know is brilliant. Loving husband. Nice fellow."

"Perhaps it would be best if you didn't introduce us," she said, and nodded toward Frank. "Then again, I've never seen a dragon consent to being ridden, either, so what do I know?"

"He came along as a favor to me. Seriously, we work together."

"Strange. And you still haven't told me why you're here."

"Because I'm an idiot sometimes," I said, and sighed as I leaned back on my elbows. "Thought I might find someone here. Nath gave me three days to get in and out, or else, Frank and I are stuck with her."

Hope grimaced at that. "It's best to avoid dealing with the tennuwaya, or so I've heard. Never been that far south. Who are you searching for?"

"Long story."

"Short version, then?"

I thought of where to begin. "Fifteen hundred years and change ago, one of your people went into my realm for sanctuary. She landed in a place called Afallon. Sometime later, the king was badly injured, and she brought him, uh...well, actually, the king's a she. She brought the king back here to try to heal her, and they were never seen again. As it so happens, the king's my sister."

Hope's eyes softened. "The woman who brought her here, do you know anything about her? Name, rank, territory?"

"Not much," I admitted. "She was a lady of some sort, and her name was Morgen. That's all I—"

"*Morgen?*"

I sat up, frowning. "You know her?"

"I know *of* her. Morgen's been dead for hundreds of years. Imprisoned and executed after the Three-Clan War." Seeing my befuddlement, she said, "Long and bloody. Her clan lost first, and then the two remaining ones turned on each other, but that's all history. Here's the interesting bit," she continued, leaning closer. "Morgen's tower still stands. One of her grandnephews holds it now—he's sworn to my father, so I know the place. Fairly ordinary as towers go in

High Vale. The area is a wide valley in the mountains, you see, and our towers are partially built into the ringing rock, so they tend to last."

"I'd heard that your people live underground," I replied.

"Many do, but High Vale is a prime location. You can't raise chinols in a cave, you understand. But back to Morgen. She fled for a time, but when she returned, she brought with her a woman from your realm—the Sleeper."

She said it so intently that I had to assume it was capitalized.

"She's held asleep by sorcery," said Hope. "No one knows who she is or why Morgen brought her home with her. But Morgen put a complicated ward around her to protect her...and then Morgen was executed, leaving the Sleeper where she lies in the tower."

By then, my heart had begun to thump in double-time. "What sort of ward?"

"There's none like it. And it can't be broken because Morgen built a defense mechanism into it. If the ward is dismantled, the tower comes down...and if that one falls, the shock will probably take out the ones around it. No one wants to risk that."

"So they've left the Sleeper alone?"

Hope wiggled one hand. "Yes and no. She continues to sleep in the tower, but she's, um...she's been put to use."

"How so?"

"Well...Morgen must have truly wanted to protect her, since there are five hundred copies of her in the tower room."

"*Huh?*"

"The original and four hundred ninety-nine copies, I mean. The story says—and the wards suggest—that if you touch the real one, she wakes. If you touch any of the others, however, you fall asleep, too. It's used instead of imprisonment for the highest born," she explained. "The ones who can't be locked away with the commoners or executed are taken to Morgen's tower and left with food and water for three days. Some hold out longer, but in the end, they either starve themselves or sleep. I've never seen the room, but I understand that the floor is littered with sleepers. They're left wherever they fall." Wide-eyed, she whispered, "Is the Sleeper your sister?"

"I have no idea," I confessed. "I've never met her. Don't even know what she looks like, to be honest."

Hope gripped my shoulder and smiled. "A sister would know her sister. I'm sure you'll feel it once you see her. I'll take you before we leave."

"Hang on, now, we've got to get out of here before—"

We have two days, Frank thought. Evidently, he hadn't been as deeply asleep as I'd imagined. *It can't hurt to check, can it?*

"The important thing is to get you home intact."

He stretched his mended wings and showed me his teeth. *I'm fine. Much better. Climb up, we'll get moving. Hope, are we to follow you?*

She paused, considering her sleeping mount, then looked anxiously at Frank. "You can probably fly faster than she can run. Any chance that I could steal a ride? She knows the way home."

Frank and I traded looks, and he thought, *Can you ride bareback?*

"Of course," said Hope, regarding him quizzically. "Who *can't?*"

"Not one word," I muttered, and heard Frank's laughter in my mind as I climbed up his leg and Hope steered her chinol toward the north. *And seriously, we don't have to do this. I promised to get you home.*

And I promised to get you to Artur, he countered. *We've come this far, Kitty—we have to <u>try</u>.*

Unless this is a trap.

Does it feel like a trap to you?

No, I admitted as Hope jogged toward us. *But if I'm wrong...*

Yes, yes, we die horribly. Think happy thoughts. He waited while Hope slid into the spot in front of my saddle and made herself as comfortable as possible, then thought to us both, *Ready? North?*

Ready, came Hope's reply—an actual broadcast thought, not the passive communication to which I had to resort in the Gray Lands. *And yes, head north. I'll guide you in.*

A few minutes in the air was all that Hope needed to copy my oilcloth coat and goggles, but unlike me, she seemed perfectly at home straddling Frank's neck, unbothered by the undulations that made my stomach flip. She *was* a rider, I told myself, trying not to compare our performance. With two days' experience under my belt, I still clung to the saddle as if I were liable to fall off at any moment, whereas Hope trusted her knees and looked around, thrilling at the sensation of being airborne.

Isn't this great? she thought, turning slightly to smile at me. *The view! And it's so smooth. I love my chinols, but the saddle sores those babies can give you…ugh.*

How far have we to go? Frank asked.

Hope leaned over his neck to study the horizon. *At this speed…we should arrive around nightfall. Maybe a little after, I'd think.*

Then Kip underestimated, he replied.

I could only shrug. *Kip's never been to the Fash Henare. He gave me the best information he had, but—*

Fash Henare? came Hope's thought.

Like Frank, she had learned to listen to me, and I could sense them almost in duet on the fringes of my mind. *Kadalin name for your mountains. Translates to "the Dragon's Tail," I think he said.*

Oh. I didn't realize that they had named them. Her reply carried a twinge of embarrassment.

Doesn't everyone name landmarks? I asked. *What do you call them?*

Heluweya.

What does that mean?

"Homeland." She shifted and leaned forward, resting her forearms on Frank's neck. *Before we approach, let's decide how we're doing this.*

You anticipate trouble? asked Frank.

If you land in the middle of High Vale, yes. I can't guarantee your safety. Plus, that would make a huge scene, and we'd be better off keeping this quiet. My first inclination is for you to land higher in the mountains, and Kitty and I will descend on foot.

In the dark? he replied, sounding doubtful.

I know the path well. You stay there, I'll take Kitty to Morgen's tower, and once she wakes the Sleeper, we'll rejoin you and head for the gate.

And this lord's just going to let us wander in and try? I pressed.

Let me do the talking, thought Hope.

As doubt flashed across my mind, she hastened to reassure me: *I'm intended for him on my next birthday. He knows me, and as I mentioned, he's sworn to my father, so—*

Back up. He's your fiancé?

Hope pondered the term for a moment, then shook her head. *No, I'm not to be his wife. He's married, anyway. I'm to be one of his concubines.*

I couldn't hide my horror at that notion, and her response sounded resigned. *He's highborn—it's an honorable arrangement. The best I can anticipate, anyway. Likdenfi seldom marry lords, and with my mother's blood, I'm particularly questionable. Father probably paid him well. It could be far worse, though. Warohn is old, but he's always been kind to me. I shouldn't have much difficulty getting you to your sister.*

And you're okay with this…arrangement?

Her reply came only after a long hesitation. *Not really. And I know he'll never let me go to find Mama once I'm installed in his household, so it's now or never for me. Honestly, I'd prefer to be a wife, even to someone lowborn. Do you think Mama could arrange that in Oklahoma?*

You would have to ask her.

Maybe not immediately, but someday. I'm only twenty—I wouldn't mind remaining single a few years longer. Are you a wife?

No, I thought, wishing I could hide from her the emotion attached to that answer. *I had a boyfriend. We argued and broke up.*

It took her a moment to understand the nature of our relationship. *So…your father didn't give you to him?*

No. That's not our way. And he and I…it's complicated. We both said some things we shouldn't have, and I'm here now, so… I laughed weakly to myself. *Maybe it would be easier if we did it your way. Then again, my dad's dead—well, Dad was my adopted father,"* I clarified—*"and my actual father doesn't seem to care much about what I do, so I might be single for a while if I left it up to him.*

Why not ask your dad's wishes, then?

I frowned. *Because he's been dead since I was ten.*

And?

I remembered then what Myrddin had said about Morgen's necromantic talent. *Most people can't just chat with the dead.*

No? Hope sounded surprised. *They visit me frequently. I don't try to seek out a particular one often—it's tiring—but for a situation as important as marriage, I would make the attempt. If that failed, the task of arranging your future would go to your father's lord.*

Picturing Coileán trying to pair me off with some poor boy, I laughed in earnest. *It's probably for the best that we do things differently, then.*

That may be, she replied, *but I hope that you and your…boyfriend?*

Ex-boyfriend, technically.

Well, I hope you make amends. I sense that you love him.

Trust me, it's mutual, Frank chimed in.

I cringed and sank lower in the saddle. *Y'all ever heard of privacy?*

Hope reached back to give my knee a friendly pat.

Difficult under these circumstances, but I'm good with secrets. Which is why Warohn isn't going to have the faintest idea of who you are.

We flew into the mountains at twilight, the sky a uniform navy, and landed in a small valley between two peaks. "You'll be safe here," Hope assured Frank as she slid off. "Kitty and I will descend, we'll call upon Warohn's hospitality overnight, and we'll be back tomorrow."

As I fumbled my way out of the saddle, I heard Frank speak to my mind: *If she can work a transformation bind, I'll go with you. You may need backup.*

I need you safe, I replied. *And if we're not back by tomorrow afternoon, leave without us.* Frank started to protest, but I ignored him as I formed my thought. *The gate's somewhere to the north, right? Find it. Go home.*

Not without you.

You're not going to get stuck here over me, bud. When my feet hit the grass, I turned and pressed my hand against his leg. *I'm serious, Frank. If you don't see us coming, don't risk it. Get out of here while you can.*

He gave no reply for a few seconds, then thought, *I'll be watching. If you need me, signal.*

Here's hoping we don't. I stepped back, adjusted my bag, and turned on my flashlight to find Hope waiting with a red orb to light her path. "Okay, let's do this," I told her, and looked around for a trail. "Where, uh…how do we get out of here?"

The trail was barely larger than a goat path, and just as steep. I'd had similarly hairy hikes in the field, though seldom in full darkness, and I was silently grateful that Hope took the lead in case I should fall and start sliding. As for my guide, she moved with practiced grace, stopping every few minutes while I clumsily caught up.

After perhaps half an hour's walk, we rounded a bend in the path, and I saw lights twinkling below us. "The towers of High Vale," Hope whispered, tracing her finger in a ring around them. "They mark the valley's circumference—we should reach the floor shortly. And that one's our destination," she continued, pointing to the lights at the eight o'clock position. "Morgen's tower. Looks like Warohn's home."

Soon enough, the path leveled into the grass, and Hope waited while I adjusted my belongings, checking Caledfwlch's sheath and making myself as presentable as I could after two days in the rough. With my bag re-strapped and hair brushed, she led me down a stone avenue laid across the valley, then took one branching path after another until the lights of Morgen's tower glowed directly ahead of us. Only the front of the tower looked anything like the towers I knew—that is, stone and round. The rest had been carved into the mountain behind it, giving the impression that the rocks were slowly reclaiming what had once been mined from them. A pair of guards stood on duty at the gate, and as I kept back, Hope approached with a demurely lowered head.

"Good evening to you," she said, folding her hands in front of her. "Will your lord receive me?"

The two muttered to each other, and then they stood silently, waiting for the space of a few long breaths until one nodded and stepped aside. "Lady Imaranta," he said, opening the door, then glanced my way. "And this…"

"The girl is with me," she replied, and beckoned me forward.

I hastened past the silently inquisitive guards, hoping that no one would disarm me of my translator.

Hope led me through the domed entry hall and down a low-ceilinged corridor, heading into the mountain. At each turn, guards and servants stood back to give us passage, though Hope maintained her submissive posture. *They were told to expect us*, she explained as we walked. *Word was relayed from the gate to Warohn. My father has a similar system—mind speaking to mind is often faster than sending a runner.*

I said nothing and stuck close to her, feeling the staff's

eyes on me and praying that the mental block I'd constructed with my sword's help would hold.

Finally, a guard opened a last door into a sumptuous sitting room, a circular space lined with weavings and filled with couches, floor pillows, and thick rugs. At one end, a cynaeli man in a loose white tunic and matching trousers lounged in a plush pink armchair, watching with interest as we entered. He looked barely older than Hope, but then I'd suspected that his race aged much as the fae did—or rather, did not. A woman in a gray gown sat in a smaller chair to his left, her dark hair braided into a complicated updo, her chin propped on her bent fingers. At their feet sat nine similarly attired women, each wearing a simple silver choker and curled on an overstuffed green pillow. Other men and women had occupied the remaining seats, while servants waited along the walls and behind couches with laden trays and jugs.

"Imaranta," the man in the armchair called, and beckoned her forward. "You come unannounced."

She took a few steps into the room, as docile as I'd yet seen her. "Lord Warohn. I do hope my intrusion causes no offense."

"None, pretty one," he replied. "Come closer. You have been traveling?"

"Attending to my lord father's business, my lord. While abroad, I came upon this stranger"—she barely turned my way in acknowledgement—"and I have brought her here as an amusement for you."

"An amusement?" His lilac features creased into a smile. "Of what nature?"

"My lord, it seems that news of your Sleeper has reached far beyond our borders. She seeks to try her luck."

At that, Warohn grinned in earnest, and the women around him tittered. "She understands the risks?"

"Evidently, my lord. I made them plain to her, but she remains convinced that she can wake the Sleeper. Knowing how long it has been since you've had the pleasure of seeing one test his skill, I brought her to you as a token of my esteem."

Warohn rose and crossed the distance between them, then raised Hope's chin with his fingertip and smiled down at her. "I *eagerly* await the appointed time," he murmured, and patted her cheek. "Your gift pleases me, lovely one."

"Shall I escort her to the room, my lord?" said Hope.

"Not tonight. Morning is the best time for testing," he replied, and gave me a cursory inspection. "She may remain here tonight. See to her needs."

Hope bowed her head again, and as the spectators laughed among themselves, she escorted me from the room. Not until we had put two flights of stairs between us and the assembly did Hope speak. "Please don't wander tonight. His guests know my father as well, and if you cause trouble on my watch, it will bring dishonor to my family."

"I'm not leaving your sight," I replied, following her up the spiral staircase. "The women in there—"

"The one beside him is his wife. The ones on the floor are his concubines. I'm sure he already has a collar waiting for me," she muttered.

Not wanting to prod a sore spot, I said nothing more on the subject, and Hope showed me to a small guestroom with a double bed. "Do you mind sharing?" she asked. "I don't snore."

I chuckled. "Better than a sleeping bag. Is there a bath?"

There was, in fact, a modest adjoining bathroom, which offered plenty of hot water...and, unfortunately for me, steel fixtures. I used a washrag to crank the shower on, then stood under the jets, letting the water rinse away two days of travel and massage my neck and back. The bottle that Hope had identified as soap contained a green, vaguely musky liquid, but it lathered well, and I groaned as I went limp.

By the time I emerged, pink and towel-dried, Hope had

called down for a plate of bread and several unknown meats, and I joined her at the little table by the window. Through the narrow opening, I could see the lights of the other towers of High Vale like ships' lanterns on a darkened sea. A slight breeze blew into the room, but otherwise, the night was still. I ate quickly, feeling guilty for leaving Frank alone and hungry in the mountains, and hoped that he'd found something to take the edge off. Despite the feast of raiders he'd downed the day before, Frank had a monstrous appetite, and no one I'd met could do hangry quite as well as he could.

I kept the sword near me when I turned in, and I was still awake when Hope returned from her shower. She sat on the edge of the bed and braided her wet hair, her fingers moving deftly as they tied and pinned the ends into place, and then she lay down beside me, keeping a few inches of space between us. Neither of us had brought nightclothes, and so we slept in the travel-dirty things we had.

"Kitty?" she whispered as she waved the room's orbs dark.

"Mm?"

"Will you tell me about Oklahoma?"

Honestly, I knew little about the state beyond the photos I'd seen of grazing bison and tornadoes, but I did my best to paint a picture of grassy plains and tree-covered mountains. "And it's not all big cities," I concluded, "so you'll get a ton of stars."

"Stars?"

The word hadn't translated, but I wasn't getting into astronomy that night. "You'll see. They're beautiful," I told her, then rolled over and pretended to sleep, hoping I'd make it back to see my own stars once more.

Dawn broke too quickly, gray and cool, and I packed while Hope tidied herself. As I was adjusting Caledfwlch beneath my duster, there came a knock at the door, and Hope opened it to reveal Warohn in the hallway, accompanied by a crowd of spectators. "Good morning. Is she prepared?" he asked while Hope lowered her head.

"Yes, my lord."

"Then come."

I hoisted my pack and joined the throng, winding up another five flights until we reached the top of the tower. We filled what appeared to be an anteroom, and Warohn stopped before a simple black wooden door. "Girl," he said, motioning me forward.

Giving my backpack to Hope for safekeeping, I pushed my way out of the crowd. "Thank you for the opportunity, Lord Warohn," I said softly, bowing my head as I had seen Hope do.

"Thank *you* for the entertainment," he replied, then raised my chin and studied my face. "Pale," he finally murmured. "Far too pale. Still…a pity to be wasted."

"This is my quest, my lord."

"A pity," he repeated, then opened the door.

The room on the other side was massive, cut deep into the sheltering mountain. The few windows along the front edge could hardly light the space, and hovering white orbs provided artificial illumination for the recesses. Filling the room were rows upon rows of evenly spaced cloth-draped biers, each holding a sleeping figure. The aisles between the biers were occasionally blocked with the sleep-locked bodies of those who had failed the trial.

"Choose the Sleeper, and all will wake," said Warohn. "Choose any other, and you'll share their fate."

He stepped back, and my audience gave the biers a wide berth as I approached the first to examine the form atop it. I found a woman lying there, still as death, her white-blonde hair brushed smooth and neatly placed over her shoulders. She wore no armor, but her brown tunic sported bloodstained rips in several places, as did her trousers. Her boots appeared to have been cleaned, though they were well scuffed with use. A thick gold chain hung around her neck, and an unadorned gold band rested just above her ears—a crown of sorts, I surmised, but nothing fancy. Something appropriate for battle.

Even with her eyes closed, I could see familiar echoes of my reflection in her face.

"Artur," I whispered, but she didn't stir.

I moved along the line, examining each bier, but the bodies were identical—down to the blood dried on her tunic, each Artur was the same as the one before.

And then I began to panic.

This was what I had come for, *this* was the moment on which I'd staked Frank's life and mine. All I had to do was choose my sister from the five hundred bodies before me and go home. But whatever kinship she and I might have shared offered no clue as to the original's location.

I took my time, wandering the rows and trying not to throw up as I maneuvered past dozens of fallen unfortunates. This was madness. I'd never laid eyes on Artur, never spoken to her, and now I was expected to pick her out of the funhouse from hell?

"If you're waiting for a sign," Warohn called, "don't. They never move."

His entourage laughed, but hearing his voice sparked a tiny flame of inspiration within me.

Caledfwlch.

The sword was made of magic, wasn't it? I'd unwittingly pulled it into service as a translator—perhaps I could put it to better use.

Mindful of the biers around me, I carefully drew the sword and watched it gleam in the orbs' light. "Go to your master," I whispered to the blade, then tossed it into the air. It rose like an arrow shot from my hand, reached the high ceiling...and then, as it fell, it replicated itself until each copy of Artur had a sword lying on her breast, resting above her clasped hands.

"*Fuck,*" I muttered as the audience hooted and laughed.

Warohn called out to me again, but though his tone of voice suggested mockery, I couldn't understand a word he said. Just as I began to despair, I thought of one more trick I might try. I looked back to see Hope standing by the first row of biers, nibbling her lip, and as I met her eyes, I tapped my forehead.

I felt her when she entered my mind, but her brow furrowed as she poked around. Her mental communication was unintelligible, so I formed words—*Talk to me*—and began to walk among the biers, listening as she spoke incomprehensibly. Whenever she stopped, I paused and thought again, and she tried to answer, growing more and more frustrated at my apparent inability to recognize that we weren't communicating.

About two-thirds of the way into the room, near the left edge, I finally heard words I understood: *I'm trying, Kitty, but I can't remember enough of Mama's tongue to—*

Stop.

Her surprise pinged in my thoughts, and I explained, *I have to be close to the sword for it to transmit and translate. The real sword.*

I glanced back in time to see her jaw drop, and then she snapped her mouth shut. *Right, okay. What do you need me to do?*

Just keep talking to me. I'm going to establish a periphery.

While Hope quietly prattled in my mind, I pulled a slightly crushed granola bar from my coat pocket and opened the corner. I stepped back and forth in the aisle, waiting for the moment at which Hope's thought blurred back into her language, then dropped a piece of granola on the floor. Slowly, I made my way around the biers until I'd marked off a five-by-five grid. Twenty-five biers...and one in the center.

I hurried to the middle of the square and looked down at the body waiting there. It was indistinguishable from its fellows, but when I held my hand over the sword's hilt, I felt a strange heat race from my palm to my shoulder, following the path it had once taken.

"Please be Artur," I whispered, then lifted the sword from atop her and slid it back into its scabbard. Heart pounding, I took a deep breath, then placed my hand on top of hers.

Her eyes didn't open. Her chest didn't so much as rise. But the other biers vanished like fog in the morning sun, and the previously condemned sat up and began blinking at the light. I looked back as my audience started screaming, and I saw Warohn standing in their midst, slack-jawed and silent as his dazed prisoners began to find their feet.

Hope, shouldering my backpack, ran to me and looked down at Artur. "She's still asleep."

"There has to be a second bind. If we get her into Faerie, it'll break on its own."

"Do you want me to try to—"

The rest of her offer was cut off by Warohn's angry howl. "*No!* How did she…that's impossible, how…no, she can't!"

As he babbled, Hope and I traded glances, and I hoisted Artur's limp body off the bier. Wrapping her arm around my neck and my arm around her waist, I dragged her across the room, but I only made it a few feet before I realized that she was too unwieldy to carry that way. Artur wasn't large, but she was *dense*—and the black look on Warohn's face told me that we wouldn't be walking out the tower's front door.

"Can you get us out of here?" I asked Hope. "Maybe a gate back to Frank?"

She shook her head. "I can't make gates, they're too complicated…" Her eyes darted around the room as if anticipating a hidden door somewhere in the unbroken walls.

"Can you stop a fall?"

The crowd's shouting reached a new high, and Hope cringed closer to me. "Probably. Why?"

"If I break the sword, the goal is to get back to Frank," I muttered. Dropping Artur into a heap, I pulled the sword free, prayed, and aimed at the part of the wall not built into the mountain. A bolt leapt from the tip of the blade, smashing a hole through the stone, and I slid the sword away again as the onlookers screamed and jumped aside. "Let's go."

Hope and I grabbed Artur under the arms and dragged her between us, racing for the hole before Warohn could recover. Just as he raised his hand to stop us, we reached the new ledge and leapt, Hope frantically waving her hand at the approaching ground. She couldn't quite arrest our fall, but she slowed our descent enough to let us land without breaking our legs, and we rolled to an ungraceful stop.

"What now?" she said, looking up at the angry faces in the tower.

Once again, I dropped Artur and unsheathed the sword, this time holding it in the air like a half-dressed barbarian on an old sword-and-sorcery paperback. Red light burst from the blade and rose high above the valley floor, where it formed into the letters *SOS*.

"We hope Frank's quick about it," I told Hope, and took my backpack from her. "And if he's not, then get ready to run."

Fortune was with us, however, and in less than two minutes, Frank came roaring over the mountains. He landed in the valley with a bone-rattling thump, and Hope and I grabbed Artur once again.

Even to the magically gifted, a dragon isn't an adversary to be underestimated, and Frank's teeth were sufficient to keep Warohn's guards at bay while we hoisted Artur over his neck. Hope gave me a boost up his side and into the saddle, then pulled herself up last, holding Artur between us like an oversized duffel bag. *Where to?* Frank asked as we settled in. *And I don't think you made any friends, Kitty.*

North, north! Hope replied, nudging him with her heels.

Keep that kicking up, and you're walking, he replied, then started a small fire in the grass to distract the guards spilling from the tower and rose.

Ten minutes in the air was all it took for the gate to come into view: a perfectly round hole hovering three feet above the ground in another little valley, guarded by six armed cynaeli. *You didn't tell me it was protected!* I protested.

Details, Hope thought. *Frank, can you scatter them?*

Probably, but there's a problem—that gate's far too small for me, he replied. *Kitty, if you go through first, do you think you can enlarge it from the other side?*

Forget that, I told him, and pulled out the sword again. Much of its luster had dimmed from the morning's overuse, but I only needed one thing more of it. Aiming at the gate, I focused on the hole until it ripped and spread, and the startled guards fell back. Exhaling flames for good measure, Frank tucked his wings and dove as the gate, and Hope and I screamed as we sped through.

We emerged over open water, barely skimming the gentle swells of a night-dark sea. I smelled the salt spray of Frank's wake and felt the sudden warm humidity, and as I glanced up at the clear sky, I realized where we were. "The Bermuda *fucking* Triangle!" I crowed, laughing in relief. "Damn gate's open again! That damn *beautiful* gate is open!"

As I cackled, Hope looked up and gasped. "What…"

"That's the moon!" I yelled toward her ear. "Almost full! And those are stars! Show you more later," I said, and willed open a gate into Faerie. *Let's go, Frank.*

We broke through over Val's villa and the high meadow, Frank roaring in the morning light as he circled for landing. While he was banking, I heard a gasp and looked down to see Artur's head move. She moaned, and as Frank touched down, Ros appeared beside him and floated Artur into the grass.

Artur had barely opened her eyes when she screamed, her back arching like she'd touched a live wire. The horrifying spectacle ended in seconds, and Ros looked up from her work as Artur lay motionless at her feet. "I put her to sleep. Those wounds were fatal, she needed augmentation to heal, and I don't want a lot of questions before she's whole." While Val and half the guards ran outside to investigate the commotion, Ros planted her hands on her hips and stared up at us, shaking her head for only a moment before she hugged Frank. "Good to have you back, bud. *So* good to have you back."

"Kitty!" Val shouted, running ahead of his own guards. "*Kitty*! Are you all right?"

"Better now!" I called back to him, then patted Hope's shoulder, momentarily distracting her from the foreign spectacle of the sun and blue sky, and pointed to the approaching welcome party. "Let me do the talking, eh? It's probably going to be a long morning."

With that, I slid down and almost fell onto Val as he ran up to catch me. "You're absolutely mad, child," he said as we hugged. "What did you...who is...is *that* Artur?"

I felt my sunflower pendant press into my skin as he embraced me, and my relief burst forth as sobbing laughter.

CHAPTER 13

Once Artur was carried inside for safekeeping, I had more than my share of explanation to give, starting with why I'd brought a cynaeli hitchhiker home with me.

I coaxed Hope off of Frank's back and pulled out the sword, which was looking critically dull. "Long story short, this has been powering a translation enchantment," I told Val, "and I've almost drained it. Could you—"

"Don't trust yourself?" he asked me, heading for Hope. "It comes with practice."

"I'd rather not zap her, if it's all the same to you."

"*Zap?*" Hope echoed, stiffening in alarm, but Val rested his fingertips on her temples before she could bolt and injected Fae into her mind. "There," he said, releasing her and stepping back a pace. "No zapping. How does that feel?"

Hope started to speak, puzzled over the words, then gaped as she understood what he had done. "How...how did you..."

"Enchantment and plenty of practice. Kitty, who is this?"

"This is Hope—uh, Lady Imaranta," I replied. "Who saved our butts, led us right to Artur, and is looking for her mom in Oklahoma, so please don't kick her out just yet."

"Oh, *she* can stay," Ros interjected, reaching up to rub the healed spot on Frank's neck. "Just don't stare directly at the sun, kid, you'll burn your retinas."

Val cocked his head toward Ros. "And the realm has

spoken. Your predecessor would have thrown a fit," he added with a hint of query.

Ros shrugged and circled Frank, giving his injuries her own examination. "None of them are thrilled, but this is my show now, and anyone who patches gaping wounds in Frank gets a pass with me."

Val glanced back at me and raised an eyebrow.

"Long story. Can we take this inside, maybe?" I asked. Whether from terror or exhaustion, my legs had begun to shake, and I remembered that I hadn't eaten that morning. "And Frank's probably starving, so—"

"Of course," said Val, and opened a gate onto the field near the dragon barn. "Rest well," he told Frank. "I'm sure you've had a long journey."

To my surprise, Frank didn't run toward the distant sounds of bleating sheep. *If it's no trouble...*

"Yes?"

I really want bacon.

"Bacon," Val repeated, rubbing his neck. "Approximately how many pigs' worth of it, would you say?"

Maybe just a little one, if you'd put the bind on.

He seemed taken aback, but only for a moment. "I suppose I could approximate Toula's work," he mused. "You'll probably want her to redo it, but for the moment..."

Ros unclasped the saddle and tossed it aside in the instant before the red flash. When my eyes cleared, the much-compressed version of Frank was lying in the grass. He sat up, took stock of himself, then looked at Val and pointedly cleared his throat.

"Sorry," Val muttered as clothing manifested around the target.

Frank pushed himself to his feet, took a few stumbling steps to regain his balance, then shook his head and brushed his hair out of his face. "Thanks," he rumbled. "So...bacon?"

"Absolutely," said Val, and headed for the villa. "Come on, girls, breakfast is this way."

I turned to Hope, who silently goggled as Frank strolled off after him. "Like I said, he's my colleague," I murmured.

"But…but *he*…"

"Is a much more effective researcher with thumbs. Do you know anything about Faerie?"

Hope grimaced. "Little. There's no magic, and it's ruled by three instead of by one…"

"Well, there's plenty of magic, but not the kind you can use, and *that* would be one of the Three," I said, pointing at Val's back, "but I'll give you the rest after we eat. Val's going to have questions. Uh, that would be Lord Valerius," I added, starting for the villa. "He practically fostered me, so we're on more familiar terms."

Hope hurried to keep pace. "You're highborn? You didn't tell me."

"I didn't know until about a month ago, and honestly, it's complicated. But we'll get everything straightened out, and I'll take you to the folks who have the best chance of finding your mom…"

I paused as a figure threw open one of the villa's many doors and sprinted across the field toward us, arms pumping and legs pistoning.

"Excuse me," I told Hope, then ran to meet him.

Wild-eyed, with mussed hair and well-worn sweatpants, Marcus had seen better mornings, but I didn't care. I sped toward him on a collision course, then slammed against him and buried my face in his T-shirt, listening to his heart hammering as his arms squeezed the air from my lungs. I gave as well as I got, and we loosened our grip on each other a few seconds later, forced apart by the necessity of oxygen.

Panting, I closed my eyes and rested my head on his shoulder. "I'm sorry," I mumbled. "I overreacted, and I'm sorry."

"And I'm *still* sorry," he said, locking his arms around me. "Did you, um…I sent you a message, but—"

"I love you, too. No reception in the Gray Lands."

Marcus laughed, which got me started, and my growling stomach only set him off again. We might have stood together in the field all morning had Frank not interrupted: *Twu wuv later. Bacon now.*

I looked up to find him waiting at the door with his arms folded, tapping one foot, and Hope grinning nearby. "He really is a romantic," I told Marcus, then kissed him and pulled him along to join the others.

At least Frank was adept at carrying on a conversation with his mouth full. While I stuffed myself and Hope taste-tested the offerings on the table, Frank methodically put down several slabs of bacon, liberally doused with hot sauce, and reported on our trip. Though Ros certainly knew already, she lingered in the dining room, drinking coffee and prodding him whenever he skipped a bit she found noteworthy. Eventually, I had to pick up the thread, and with great reluctance, I put down my fork to tell the others about Warohn and our unorthodox escape from the tower. All the while, Marcus kept scooting his chair closer to mine, but I welcomed the encroachment on my personal space.

When Frank and I had finished, and Hope had offered a few clarifying details, Val nodded and produced a fresh espresso for himself. "Nath will not be pleased," he said after a quick sip, "but you kept the terms of your agreement, so I don't think she has much room to protest. Ros, how soon will Artur wake?"

"When I say so," she replied. "She's intact, but what's your strategy for dealing with her?"

"Fair question…"

"Actually," I interrupted, "I have an idea. Let me get Myrddin over here to explain the situation to her. Having someone familiar on hand should help, right?"

"I second that," Marcus murmured beside me, and I squeezed his hand under the table.

A flicker of guilt creased Val's face. "Of course. Bring him here, and he can be present when she wakes. In the meantime, the sword needs to return to Amy for stabilization—"

"Immediately," said Ros.

"Tell her, if you would. I need to inform Toula."

Hope glanced around the table uncertainly. "Um...I beg your pardon, but—"

"The people you'll want to get with are in town," Ros cut in. "Kitty can take you, but there are only so many fires we can put out at once. Sword repair, waking Artur...didn't someone leave a gate open in Shapwick Heath?"

"Hence the call to Toula," said Val, rising from the table with his phone. "Marcus, would you—"

Marcus waved his father on, then looked at Frank, who, satiated, had lowered his head onto his arms and was moments away from a meat coma. "Bed?"

"Bed," Frank mumbled.

Fortunately, there was no shortage of guest rooms in the villa. Frank collapsed onto the bed Marcus offered him, face-planting in the pillows with his new shoes still on. Marcus showed Hope to the next suite, and as she cautiously examined her surroundings, he took me aside and said, "I'll watch her. Go break the news to Myrddin."

"You're sure?"

"Not a problem—wait, Hope," he called, finding her out in the adjoining garden with her face tilted skyward, "*sunglasses!*"

I laughed to myself as he created a pair and ran out to instruct her in their use, then steeled my nerve, called up an image in my mind's eye, and opened a gate to Afallon.

England was a little behind Faerie that day, but the summer sun was up and climbing when I stepped out onto the hidden island. I saw no sign of Myrddin, but that meant nothing; the morning was young yet, and it *was* Sunday. Still, I felt like a prowler as I circled the tower. Though I'd hoped to catch him by the patio fire pit, I was out of luck, which left only two places he might be: the *Nymph*, or somewhere in the building.

And so I knocked.

And waited.

Five minutes and several rounds of pounding later, having received no response, I created a second gate to the edge of the island to save myself the walk. The boat was moored and silent, and as I couldn't imagine that Myrddin would sleep aboard his yacht when he had an island at his disposal, I returned to the tower and considered my options. I didn't want to just barge in on him, but the situation warranted swift action. Telling myself that breaking and entering was okay because I was bringing good news, I stepped back, recalled what the tower's central shaft looked like, and bypassed the door with yet another gate.

Myrddin really needed to work on his wards, I thought, as I stood by Caledfwlch's former boulder and listened for movement. As the tower remained quiet, however, I finally shoved manners off the table and yelled upward toward the rings of rooms: "Myrddin! It's Kitty! Where are you?" I paused, listening to the wind outside, then added, "I'm not leaving until you talk to me!"

After another long few minutes, a door above me opened, and Myrddin, fully dressed and looking peeved, appeared at the railing. "I would have thought you could take a hint, girl."

"Sorry for the intrusion, but—"

"Stop. It's not a good time. It's really never going to be a good time. Do you understand?"

I looked up at him and folded my arms. "*Wow*. You're an asshole, but at least you're honest about it. I can respect that."

"I trust that you can see your way out," he replied, and turned to go.

"*Hey*! I'm not finished!"

He heaved a sigh and glanced down at me again. "Yes?"

"Artur's back. Thought you might be interested."

Myrddin didn't bother with the stairs. He leapt, slowed his fall—far better than Hope had managed, my sore knees noted with envy—and grabbed me by the shoulders. "*Where?*"

"Frank and I found her in the Gray Lands and took her to Faerie. She's at Val's place. Patched up nicely, I understand, but she's being kept under until you get there. We thought it would be easiest if someone familiar was there when she wakes."

He floundered for a moment as he digested that, then managed, "Why didn't you bring Artur to me?"

"Because we decided that fixing her wounds was the first consideration. Now that she's stable, do you want to go say hi?"

"Take me," he snapped, squeezing my shoulder to the point of pain. "*Now.*"

"Gladly," I muttered, and opened a gate into Val's main courtyard. Myrddin brushed past me, and as I followed and closed the hole, I heard him demand to know Artur's location from a perplexed aide. "This way," I said, tugging his sleeve. "Follow me."

When we arrived outside the bedroom door, Ros manifested and gave Myrddin a long, hard look. "I'm going to bring her up as slowly as I can. She'll be extraordinarily disoriented. If the bind on her worked the way I think it did, she won't remember anything from the time it was applied until now, so be gentle—"

"Out of my way," he said, attempting to push past her, but Ros threw him back against a pillar with an effortless burst of force.

As Myrddin groaned and picked himself up, she

planted her hands on her hips and glared at him. "Okay, one, I am *Faerie*, so back the hell off. Two, I know what to expect in these situations, and *she* doesn't need you charging around like a mad bull. Either get it under control or get out."

From his shifting expression, I gathered that he had finally noticed that Ros was glowing. "You're—"

"Stronger than you will ever be in this realm, *cupcake*," she almost snarled. "Try that again, and I'll gladly give you a demonstration."

He nodded, but that was the only wise reaction—the anger radiating off of Ros was making me uncomfortable, and I wasn't even its focus.

"Good," she said, and pointed to the door. "Go be her friend. She's going to need one."

The door opened at her will, and Myrddin scurried inside. "Why did no one put his *face* back on?" he said, then huffed and waved a fresh transformation bind into existence. The sleeping blonde morphed into a dark-haired man with a short, neat beard, and I watched as Myrddin fixed his clothing to mend the signs of battle. "Where's Caledfwlch?" he asked, spotting me waiting outside the door.

"Gone for repairs."

"*Repairs?* That's Artur's sword! He'll want it—"

"It's unstable. I practically drained it getting us out in one piece. Should be back from the crafter before too long…"

He scowled at me, then waved the door shut in my face. I heard a latch turn on the other side—not a real bar to entry, not in Faerie, but certainly an indication of his mood.

"I'm sorry, honey," said Ros, steering me down the breezeway. "You handled that well. Probably better than I would have."

"Eh, Mom's given me years of practice in parental rejection," I replied. "If you go in expecting it, you'll either be prepared or pleasantly surprised. You went snooping?"

"It was at the top of your thoughts when you came back, and I can't exactly help it. I'll keep an eye on them," she said as we returned to the courtyard. "Do me a favor and be on standby, hmm?"

At a loss for my next move, I went to my old room, closed the door, and flopped onto the bed with my eyes closed. I'd slept poorly for the previous two nights, and my fatigue was catching up with me. Artur was safe, Frank was asleep, Marcus was keeping Hope from blinding herself, Val was managing the situation with Toula…surely, I reasoned, no one would miss me for a few minutes if I caught a quick nap.

I'd barely begun to drift off when I heard a knock at the door.

Groaning, I rolled over and waved it open, then sat up in shock when I saw my little sister storm into the room. "*Beth*? What are you doing—"

She punched me in the chest, not hard enough to break anything, but painfully enough to convey her displeasure. "What the hell?" I protested, rubbing the impact site, and spotted Maria in the doorway. "What's going on?"

"*That's* for being a stupid jerk," Beth snapped, folding her arms and quietly fuming.

I looked to Maria for an explanation, but she shrugged and glanced toward Beth. "Talk to your sister."

But Beth said nothing. She stood by my bed in red-faced silence, arms clenched across her chest and jaw quivering. "Tell me what's wrong," I murmured, assuming the worst if she'd made her way to Faerie. "Are you hurt?" Still, Beth said nothing, and if my eyes weren't deceiving me, she was trying not to cry. Stymied, I remembered the option newly available to me and muttered, "Hold on, this'll feel weird."

Getting inside Beth's head was the work of an instant,

as difficult as popping a soap bubble, and with her emotions so close to the surface, I soon found what I'd come for. The memories were fresh and as raw as open wounds.

I looked out through Beth's eyes at her bedroom at the Audleys', feeling the depression that she lacked the maturity to handle. She was messing around on her computer, but she wasn't focusing; school was out, she'd barely avoided remedial summer classes, and the little Audley girls had learned to leave her alone. Someone knocked, and Piper stuck her head into the room, wide-eyed and hesitant. *Beth, honey, you've got a visitor.*

It was Maria—no formal robes, no official pronouncement, just a thick manila file folder full of paper. *Kitty's gone to the Gray Lands*, she said once Piper had left them. *She asked me to give you these if she doesn't return, but I don't see the point in waiting.*

Beth stared at her uneasily, shaken to be alone with a magus—particularly *that* magus. *Why'd she do that?*

Because she's decent, and because she's haunted in ways she doesn't like to think about. Maybe you'll be able to ask her yourself—we'll know on Monday whether she's coming back. But in the meantime, you're going to read these, and I'm not leaving until you do.

A smart remark was on the tip of Beth's tongue, but Maria's expression froze it until it died. *Read what?*

Maria handed her the folder and leaned against the dresser. *She doesn't have copies of all of them. Sometimes, she sent you postcards and such. But these are the typed letters. Go on, start reading.*

Something in Beth's stomach coiled as she skimmed the page on the top of the stack:

Hi, Beth!

It's turning cold here, but I bet it's even colder in Montana. Do you have snow? What's your favorite thing to do in the snow? I like to make snowmen, but I'm not very good at it. How's kindergarten?

After a moment, she stopped skimming and started reading, flipping through years of my one-sided correspondence until she reached the last page:

I'm so proud of you, and I know you're going to be fantastic at the Games. Don't be scared—everyone there is nervous, even the ones who look like they aren't. If you're in combat—I'm sure you are—Maria will be refereeing, and she won't let anything happen to you. I'll be up in the stands. Wouldn't miss it, sis! And while I <u>know</u> you'll be amazing, whatever happens, I can't wait to see you and give you a big hug. (You'll have to come visit my office! We've got some great trips lined up, and I'll tell you all about them. Super exciting!) Anyway, rest up, practice your casting, and I'll see you here in two weeks!

All my love,
Kitty xx

The churning mass in Beth's gut had increased its tempo as she read, and she looked up at Maria through a wet film. *There,* said Maria. *You finally got your letters.*

I found a second memory overlapping with the first, which turned into a sequence of quick flashbacks as I watched:

Typing a letter to Mom, hoping *this* would be the one that got a reply.

Hunching at a desk in the back of a classroom, sweatshirt hood raised as if she could block the stares from the girls who had once been her friends.

Sitting on a wooden chair across from the principal, sulking through another lecture about not fighting.

Slouching at the Audleys' dinner table, looking away as I caught her eye and smiled at her.

Standing by the couch as Mom read over her progress

report from night class, muttering, *You have to try harder, Elizabeth. Is that really the best you can do?*

Sparring with a boy in class and losing, only to spot Mom standing by the door with pursed lips.

Proudly showing her first wand to Mom, who dismissed it as a beginner's tool.

I felt Beth's swell of disappointment as I withdrew from her thoughts, and then I saw her through my own eyes again—still flushed, but now poised to break. "You weren't good enough, either, were you?" I said softly.

She shook her head, and then the tears began to flow.

I stood and cautiously wrapped my arms around my sister. She stiffened at first, then relented and hugged me, crying in earnest with heaving, choking sobs. "It's okay, sweetie, it's okay," I said, rubbing her back while she soaked my shirt. "It doesn't matter what she thinks about your talent."

Beth mumbled into my shoulder, then lifted her face enough to be understood. "She said you were lying. That you didn't write any letters. But you did, and…and…"

The rest was drowned in fresh tears, and I held her closer, hearing the unspoken: *If she lied about that, what else was untrue? She used to say she loved me, and now she won't say anything to me.*

I'd known Beth's heartbreak—and then some—but I'd had people around me who cared. Beth had kept this bottled up and festering, withdrawing a little more every time she was reminded of her absent, silent mother. Mom had said I was bad, wrong, that I didn't care about them…and yeah, I consorted with faeries…and okay, *yeah*, I was witch-blooded…but now Beth had a folder of letters proving Mom a liar.

She wanted to talk to me, but she was fourteen and so very lost, and most of her too-big feelings came through as anger. And there was Maria, telling her that I might never be seen again.

"I promise you, it's okay," I murmured as Beth's fit ran

its course. "I'm here, I'm not going back to the Gray Lands, and you've got nothing to worry about." I pulled away to see the state of Beth's splotchy face, then plucked a wad of tissue from the ether and offered it to her. "I'm sorry, Beth. Didn't think you'd be upset to see me go."

She dried her face as she hiccupped her last sobs, and while she didn't refute my assumption, her tears didn't exactly confirm it.

"Look, I'm probably going to be here for a few days," I told her, "but you still have time until school starts, right? Want to come visit Glastonbury again? Maybe stay over when you come for the Games, huh? You, me, borrowed car? Or bad TV, I'm not picky."

Her head bobbed a fraction of an inch, but she gave me a hard look. "Is *he* going to be there?"

"Who, Marcus? Probably."

"*Why?*"

"Because he's my boyfriend...or something. Ish," I amended.

Beth had inherited Mom's tendency to compress her lips until they turned white when she was displeased. "But he's—"

"Just as fae as I am." That threw her, and I nodded emphatically as she scowled. "Technically, I'm a lady—did anyone mention that?"

Beth let out an exasperated sigh. "Why are you being difficult, Kitty?"

"Because that's what big sisters do. And whatever has happened, whatever will happen...I'm still your sister. Half sister, I guess, but...is that okay? Maybe?"

She said nothing, and when I peeked again, I saw her question and grinned. "I think you'd like school at Arc 2. Fresh start. You could board, if you wanted, but I could give you your room back."

"But where will Marcus sleep?" Maria asked.

The look of confusion, then horrified comprehension, on Beth's face was priceless, but I resisted the urge to laugh. "He'll manage. Come on," I said, slinging my arm around Beth's shoulders, "let me introduce y'all properly. Oh, and Hope! Uh…try not to stare, she's half cynaeli."

"Huh?"

"In brief, she's purple. Be nice."

I released Beth as I neared the door, then gave Maria a long, tight hug. "Thank you," I whispered.

"Happy to. So glad to have you back," she replied. "And *why* is there a cynaeli here?"

"I'll explain on the way," I said, reaching for Beth again, then tugged my sister into the corridor and pulled Maria along. "Long story short, I need to know what the Fringe has on folks in Oklahoma, and I'm going to need someone to give Hope the crash course in passing for human."

"She's…wait, *what* is she?" Beth pressed.

"From the Gray Lands. And since she's much of the reason why Frank and I made it out, I'm going to help her find her mom."

"And where's Frank?" Maria cut in.

"Sleeping it off, last I saw. Val fed him, and we put him to bed. Poor guy's exhausted."

"Who's Frank?"

"Tell you later," I said to Beth.

"And what were you doing in the friggin' *Gray Lands*, anyway?" she continued. "Magus Corelli wouldn't tell me."

I cut my eyes to Maria, whose face betrayed nothing. "We were trying to find someone. My, uh…my other sibling."

Beth stopped in her tracks and caught my arm to stay me. "*What* other sibling?"

"My biological father had…well, she was born female and raised male, so I don't know what to properly call her right now," I replied, slightly flustered, "but anyway, she's been asleep over there since the late fifth century, so I thought it was past time to find her. And since Frank's a better friend than I deserve, he went with me."

She sucked on her bottom lip as she considered that. "You've met him? Your...bio-dad?"

"Yeah."

"Is he nice?"

"I don't know him that well," I replied, which wasn't a lie. "He's with, uh...his other child now, so we may bump into him in a bit."

Beth said nothing but seemed to be wrestling with herself, and once again, manners be damned, I looked at her thoughts. "Of course I'll tell you about Daddy," I murmured. "Whatever you want to know."

The question I'd seen was tinged with jealousy—I'd had a father, she hadn't, and he wasn't even my father to start with—but I didn't tell her I'd picked up on that.

She smiled slightly, and we continued around the courtyard. "What's this sibling like, then?" she asked.

"Don't know. She's been unconscious the whole time I've been around her."

"Is she going to stay here?"

"Don't know that, either."

Maria peered around me at Beth. "You're inquisitive today, aren't you?"

I glanced at Beth in time to see the incredulous look she shot Maria. "Wouldn't you be?"

"And here we are," I interrupted, stopping outside Hope's room. "Seriously, Beth, be nice," I warned, then rapped and cracked the door open. "Hope? Marcus—hey," I said as he approached, moving aside to let him out of the room. "How is she?"

Marcus stepped into the corridor, nodded to Maria, then caught a glimpse of Beth and did a double-take. "Uh...hello?" he said, switching to English and silently querying Maria and me.

She's trying. Behave, I replied, and looked for my sister, who had slid a few inches behind me. "Beth, you remember Marcus, yeah?"

She nodded. "Hi."

That was better than nothing, I decided. "How's Hope? Sleeping?"

"Garden, actually," he replied. "She found the fish."

"Have we talked about sunscreen?"

"She's *violet*. Can she get burned, do you suppose?"

"I don't know, but seeing as she's being exposed to direct sunlight for maybe the first time in her life, we should take precautions. How about a hat, at least?"

Before we could pursue the matter further, the door opened again, and Hope beamed when she saw me. "Kitty!" she cried, her Fae as oddly accented as mine. "Did you know that the mosaics move? They're charming." Noticing Maria and wide-eyed Beth, she smiled again and raised a hand in quick greeting. "Howdy!"

Beth blinked hard, then turned my way. "*Howdy?*"

"Her English is kind of limited," I explained, and ushered everyone into her suite. "Here, come look at the fish mosaic in the fountain. I'll try to explain."

Ten minutes later, with Maria brought up to date and Beth still goggling at her surroundings, I left Maria in charge and stepped out into the main courtyard with Marcus for a breather. "Too much at once, isn't it?" he said, rubbing my shoulders as I perched on the edge of a fountain.

"It's a bit overwhelming," I admitted. "But this is nice. You could keep doing this, and I wouldn't mind."

He chuckled and kissed my neck. "You'll fall asleep sitting here, and then you'll wake up in the fountain, and you'll be cross because you'll be soaked. *Rest*. Surely Maria and I can keep Hope and Beth from walking off a cliff while you sleep."

That wasn't a bad idea, but Marcus kept kneading the knots in my back, and I was melting under his hands. "You still haven't tried out my new mattress. It's *fantastic*."

"So you said. Is that an invitation back to the flat?"

"Mm-hmm."

"Am I forgiven, then?"

"Are you going to try to order me to stay in the subbasement?"

"And risk you running away to the Gray Lands again? I learned *that* lesson."

I turned and kissed him properly, my blood stirring even with my exhaustion, and was poised to invite him back to my bedroom across the courtyard when the door to Artur's room burst open and slammed shut. Myrddin marched toward us, his face dark with an emotion on the cusp of anger, and jutted his thumb over his shoulder. "He refuses to listen to reason," he barked. "I can do nothing with him."

"Is Artur…*sane*?" I asked. I'd seen a few of the Fringe's barely stable members around the settlement, the ones who'd recovered enough of their wits after being frozen alive in the darkness to leave the rest home where their companions lingered. They were pitiable creatures, the newly recovered, frail and jumpy, and prone to all-encompassing flashbacks. If eleven years could so break a mind, I hated to imagine what Artur's long span could have wrought.

But Myrddin snorted. "Sitting, talking, weeping like a woman. I told him about the island, but he won't go. Revealed myself as his father, and he ordered me out." He shook his head and glowered at me. "Let me know when my son's himself again, won't you?"

Before I could stop him, Myrddin ripped open a gate and stormed off, leaving Marcus and me to stare at each other in shock. After a moment, I gathered myself and rose. "I should look in on Artur…"

He caught my wrist before I could hurry on my way. "Let me."

"But she—"

"*Please*, Kitty. Let me do this." While I wavered, he stood and kissed my forehead. "Take your rest. I'll do what I can."

CHAPTER 14

Marcus saw me back to my room, turned down my bed, and waited until I was burrowed beneath the covers before slipping out, every inch the doting boyfriend. I didn't have the heart to tell him that I wasn't going to sleep. Though I'd acquiesced, I felt awful for it, and I couldn't just take a nap if Artur was having a come-apart in the next wing.

It was almost a relief when Ros appeared. "You're going to want to see this," she said without preamble, and a shimmering image manifested in the air beside her shoulder—the realm's omniscient view of Marcus as he approached Artur's door. Anxious, I sat up in bed and leaned closer to the picture like a child scooting toward the television.

Marcus knocked twice, and a muffled baritone from the other side shouted incomprehensibly in reply. He let out a long breath, then squared his shoulders and opened the door. "Artur?" he said, looking around the darkened room. "Do you understand me?"

I spotted Artur—well, the transformed version—sitting on the side of the bed, slumped with his head in his hands. He raised his face when Marcus spoke, and even with the low light through the curtains, I could see the moisture on his cheeks. He voiced a reply, but he seemed more confused than angry to find the stranger in his presence.

Marcus raised his empty hands and slowly turned them back and forth. "No weapons, no tricks. But this will feel strange, and I'll apologize properly once you know what I'm saying." He crossed to the bed, and as Artur drew back in alarm, he put his fingers to Artur's temples and closed his eyes. His target cried out in surprise, and Marcus withdrew, muttering, "Sorry, sorry. I couldn't exactly warn you."

Artur stiffened. "Warn me of…of…*wait*…"

"The feeling passes," he replied as Artur frowned in bewilderment. "That's the tongue of this realm I gave you. Myrddin left, and we don't have another translator available, so…" He spread his hands and shrugged. "Quick and painless, yes?"

Artur rubbed his head, blinking slowly as he considered that, then managed, "Who *are* you?"

"A friend. Possibly the best friend you'll have today. Call me Marcus. You're in my father's house."

As he spoke, Artur seemed to recover his footing. "Your hospitality is appreciated, but your company—"

"Is necessary." Marcus beckoned to a chair, which moved into position behind him as he sat. "I'm the one man in this realm who knows what you're going through. You shouldn't be alone."

Though apparently shaken by the moving chair, Artur responded with disbelieving laughter. "You have no idea—"

"I was you last year." Artur's mouth snapped shut, and Marcus quietly continued. "One minute, the world makes sense. The next, you're in a future so distant that you've never imagined it, and everything and everyone you know and love is gone. Sound familiar?" He pulled his chair closer to the bed and held Artur's watery gaze. "I'll be plain with you. This may be the most difficult day of your life. Mourn your dead, Artur. There's no shame in it. You'll be mourning them for months to come, but the pain's at its most acute right now. And the physical pain, too—you were badly wounded, that sort of thing takes augmentation to heal, and believe me, that's not a process I'd wish on my worst enemy." He produced a cloth from midair, the classier version of my wadded tissues, and handed it to

Artur, who wiped his face and honked his nose clean.

"What do you last remember?" Marcus prodded.

Artur pressed on his eyelids as he thought. "Monstrous things. Like smoke made flesh. They killed everyone who approached, they…oh, *Kei*…"

"You charged them?" Marcus prompted before Artur could break again.

"I had to try. They slaughtered my men, the horses…one of them raked through me, I remember that, and I was on the ground, and Myrddin…he was saying something to me, but everything went dark, and then I woke here, and…" He raised his head again, his tears spilling over. "Myrddin said that everything is gone. Afallon's been conquered. All my men are *dead*. I've lost my kingdom—"

"And I lost my son," he murmured. "A small loss to you, I suppose, but he was the most precious thing in the world to me. *I understand.*"

Artur's face contorted, and he swallowed hard. "My sympathy for your boy."

"And mine for your men. Kei, was it?"

"Kei," he repeated. "Bedwyr, Medraut, Madoc, my own blood…or…no…"

"Madoc was your cousin?"

"My father's blood," he mumbled. "But if Myrddin—"

"My advice to you would be to put Myrddin aside for now," Marcus interrupted. "Take care of yourself first." He leaned back in his chair and folded his arms. "These hours are hell, while it all sinks in. I panicked at first, and then everything was explained to me, then I panicked some more once I had a moment's privacy. Thought about killing myself, jumping in a fountain face-first and holding myself under," he added, nodding toward the curtained door. "Then my distant granddaughter dragged me to a tavern, and I got *thoroughly* drunk, and I woke up and understood that this wasn't all some terrible dream. I had to face it."

"How?" said Artur. "I barely know where I am, much less what I'm meant to be doing."

Marcus held out his hand, and a glass of red wine appeared. "Take off the edge, to start," he said, offering it to him. "Not too much, but it can help. Honestly, your sister's done more to help me than anyone else. Well, her and my counselor," he allowed. "You'll meet Wanda soon enough, I trust."

Artur drank, then frowned bemusedly. "What sister? I have no sister."

One of Marcus's eyebrows inched upward. "Did Myrddin not mention...no, of course he said nothing. *Scelus*," he muttered under his breath. As the furrows in Artur's forehead deepened, Marcus asked, "What did he tell you about how you came to be here?"

"Little. He said he gave me to Morgen for protection, and I slept for several years in her care, and now all is lost in Afallon—"

"Wait—*several* years?" Marcus interjected, incredulous.

"So he told me. How long, exactly?"

He linked his hands behind his head and gazed at the ceiling as he thought. "By our best estimation," he said slowly, "that battle you last remember occurred around the year numbered 490 in the present reckoning. Late in the fifth century. We're now midway through the twenty-first, so...one thousand, five hundred, sixty-nine years, I think."

Artur stared at him, motionless but for his descending jaw.

"Myrddin told us that he gave you to Morgen when you were at the point of death. He couldn't heal you, but Morgen thought she could protect you in the Gray Lands, her home. She took you across and basically locked you in sleep. It's not a true sleep—nothing about you changes except your talent," he explained. "But Morgen died without fixing or freeing you, and so you've been a trophy of sorts for the last fifteen centuries." He paused, noted Artur's horror, and pressed on. "Yes, Afallon fell. So did all of your little kingdoms. The Saxons were triumphant until a Norman lord decided that he had a better claim to your island than its king and conquered it. *Much* of it," he amended. "And in the millennium that's followed, that kingdom has grown strong. It's not as strong now as it was, but it endures. Your people's blood endures, though intermixed with others'. I'd give you more, but I'm still learning much of this myself," he added apologetically. "I slept for twenty-two centuries and woke to find that Rome had fallen, and I've been catching up ever since. As I said, this will be a difficult day for you."

Artur's fist balled around the handkerchief. "And Afallon? Is it…"

"Long gone and passed into legend. As has your name, but that's a matter for another time." While Artur wrestled with that news, Marcus sighed and created a glass of wine for himself. "I wish I could make this easier for you, but I know of nothing that would soften this blow."

He drank in silence, giving Artur a moment.

Finally, voice cracking, Artur said, "Myrddin claimed to be my father. Is this true?"

"He believes it to be so. He says you have a talent for magic."

"Because I was born from it—"

"From *him*, more likely. There are ways of finding the truth. My aunt is skilled in that regard—"

Before he could finish, Ros flickered out of my sight and appeared in Artur's room, causing both men to jump and almost spill their drinks. "He's your father," she told Artur. "I'm certain of it."

When she vanished, Artur, who had automatically reached for a sword that wasn't at his hip, wheeled on Marcus in alarm. "Who…what…"

"Ros. I'll explain later. And I'd believe her about Myrddin."

"So…my mother…"

"From what Myrddin told us, it sounded like Uther

couldn't get a child on her. She lay with Myrddin for lack of a better option."

"And they deceived Father." He stared into space, barely shaking his head. "Myrddin never told me until now."

"Because you needed to be Uther's son, I suppose. Now that you're here, the truth was bound to come forth." Marcus drained his glass, and it vanished. "I always thought my father died in battle before I was born. Turns out he's a king in this realm. Something of a shock, that."

"I can imagine. Suppose it's easier if you're born to it," Artur replied, accepting the momentary distraction. "I always knew I was destined for Father's throne. Have they been training you, then?"

"Training, yes, but not what you might think. And with any luck, I'll have millennia to go before the throne falls to me...but we're getting off point." He leaned toward Artur and said, "Myrddin claimed an island for himself, called it Afallon, and hid it from the rest of the world while he waited for Morgen to bring you back. She never did. About a month ago, we stumbled onto him, he told us about you, and your sister and a friend of ours risked their lives to find you." Seeing Artur's confusion, he explained, "Myrddin had another daughter twenty-four years ago. He didn't know, she didn't know, and I think he'd prefer to pretend that Kitty doesn't exist...*oh*. Sorry," he mumbled as the blood drained from Artur's face, "Myrddin had *a* daughter. Your sex is supposed to be a secret, isn't it?"

"You...who told..."

"Myrddin. Only a few people know—"

"I'll *kill* him," Artur whispered. "He swore never to betray me, he *swore*—"

His wine glass shattered in his hand, and Artur jerked, staring at the fresh scratches on his palm as the blood welled.

"Try to be calm," Marcus soothed, producing a wet towel. "You have talent, and it grew while you slept. Hold it inside until you've had training, if you can." He inspected Artur's hand, pried a shard free, and wove together a healing enchantment to close the wounds. "There, let that work."

I wasn't sure what upset Artur more, the fact that his secret had been spread or that his anger had resulted in broken glass, but Marcus went with the former. "How you choose to glamour yourself is none of my business," he said as the towel disappeared. "If this is what you prefer, keep it. There's a dragon working under a transformation bind in human guise two offices down from mine— believe me, *this* is nothing," he added, waving one hand toward Artur.

"*What?*"

"Frank. He's the one who went after you with Kitty. Good man. But look, do what you like with your appearance, and I'm sure that Kitty will respect your wishes. All of that aside, yes, you have a sister. She risked herself to rescue you, which is a hell of a lot more than Myrddin ever did." He paused, then asked, "Would you like to meet her? She's just gone for a nap, but I don't think she would mind—"

"No. Please…no."

Logically, I knew that Artur was having a bad day, but the words still hit me like a punch to the gut. Ros pursed her lips at the image but said nothing while I listened in.

If Marcus was at all surprised at the answer, he didn't let on. "Probably wise. She needs her rest, anyway," he said, gesturing toward the bedroom's two-top table, "and you need to eat." A sumptuous spread manifested, covering every inch of the tabletop, and as he held out his hand, an empty plate appeared atop it. "You're weak. This will help, believe me."

Artur hesitated, then took the plate from him, slowly pushed himself from the bed, and approached the buffet. "Thank you for your counsel. You may leave me."

"I don't think so."

He turned, surprised at the refusal, but Marcus merely shook his head. "I don't trust you not to do something rash once my back is turned. Allowing you to stew alone in here isn't on the day's agenda."

"Then what is, pray tell?"

A fresh pair of wine stems appeared in Marcus's grasp. "More of this. I can't guarantee amnesia, but it won't hurt you any worse than you're feeling now."

Artur sighed, then accepted a glass and drained it in a long gulp. "Not bad. Can you make beer?"

"Nothing you'd want to drink. I've been told that I need practice and a better palate. Mead?"

"Mead," Arthur agreed, and a pint glass of golden liquid appeared in Marcus's hand. Artur gave it a test sip, then nodded and put it on the floor while he retrieved his plate. "You're joining me, then?"

Marcus lifted his glass in acknowledgement and drained it. "Do try to keep up."

Ros cut the feed as they started on their second round of mead. "I'll let you know if you're needed," she promised, shooing me back into bed. "Now get some rest, kid. Frank has the right idea."

Though disappointed to be excluded from Marcus and Artur's commiseration session, I gave in to my exhaustion and might have slept all day had Maria not come knocking that afternoon. "Amy Levey called," she said as I yawned back to consciousness. "She's cleared her workshop, and she's prepared to tinker with that sword now. Val asked me to take it to town—did you want to come along? Maybe find Vivi and figure out what's to be done with Hope?"

I stretched, willed myself unrumpled, and emerged to find Hope, now sporting a hooded sweatshirt, and Beth waiting with Maria in the corridor. "You're still here?" I asked my sister.

She shrugged. "It's either this or hang out in my room. Do you want me to go?"

"No—no," I replied, squeezing her shoulder. "Just surprised, that's all."

"I can be surprising," she mumbled.

"I'm sure."

"Like, fun and full of surprises."

Superficially, Beth wore a hard façade of nonchalance, though I thought it might be cracking to expose something softer beneath, and I tried to be gentle. "I'm glad you haven't run screaming yet."

"Eh, the day's not over," she retorted, but she flashed a small, shy smile as she shoved her hands into her pockets. "How far is this town, anyway?"

Maria opened a gate onto the main square. "About a meter from where you're standing. Close enough?"

"Show-off," Beth muttered.

"Brat," said Maria, giving Beth's ponytail a tug as she passed.

I shook my head at the two of them, and Hope, who was too excited to care about the sniping, hurried after my sister.

The Fringe settlement had grown from a refugee camp to a planned community with a population of several thousand, a neat downtown of manicured parks and charming storefronts surrounded by leafy residential avenues. Much of it smacked of fantasy small-town Americana in design, if one overlooked the absence of automobiles. Other than the trolleys, the streets were empty of all but pedestrians, bicyclists, and a couple who skated by us on matching rollerblades. Maria had dumped us out by the ornamental fountain in the park at the center of town, generally a safe place to make a gate without causing a fuss, and Beth and Hope stood on the sidewalk and took it all in: the green lawn, the band shell, the teenagers with their Frisbee, the old woman handing out ice cream from a cart a few yards away.

There was no economy to speak of in the settlement—with an endless supply of magic and practitioners on hand to see to the Fringers' needs, there was no need for money—but people found their own ways to stave off tedium. I'd been out to hear the orchestra one night, and a few restaurants had flourished downtown, overseen by chefs, their apprentices, and a rotating crew of volunteer staff. A market held nearly anything that one could wish for, and a Stowe or two handled special orders. Mal's dad oversaw the school two blocks away, which taught the mundane subjects, plus the rudiments of spellcraft and enchantment at a level appropriate for the less talented students. And just across the street from the park were Amy's and Kip's shops, the latter equipped to handle the Fringe's technological needs and the former serving as the source of the finest wands in any realm. It had taken work on Toula's part to convince Amy to craft for the Arcanum, and I suspected that they would have given Amy whatever she wanted to keep their supply of Levey wands coming. Fortunately, she seemed to enjoy her work—either that, or she'd worked out one hell of a deal.

Amy was waiting beneath her blue awning as we left the park. "Honestly, Kitty," she called across the street, "I fix your sword, and you turn around and break it again?"

"Desperate times," I replied, lifting the sheathed weapon. "I'm sorry."

She waved it off. "Y'all come in. No stunts, now," she warned, and led the way into her workshop.

Kip's space next door was airy and neat, well organized and comprehensible. Amy's, however, veered toward controlled chaos: a wooden workbench at least ten feet long, piled with dowels, scales, scoops, a marble mortar and pestle stained brownish-green, and an array of tiny jars filled with powdered stones and organic matter. The shelves lining two walls were similarly cluttered with the implements of her trade, while a pile of wand boxes occupied a wall of their own. The plate-glass window overlooking the park was tinted to begin with, but Amy hit a switch, and the glass clouded to black opacity as a red bulb in the ceiling flicked on. "Precautions," she explained, and pulled Caledfwlch free of its scabbard to examine it with her practiced eye. After a low whistle, she muttered, "Jesus, hon, try to leave a *little* magic in it next time, okay?"

"Salvageable?" I asked.

"Yeah, but barely. It would have started to eat itself, had you kept up whatever you were doing for much longer. Congrats on surviving, by the way. Find what you were looking for?"

"And then some," I said, and slung an arm around Hope's shoulders. "Do you know if Vivi's in today? I don't want to interrupt mayoral stuff, but we need someone with full access to the Fringe database."

"She should be in. Check City Hall..." Her voice faltered as she studied Hope in the red light, which made all of our eyes seem just slightly demonic. "Uh...hi?"

"Howdy?" Hope replied tentatively.

"You're—"

"Cynaeli," I interjected. "And a large part of the reason we made it out of there."

Amy considered her for a moment longer, then grimaced and turned her attention back to the sword. "Huh. Maybe don't go next door—oh, shit," she muttered, glancing past us at the monitor on the wall, the twin of the one in Kip's shop. There was Kip, wide-eyed, gesticulating, and ready to charge, and Amy lifted her hands to stop him from running into the room. "Sorry, girls, I'm going to need you to go outside," she said, pointing toward the street. "I can't afford stray enchantment or flying elbows in here."

Reluctantly, we filed out—Beth dragged her feet to get a good look at the wands on display—and as soon as the door closed, Kip joined us on the sidewalk. "What the *hell*?" he cried, pointing at Hope, who cringed toward me in her hoodie. "Why would you bring one of those—"

"She saved our lives, and she's trying to find her mom in Oklahoma," I began, but Kip was having none of it.

"That's a fucking deep dweller!"

A few of the Fringers around us turned at his shout, slowing to see the show.

"Half," I protested. "And completely without useable magic in this realm. She's not a threat."

He ignored me, instead launching into a shouted tirade in a language I couldn't understand. Neither, it seemed, could Hope, who cocked her head and bit her lip as she tried to puzzle it out. When he came up for air, she said, "I'm sorry, but I don't know that tongue. How have I offended?"

"He's the kadalin I was telling you about," I murmured. "Under a transformation bind."

"*Oh*," she breathed, and held up her empty hands. "I mean no harm—"

"Sure," he snapped. "Here, with an entourage watching you." He swept one finger across our little party. "They're vile monsters," he said, glancing my way. "Half-blooded or not, that thing is a killer."

"Kip—"

"No, stop," said Hope, cutting me off. "He has a right to be angry. I won't trouble you," she told Kip, "or your neighbor—"

"My *wife*," he growled.

Hope shrank under the force of his anger. "Your wife, then. And to be clear, I have *never* hunted your people. I raised chinols for my father, that's all."

"Guronts," I offered.

But Kip remained unyielding. "Leave. If I see you near us again, you won't be so fortunate. And I would suggest that you choose better company," he added, looking at Maria and me.

"We're going," said Maria. "Off to find Vivi. Stand down."

He kept watch in front of Amy's door, blocking it until

we had crossed the street and were well into the park. "So…" Beth began, glancing back at him, "is someone going to tell me what the heck that was all about?"

Hope kept her hood up and her head lowered, and so I pulled Beth back and whispered, "How do you suppose a rhino would feel about having a big game hunter around?"

"Not great."

"Exactly. Her people hunt his."

Beth looked toward the shops again in confusion. "He's not Fringe?"

"Kadalin. They're centaurs native to the Gray Lands."

Her dark eyes grew saucer-round. "Wait, but he's married to—"

"Best not to think too hard about it, okay?" I said, and hurried to catch up with the others.

"City Hall" was nothing so grand, but it was where Vivi Stowe kept her office, and as she had been the de facto mayor of the settlement for more than forty years, the nickname had stuck. Vivi was one of the few remaining coordinators, the Fringers tasked with keeping the rest of the organization in running order, but then, with their members largely centralized, the Fringe didn't need much bureaucracy. In the past, most countries with a Fringe presence had at least one coordinator—there had been three in the States alone—but when the Arcanum turned on its cousins, the assassins had managed to kill all but two: Slim, who'd been taken captive instead, and Badger, who'd slipped their nets and gone on the run. It was Badger who'd made Vivi a full-fledged coordinator to oversee the Fringers taking refuge in Faerie. Though the child of two half faeries, Vivi had seemingly inherited all of her parents' mortal attributes and virtually none of their talent, but she also had a dozen talented older brothers, who had proved willing to help their baby sister maintain peace in the settlement.

By the time I came of age, Badger and Slim had retired to Faerie, the former taking a well-earned break and the latter eschewing all leadership responsibilities beyond his bar. The few Fringers who had never left the mortal realm, had returned, or had struck out to seek their fortune over the border had chosen their own leaders, less experienced coordinators who kept closely in contact with Vivi.

I had two strategies for finding Hope's mother. Toula could set up a blood trace using a donation from Hope, but before I embarked on that route, I wanted to see if the Fringe had any information beyond a location. Knowing where someone was living was one thing; knowing *how* they were getting on was another matter entirely.

Vivi looked up from her triple monitors at Maria's knock and beckoned us into her spacious office, whose windows would have afforded her a lovely fourth-floor view of the park had she not installed light-blocking shades. The harsh glow of the screens gave her youthful face a grayish tint, but she dialed up the recessed lights as we filed in and filled her sofa and wingback chairs. "Little bird warned me you were coming," she said, lifting her phone. "Kip's not a happy camper."

"And Hope's not going to be here long," I replied. "Especially not if you help us out. We're trying to find her mom."

"Could do." She pulled a notepad out of her desk and clicked open a pen. "Okay, exactly what do we know about this woman?"

Precious little, as it so happened. Hope could provide her mother's name, hometown, and a vague description of her appearance, but she had little else to go on and only a five-year-old's understanding of who her mother had been. Still, Vivi promised to investigate—if nothing else, the Fringe maintained extensive files on unexplained activity in the mortal realm, anything that could inadvertently draw attention to them. "Might take a few days," she cautioned as we rose to go. "And I know how this sounds, but Hope, it would be best if you didn't go wandering around town in the interim."

We returned to the villa through a gate made outside Vivi's office—it was only courteous to keep the magic to a minimum around her computer, shielded though it was— and settled in my old room. There was no sign of life from Artur's side of the complex, and Frank remained unconscious, so I felt rather like a bad hostess as I looked at Beth and Hope. "Sorry, it's kind of boring right now," I said apologetically. "Um...there's the gardens, or there's the beach..."

My sister perked at that. "Beach?"

"Yeah, it's not far. The water's a little chilly, but it's swimmable. Interested?"

She stared at me in disbelief. "I've never *been* to a beach. Mom always kept me in Montana except for the Games in Glastonbury."

"I like water," Hope quietly added. "Unless I would cause more problems by being out..."

"No, I don't envision any trouble," said Maria, kicking off her shoes. She opened a fresh gate onto the shore, and the salty breeze fluttered my curtains. "After you."

Barefoot and with her jeans rolled up to her knees, Beth stepped out onto the beach as if she were expecting to sink, then grinned as she scrunched her toes in the sand. "Here," I offered, producing a bottle of sunscreen, "don't get burned—"

There was no point in finishing that thought. Beth was already running for the surf, laughing at the wind in her face and kicking up grit with every footfall. Hope raced her, while Maria and I stood back and watched as they plunged into the waves, shrieked at the shock of cold water, and retreated briefly before braving the sea again.

"You did that once," she reminded me.

"I was *ten*, and it was my first beach trip." I willed a wooden lounger into place near the tide line and added an oversized umbrella to shield my pale skin from the clear sky. Even with the sun beginning to sink, nightfall was hours away. "Join me?"

"Don't mind if I do," said Maria, copying my work. We flopped onto our respective chairs, and she brought forth a pair of respectable daiquiris, which we sipped in silence while we supervised.

After a time, Maria murmured, "Artur's going to be fine. Marcus won't let anything happen."

"Yeah, I know," I replied, my voice small, "but what if Artur still doesn't want to see me once the shock is past?"

"Then you move on, I guess," she said, reaching for my hand. "And you look around at the people in your corner and know that you're loved." She dipped her drink toward my sister, whose jeans were soaked black, and gave me a slight smile. "She cried when she read those letters, you know."

"Oh?"

"*Bawled.* Cursed Eva, cursed me for not stopping you, then cursed her fosters when they told her to watch her language with the children in the house. There's a lot of anger in that one. A lot of hurt. And she's only—what, fourteen?"

"Yeah. Remember how well we got along the last time she lived with me?"

"Vividly, but a lot can change in a year, you know?"

"Sure. She still doesn't like the idea of Marcus and me as a couple."

"Maybe not, but did you ever think you'd see her hanging out with a Gray Lander on a beach in Faerie?" Maria clinked her glass against mine and smiled in earnest. "Progress, right?"

I watched Hope and Beth splash each other, then freeze and look up in alarm as Frank's brothers flew by overhead. "Progress," I replied, bracing myself as Beth sprinted back up the beach, pointing to the sky for an explanation.

A knock at my door pulled me from sleep, and I squinted through blurry eyes at my bedroom, assigning meaning to the pile of bodies around me.

My bed was wide but crammed—I'd taken the spot on the far left, and Beth was spooned against me, drooling on the pillow and hogging the blankets. Beside her was Hope, flat on her stomach with one arm flung toward the headboard, then Maria on the far right, clinging to the little of the covers that hadn't been sucked in by Beth's personal gravity. The door to Maria's adjoining room was still open, but no one had wanted to sleep in there. One of the kitchen staff had brought us dinner once we'd coaxed Beth and Hope, both shivering, off the beach, and Frank had awakened enough to join us. Introducing him had led to a long, awkward explanation for Beth, but to my pleasant surprise, she'd acclimated rapidly, *particularly* once Frank started telling embarrassing field stories. Hope had tried to keep up—she'd missed most of the references but had been happy to laugh along—and Maria had kept the sangria flowing for everyone but my baby sister, who'd grumbled but accepted several Shirley Temples as a peace offering. In the spirit of sorority, I'd sneaked her a glass of sangria late in the evening when Maria's back was turned.

I stood and peered around the bed to find Frank curled up on the rug beneath a spare blanket from Maria's room, one foot twitching in his sleep. While I'd never seen him turn down a proper bed, Frank could and did sleep anywhere, and he hadn't wanted to leave the impromptu slumber party. Maria had slipped back to Glastonbury for her computer, and we'd projected movies onto a screen conjured for that purpose until the wee hours. Again, Hope hadn't understood everything, but once I got English into her head, she'd seemed to enjoy the show.

At least the night hadn't devolved into makeovers and a pillow fight, I mused. Maria and I had pulled together the necessary pajamas, and there had been cheese fondue at some point—I spotted the pot and leftover bread on the table, long since gone cold—but as far as I could tell, Frank's fingernails remained unpainted, which suggested that we hadn't done anything completely embarrassing before crawling into bed.

The knock sounded again, reminding me of why I was conscious, and I hurried to the door in my tank top and plaid flannel pants, still tasting the ghost of sangria in my dry mouth. I flipped the latch and pulled the door open, expecting to find Val on the other side, checking on us, or perhaps Marcus, who'd sent no word all day.

"Oh!" I said, surprised to instead see Artur in the corridor, washed, dressed, and relatively clear-eyed for dawn. "Uh…hi."

"Kitty," he said, and smiled—a real smile, oddly enough—as he gripped my arms. "It's good to meet you. Did I wake you?"

"No," I fibbed, my bare skin starting to prickle into gooseflesh in the early morning chill. "No, I was…up…"

His raised eyebrow suggested that we both knew otherwise. "My apologies. It seems that the sun and I are in disagreement." He glanced over my shoulder at the packed bed, then back at me. "You're entertaining?"

"It just sort of happened." I closed the door before we could wake the others and shifted my weight, trying to keep one foot off the cold tile at all times. "I'm *really* sorry about…this…"

"Why would you apologize? You freed me. The debt I owe—"

"No, no, uh…I'm sorry that, you know, everything's kind of awful right now," I fumbled.

His shoulders rose and fell in a resigned shrug. "I've been informed that time travel is impossible, so there's nothing to do but make the best of it."

"We had to set Marcus straight on that, too."

"So he said. A good man, your Marcus. He *is* yours, is he not?" he asked with a quizzical tilt of his head. "He's obviously in love. No one speaks of a woman as he did you unless he's fallen for her."

I grinned. "We're working on it. What did he say?"

At that, Artur glanced toward the ceiling and sucked his teeth. "I remember the tenor of it, but the actual words have slipped my mind. Marcus and I got *thoroughly* drunk. He said you had a word for it that I quite liked..." He snapped his fingers as he dredged up the memory. "Shit-faced. Yes, that was it. Much funnier yesterday..."

"Look," I said, patting his shoulder, "it's okay. You don't have to pretend—"

"Oh, I feel fine," he insisted. "Physically, I suppose. My wounds seem to have healed, and our host found me wandering this morning and made the hangover go away. Remarkable skill."

"No, I mean, if you'd rather not do this..." Seeing his bemusement, I tried to coax my foggy brain into producing words that made sense. "Myrddin doesn't have much use for me, and I understand if—"

"Myrddin," he interrupted, eyes narrowing, "allowed me to languish in captivity for fifteen hundred years. You learned of my existence and sought me after a matter of days. I knew he was a coward, but...well, frankly, whatever Myrddin thinks of you is irrelevant, as far as I'm concerned."

The knot in my stomach began to unravel. "Did Marcus tell you that I'm—"

"He mentioned the mixed blood thing. Ridiculous," Artur muttered. "I still can't believe that, in all likelihood, Myrddin bedded a woman of Saxon lineage."

"Which I share," I pointed out.

He smirked. "Forgivable, under the circumstances. But in all sincerity, thank you. I'd rather face the truth than sleep for eternity. Of course, I have nothing to offer you in reward. I seem to have lost a kingdom in the last two days..."

"A sibling would suffice, if that's a possibility."

He regarded me closely, then gave me a slight smile.

"You didn't say 'sister.'"

"That's up to you. I'm just glad you're here." Folding my arms against the cold, I said, "Did Marcus tell you anything about where you are and what's going on?"

"He told me much—I remember most of it, I believe. And…Valerius, was it? He said I'm to begin training this morning."

"I had to go through the same thing. So did Marcus. You're a danger to yourself until you learn some basics."

"That was the impression I got. You know, Myrddin expected me to go back to his island yesterday."

"*Seriously?* Without any instruction?"

"And he seemed perturbed that I was somewhat emotional about a battle that happened two days ago for me. What the hell is wrong with him?"

"He's fae," I replied, shrugging. "I'm sure we have more than a touch of it."

He rolled his eyes and sighed. "Wonderful. So, your mother's a traitor, mine was unfaithful, and you and I share *him*. This family is—"

"Fucked up?"

"I was going to say problematic, but yes, that'll do."

A flash from the corner of my eye heralded Ros's arrival, and Artur jumped when he noticed her. "Give it time, you'll get used to me," she told him. "And stop calling your mother unfaithful. She wasn't."

He frowned at that. "Myrddin told me—"

"Myrddin tells versions of the truth that are convenient for him. But here's the kicker: as long as you're in this realm, *I* know what's in your thoughts. And I can filter through his bullshit with ease." She cut her eyes to me long enough for a blanket to appear around my cold, bare shoulders, then looked back at Artur. "Yes, Uther and Eigyr had trouble conceiving, and yes, it's entirely possible that Uther was infertile. Myrddin gave him some fake magical objects to help the process along, and then, when Eigyr was sleeping alone, he made himself invisible, went to her bed, and forced himself on her."

Artur's face blanched but for twin spots of color on his cheeks. "You're certain?"

"Oh, I'm just getting started. The poor woman couldn't fight him off, and she told Uther that she'd been raped by a demon. Myrddin stepped in to explain to them that the amulets he'd given Uther caused Uther's spirit to leave his body in the night and go to his wife, making his seed all the stronger. So, for the next couple of months, Uther got with Eigyr as often as he could, and Myrddin helped himself until she came up pregnant."

While Artur seethed, I muttered, "What about Mom?"

Ros's expression was almost pitying. "She was willing. A little tipsy, but so was he. But Artur, hear me. As far as Myrddin knows, your mother believed his lie, and she thought she was being faithful. Don't think ill of her now because she was deceived."

I stepped back as tiny flames began to dance around Artur's clenched fists, and Ros pointed to the manifestation of his rage. "Calm down. This is why you're not leaving here without training."

"What if I castrated Myrddin first and returned straightaway?" he replied through clenched teeth.

"Sorry, honey, but *no*. Take a few deep breaths, that seems to help."

He did as instructed, and after a moment, the fire died. "You can't castrate him now, anyway," I said once Artur's rage had cooled to a simmer. "Caledfwlch is gone for repairs. Sorry, I drained it in the Gray Lands."

"Again, forgivable." He squeezed my shoulder, steadying himself, then looked up and realized that Ros had disappeared. "She does that often?"

"Constantly. Privacy is a relative term in Faerie."

Before Artur could comment, the door opened, and Beth, rubbing the streak of dried spit off her face, shuffled out of my room. "Hey," she mumbled, taking us in. "Who's this?"

"Uh...well, this is who I went to the Gray Lands to find," I told her, wishing I knew how much detail Maria had given her. "My other sibling. Artur, this is Beth, my little sister."

They sized each other up briefly, and then Beth, to my surprise, stuck out her hand with semiprofessional courtesy. "Beth Stanhope."

He hesitated, then met her grip. "Artur."

"Just Artur?"

"He doesn't have a surname," I explained, "but if you wanted something a little more formal...Artur Pendragon."

She laughed, waiting for the punchline. "Yeah, right. Very funny."

I met Artur's glance and muttered, "Did Marcus mention—"

"Some of it. He was unsure of the details, but there was something about a grail?"

"Yeah, that's right." Turning back to Beth, I said, "No joke. High king of the Britons until he got shipped off to the Gray Lands. Our father's name is Myrddin—it ended up as 'Merlin' somewhere along the way."

Beth stared at us, still waiting for someone to break, and when no one did, her jaw dropped. "Oh, my God," she whispered. "Oh. My. *God.*"

"Whatever you've been told," said Artur, "I assure you, I'm a disappointment."

She floundered briefly, then squeaked, "I've read *The Once and Future King* seven times. *Seven.* Oh, my God, this...you..."

"Would it help if I told you I pulled a magic sword out of a stone?" I interjected.

Beth shrieked, the kind of high-pitched, higher-decibel sound produced only by teenage girls on the verge of hysterics, and I patted Artur's arm as we flinched. "Well," I said once Beth came up for air, "if nothing else, at least you have a fan."

CHAPTER 15

I accompanied Artur out to the training field as moral support. Though he recognized the necessity of the exercise, he was reticent on the walk, stiff-shouldered and tense, and I suspected that Marcus had given him a preview of what to expect from Mina. Maria had offered to come along and lend a hand, but I'd begged her to stay behind with the others. While I trusted that Hope had sense enough to keep herself out of trouble, it was going to take some convincing, if not strong-arming, to pry Beth away from the object of her awe. Having never had a talk with my sister about her interests that didn't devolve into grunted non-responses or shouting, I'd had no idea that she was *deeply* into all things Arthuriana—that is, as deep as one could go without slogging through Middle English or medieval French. She could rattle off the stories, the players, the convoluted relationships—and poor Artur could only shrug and try to let her down gently. Still, she followed him around until breakfast with stars in her eyes, and it took a distraction from Maria before I was able to sneak him out of the villa.

Mina was waiting for us, chipper and smiling in challenge. "I do so love fresh meat," she announced as we neared. "This is going to be delightful." She produced a bronze sword from the ether and extended it to Artur, then pulled her own free from its place at her hip. "Let's warm up. I hear you're an adept of sorts."

"Some would say," he replied, taking his stance and watching her warily.

"Shall we test that? Kitty, move out of striking range."

To his credit, Artur was quick and light on his feet, able to parry without losing his balance and almost preternaturally aware of the trajectory of the incoming strikes. But Mina, even to my layman's eye, was *scary*. She barely broke a sweat as she brushed off his attacks, maintaining her Cheshire-cat grin all the while, then moved for the kill and sent Artur tumbling onto his back, disarmed. "Get up," she said, stepping back while he scrambled for his footing and his blade. "Again. That last attack of yours was sloppy."

Around and around they went, thrusting and parrying until both were red-faced and Artur was surely bruised from making repeated contact with the ground. Mina called a halt and underhanded him a bottle of water, and once he figured out the cap, he drained it and wiped the fresh sweat from his eyes, panting. "Impressive," he said as she drank. "I thought myself to be nearly a master, but you—"

"Have been doing this for a long time," she interrupted. "You're quite good, child, particularly for your age. A natural, I would think. Give yourself a few decades of practice, and you'll be my equal."

"I was handed a sword at two," he protested. "This has been my life, and *you*…"

She smiled to herself at his frustration. "How old are you? Not actually," she amended before he could panic at the calculation, "but in your head."

"Twenty-five."

Mina folded her arms. "Oh, you're a *babe*. I've been doing this for more than twelve centuries. Don't be so disappointed."

Having heard what Marcus had gone through, I'd expected Mina to rub Artur's face in his defeat, but she did nothing of the sort. "Now, I know a fair bit about magic as well," she continued, chucking him a towel. "And I think you may be trainable. Let me guide you through this, hmm? It will hurt, but you'll be stronger for it."

He nodded, and while he rested and cleaned himself up, she pulled me aside. "That was all the breaking he needed," she murmured. "Just enough to show him that I have skills he lacks. Don't fret so much, this won't be a bloodbath."

"He's only just awakened, and—"

"I'm well aware. Valerius told me the basics, and Ros filled in the rest. I assure you, I'm not going to crush Artur, if you'd rather go back to the house. You may stay," she added, "but try to keep clear. I'm assuming that whatever he knows of enchantment is rudimentary."

Once Artur had caught his breath and hydrated, Mina beckoned him closer and took a long, hard look at him. "First thing," she said, "that bind has to go." Artur stepped back, but she pressed on. "You're starting from basics. I don't need a complex enchantment potentially interfering while you sort yourself out, understood?"

"I'll take the risk—"

"*No*, you won't. Don't be stupid. This isn't life or death, it's…"—she flipped one hand dismissively— "cosmetic. And for training purposes, it's coming off."

Artur began to protest, but Mina's impassive face made it clear that further argument would not be tolerated. He took a deep breath, gave her a last, uncertain glance, then scrunched his eyes shut and waited.

"It won't hurt," Mina assured him, then effortlessly overloaded the bind until it crumbled.

And there was Artur—the version I'd seen in the Gray Lands. Though she was as muscular as she'd been seconds before, she'd lost a couple of inches and was now roughly my height, with the same whitish-blonde hair still tied back with a thong. Her eyes, though, were blue and nervous, and she started to unconsciously hug herself before she felt small breasts and jerked her arms away.

Mina inspected the result. "Not bad. And *there's* the familial resemblance. I'd wondered."

Artur looked at me inquisitively—and yes, with trepidation. "We've both got Myrddin's coloring, more or less," I explained.

She took a tentative test step, realized that her clothing was now too long, and knelt to roll up her trousers. "I hope you're happy," she started to say, then froze. "My voice. What did you…"

Her baritone had risen an octave, still lower than mine but definitely female. "Part of the bind," said Mina, unbothered as Artur quietly panicked. "Don't tell me you've never taken it off." Artur shook her head, and Mina's eyes widened. "Truly? Not once?"

"No," she muttered.

"You weren't even curious?"

Cuffs adjusted, she stood and planted her hands on her slim hips. "Tell me, how am I supposed to be a king looking like *this*?"

"Myrddin put the bind on at birth," I quietly interjected. "And he put it back together before Artur woke, so…"

I left that thought unfinished, hoping for mercy, but Mina was unmoved. "Interesting. Well, then, Artur, you may have your security blanket back once you learn to remake it. Until then…do yourself a favor and find a mirror. Really, you could be *so* much worse."

Mina worked Artur until sunset while I stood by with water and sweat towels. Artur didn't complain, even when Mina hit hard, and she made good progress, but as Mina called a halt, she frowned with worry. "You still haven't taught me to replace the bind," she pointed out.

Mina drank and rubbed a kink out of her shoulder. "So I haven't."

"Teach me, then."

"You're exhausted, and binds are complicated. Maybe tomorrow."

"But—"

"Not now, child."

As Mina returned to her quarters in Coileán's palace, Artur limped back to the villa with me. "What am I to do?" she mumbled. "Can you—"

"I can't work a bind like that—I'm still too young. Sorry."

She sighed softly. "It's not your fault."

While we walked, I concentrated on Artur's soaked tunic, which morphed into an oversized hooded sweatshirt. She paused, saw what I had done, and raised the hood with a grateful smile. "Beth will be *so* disappointed," she said.

I chuckled and flung my arm over her shoulders. "Let me worry about Beth. I'll bring dinner to your room—that way, you won't have to deal with anyone tonight if you don't want to."

"Thank you."

"I mean, if you *want* to come hang out, you're welcome, but I understand."

The invitation was accepted politely but without enthusiasm. "Perhaps sleep would be best."

"Sure," I replied, and hustled her in through a side door. With Artur settled, I stopped by the kitchens, begged Val's cook for an early helping of the meal on offer, and slipped back into my sibling's bedroom through the adjoining garden. "Smells like beef," I announced, uncovering the tray. "And if you don't want that cake, let me know now. I'll gladly spoil my dinner with German chocolate."

Artur frowned at the plate, tasted a small bite, then shook her head. "No, this is mine. Nice try, Kitty."

"Can't blame you." I gave the room a cursory inspection—rumpled bed, half-full pitcher of water sitting on the floor, an untouched flagon of mead on the table—and waited as Artur sat to eat, still sporting her hoodie. "Do you want company?"

She hesitated, knife raised over the meat. "No, thank you."

Dismissed, I joined the others for dinner—Beth was by turns disappointed not to see Artur and frightened to see Val—then retired to my room with Marcus, slightly sunburned from my day outside and bone-weary. Maria dragged Beth back to Arc 1, promising to retrieve her if Lancelot should surface, and Frank took Hope into one of the many sitting rooms to teach her to play cards. As I stretched out beside Marcus, who spooned behind me in the darkness, I murmured, "Thank you. Whatever you did yesterday with Artur—thanks."

"Of course." He inched closer until I could feel his breath on my neck. "I'm always up for getting drunk for a good cause."

"*Marcus.*"

He laughed softly and wrapped one arm over my waist. "I've missed you."

I rolled over and found him giving me a look that meant only one thing. "Missed you, too," I whispered, and kissed him.

But before we could get too comfortable, someone knocked, and I hastily threw my T-shirt back on as Marcus groaned his disappointment. "Coming," I called, feeling my way toward the door, and threw it open, expecting to see well-meaning Maria in the corridor.

The woman waiting outside was a slender redhead with brilliant green eyes, wearing a pale blue tunic over white leggings, and after seeing me, sporting a knowing grin. "Ooh...am I interrupting?"

"Lady Eleanor," I said, retreating a step into my room, and glanced down to find that my shirt was both inside-out and backward. "Uh...sorry, no, just, uh...changing clothes."

"*Right,*" she replied, and waved over my shoulder. "Hello, Marcus. Just a minute, I'll have her back soon enough."

Blushing, I willed my clothing straight, then joined the queen in the hall and closed the door. "Can I help you, my lady?"

She clasped her hands and smiled. "Where's Artur?"

Eleanor was looking at me like I might be hiding Artur in my back pocket with a bottle of tequila, a box of chocolate truffles, and a male stripper in a birthday cake. I recalled that in a previous life, she'd been a professor of British history, and I did my best to prevent another Beth-level freak-out. "Artur's had a long day, you know, Mina worked her half to death—"

"Yes, Coileán gave me the condensed version. Where is she?"

Suspecting that the queen was not to be denied, I reluctantly led her to Artur's room and knocked. After a moment, the door cracked open, giving me a glimpse of one blue eye through the gap. "Hey, sorry," I said, keeping my tone light, "Lady Eleanor is here, and she'd like to—"

"I'm here to help," said Eleanor, breezing past me into the room. Artur moved aside to admit her, then latched the door behind us as Eleanor took in the mess. "Oh, pet, this *is* depressing," she said, then gestured the bedroom tidy and pulled out one of the pair of chairs. "Right, then. Let's have a look at you."

Still hooded, Artur kept her distance from the queen and tucked her hands into the sweatshirt's pouch.

"No?" said Eleanor. "Would you prefer this, then?"

The redheaded woman was gone in the space of a blink, replaced by a black-haired man with a handlebar mustache, a dark green turtleneck, and a tweed blazer. "Simple, really," he said, his voice dark and rich enough to give Frank's rumbling bass a run for its money. "It's called glamour, child. I trust that Mina didn't mention it."

Goggling, Artur managed, "How...the bind—"

"No bind at all." Eleanor stood, did a slow twirl, then tucked his hands into the pockets of his pleated trousers and grinned. "Personal glamour. An illusion you control, indistinguishable from reality to all the senses *and* electronics, which, let me tell you, came as a relief." Artur stared at Eleanor blankly, and the queen waved the matter aside. "Easy to manipulate," he continued, instantly going bald and paunchy, then reed-thin and blond. "And vastly simpler than working up a bind. Don't get me wrong, binds are useful things, but it's best to go to the trouble only when you're trying to disguise someone else."

"Or shrink Frank," I added.

"Or that. For daily use, though, glamour's all you need." Eleanor shrugged and watched Artur struggle as Eleanor flicked through several faces and forms. "As solid as your true body, and able to work in the fashion to which you've grown accustomed. I can't tell you how many partners I've bedded glamoured in this fashion, and none were the wiser."

"You…um…"

Eleanor smiled in conspiracy. "I could drop trou, if you don't believe me, or you can trust me that the equipment is as expected. Somewhat desensitized, but that's a matter of preference. I've never seen the benefit in walking about with a target between one's legs."

While Artur continued to grapple with the spectacle before her, Eleanor took her hands and slouched to look her in the eye. "Mina is brilliant at what she does," he said gently, "but in this case, I thought someone should step in. You have enough on your mind without being trapped in a body you don't know."

Relief washed across Artur's face. "You can teach me this?"

"Heavens, yes. Come to the mirror, let me show you…"

I stood aside and watched as Eleanor guided Artur through the basics of glamours. Artur tensed every time she had to stare at her reflection, but I couldn't blame her. Piece by piece, Eleanor helped Artur put herself back together, and then there were two men before the mirror, one with a knowing smirk and the other seemingly poised to kiss the glass with joy. "There," said Eleanor, patting Artur's shoulder. "Feel better?"

"Much," he replied, his voice once again in its deeper register.

"Good." Eleanor's glamour evaporated, and she waited while Artur took a few tentative steps around the room, readjusting. "If you choose to keep up that glamour, I understand. I've spent most of my life as a man."

Artur stopped in his tracks and stared at her. "I'm sorry, *what*?"

"Necessity, you see. Until recently, a woman's options were limited. I was born in the mortal realm and spent seven hundred years there—I *had* to disguise myself. Went into academia, went into commerce, bought property, married heiresses and younger daughters, was intimate with my share of them…I've lived many lives, most of them in a body rather different to the one into which I was born. But society finally started to evolve, I fell in love with a man, and I let myself be myself with him. Such a liberating experience, though honestly, I'd almost forgotten by then how it felt to be female. It comes back to you—not all at once, but you can stumble your way through it." She crossed her legs and propped her arm on the table. "What I'm saying is that I'd encourage you to experiment. Play with your glamour until you find something that makes you comfortable. Not tonight, of course," she hastened to add, "but once you've begun to sort the rest of your life…think about it. You're no less *you* because of the face you wear. Now, if I were you, I'd retire. Mina won't be any kinder in the morning than she was today."

Eleanor was on her way out when Artur said, "Thank you. How can I repay you?"

She turned back to him and grinned. "Once you've finished with Mina…come have tea with me some afternoon, won't you? I have *loads* of questions."

The queen saw herself out, and Artur stripped off the sweatshirt and ran his hands over his flatter pecs and returned beard. "You heard her," I teased, turning the sweatshirt back into a tunic. "Don't stay up all night ogling yourself."

He smirked and made a shooing motion, and I returned to find my room as I'd left it, except that Marcus was out cold. I slid in beside him, kissed his brow, and, more at peace than I'd been in weeks, fell into a dreamless sleep.

While I'd decided to accompany Artur out for the second day of training, my plans were derailed before I'd had my first cup of coffee.

As I settled in at the dawn breakfast spread—Val, ever the gracious host, had instructed the kitchen staff to see to our needs, no matter at what ungodly hour we slunk in—I caught the flash of an opening gate in the courtyard through the door. I could just make out the contours of Vivi's office before she, one of her many brothers—I could never keep them all straight—and a black woman in an orange windbreaker slipped through. The newcomer was no stranger. "Yolanda!" I called, waving to get her attention. "Hi, over here!"

Yolanda Ford, a settlement-born Fringer who'd returned to the mortal realm to pursue archaeology and her PhD, had recently become the Fringe coordinator for the Americas on top of her other duties. Though her parents were American-born Fringer refugees, she spoke English with a faint accent, unidentifiable unless one knew what the settlement patois sounded like. While Fae was the lingua franca of the Fringe town, the first-generation settlers had, naturally, taught their children their native languages, and kids being kids, they'd been happy to share with each other.

I'd crossed paths with Yolanda on several occasions in

the last year, but it was strange seeing her in Faerie. Though only in her mid-thirties, she appeared to be older than everyone around her, the unfortunate side effect of leaving the realm and losing its time-freezing qualities.

"Morning!" she said, crossing the courtyard with long strides. "It *is* morning, right?"

I lifted my coffee as proof. "Hungry?"

"Eh, why not?"

Tall, lanky, and blessed with the metabolism of a marathoner, Yolanda seldom turned down a meal, even if her body clock was surely confused. She pulled up a chair and helped herself to toast, but she pushed her plate to the side and gave her computer pride of place on the table. "Found your Hayleigh Lozano. Where's the Gray Lander?"

I ran to fetch Hope, who practically sprinted back to the dining room, her new bathrobe flapping behind her like a cape. "You found Mama?" she demanded, not bothering with the trivialities of introductions.

But Yolanda didn't seem offended by Hope's single-mindedness—and if she was unnerved to be in proximity to a cynaeli, she didn't let on. "We don't have recent visual confirmation, but she's in our files. Take a seat, I'll give you our notes."

Hope dropped into the chair opposite Yolanda's, as taut as if she were poised to leap across the table.

Yolanda accepted a cup of coffee from Vivi, then turned her attention to her computer and began scrolling. "The Fringe keeps an ear to the ground at all times. If something weird arises, we need to know whether it's dangerous, yeah?"

Hope nodded expectantly.

"There's a team back here that does a lot of the initial research for us—the web searches and such." She flipped the computer around to show Hope a saved story. "Look familiar?"

The picture showed a tanned teenage girl with large

brown eyes, her dark hair pulled into a high ponytail with a ribbon. She was dressed in a green cheerleading uniform and appeared to have her arms wrapped around other girls, who'd been partially cropped from the photo.

Hope's face split in a smile of pure joy. "That's Mama! That's her, you found her! Is she in Oklahoma?"

"Her last address is." Yolanda took her computer back and scanned her notes. "Approximately twenty-two years ago, Hayleigh Lozano went missing from the town of Pauline, Oklahoma. It's basically the nexus of a bunch of farms in the northeastern part of the state—a wide blip in the road with a main street and some municipal services. From the looks of it, the Lozanos were a prominent family. Adam Lozano was one of maybe three doctors in town—one of these guys might actually have been a dentist—and Jessica Hogan-Lozano was a realtor and four-term mayor. Hayleigh was their only child."

She tapped at the screen, then turned it to Hope again, revealing a missing person poster. "When she was sixteen, Hayleigh went for a walk after school and never came home. The sheriff's dogs tracked her to a wooded area where the kids hid out to smoke and drink, but the trail went cold. There was a three-state manhunt, national alert, the whole deal. Hayleigh was, by all accounts, a good kid, so her parents believed she'd been abducted—she wouldn't have run away. They put up a massive reward for her return, but no one had any leads."

Yolanda pulled up a different photo: still Hayleigh, but older and looking disoriented. "Seven years later, a young woman walked into a police station in Miami and said she'd been kidnapped. That's Miami, *Florida*—fifteen hundred miles away. They checked her prints, called her parents, and the Lozanos had their reunion at the hospital. Hayleigh was fine physically, but it seems she had a mental breakdown."

Hope cocked her head. "Breakdown?"

"They thought she'd gone crazy," Yolanda explained.

"Her parents and the authorities were trying to figure out what had happened to her, and Hayleigh was telling them she'd been abducted by purple humanoids and held as a sex slave. When you don't know that there are multiple realms, that sounds absolutely insane."

"Oh," Hope mumbled, her shoulders hunching.

"*Yeah.* Apparently, she insisted that she'd had a baby, and that the purple people had kept her. She said she could speak their language, and of course, that was no known human language, so there's another point in the 'crazy' column. Physical exam revealed that she had indeed given birth at some point, but that was all."

I cleared my throat. "How do you know all of...*this?*"

The corner of Yolanda's mouth ticked, but she didn't smile. "As I said, there's a team back here that looks for the weird reports. Hayleigh's case pinged on someone's radar, and they saved all of the stories from the reputable sites and the gossip rags, then hacked into the hospital's system to pull her chart. *Hospitals*, I should say. She was transported back to Tulsa and held on a psych ward for months. Intensive therapy and antipsychotics until she was cured of her delusions. Her doctors' conclusion was that she was kidnapped by *someone*, and the experience was so traumatic that she severed contact with reality as a defense mechanism. Might be plausible if you didn't know better. But more to the point," she told me, "when someone starts talking about being taken by purple people to a place where the sun never shines, the Fringe pays attention."

Although she'd been ebullient moments before, Hope seemed to sink into herself as Yolanda spoke. "Mama's not crazy," she murmured.

"Undoubtedly," Yolanda replied. "But she's had a rough go of it. We've kept tabs..." Again, she consulted her notes. "Still lives in Pauline as of her last income taxes. Her parents died a few years ago—he went by stroke, she had an aggressive cancer. Never married, no known children. She's a small-business owner—a store called

Tequila Sunrise—and I've got the address, but that's all."

Hope hesitated, then spoke slowly, as if forcing the words out. "Do you think that Mama…that she wouldn't want to…to see me?"

Yolanda's face moved into a quick grimace before softening. "Hard to say, kid. From the sound of things, she was desperate to find you in the beginning, but then she went in for treatment. Seeing you might make her happy, relieved, vindicated…or it could be the most traumatic thing to happen to her in years. I'm no expert. There are counselors in town, you might check with them—"

"Probably better if she doesn't go back there," Vivi interjected.

She rolled her dark eyes and snorted. "*Jesus.* People can deal with themselves—what's *she* going to do?"

"Kip has strong sentiments."

"Yeah, well, this is friggin' Faerie. Remind him that no one's coming after him and tell him to get over it. And don't tell me I'm young," she added as Vivi patted her shoulder. "You're just set in your ways."

"Respect your elders," Vivi replied primly, but there was fondness in her tone.

Yolanda turned back to Hope, who was looking more unsettled by the minute. "I hate to be the bearer of bad news, I really do, but that's the truth of the matter. She might be thrilled to see you, or she might end up checking herself into the hospital to have her meds reupped." Hope stared at her lap and raked her teeth over her lip, and Yolanda pushed her computer away to reach across the table. "Hey, look at me."

She slowly lifted her watery eyes, and Yolanda beckoned until she gave the coordinator her hand. "Don't think I introduced myself. I'm Yolanda. What's your name, anyway?"

"Hope," she whispered.

"*Hope?*"

"Imaranta, if you prefer. Mama called me Hope."

A strange, sad smile creased Yolanda's face. "You know what that means?" The younger woman nodded—I *had* given her English, after all—and Yolanda's smile widened. "I'm not even going to pretend that I have the first clue what Imaranta means, but if your mother called you Hope, that probably wasn't a fluke. The baby she had in captivity...maybe she had hope for both of you."

Hope's tears began to fall, and Yolanda squeezed her hand. "Chin up, girl. Whatever happened to Hayleigh wasn't your fault, you know."

"But if she doesn't want to see me—"

"We don't know that for sure."

"We could go scope it out today," I offered. "Work up a glamour for you, have a look around Pauline, and if you want to approach her, we can do that."

Hope wiped her free hand over her eyes. "A glamour?"

"You're pretty," said Yolanda, "but if you went walking down the street, it would be a disaster. Folks in the mortal realm don't have skin that color...and they normally have ten fingers, not eight," she added, glancing at Hope's hand. "Can you do glamour?"

She nodded. "But not here. Nothing works here—"

"Lack of dark magic. There's probably enough across the border to do you, and if there isn't..."

"I can handle it," I told her.

Yolanda started to question that, then raised her eyebrows and mouthed a silent *Oh*. "Forgot about you. You're in control of your talent?"

"Sufficiently."

"Good. I don't need anything magical on my turf to explain away, got it?"

"Understood," I said, and looked up at the sound of footsteps to see Artur in the doorway—surprisingly, unglamoured. "Did it fall apart?" I asked, rising to hurry her out of the room if she needed help.

But Artur stood her ground. "No. I dropped it for training—there's nothing to be gained by depriving Mina of her fun, is there? And I smell meat," she said, her eyes lighting with a hungry gleam as she slid past me, but she stopped when she saw Yolanda. "Ah. Another Roman?"

Yolanda's brow furrowed. "No...why would you think—"

"Because she's a fifth-century Briton," I interjected. "Sorry. Did Vivi not mention anything about it?"

"I didn't know how quiet we were keeping this," Vivi replied. "Yolanda, this is Artur. She spent the last millennium and a half unconscious in the Gray Lands."

"*Damn*," she muttered, and whistled low. "To answer your question," she told Artur, "my ancestry is mostly sub-Saharan African, but my parents are American...and you have no idea what any of that means," she said, watching Artur's expression. "Is someone going to give her the short course, or what?"

"Marcus told me much," Artur began, but Yolanda smacked her forehead.

"Blind leading the blind. Can you read?"

Artur shrugged. "The Roman tongue, yes. My, uh...*advisor* thought it useful."

"Mm. Well," she replied, biting into her neglected toast, "*someone* is going to have her homework cut out for her. Hope you like history."

I might have imagined it, but I thought I caught a flash of anxiety from Artur—quickly subdued—when I informed her that I wouldn't be along for training that day. "I owe this much to Hope," I explained, catching her up. "Not sure how this is going to go, but I should be back in a few hours, regardless."

"You're certain?"

There it was again, the ripple beneath the stoic façade, and sensing the cause, I almost asked Hope to postpone. Of course Artur was anxious—she'd been stranded in a foreign land and left at Mina's mercy, and now, one of the few people with whom she'd spent any time was going away. "I promise," I told her, trying to sound reassuring. "And Marcus knows how to reach me in case of emergency. You have fun without me, okay?"

"Yes, *fun*," she muttered, but walked off to face Mina alone.

With that sorted, I waited as Hope cleaned up and packed her few belongings, then opened a gate into my quiet flat. "After you."

She stepped through the rift and examined my den while I closed the gate behind us. I thought she was trying to puzzle out the mystery of the television hanging on the wall until I saw a glowing orb manifest over her hand. "Not as much, but enough," she said, and sighed with relief.

"You can see dark magic, huh? The raw stuff?"

She nodded, and the orb disintegrated. "Why do you call it dark?"

"Because…well, for one, it's darker than magic," I said, hearing how lame that sounded. "You know, magic is iridescent, and dark magic is just…dark. Like smoke."

Hope regarded me strangely. "Just the opposite, don't you mean?"

"Huh?"

"The magic I use…it's brilliant to my eyes, vivid, colorful. *Your* magic looks like dark fog." She dropped her bag beside the couch and shrugged. "All things relative, I suppose. Now, what am I to do with glamour?"

I led her into my bathroom, and together, we came up with a passable illusion. Overall, Hope didn't have to change much—her skin tone shifted toward her mother's deep olive complexion, and she sprouted extra digits to make up the difference—and when we'd finished, she looked sufficiently human, a black-haired young woman with striking blue eyes. I put together an outfit for her that could have come from a high-street shop, jeans and a flowing pink shirt with cute yet sensible flats, then checked the time. "Slight problem," I told Hope. "Faerie's about two hours ahead of here right now. Glastonbury is...six hours ahead of Pauline, I think, so it's still the middle of the night in your mom's neck of the woods."

That concept made little sense to someone who had never dealt with the nuisance of time zones, which detoured into a discussion of astronomy and the oddity of seasonal time shifts. With hours to kill, I settled Hope on the couch with old science documentaries while I located my computer and attended to my neglected inbox—menus from the Arc 2 dining hall, notices about social clubs and the castle's coed football league, scheduling reminders from Lakshmi, job openings at other installations, and one of the usual vague messages from security that never named names but hinted at idiocy. This time, it was a gentle reminder to conduct one's hookup at a hotel instead of trying to sneak a drunk mundane into the castle.

The morning dragged, and with every passing episode, Hope seemed to grow glummer. I put out lunch, but she barely touched a bite. "Eat something," I urged, taking a seat beside her. "Your mom's shop probably doesn't open until nine or ten, so we'll be here until midafternoon. You don't want to be cranky from hunger, do you?"

She gave in and reached for a piece of bread, but she paused before she could touch it. "Maybe we shouldn't do this," she mumbled.

"Why not? It's what you came here to do," I countered, trying to sound more optimistic than I felt. "We'll pop over, take a look around, see if we can't find her, and if you want—"

"Yolanda said she was a sex slave." Hope spoke just above a whisper and stared at her lap. "I knew she didn't come to Father willingly, but once she became one of his concubines, I...I suppose I thought she was like the others. She would have been happier as a wife, but there are many concubines of status, and..." She paused, then risked a glance at me. "Is that what you think of concubines? Be honest."

I thought of a dozen tactful ways to answer that question, but I settled on the truth. "If you're forced into a sexual relationship against your will and not allowed to leave, then yeah, that's sex slavery. What your father did to your mother, that's a crime here. And she was only sixteen when she was kidnapped—she would have missed finishing high school, going to university, starting her career..." Thinking of what Hayleigh must have endured made me shudder. "I mean, maybe I'm reading too much into this, but the fact that she's still alone could mean any number of things. She might actually like being single, or maybe no one wants to be with the crazy girl...or she may have been so traumatized by her time in the Gray Lands that she can't bring herself to be with anyone. But all of that aside, Hope, you should at least try. We can find her and take it from there."

Hope said nothing for a long moment, then murmured, "What if she doesn't want me?"

Welcome to the club was on the tip of my tongue, but I bit it back. "Disappointing, but not the end of the world."

"Where will I go?" she pressed, picking up speed. "I have nothing here, I know no one, I can't even show my face. And I can't go back to Faerie—there's no magic for me, so I'd be at everyone's mercy."

"Not in the settlement."

"Oh, yes, because I was *so* well received there. They probably all think I'm some sort of monster." She pulled her feet onto the couch and tucked her knees to her chin. "And I can't go home. I *won't* go home," she insisted. "I don't want to be with Warohn. He might not even have me now, not after what we did with Artur..." Glaring at the coffee table, she said, "If he won't take me, then Father will be shamed. If I won't have him, then Father will be shamed. Either way, Father will be furious with me, and he might give me to someone...unpleasant. Maybe give me to the brothel as punishment."

I rubbed her shoulder in reassurance. "You're not going back there, I swear. Look, let's not start catastrophizing until we have to, eh? Cross those bridges as we come to them."

Hope sighed, her eyes troubled. "If you like."

"Food?"

She accepted the sandwich I made for her, but she barely nibbled on it as the afternoon passed.

Around four, with Hope by turns pacing the flat and curled into a ball on the couch, I found a selection of street-level images of Pauline and decided where we could land with the least chance of scaring anyone to death. "All right," I said, moving the computer into the middle of the den, "do you want to do this?"

Hope wavered, then screwed up her face as if she were preparing for a blow and nodded. "Might as well, right?"

"That's the spirit." Keeping my eyes on the screen, I concentrated on the picture of a narrow alley between two brick early-twentieth-century buildings, then willed the gate open. To my relief—and yeah, my continued surprise—the alley appeared on the far side of the gate, and I hustled Hope through before she could get cold feet.

I'd anticipated heat—we were a week from July, after all—but not precipitation. We stepped out from my comfortable, climate-controlled flat into a sixty-degree morning with heavy rain, and I was soaked before I managed to produce umbrellas from the ether. With the gate closed and the coast clear, I enchanted us both dry, and we huddled together by a ripe-smelling Dumpster to contemplate the empty, wet sidewalk.

There were cars in the diagonal spaces along both sides of Main Street, a good sign, but no one was crazy enough to be out walking among the two- and three-story shops, architectural remnants of a time when local commerce was everything. Water pooled in the depressions around the bases of the trees pocking the sidewalks and flooded the flower boxes with their anemic vegetation. A small river flowed through the gutter and made rapids around the litter, giving anyone coming in from a car the option of fording it and drenching their shoes or jumping across like an ungainly gazelle. The sky was leaden but for the occasional distant flash of lightning—and from the sound of the thunder, the worst of the storm was coming out way.

Hope slouched beside me, her clothes dampening with the blown rain. "Are we close?"

I stuck my head out of the alley and pointed to the orange awning two doors down. "Right there. Come on, let's get out of this mess."

We hurried through the storm, my blue leather shoes darkening to black as I navigated the puddles on the uneven sidewalk, and then we reached the shelter of the awning and leaned our umbrellas against the fogged window to drip off. Giving Hope a last smile, I opened the door and squelched inside, and she followed on my heels into the store.

Tequila Sunrise's trade seemed to be in equal parts whimsy, sauciness, bar accessories, and scented bath paraphernalia. A planter in the shape of a plastic flamingo guarded the door, a slightly sallow peace lily erupting from the cavity in its back. Strings of colorful Christmas lights hung from and among the arms of a trio of mismatched chandeliers. No two walls were painted the same color— one red, one pink, one yellow, the last an earthier peach around the door and window—but the warped hardwood floors suggested that the building had once sported a more conservative appearance. Tables of various shapes, sizes, and pedigrees dotted the floor; a card table draped with a picnic blanket offered an array of koozies, decorated wineglasses, and packaged beverage napkins, while a former dining room table played host to a selection of cheeky wooden signs, the sort over which one would titter, then buy only as gifts. A sky-blue bookshelf beside it held lotions, soaps, and a metal ice tub full of fragrant bath bombs wrapped in pink tissue paper and labeled with the names of fruity cocktails. Across the room, a reclaimed piece of iron pipe ran the length of the store, serving as a clothes rack for vaguely boho blouses and trousers. An oversized fabric-covered tack board hung nearby, displaying necklaces and earrings on pushpins.

I was investigating the offerings in the glass case near the front—more expensive jewelry, from the look of it— when one of the pink velvet curtains in the back wall stirred and parted as a woman emerged carrying a large glass bowl full of cans of flavored seltzer. "Morning, y'all!" she called as she lugged her burden toward the front, skirting a three-legged table of picture frames and a leaning pile of shoeboxes topped with a marabou-bedecked mule. "Heck of a storm, isn't it? Are y'all just soaked?"

The woman's face was softer and fuller than the cheerleader's had been, but she was unmistakably the same person—Hayleigh Lozano, now in her late thirties, her thick black hair threaded with silver strands that glimmered in the light. She sported a white cotton blouse over tailored jeans, the colors far too muted for the warm extravagance of the shop and its wares, but her carnelian-studded drop earrings brought a touch of brightness to her look.

"Just drippy," I replied. "You've got some fun things in here."

Partly hidden behind a display of candles, Hope looked on with wide, unreadable eyes.

"Thanks!" said Hayleigh, flashing a cheery smile. "Help yourself to something to drink while you look around. Y'all visiting?"

"Passing through," I said, trying to inject a touch more of my childhood drawl into my accent.

"Gotcha. Bad day to go shopping, though."

"On the plus side, we have the place to ourselves," I countered.

"True. Still…" She glanced past me at the cloud-covered sky and grimaced. "I hate days like this. Got to have my sunshine, you know? Probably should have set up in San Diego." Grinning at her own joke, she removed a half-empty tray of necklaces from the glass cabinet and opened a small carton on the counter, from which she pulled a dozen bubble-wrapped bundles. "Let me know if I can help you with anything," she said, attacking the packaging with a pair of scissors. "Take your time, and if you have any questions, I'll be right here. Honestly, with the amount of padding these folks put on their jewelry, you'd think they were shipping them by cannon."

While Hayleigh worked, I maneuvered around the store to Hope, who stood behind a display of margarita kits, breathing rapidly. *Okay?* I asked.

Her head barely dipped. *That's Mama.*

I know. Are you okay? We don't have to do this right now. There's no rush.

But the sheen of desperation in Hope's eyes told me there would be no second attempt. Brushing past me, she made a beeline for the glass cabinet, and I rushed toward the door, ready to step in.

Hayleigh looked up from her unwrapping with polite interest as Hope neared. "Something you'd like to see?" she enquired, putting the scissors aside.

Hope swallowed hard, her hands clenching in nervous fists, then whispered, "Mama."

The woman frowned. "Come again?"

"Mama," she said more insistently. "Mama, it's me. It's Hope."

Hayleigh stepped back from the counter, the blood draining from her face. "You...I think you've got me confused with someone else..."

"It's *me*, Mama," Hope pleaded. "I've wanted to find you for so long, I—"

"Stop. You're mistaken—"

Whatever else Hayleigh would have said was drowned in the torrent that came pouring from Hope—excited, yearning, and all of it unintelligible to me, though I thought I detected a glimmer of comprehension on Hayleigh's face before she covered her ears and squished her eyes closed. "Not real, not real, just your mind, it's not real," she muttered like a spell, doing her best to block her daughter out.

Hope fell silent, her face crumbling, and then she unclasped her necklace chain. "*Remember me,*" she begged, then pulled one of Hayleigh's hands down and pressed the turquoise heart into her palm. "Please, Mama, please remember me…"

Hayleigh dropped the pendant onto the glass like a burning coal, and Hope, eyes brimming, retreated from the counter. "Come on, hon," I coaxed, gripping Hope's wrist, and she let me lead her out of the store. I opened both of our umbrellas, fit one into Hope's hand, and wrapped my free arm around her, steering her down the street. "It's going to be all right," I said, raising my voice to be heard over the incessant patter of the rain. "Let's go back, we'll regroup, we'll figure something out…"

But Hope couldn't go any farther. She stood beneath a dripping tree and wept, shaking with hitching sobs, and I hugged her as well as I could, considering the unwieldy umbrellas. I didn't need to look at her mind to see her heartbreak—I'd cried like that, and I knew too intimately the wrenching pain of rejection. "This is not the end," I said as she clung to my shoulder. "And it's not about you. Let me take you somewhere dry—"

"*Imaranta!*"

We turned at the shout to find Hayleigh standing beneath the awning of her store, the silver chain of Hope's necklace dangling from her tight fist. Hope straightened, wiped her sleeve across her face, and called, "Mama?"

Hayleigh let out a strangled cry somewhere between a gasp and a sob, then ran toward us through the pouring rain. She threw her arms around Hope, who dropped her umbrella in surprise, and they clung together, crying and talking over each other. I did my best to keep the three of us dry, and after a few minutes, Hayleigh cupped Hope's face in her palms and stared at her as if witnessing a miracle. "Hope, baby?" she murmured, and hiccupped. "You're really here?"

Dripping but laughing, Hope nodded and put her hands over her mother's. "Howdy, Mama. I missed you."

Hayleigh had barely locked up and flipped the store's sign to CLOSED before she had us in her Volvo, heading out of town to a renovated two-story farmhouse on several acres. Hope rode shotgun, and mother and daughter kept their hands entwined for the duration of the journey.

After warning Hayleigh not to panic, I willed the three of us dry again, and we settled around her rustic kitchen table with glasses of iced tea. I didn't want to intrude—and in truth, given Hope's tendency to segue into her native language, I couldn't follow half of what was said—but I remained on hand to fill in the gaps as Hope recounted how we'd come to be in Pauline. "The Fringe is there if you want them," I told Hayleigh, copying Yolanda's number onto a scrap of paper. "Few of them have any experience in the Gray Lands, but you've been in their files for some time, and if you need help, you can turn to them."

She took the paper from me, scanned it, and smoothed it flat on her placemat. "They almost had me convinced that I was crazy," she murmured, and Hope reached over to stroke her arm. "All my doctors...the pills...the looks people still give me when they think I don't notice..." She laughed weakly and lifted her tea with a tinkle of ice cubes against glass. "Part of me believed them. Part still wants to."

Hope waited until she had slaked her thirst, then softly said, "I'm sorry, Mama."

Hayleigh's dark eyes widened, and she gripped Hope's

hands in hers. "No, baby, *no*. None of this is your fault." She lifted Hope's hands and kissed her bent fingers, then stroked her daughter's cheek. "You look...different...than I'd expected."

"Glamour," Hope explained. "Kitty said I'd cause a scene otherwise. I could drop it, if you want, but—"

"Show me."

She hesitated only a moment before allowing the illusion to fall away. I'd expected to see a sign of fear from Hayleigh—nothing like having *those* old memories dredged up—but instead, she smiled and leaned over to kiss Hope's forehead. "*There's* my pretty girl," Hayleigh said, studying her violet features. "I was wondering what had happened, if your father..."

Though Hayleigh's voice trailed off, Hope seemed to know where her thought had been going. "No, he hasn't abused me—he's not cruel to any of his likdenfi. But..." She hesitated, then explained in a rush why she had come when she did: how her father had arranged for her to go to Warohn, and then how she and I had run off with her intended's prized toy. "Even if he would have me now, I don't want to be Warohn's concubine," she said. "Could I stay with you? Please? I could tend your herds—"

"Not here, you can't," I interrupted. Hope regarded me quizzically, and I explained, "Animals in this realm are sensitive. They don't like faeries, and I think Kip had trouble with them as well."

"I could cook and clean, then," Hope offered. "Or anything. Whatever you'd like—"

"*Baby*," said Hayleigh, sounding almost hurt, "of course you can stay! Why would you even ask that?"

"Well, you know, the situation with Father," she mumbled.

Hayleigh rose and pulled Hope into her arms. "Imaranta, darling, I am your *mother*. You will always have a home with me."

Hope wrapped her arms around Hayleigh as her

mother stroked her hair. "It's just…you left, and the woman from the Fringe told me what had happened to you, and—"

"I didn't leave," said Hayleigh, pulling her closer. "He threw me out. I begged him to let me take you, and he refused. And then I begged to stay there as his whore, and he turned that down, too. Said he was tired of me, and you were weaned, and that was that. I was set on finding a gate back to you, but…"

"They said you were crazy," Hope finished.

"But I wasn't," she replied, tearing up. "I *wasn't*. And you're here now, and everything's going to be okay, Hope, I swear it. You're with your mama now, and no one's going to take you away."

I wrote down my number for Hope and told her to call at any time, but I think my departure barely registered.

CHAPTER 16

Over the next week, I saw less and less of Artur's male glamour, but I knew damn well not to mention it. She came in exhausted every night, sweat-soaked, bruised, and often babying a healing limb or two, then stuffed herself and fell asleep. Marcus had begun going along to assist—or at least to provide a second target for Mina's painful lessons—and between the two of them, Artur made excellent progress. "A far better student than Marcus," Mina reported to me one evening after Artur had collapsed in bed. "She came to me with a few basics mastered, and much of the rest she understood in part, which is vastly more than I can say for him. Quick study, barely complains, doesn't give me a lot of pushback. She's tougher than I'd anticipated."

"Myrddin trained her as a child, and as for the rest, much of her previous career *was* military," I pointed out.

"True," Mina conceded. "In a few years, assuming she masters her talent, she might be fit for the guards…though something tells me that wouldn't be an ideal transition for her," she added with a smirk. "Surely no one who's worn a crown is eager to take orders."

By the end of the month, Mina deemed Artur suitably skilled—or at least less likely to accidentally kill everyone around her—which left Artur's schedule open for the second-most pressing item on the agenda: quality time with Wanda.

When I escorted her to the settlement that Monday morning, she was in good spirits. Amy had called to say that Caledfwlch was ready for pickup, and the statistical odds of Wanda breaking any of Artur's bones were virtually nil. I made the introductions, took a cookie from Wanda's tray, and set off into town to answer my mail at my favorite coffee shop for a few hours. Frank and Maria had gone home days before, and both were keeping me posted as to the Team's doings in my absence, including research assignments ahead of the autumn fieldwork. But when I returned to Wanda's office, repaired sword in hand, Artur was puffy-faced and red-eyed, and Wanda hugged her before she returned her to my keeping. "Thursday, okay?" the therapist said, pressing more cookies upon us. "And you call me if you need to talk between now and then."

I hurried Artur back to Val's, and while she washed her face, I unwrapped the butcher paper that Amy had taped around the sword. The blade glittered like new when I pulled it free of its scabbard, and after a cursory inspection, I sheathed it again and carried it into the bathroom. "Amy did a nice job. I don't think you'll notice a difference," I said, offering the sword to Artur.

She blotted her face dry, then saw what I was holding. As I had done, she slipped a few inches of the blade out for inspection, then nodded. "As always."

"Feels good to have it back?"

Her response was slow in coming. "Yes and no," she finally said, and leaned it against the wall while she finished cleaning up. "It's been an extension of me for so long that I've almost missed it like a hand, but…"

"It came from Myrddin?" I guessed.

Leaving the sword where it rested, she cut the lights, and we returned to her bedroom. "I trusted him, Kitty. I *trusted* him. My father trusted him. And what does he expect of me now? That I should be pleased to know he sired me?"

"He seemed to truly miss you when we met him—"

"He *seems* many things," she retorted. "He *is* a coward.

And if he cared about my wellbeing, then why am I just now free of the Gray Lands?" The anger in her voice was sharp and raw, brought forth by Wanda's long-practiced arts. "He claims to be my father, but not once in fifteen hundred years did he even *try* to find me. Or did he?"

I could only shrug. "Not that he mentioned."

"Assume he didn't, then. I suppose he liked the narrative well enough: the grieving father, waiting for me to miraculously stumble across the border and onto that damn island of his. And he has the *gall* to name it Afallon." She clenched her jaw and glared out at the garden. "As if he has any claim to Afallon. He ran and let it fall."

"To be fair," I began, earning a pointed look for my pains, "he couldn't have saved you on his own. I think he was hoping that Morgen could. The only reason you lived after we yanked you out of there is because Ros worked on you. If Titania had still been on the throne when you left the Gray Lands—assuming he'd been bold enough to bring you here—then you probably wouldn't have been as lucky."

Artur considered that for a time, then reluctantly muttered, "Perhaps."

"Doesn't make it hurt any less, though," I said, sitting on the bed beside her. "I get it."

We sat together in silence for a long moment, and then Artur sighed and flopped back onto the duvet. "What the hell am I to do?"

I stretched out as well and stared at the ceiling mosaic. "What do you want to do?"

"I don't know." She huffed and tucked one arm behind her head. "I'm good at leading armies. Killed more than my share of men. Is there a need?"

"Not for the kind of weapons you know." I thought briefly, then said, "You don't have to figure yourself out right now. Come back to my place, take your time, see what interests you. I've got room. It's just Marcus and me there now."

"And Beth?"

"Maybe in a few months. Come on, it'll be more fun than letting Mina punch you."

"A sword to the gut would be more enjoyable than her lessons," she replied with a grunt. "I don't want to tax your hospitality, Kitty—you've given me far more than I can repay."

I reached for a pillow, then thwacked Artur in the head. "You're my sibling. It's what we do, right?"

She was quiet for a moment, then murmured, "Sister."

"Hmm?"

"I'm your sister."

I rolled onto my elbow, and Artur did likewise to face me. "Are you sure?" I asked. "Really, you don't have to make any huge decisions right now—"

"This is who I am," she said, her voice low but firm. "All my life, I've been masked, to the point that I was terrified to even acknowledge the mask, much less peek beneath it."

"Prospects for women in your day weren't all that great."

"Beyond that. Myrddin treated the matter like a terrible secret. This shame I carried. I spent *so long* trying to be someone I'm not and feeling like an imposter at every turn. And then Mina ripped the mask away, and I saw myself for the first time, and...well, aside from the, ehm, *differences* in the lower bits," she said with a grimace, "it's felt...good. Surprisingly good. I thought I'd be weak, but I'm stronger than I've ever been, and this body...it *fits*. Do you understand?"

"I think so," I replied, and smiled. "Did Wanda make you talk about it?"

"Among other things. She has a way of getting into your head."

"Well, she *is* a psychologist. That's what they do." I entwined my fingers with hers and squeezed. "Come with me to Glastonbury. You can always slip back here for therapy."

"Glastonbury." She pronounced the word slowly, as if feeling the shape of the letters on her tongue. "Marcus said that's what you call my capital."

"Yeah. The Arcanum is headquartered there now...wizards, hippies, neo-pagans, and a bunch of townies trying to go about their lives. You're supposedly buried nearby, you know."

"Sorry to disappoint. Are you certain that I wouldn't be a burden to you?"

"Not at all." I grinned to see relief on her face. "Though I'm sure it won't be what you're used to," I teased. "It's just an ordinary flat. No servants. Your Majesty might actually be called upon to get off the couch and get your own beer from the kitchen."

"Mm." Artur frowned in feigned deliberation. "Does this flat of yours have running water like the baths here?"

"Hot *and* cold."

"Then I can see to my beer." She sat up and closed her eyes as she rolled her shoulders. "And you needn't be so formal. I suppose I don't merit any particular address these days, do I?"

"I don't know. Once a king, always a king, right? Or is it queen?"

"King," she replied without hesitation. "Perhaps a king without a people now, but I've never been a queen. Wouldn't know where to begin." She paused, then gave me a sidelong glance. "Your Marcus is a prince of sorts, is he not?"

"He's still getting acclimated to the notion."

"Ah. It's to be a royal wedding, then?"

"There is *no* wedding," I protested, hitting her with the pillow again. "We're just dating."

"What are you waiting for? Permission? Granted."

"Don't need it, but thanks," I said, pushing myself off the bed. "You don't have a problem with premarital cohabitation, do you?"

Artur raised an eyebrow. "As long as it doesn't keep me awake."

"No worries," I replied, patting her shoulder. "That's what magic is for."

When Val held court the next day, Artur tidied up, belted on her sword, slipped on her crown, and made an appearance. "I thank you for your hospitality," she said, standing before the throne in the courtyard while a gaggle of highborn and lowborn petitioners mingled among the fountains. "Truly, I am in your debt—"

Val rose, and Artur fell silent. "There is no debt," he said, loudly enough for those standing by to overhear. "I'm pleased to see that you've recovered your strength. Mina's reports have been…colorful."

"I'm sure," she replied, reciprocating his knowing smirk. "This is your land, and I am a guest here. With your leave, I'll take mine."

He spread his hands. "You're free to come and go as you like. Regardless of whether your father chooses to use it, you have a birthright in this realm, just as your sister does. Should you someday elect a court, you would have further rights and restrictions, but I certainly won't force that upon you. You've been awake a bare ten days—it is, perhaps, too soon to ask you to swear fealty to another sovereign."

"I hope I give no offense if I concur."

Val smiled in earnest and sat. "Go as you will, Artur. I hope you find peace. May I offer one bit of advice?"

"Please."

I thought I detected a sudden cast of wistfulness in his eyes. "Marcus says you're going to Glastonbury. I'd caution you to bear in mind that the world you know isn't waiting for you on the other side of the border. The land is there, but…much changed. Don't be disappointed if it's not the home you remember."

Artur nodded. "You speak from experience."

"I do." He leaned back against the throne and crossed his legs. "There are wonders in that realm beyond anything you could have imagined when you last saw it. But the current civilizations are built on the bones of the ones that came before, and so much of what you and I knew is long buried. Home…" He paused, thinking. "Home may be unrecognizable. The trick is to decide where home is to be now. But I wish you good fortune."

Artur was making space for the next petitioner when Val called her back. "One more thing. Have them take you to Ted," he said, waving toward Maria, Marcus, and me. "He's an excitable fellow, but he might be of help to you."

As Artur walked our way, Marcus muttered, "Assuming Ted hasn't revoked my basement credentials, that is."

"I'll put in a good word for you," I offered, squeezing his arm. "And since I've missed almost as much work as you have this summer, we may both be spending the winter in Siberia."

"Hmm. You, me, a sad little tent, depending on body heat to survive…"

"Which is why we'd have to bring Frank."

Marcus glared at me in exasperation. "There is *no* room for Frank in this two-person tent."

"But he's warm," I protested. He mock-pouted, and I linked my arm with his. "I *suppose* we could make do."

Under ordinary circumstances, moving a third person into my two-bedroom flat would have necessitated someone either bunking up with a partner or camping on the couch. Fortunately for us, Maria had the technical wherewithal to design an expansion that didn't break through the castle's wards, and Marcus had the oomph to put her plans into action without bothering with the preliminary work of focusing. In short order, my two bedrooms had become four, the new pair accessible via a hallway cut through a hole in one of the dining nook's walls. The expansion violated at least a handful of the laws of physics, but it was stable, a bubble of space that shouldn't have existed between my flat and my neighbor's. One of the rooms even had a window, though I was sure that no such opening would have been visible from outside the castle.

While Maria and I saw to the furniture—I fixed Artur's room into a more neutral version of mine and left the fourth room bland until Beth could decide whether she was moving in—Marcus put English into Artur's head, then gave her the quick tour of the place. I overheard snippets of his commentary as we worked: *This is the refrigerator, that's the freezer, and push this lever for ice. This is the microwave, do not put metal inside. Oh, you're going to like the television, let me show you…and she's been watching animal documentaries again, I see. Wait, I'll find something better…there. Remarkable, isn't it? The fascinating thing is that none of this is done by magic.*

He took her up the tower and onto the roof while we put the finishing touches together. When they returned, Artur seemed overwhelmed, but she put on a brave face. "It's nearly unrecognizable," she said. "Had you not told me where we were…"

"Come with me," Maria smoothly interrupted, beckoning for Artur to follow her into her newly furnished room. "Tell me what's missing. You can change this on your own, you know, but I've had experience…"

I waited until the door closed behind them, then glanced at Marcus. "How'd it go?"

He stuffed his hands into his pockets and made a face. "Saw a plane *and* a helicopter. She kept trying to figure out where a missing swamp went."

"Is she okay?"

"Relatively, I think. Just be glad she wasn't previously based in London, eh? And some of it may be the new language on top of everything else—she's had a long morning already."

Maria and Artur emerged a few minutes later, the room having passed inspection, and I was about to suggest we head out when there came a knock at the door. I opened it to find Toula waiting, a formal purple robe and her chain of office thrown on over leggings and an old *Doctor Who* T-shirt. "Welcome back, you little lunatic," she said, giving me a quick hug. "Val said you were inbound. No lasting damage from the Gray Lands?"

"None. You've spoken to Frank?"

"Fixed his bind. My brother has many talents, but my binds are *so* much neater," she said with a hint of smugness. "Glad to see you two safely home...and aren't you going to introduce us?" she asked, looking past me into the flat.

I turned to find Artur standing by the couch, still wearing the clothes in which I'd found her, plus her sword belt. She regarded Toula warily, and her right hand seemed to creep toward the hilt at her hip in preparation for an attack.

"Grand Magus," I said, "this is my sister—"

That was as far as I got before she swept past me into the room, hand outstretched. "Hi, Toula Pavli. I run this joint."

Artur gripped her hand and nodded as she made sense of the unfamiliar words. "Hello. Artur."

"Artur *Pendragon*?"

"Some have called me such."

"No need to be coy." Grinning, Toula released her. "Not with me, at least. I wouldn't go announcing myself like that in town, now, but Val has kept me well apprised. So, decided to cross the border?"

She paused, sizing Toula up. "Am I to understand that I'm trespassing on your—"

"Technically, yes, but since you're with Kitty, I don't mind. Just remember that Arcanum policy frowns upon letting outsiders know of our existence, so do us all a favor and don't tell anyone outside this place about the hidden castle full of wizards, eh?"

"Would anyone believe me if I did?"

"Who knows? This *is* Glastonbury," she said, and shrugged. "Anyway, I was passing by. Come see me once you get settled—and hey, kid," she added as Marcus peeked out from the kitchen. "Behaving yourself?"

"For now," he replied, lifting a mug in salute.

"Good. Welcome back. Maria, the Council meeting's been pushed to tomorrow afternoon, in case your aides don't mention it. See you then," said Toula, and departed.

When the door closed, Marcus quietly explained to Artur, "That's the aunt I mentioned."

"Also my boss," Maria added, conjuring a double shot of espresso from the ether. "And since family has its perks, she didn't give me trouble when I suggested bringing you here. Please don't kill anyone on the premises."

Artur looked mildly unnerved. "I wasn't planning to…"

"Glad to hear it." She sipped her coffee and sighed with all-too-familiar pleasure. "Maybe you could leave the sword in here, then, hmm? Wouldn't want to give anyone the wrong impression."

The walk to the office was slower than usual, as Artur kept dragging her feet, dawdling to stare at her surroundings. I reminded myself that she had never seen a castle; sub-Roman Britain had hill forts, but true castles had been a medieval development. The nucleus of the Arcanum's headquarters was constructed in the twelfth century, and since that time, it had grown and sprawled, its occupants throwing up annexes as required. By the time I arrived in Glastonbury, it had stretched into a twenty-four-tower complex, and visitors from other installations were given a map upon arrival. As for Artur, she lagged as we led her through the maze, slowing to look out the windows and run her fingertips along the stonework.

And, I noticed, kicking myself, she drew her fair share of curious glances. While she'd left the flat unarmed, I hadn't insisted that she change her outfit—as far as I knew, she had only the clothes on her back, which, while clean, made her look like an escaped reenactor. Deciding to take my battles one at a time and making a mental note to augment her wardrobe that night, I tried to hustle her along as we scanned ourselves into the Archives and made our way down the spiral staircase to the Team's subbasement lair.

"I hope Ted's in a forgiving mood," Marcus muttered as he pushed the inner glass door open. "If he—"

The rest was drowned out by a soprano battle cry and the sound of popping plastic weaponry as Allie Copeland, Antony's twelve-year-old daughter, jumped out from her hiding place against the wall and began rapidly firing orange foam balls at us. The barrage was brief—seconds, really, the time it took for her to register that she'd shot the wrong target—and she cringed as she lowered the gun. "Sorry, sorry, thought you were—*hey*," she said as Marcus, grinning evilly, motioned the spent balls off the floor. "No fair!"

Allie ran for cover, a dozen balls chasing her around the corner, and yelped with laughter as they found their target.

Footsteps rang off the stone behind us, and Antony emerged from the staircase with a short stack of books. "Ambush, right? It's her new favorite tactic. Welcome back."

"Skipping school?" Maria asked.

"Just for a bit," he replied. "Ted's letting her come along on the Iceland trip in August before the new term, and he's going over the details this morning, so I told her she could sit in. I did *not* tell her to shoot anything that moved," he added, raising his voice as Allie peeked out from around the corner.

"Sorry, Dad," she repeated, all big-eyed blonde

innocence.

"And *this* is why we have supervised wand use," he said, shaking his head.

Allie didn't have much to worry about—she'd grown up around the Team, and since Lakshmi's sons were quite a bit older, Allie had been our child mascot by default. Before I could reassure her, however, Ted emerged from the breakroom, all smiles. "The prodigals return!" he announced, gesturing toward us with his chipped tea mug. "You're in time. Meeting at ten, eh?"

Marcus stepped forward and cleared his throat. "Ted, I apologize for running off, I—"

"Don't worry about it. Your dad told me what was going on."

That took him aback. "He did?"

"Sure. I gave him a call to check on you." Seeing our faces, he chuckled. "Don't look so surprised. He's reached out to me enough times over you miscreants—phone works both ways, doesn't it?"

There are few wizards who would be so completely blasé about calling to chat with one of the Three, and I was fortunate to be working for one of them. "Thanks for not giving our jobs to Allie just yet," I said.

He tugged her ponytail good-naturedly as she reloaded her gun. "Kid needs to work on her aim first. And *hello*," he said, noticing the fourth member of our party, "you are…"

Marcus and I shot each other quick looks. "Ted," I began, "I'm going to need you to be cool, okay?"

Understanding dawned on his face, and his eyes flew open wide. "Is…is that…"

"This is my sister."

He clamped his free hand over his mouth, which only somewhat muffled the happy squeal that followed, a sound much like air being squeezed from a balloon through a pinhole.

I turned to Artur, who, having already been shot at

once that morning, observed the proceedings with concern. "This is Ted," I told her. "He's going to have a few questions."

"A *few?*" Marcus asked under his breath.

"Many. He'll have many questions. Let's, uh...let's get out of the hallway, okay?" I said, and steered her toward my office before Ted could start flailing with excitement.

The Iceland planning meeting was delayed that day because Ted couldn't stop talking—judging by her expression, I think Artur doubted his sanity—but even with the scheduling upset, Antony still found time to stop by before lunch with a spare computer. At first, Artur regarded it as one might contemplate an unexploded grenade, but Antony was gentle and persistent. While I caught up on my reading across the room, they sat on my office couch with the computer on the coffee table, slowly going over the basics of operation. Having done the same for Marcus, Antony had carved out a niche for himself as tech support for the temporally displaced, and I eavesdropped as he guided her online, pointing her to the information she needed the most.

And there she remained. For the rest of the work week, I seldom saw her without the glow of the screen on her face, excepting meals and her trips to and from her Thursday session with Wanda. Having never considered reading to be more than a semi-useful skill, Artur suddenly found herself doing little else, scanning and scrolling for hours and punctuating her research with a litany of questions. I kept her with me in my office during the day, but at night, she sat at the kitchen table with beer and her electronic tutor, playing catch-up. In that respect, at least, age was on her side; regardless of her centuries in stasis, she was old enough to need little sleep unless she worked herself to exhaustion, and I found her napping with her head on the table when I shuffled out for breakfast.

Marcus, who shared her stamina, sneaked out of bed after I dozed off to sit up with her and fill in what gaps he could. Firsthand experience made him an excellent guide, as he knew what to show her that the rest of us would inadvertently overlook as common knowledge. On Friday morning, en route to the tea kettle, I found them hunched over Artur's computer together, Marcus smiling faintly and Artur with tears streaming down her face. "Oh no, what's wrong?" I asked, hurrying over to help.

She looked up at me, wiped her new bathrobe's sleeve over her eyes, and wordlessly turned the screen around to show me a photo of Earthrise from the moon.

I had to remind myself that everything was new to her—that the satellite imagery I took for granted was virtually miraculous, that the notion of seeing the contours of Great Britain from the air would have been ludicrous to her two weeks before, that it was mind-boggling that the castle ran partly on magic and partly on a force Marcus described as controlled lightning. There were mysterious tropical fruits in the fridge and people on the television going live to their colleagues in Japan. On Sunday, Marcus pulled up an oceanic documentary series, and Artur watched the whole thing with her computer nearby, trying to look up locations and species by phonetic spelling.

By then, she needed a day of fish and soothing music. Wanda had scheduled her for a long session on Saturday afternoon, and Artur had returned somber, then curled up on the couch with the lights low and said little to anyone. I put a blanket over her that night and went to bed, but when I woke in the wee hours to a cold spot beside me, I peeked out and found Marcus with her, several empty beer bottles on the table, and Artur sobbing into a pillow to muffle the sound. I started to show myself, but Marcus noticed me and shook his head. *She doesn't want you to know*, he thought. *Pretend.*

I ached for her, but there was nothing I could do to ease her pain but offer distractions. On Monday, I left the office for the afternoon and walked Artur into town, hoping the warmth of July might lift her spirits. We went up the Tor for the view, and she rested her palm against the stone wall of St. Michael's Church, a centuries-old edifice that had been erected and ruined in the time she'd been away. "Marcus said I'm supposedly buried around here," she remarked as she studied the lonely tower.

"At the abbey." I angled her to the west and pointed toward town. "It's only ruins now. The monks needed funds at one point, so they claimed to have found you and Guinevere. Turned it into a tourist attraction, and this town's never been the same."

"Happy to be of service." She sighed. "Remind me, who is this Guinevere?"

"Your supposed wife."

"Ah. And Medraut was supposed to have been our son?"

"No—the stories vary, but he was either your nephew or your child by your half sister."

Artur shuddered at the latter notion. "Medraut was my friend, one of the finest swordsmen I've ever known. He deserves better than being remembered as my incest bastard."

"Traitorous, regicidal incest bastard," I added. "But that's the legend. You're not going to be able to wage a successful campaign to correct the record. As far as most folks are concerned, y'all probably never existed."

"*Probably*?"

"The records are bad, and the stories don't help." I leaned against the tower, letting the stones warm my back. "Given Ted's penchant for Grail quests, I've read arguments for and against an historical King Arthur. The consensus seems to be, 'Eh, maybe.'" Artur's expression was inscrutable, and I continued, "The stories agree on this: you were one heck of a warrior, probably a decent ruler, and you were either mortally wounded or died in battle."

"I should have died," she murmured.

I took her hand. "Glad you didn't. Look, I…I know this is hard for you. I'm not going to pretend that I understand the half of it. But if there's something I can do to make it easier, tell me."

She said nothing for a time as she contemplated the sprawl of Glastonbury, shielding her eyes and squinting into the sun. "If I could remain with you for now…"

"Of course."

"Not indefinitely," she hastened to add. "I've been the beneficiary of far too much hospitality of late."

"I'm happy to have you," I protested.

Artur gave me a small, lopsided smile. "I know. But Beth will need a place to stay—"

"Which is why there's a fourth bedroom."

"Do you *really* want both of your sisters crowding your flat?"

I could see it in my mind's eye: Artur waking up at the table to find Beth sitting across from her, gazing in adulation, while Marcus hid out with the coffee in the kitchen.

"Wouldn't bother me," I told her.

"You're mad," she replied, but squeezed my hand and nodded toward the downward trail. "Shall we?"

As we descended, Artur said, "If Beth is truly planning to move in, then I should read the stories so I know what the hell she's talking about."

That night, I pulled copies of White and Malory from the library, cautioned her that Middle English was a pain, and left her to her own devices in the den while I scratched my baking itch. Mixing up a simple cake, I heard her mutter and snort in disbelief, until finally she called, "This is insane! Where did this come from?"

I glanced through the cut-out and saw her waving *The Once and Future King* over the back of the couch. "Have you gotten to the bit where Myrddin transforms you into animals for educational purposes?"

"*What?*"

"Honest to God. There's a movie version, too."

She tossed the book to the floor and cackled at the absurdity, and I brought her a beer. "Might need this."

"Oh, I *will*," she replied, accepting the offering and swigging back a long gulp. "Do you suppose Myrddin has read this nonsense?"

"Probably. In some of the versions, he gets stuck inside a rock or tree for all time."

Artur considered that as she drank. "Fitting."

I hesitated, then asked, "You're not planning to go see him, are you? He told me to let him know once you were feeling better—"

"He wouldn't be of any help in that process." She leaned back against the cushions and studied the ceiling fan. "I suppose I should be grateful to him for my existence, but knowing what he did to my mother...my father...*me*..."

"At least he likes you," I replied, flopping onto the seat beside her. "Once he realized what I am, *poof*, that was it. You know, I met him over breakfast, when he was masquerading as an old man, and I'm pretty sure he was flirting with me."

"That's disgusting."

"Yeah, well, at least I didn't have a baby with my sister."

She punched me in the shoulder, but I caught her brief grin before she sobered. "He's always been an ass," she said, swiveling onto the couch to face me. "I knew he was talented with magic—he did the odd bit to assist Father and me—but knowing now what he was truly capable of doing..." She drank and stared at the wall for a moment before resuming. "We were constantly at war with the Saxons, you understand. There were so many battles, so many lives lost...and he could have prevented it all. He could have called down lightning from the heavens, or turned the fields to fire, or...or put up a wall around their armies until they starved. *Anything*. And he was so afraid that his damn queen would find him that he did nothing. He could have saved Afallon," she continued, slowly shaking her head. "My people. That gate…surely he could have found a way to close it before those *things* attacked us. But he stood back and let us die, and now he expects gratitude from me? If he had helped us, we could have driven the Saxons back across the sea, made them Rome's problem…we might have had peace. Instead…"

"I'm sorry."

Artur brushed that aside. "I don't mean to be so depressing, Kitty, but—"

"*Stop*. You're allowed to be depressed, though the beer probably isn't helping."

"It isn't hurting," she countered. "So…Myrddin has nothing to do with you, does he?"

"He hasn't yet, but…" I shrugged. "My dad and I were really close. I mean, he never knew that he wasn't actually my father, which might have changed things, but…Dad was good to me. I'm not exactly holding my breath waiting for Myrddin to step into his shoes."

"My father was a good man," said Artur. "A good king. I would have done anything for him. Murdered by Saxons when I was ten, but—"

"Myrddin mentioned that." I concentrated, then pulled a glass of barely passable rosé from the ether and took a long sip. "Mine died when I was ten, too. Mom didn't want me, so she shipped me off here."

"She lives yet?"

"Yeah, in the dungeons here. Treason is frowned upon, you know."

Artur lifted her bottle. "To family."

I clinked my glass against it and smirked. "Cake should be out in a few minutes. If you want, I could put on the movie version of the first part of that book and save you the reading. It's a kids' cartoon, but it's not bad."

She glanced at the discarded book, then hoisted her

bottle again in thanks. "You've seen it, have you?"

"Grew up with it," I replied, returning to the kitchen to check on my project. "And then I had a class in Arthurian literature at uni, so yeah, this isn't new to me."

"Then you've read these damned books?"

"Yep." The oven light revealed good progress. "I still have my lecture notes saved…"

When I stood and turned, planning to whip up a quick frosting, I found Artur marching into the kitchen. She slammed her beer onto the counter, gripped my shoulders, and looked me dead in the eye. "For mercy's sake, woman, give me the short version."

While the Team did report to work that week, we anticipated accomplishing little of substance. Arc 2 was busily gearing up for the annual Games, when students from all seven installations converged upon Glastonbury for three days of competition in mid-July. Although we were still days out, there were dorms to be set up, meals to be prepped, and last-minute safety drills to be run, as teenage wizards aren't always the most accurate in their casting. Beth sent me a message with her travel plans: she would be arriving with the Arc 1 contingent on Monday, but could she stay at my place? I warned Marcus and Artur, then told Beth she was welcome. I couldn't imagine anyone else wanting that room for the week; the only other houseguest who ever spent the night was Maria when she couldn't be bothered to go back to her flat, and with her referee duties keeping her booked, I doubted that I'd see much of her until the Games ended.

As for the subbasement, Artur continued to camp out in my office on Tuesday morning, quietly reading on her computer. Down the hall, I could hear Antony, Marcus, and Mal discuss Allie's competition plans—she'd signed up for technical on Wednesday, academic on Thursday, and combat on Friday, and her proud parents planned to be in the stands as often as their schedules allowed. "Come on, now," said Mal, "do you really think Ted would complain if you bailed on us for a few days? Hell, he'd probably go with you. We could make posters and embarrass Allie again…"

Mal's voice cut off as rapid footsteps neared. "Aunt Toula?" said Marcus. "What's wrong?"

"Later," I heard her say, then looked up as she rapped her knuckles against my doorframe. Oddly enough, she wore a black pantsuit under her green robe, a far more formal look than she regularly sported. What struck me, though, were the lines of tension around her eyes and mouth.

"Grand Magus?" I asked, closing my computer. "Can I help you?"

"I don't know if it'll help, but I need you upstairs, now. You, too, Frank," she said, glancing over her shoulder and calling toward his office.

I rose and absently smoothed my hair. "What's going on?"

"Tell you on the way. Artur, stay down here," she ordered, and escorted Frank and me past our concerned colleagues and through a gate into her suite. When the three of us were alone and the gate was closed, she leaned against her desk and folded her arms. "Nath's sent an envoy."

"*Here?*" Frank replied. "How?"

"Glamoured, I hope," I added.

Toula nodded. "Yeah, he looks normal enough, but I'm pretty sure it's glamour. His Fae is too accented for him to be anything but a Gray Lander. And as for how he got here…well, simple," she said, scowling. "I put a deterrent on that gate at Shapwick Heath and posted a guard while you two were gone, but no one bothered to tell me until now that one of the guards sneaked off for a nip at the pub during his shift. More than a nip," she muttered. "That idiot was away for most of the night, and it seems that someone did a little reconnaissance while he was drinking. A gate from the Gray Lands opened just outside our wards half an hour ago."

"Fuck," I muttered. "What does the envoy want?"

"Don't know, but he's waiting next door with five of the guards that I *haven't* sacked today, so let's find out." She stood and headed for the door. "If I had to guess, I don't think Nath's offering us a fruit basket."

The three of us stepped into the grand magus's small conference room, a windowless space accessible only from the main office. The promised guards ringed the walls, wands very much out and at the ready, while the object of their attention sat stiffly at the table with his hands folded in front of him. Other than his clothing, he seemed unremarkable—a dark-haired, dark-eyed young man in a sleeveless orange shirt with a deep V at the neck—but as Toula closed the door behind us, the image shimmered and fell away to reveal the hairless blue head and pointed ears of a tennuwaya.

"At ease," Toula said to the guards, then took the seat opposite the envoy. Once Frank and I had seated ourselves in the chairs flanking hers, Toula spread her empty hands over the polished tabletop and nodded to the stranger. "I understand that you bear a message from your queen," she said, segueing into Fae. "I would hear it."

The envoy maintained his perfectly rigid pose. "You have permitted the abduction of one of my lady's people," he replied. "She graciously allowed your representative"—his eyes flickered toward me, though he seemed not to recognize Frank—"to enter her realm and seek out one of your people who was allegedly being improperly held. In the process, your representative murdered a band of jinoda, damaged the ancestral home of a lord of High Vale, and abducted the daughter of High Vale's paramount lord. What say you to these charges?"

Toula didn't flinch, but I felt her in my mind, searching through my thoughts, and I opened my memories to her probing. "The jinoda are not Nath's people, are they?" she asked the envoy.

"No," he admitted, "but the slaughter has created unrest among them, which puts my lady's people at risk."

"Understood. However, the jinoda were attacked in order to assist a band of kadalin, and those who survived were killed in defense. I have authorized no needless assault on the tennuwaya or the cynaeli."

"The damaged tower?"

"Unfortunate, but easily repaired with magic. My representative was put in fear for her life when she successfully woke the one called the Sleeper—who, incidentally, was held against her knowledge and will for more than fifteen hundred years. Nath permitted Kitty to seek her out," she continued, nodding toward me, "and that is precisely what she did. The property damage is unfortunate, but I have full confidence in Nath's ability to restore the tower to its former condition."

"Which leaves the matter of the abducted girl."

"And who would that be?"

"Lady Imaranta of High Vale."

Toula cocked her head. "An abduction implies that the target was taken unwillingly. Imaranta asked for my representatives' assistance in journeying to this realm. She is half human…and a likdenfi," she added, feeling out the strange term, "about to be given away as a concubine. She was opposed to the arrangement and desired to seek her family here."

"She was taken without my lady's permission," the envoy protested. "Her father and all the lords of High Vale are incensed, and my lady will see her safely returned."

"I'm afraid that's impossible."

The envoy blinked. "Excuse me?"

"Imaranta has left my custody to search for her kin. I don't know where she is at this moment, nor am I inclined to seek her out." Toula leaned across the table and lowered her voice. "The girl's mother was kidnapped and held as a sex slave for seven years. The girl was poised to be pushed into the same system. You can go back and tell Nath that I won't stand for it, and if Imaranta's father is upset at her departure, then he can consider this compensation for everything he did to her mother—who is one of *my* people."

The last part wasn't strictly true—as far as I knew, Hayleigh wasn't even a witch—but I wasn't about to correct Toula when she was on a roll.

"The lords of High Vale held two of my people captive," said Toula, her voice low and dangerous. "One has been freed, and the other has been reunited with the child she was forced to bear as a concubine. If recompense is due, it isn't from me."

To his credit, the envoy stood his ground. "My lady will be exceedingly displeased to hear of your refusal to her terms."

"Your lady doesn't frighten me," Toula replied. "Faerie knows better than to take changelings from this realm. Nath could stand to learn that lesson."

He nodded curtly, then stood. "In that case, I have been authorized to inform you that you have until this time tomorrow to return Lady Imaranta. Should you fail to do so, my lady will consider it a declaration of war."

"Is that so? Then I ask that you convey to your lady my exceeding displeasure at the way my people have been treated in her realm and the insult she delivers by sending demands in this fashion. You may leave," she said, and kept her seat until the guards had escorted the envoy from the room.

When the doors closed and the sound of footsteps had faded, Toula exhaled slowly and turned to look at Frank and me. "Well, that does put a kink in my schedule, doesn't it?"

"I'm sorry," I hastened, "I didn't mean to start—"

"If I didn't think you two had done the right thing, I'd have sent Imaranta home," she interrupted, and pushed back from the table. "Okay, new plan. We're going to quietly go on high alert and hope for the best."

"Meaning?" asked Frank.

She sighed and stood. "Meaning that I'd sleep now if I were you."

CHAPTER 17

"**G**ood morning, Ms. Lozano," said Toula through the screen door.

Morning was a technicality. It was barely four in Oklahoma, and even in July, sunrise was still hours away. The porch light shone bright white overhead, throwing us both into stark relief and dimming our view of what waited inside the house.

"I'm Toula Pavli from the Arcanum," she continued. "I believe you've met Kitty, haven't you?"

"Yes," Hayleigh admitted, her voice sleep-froggy but sharp with caution.

"Well, I hate to bother you at this hour," said Toula, "but we may be going to war with the Gray Lands in the next day or so, and I'm convening a strategic planning meeting. Time is of the essence. I'd greatly appreciate it if you and your daughter would attend."

No answer came from beyond the door.

"Hayleigh, they want Hope back," I tried. "Toula said no. Since you two have more insider knowledge here than anyone else in this realm, we could really use your help."

"They can't have her," came the terse reply.

"Our point exactly," Toula soothed. "I know you've been through hell, and the Gray Lands is probably the last thing you want to think about, but we're staring down the potential of an all-out invasion. I'll do whatever I can to protect your daughter, I swear, but right now, I need you to put on some pants and help us protect the world. And maybe put that pistol down, okay?"

The foyer light flipped on, and I saw Hope standing behind her mother, clutching her bathrobe closed. "What do you need me to do?"

"Hope," Hayleigh began, but her daughter shook her head.

"The tennuwaya have ways of tracking. If they're sent here to find me, they will, and then we'll both be in danger. So, what can we do?" she asked, staring at us through the mesh.

"War counsel in Faerie in twenty minutes?" said Toula.

"All right. I'll get dressed. Come on, Mama," she insisted, tugging Hayleigh away from the door as her mother sputtered her protestation.

The crowd that gathered around Val's largest dining room table half an hour later was certainly one of the strangest I'd seen.

The Arcanum party was small, but then again, Toula wanted a plan before she let the rest of the magi know what was coming. The only representatives of the Council were Maria and former grand magus Arnold Lowe, both of whom could be trusted to keep their mouths shut. Frank and I sat with them, while beside me, Artur drummed her fingers on the table and scanned the room with solemn eyes. Hope and twitchy Hayleigh sat beside her, followed by Carey Jones, the Minor Arcanum's elderly spokeswoman, and Tanner Adler, the even more senior head of the Dark Company, who alone of the assembled sported a three-piece suit and fedora. Badger took the chair to his right, followed by Vivi, Yolanda, and Kip, who glowered every time his gaze drifted toward Hope's end of the room. Completing the ring were Eleanor, Val, and Coileán—whose touch on Toula's shoulder had spoken of more than mere collegiality. That the grand magus had been involved with one of the Three for close to four decades might have been a secret known to few in the

Arcanum, but it was surely common knowledge to most of the assembled.

"I wish I had packets prepared for you, but this just came up," said Toula to the room. "In brief, Nath is threatening war unless I send Lady Imaranta here back across the border."

All eyes went to Hope, who, rendered unglamoured in Faerie, flushed a dusky purple.

"And while I'd rather not dredge up unpleasant memories for Ms. Lozano," Toula continued, gesturing toward Hayleigh, "you should be aware that she was held captive by a cynaeli lord, gave birth to his child, and was expelled a few years later without her daughter." Turning to Coileán, she murmured, "I shouldn't have to tell you why sending the girl back isn't an option."

"Understood," he muttered. "She's just Nath's excuse, anyway."

Hayleigh—who was doing remarkably well for a woman pulled from her bed, dragged into Faerie, and given the language ten minutes before the meeting began—went to her feet. "You have to protect Hope," she pleaded as she looked around the table. "*Please*. She's all I have, and I just got her back, and…and her father—"

"She may stay here until the matter is settled," Val gently interjected. "Whatever tracking ability they have will be useless across our border, and Nath wouldn't be foolish enough to invade this realm. Stay here with her," he offered as Hayleigh's shoulders sagged in relief. "I'm sure she would prefer to have your company."

"Thank you," she whispered, and fell into her seat. Hope wrapped her arm around her mother's shoulders, and the two leaned together.

With that settled, Toula cleared her throat and resumed. "Some of you I've asked here because you and your people are at immediate risk. While Faerie is presumably outside the direct line of fire, if I have any favors to call in, I'm asking now," she said, looking at the

Three. "If the Fringe could assist us—"

"Say the word," Vivi interrupted, and Yolanda nodded beside her. "We've got people in that realm, too."

"Thanks. As for rest, I've asked anyone who's spent more than a few minutes in the Gray Lands here to help us strategize. What do we know about Nath's forces, how do they fight, what could we be facing…"

Artur lifted a finger to draw her attention. "I'm sorry to disappoint you, but I was asleep the entire time I was there."

"Sure, but if I've got the story straight from them," she replied, indicating Frank and me, "you had to fight off whatever came wandering through a gate, right?"

"Not an organized army."

"No, but God only knows what she could ultimately send our way. And with that sobering thought," she said, standing, "let's see what we know." One long wall of the dining room shifted from a fresco of trees and distant mountains to a white dry-erase board, and Toula held up a hand to stop Val before he protested. "I'll put it back. Right," she said, a red marker manifesting in her hand. "Who'd like to share with the class?"

An hour and a good deal of coffee later, Toula had covered two-thirds of the wall with neat notes on everything we could think of: dragons, cyclopes, trolls, jinoda, yeti, and several creatures for which we had no set name and Kip and Hope couldn't agree on a term. When one of them tried to describe something unknown to us, both ended up sketching it on the board, comparing information and terminology as they went. Though he initially seemed opposed to sharing a room with her, let alone the markers, Kip grudgingly relented as Hope kept deferring to him. Kip knew the land and its dangers, describing in gory detail what a pissed-off hydra could do and how to best attack the beasts known to most of the room as scent hounds—as far as I could tell, a giant cross between a wolf and a praying mantis. Hope, on the other hand, knew something of the ruling class's politics and alignments.

"The tennuwaya have always been stronger than the cynaeli," she explained, adding details to a rough map on the far third of the board. "There are more of them, their magic is better in battle, and they have the realm's favor— Lady Nath is daughter to the realm, you understand."

Ros, who had popped in during the discussion, lifted her hands and shook her head as people looked her way. "Don't ask me, I don't know the mechanics," she insisted.

"Our forces don't always work together," Hope continued. "The tennuwaya have their territory, and the cynaeli have theirs. But if the queen called out a full army, then our lords would send forces to join hers."

"It happened once when you were a baby," Hayleigh added, nursing a doppio. "There'd been a massive fire in the far south that summer, and with so much wildlife crisped, the dragons were starving and started attacking the tennuwaya holds. Enogi ordered out a squadron from all of the towers of High Vale." She grimaced and held her tiny cup closer. "Those monsters raided all the way to our doorstep. I hid you inside for weeks."

"You know," Frank rumbled to my left, "maybe we could watch it with the whole 'monsters' thing, hmm?"

Hayleigh peered around me. "If you'd seen one, you'd understand. Flying, fire-breathing terrors—"

"Who, as you just said, were starving."

"Excuse me," she snapped, "have *you* ever been terrorized by a dragon?"

Frank's smile showed far too many teeth. "My clutchmates liked to roughhouse, but that's probably not what you had in mind."

"*Mama*," said Hope, cutting her retort off, then tugged her into the garden for a quick chat.

A few seconds and a distant, yelped, "*What?*" later, Frank snorted.

When they returned, wide-eyed Hayleigh took Kip's

abandoned chair, and Frank propped his chin on his fist, staring at her until she squirmed. "Can't actually breathe fire here," he said in an almost conversational tone. "Only a trace of dark magic."

Ros stepped behind him and squeezed the back of his neck. "Come on, bud, don't be an asshole," she murmured.

Frank started to object, then huffed and folded his arms on the table. "You heard—"

"She's a mundane from friggin' Oklahoma. If Kip can put aside his blood feud for the moment, then you can be the bigger person, okay?"

"What's wrong with Oklahoma?" Hayleigh demanded.

"And it's not a blood feud," said Kip, scribbling a few additional details onto the map that he and Hope had been sketching. "I just harbor an inherent mistrust of anything that considers me prey."

"Likewise," said Hayleigh, jabbing one hand toward Frank.

My colleague sighed and rolled his eyes. "Honestly, you eat *one* human, and suddenly, you're on everyone's shit list."

Ros put her head in her hands and sighed. "Frank, sweetie, you're not helping."

"And when did you—oh, right. Colombia," said Toula. "I think there's an understood exception for self-defense."

As Hayleigh sputtered, Tanner waved for her attention. "My dear girl, the collective kill total in this room is *significant*," he said, drawing the last word out. "Some of the top magical talent in two realms is sitting around this table, and believe me, you don't last in this game if you can't fight back. Now, I know we have our differences," he continued, lazily gesturing toward Kip and Hope, "but I probably don't have to tell you that letting Nath conquer the mortal realm would be a mistake."

She shuddered in agreement. "You don't know what they're like."

"I know enough. For the moment, in here, we're on the same side. And since *my* people don't have the luxury of hiding out in Faerie, the Company will assist as it can."

"What company?"

"*The* Company," said Tanner, leaning closer to her. "Shifters, all of us. And unlike them," he said, pointing to Frank and Kip, "we don't have to wait for someone to break a bind." His voice softened and deepened as he stared Hayleigh down. "Much of this is new to you, and most of us appreciate that, but if you were wise, you would keep your mouth closed and your eyes open until you had the lay of the land."

Chastised into silence, Hayleigh slumped at the table, and I stood to stretch my legs while our amateur cartographers finished. While I refreshed my coffee at the side table, I heard Kip mutter to Hope, "My wife chewed me out for my behavior the other day. Apparently, I owe you an apology."

"None needed," she replied, marking settlements around a lake. "I'd hate me, too."

"Seeing as you're willing to betray your father's people and your queen, though, I suppose we could at least pretend to be on the same team for now."

The corner of Hope's mouth twitched. "I'd like that."

"Good." He glanced over his shoulder and lowered his voice. "Is your mother going to be okay?"

"Eventually," she said, stepping back to examine her work. "We're fighters—"

"Are you *serious*?" Hayleigh cried, her eyes almost bugging out of her head. Vivi's expression had turned guilty, and I realized the cause when Hayleigh stared across the table at my sister, slack-jawed.

Oh, good, a distraction, Frank thought to me as Artur weakly waved at Hayleigh. *I knew I liked the Fringe.*

After a few hours of strategizing, the Fringe's database had been improved, but we had no firm plan for beating back a full-scale invasion from the Gray Lands.

The problem was that no one had any record of engaging that realm in combat. Coileán's extensive library contained nothing helpful, and while Maria had remotely trolled the Arcanum's resources that morning, she'd found nothing of use. There'd been notes of skirmishes, short-lived battles with rogue bands who'd come through gates to hunt, and Artur had described in detail what her men had seen and fought, but there was simply no entry in anyone's history of the Gray Lands engaging either of the other realms in all-out war.

The closest we'd come was some forty years prior, when Badger and the Minor Arcanum had stopped an invasion by trickery. "That only worked because Nath was careless enough to catch a nap on my turf," Badger explained. "I got to her and worked out an arrangement before the first shots were fired. She won't make that mistake again." Spreading her hands, Badger added, "If I could catch her unawares in the Gray Lands by sleepwalking, I'd consider it, but—"

"But you can't sleepwalk outside of the mortal realm," Val interrupted, "and you're not taking the risk of crossing for a fool's errand."

She grimaced. "I'm ninety, but I'm in fair condition. Wizards tend to be longer-lived than mundanes…"

"Ninety is still ninety," he said firmly. "Not unless the end of the world is nigh."

Eleanor, who'd been taking copious notes of her own, piped up. "What about another sleepwalker? If Nath crossed the border, and someone were able to knock her unconscious, could a sleepwalker reach her?"

"Theoretically, yes," said Carey, who, unlike Badger, looked her age. She was still spry for a woman in her eighties—white-haired and sun-weathered, perhaps, but sharp and strengthened by a lifetime of wrangling large animals in her veterinary practice. "Pulling her into the dream space would be no problem, no matter how she lost consciousness. But there's nothing we could do with her once we got her there beyond give her a stern lecture. There's no one I know of besides Badger who can cast in the dream space."

"Have you checked all of your people?" Yolanda asked.

Carey glanced at her impatiently. "Of course. Once we realized what Badger could do, we tested everyone. I've overseen all new sleepwalkers for years, but no one else has that talent. I know of exactly one other wizard who had the skill, and that was Simon Magus, so unless the Fringe has a time machine…"

"Not even a prototype," she muttered.

"And anyway," said Val, "all of this is predicated on the assumption that someone could get close enough to Nath to affect her. It's not a viable plan." Tapping his pen on the table, he scowled in thought, then released a frustrated sigh. "There's no clear way to stop this short of returning the girl, which isn't an option," he said, speeding up at the end before Hayleigh could protest. "If I were coordinating this…" He paused and looked to Toula, who motioned him on. "I would concentrate my forces in Glastonbury. We know that she has a way to make a gate to your front door. Send your children and your infirm to the other installations—*not* Arc 1, we've seen that place under siege—and pull anyone with significant talent into the castle."

"And if I may," said Eleanor, "I've never seen a gate sufficiently large to admit an entire army. If your forces are there quickly enough after it opens, you could Stirling Bridge her."

Artur frowned. "There's no bridge at the castle—"

"No—sorry," she replied. "September 1297. The Scots were fighting for their independence, the English mustered on one bank of the River Forth near Stirling, and the Scots took the other side and waited. That bridge was the only safe crossing for miles, and it was barely large enough to let two horses pass abreast. The Scots were outnumbered, but the English, like fools, decided to send their army across the bridge. All the Scots had to do was wait, allow a few thousand English to cross, then swoop down and pick them off. Easy victory. The English lost thousands, and Wallace had the body of one of their commanders flayed for souvenirs—"

"Easy, Professor," Coileán interrupted.

Eleanor ignored him. "The principle is applicable here. Nath makes a gate, she starts to send her army through, and the Arcanum can pull a page from Wallace's playbook."

"Which would be fine and dandy if we only had one bridge to deal with," said Toula. "What's to stop Nath from ripping open two? Ten? Fifty gates, all aimed at the castle?"

"*Ooh.*" Vivi winced. "The structural stability…given the inter-realm traffic through Glastonbury to begin with…"

Befuddled, my sister lifted a finger. "Pretend that I have no idea what you're talking about and explain the problem, hmm?"

"Allow me," said Toula, and whispered as she traced a pattern in the air. A translucent red sphere appeared over the middle of the table, slowly spinning in place, and was joined an instant later by similar blue and yellow spheres. "The three known realms are distinct entities unto themselves," she explained. "We're not entirely certain of how they physically coexist, and there isn't a perfect way to visualize it, but this is the best model our theorists have devised."

"They must be delightful at parties," said Coileán.

"Anything can be delightful with sufficient alcohol," she replied, and flicked her wrist. The three spheres slid together until their component colors blended into white light. "Imagine that we exist on top of each other. Keep that in mind, but I have to separate them just a bit…"

The blue sphere shrank until it was inside the yellow,

and the red grew to encompass both. "Pretend that the yellow layer is the mortal realm, the red is Faerie, and the blue is the Gray Lands. Inter-realm gates join these layers." Lights flickered over Toula's concentric spheres, leaving behind smudges of green and orange, and at each gate, red and blue began to flow into the yellow layer. "Wherever we have gates, we have an etheric outflow into the mortal realm. Following me?"

Artur's brow furrowed, but she nodded.

"Now," said Toula, "gates just *happen*. There are simply spots in the mortal realm where the skin between the realms is thinner, and we get natural gates. These are often fairly small and stable. And we can make our own gates, of course, but those tend to be less stable. Left alone, most would eventually close, but we patch them anyway. We don't want random mundanes stumbling into Faerie and getting themselves in trouble, see?"

I cut my eyes to Hayleigh, who hunched low in her chair and clutched her coffee like a worry stone.

"But even though we close our gates, it doesn't leave the barrier quite as we found it. It's like a scab over a wound. Maybe it's a little scab, but it's still a weak spot. The area will heal if you leave it alone, but that takes time. And since the *highly* transitory fae population of Arc 2 has been on the rise in recent years, we have more and more of those scabs. Accumulate enough of them, and natural gates can start opening."

Toula glanced toward her demonstrative illusion. "Another natural gate into Faerie wouldn't be that bad for us—even if we couldn't keep it closed, at least we'd be getting more raw magic. But a thin spot means we could have natural Gray Lands gates, too."

Another burst of flashes enlarged the green streaks between the two inner spheres. "Nath is no weakling, and she has the force of that realm behind her. If she opened enough gates in a short span, she could cause lasting damage to Glastonbury. It's tough enough closing Gray

Lands gates on a good day," Toula explained. "Faerie gates are pretty simple because the magic we need to make the patch is literally flowing out at us. But when you're closing a gate to the Gray Lands, you've got to work around an outflow of dark magic, which makes everything you do exponentially more difficult."

"In sum," Val offered, "if Nath creates too many gates, particularly if she weakens the barrier between the realms, then we may not be able to close them all."

"Can they coalesce?" Artur asked. "If they're unstable and the skin is thin, can they rip into each other and form larger gates?"

"Theoretically, yes," Toula replied with reluctance. "But let's hope we don't get a chance to prove that."

With the mood somber, the meeting soon broke up. As I prepared to depart, I saw Toula remove the white board and faintly smile at her brother as the fresco reappeared. "See? No damage."

Val moved close and kissed her forehead. "You know you have a place to retreat," he murmured.

"That may be," she said, patting his cheek, "but the rest of the realm doesn't. If we fail..."

I glanced toward Hope and Hayleigh, who had taken a spot in the corner of the room and were watching uncertainly as the rest of us scattered. Studying them, I wondered if Toula was reconsidering, weighing the risk to our world against the future of one young woman and her traumatized mother. Prudence cautioned that it would be a bad idea to pry in the grand magus's head without an invitation, and Toula was a master of the poker face.

"The others can do as they like," said Val. "You'll have whatever I can give you."

Artur and I returned to the flat and brought Marcus up to date while Frank headed to the basement to quietly fill in the Team, secrecy be damned. While I put on water for tea, needing something to do with my hands, and Marcus began searching the Arcanum's electronic records for gate-closing techniques, Artur paced, treading up and down the den in her thin boots and wrestling with her thoughts.

When the kettle whistled and the comforting smell of orange pekoe filled the kitchen once again, I fixed my mug, then caught Artur's arm to stay her long march. "Come on, sit down," I urged. "We should probably make it an early night, you know?"

"It's not even sunset," she grumbled, but followed me into the kitchen. As I started on her tea, she murmured, "Our Gray Lands gate was quite near this place."

"Yikes. Sugar?"

She shook her head. "I was sixteen when it opened. A hole in the world wide enough to let ten men pass abreast and equally tall. Myrddin tried for years to close it, but he never could." She leaned against the counter and took the mug I passed her, staring into her drink as if the answers were hiding in the teabag. "So how was it closed? If it was a natural gate, if the skin here is thin, then what came along to heal it?"

Something she said made me pause. "Myrddin didn't try to close it."

"Yes, he did. He tried all manner of craft, but—"

"He told us that he didn't even attempt it."

Artur's brow knit. "Perhaps he's forgotten."

"Or perhaps he's not been entirely honest with one of us." I stood opposite her, clutching my mug as my mental gears turned. "He talked about the gate when he told us about you. He said it was natural and large, and he wasn't strong enough to seal it—"

"As I just said."

"Right, but he also told us that he didn't try to fix it. He thought it was too risky—that Titania might notice the amount of enchantment it would have taken to plug the hole. He couldn't afford to blow his cover."

The look on her face told me that the trajectory of

Artur's thoughts was lining up with mine. "He had no reason to lie to you."

"What if he didn't attempt to close the gate? What if he told you he was trying but only went through the motions? You'd have been satisfied that he was doing his best, and he wouldn't have had to take a risk."

"But...*no*," she insisted vehemently, "if he'd had the skill, he would have helped us. You heard what I said today about the creatures that attacked us from the Gray Lands. We lost people, crops, homes...no, Myrddin would have done something if he could."

Though she spoke with conviction, her eyes were troubled.

"We could ask him," I quietly suggested. "See what he remembers about it. Maybe he knows how it eventually closed up." Putting my drink aside, I gripped her arm. "You don't want to see him, I understand that. I'm happy to go by myself. But right now, we need all the information we can get. Maybe he'd even be willing to help out."

Artur seemed poised to object, but she clenched her teeth, sat her mug back on the counter, and nodded. "You're right. I'll dress."

"Dress?" I asked as she retreated to her room.

I waited, reading over Marcus's shoulder in the den, until she emerged with Caledfwlch belted on. "Habit," she said. "I feel naked without it."

"No judgment here," I replied, and bent to kiss the top of Marcus's head. "We'll be back. Going to go have a word with Myrddin."

He looked up from his research, took in Artur's weaponry, and frowned. "Do you want me to come along?"

"Nah," I said, smirking. "Whether he likes it or not, he's my father. Surely he can spare ten minutes."

I'd aimed for the patio of Myrddin's tower, which I found deserted in the cloud-patchy afternoon light. Artur closed our gate and inspected our surroundings, taking in the laden trellis, the fire pit, and the spectacular ocean view. "He's improved the island since I was last here," she said, pulling a grape from a dangling vine.

"I mean, it *has* been a few years..."

She chewed thoughtfully and spat the seed over her shoulder. "Do we knock?"

"Well, I wasn't planning on standing outside like an idiot all day," I retorted, and headed for the tower door. "If he's not in, he's either on his yacht or hunkered down in Port Warren. I can get us there, if need be..." My pounding on the door was met with silence, but I tried the handle and found it unlocked. "Maybe he's in. Let's see."

The tower was as I'd last seen it—Caledfwlch's empty boulder standing like a tombstone in the center of the floor, a staircase spiraling around the central shaft toward Myrddin's quarters, and no indication of welcome. "It's us!" I shouted up the tower. "Need to talk to you!"

A door above us creaked open, then slammed, and a gate blazed open at the bottom of the staircase. "Kitty," Myrddin muttered as he strode through, then gave my sister a long, hard look. "Artur. You've changed your appearance."

"I didn't feel a need to replace the bind," she replied.

He pressed his lips together as he studied her. "Doesn't suit you. Let me—"

"*No.*" She lifted a hand to stay him. "That won't be necessary."

Myrddin shrugged and folded his arms. "You've finally decided to come home, then?"

"Indeed. I'm staying with Kitty in...what do you call it, again?"

"Glastonbury," I offered.

"Yes, that. Her people have been most kind."

I'd expected Myrddin to be upset at the news, but he

showed no more concern for Artur's living situation than he would for a stranger's. "Then what do you want?"

"We've got a situation brewing with the Gray Lands," I began, but Artur cut me off.

"Answers," she said, staring Myrddin in the face. "I will have complete honesty, is that clear?"

One of his pale eyebrows rose. "Issuing commands without a throne? Do you suppose that's wise?"

"All I want is the truth," she replied, her voice low but sharp, a razor hidden in velvet folds. "You owe me that much."

By then, I knew damn well that my planned quick outing had gone off the rails, and something told me that Artur wouldn't be denied. Still, I tried to get us back on track. "We need to know about the old Gray Lands gate in Afallon," I said, hoping the segue would work.

Myrddin glanced my way. "What about it?"

"For starters, you told me that it was naturally occurring. How did it finally close?"

"You told *me* that you were unable to manage it," Artur added.

He looked back and forth between us for a moment, then shrugged. "I...*massaged* some of the details in the telling. Why does it matter?"

"Because the queen of the Gray Lands is threatening war, and we're concerned that she's about to invade Somerset," I replied before Artur could get a word in. "So how did the gate close?"

"Honestly? Morgen took care of it when she left."

"She could have managed it all along?" Artur cried. "Why didn't she say so?"

"Because I asked her not to."

Myrddin seemed as nonchalant as if he were discussing the weather, and I watched his face, wondering if mine looked like that when I was bored.

While Artur sputtered, Myrddin pulled a pint of ale from thin air and drank. "You want the truth of the gate?

Fine," he said between sips. "I found it open one night when I went walking to clear my head. A pair of cynaeli had come through, probably running from their war. They were making camp, as I recall. I killed them before they knew I was there, but that left the matter of the hole. Closing a gate into the Gray Lands means working against dark magic, which takes a fair bit of enchantment and technique. Had I patched it, I might as well have set off a flare and waited for Titania to find me—or so I worried at the time. Perhaps she'd called off the active search by then, but I wasn't going to chance it. She was unpredictable when enraged." He sipped again, staring off into space. "So instead of trying to close it, I used it to our advantage."

"*Advantage*?" Artur shouted. "My people *died* because of that—"

"Yes, and we both lived, and you kept your kingdom for a time. Look at the bigger picture, child."

"How—"

"If you'll stop yapping, I'll explain," he retorted. "I expanded the gate and stabilized it, increasing the dark magic flow into the area. That way, unless she was actively hunting me, Titania would have no incentive to come near the gate. As for you, the benefits were twofold." He smiled at her over his beer, but there was nothing kind in his expression. "You were made high king only because those other simpletons knew you had a gift for magic. They feared you, and at first, they resented being subject to a mere boy. With the gate open, however, all manner of training opportunities came wandering in for you. Every time you slew a monster, your reputation grew. The skills presumably translated into battle with your Saxon friends," he added. "In sum, yes, I could have closed the gate, had I wanted to risk my head, but instead, I made it work for us both. You're welcome."

Artur stared incredulously at him. "Afallon fell because of that gate," she managed, her voice shaking. "My men were *slaughtered*. And you tell me now that you could have prevented everything?"

"I didn't anticipate the smoke creatures," he admitted. "Even Morgen was surprised to see them—they're rare in that realm. If you'd been wise and waited for her to do her work, you wouldn't have been hurt, and you'd still have had a kingdom to rule. Oh, Afallon would surely have fallen in time," he said as her face crimsoned, "but you'd have had it to play with a while longer. But you were foolish, I was sentimental enough to send you with Morgen when you were on the brink of death, and then, when you didn't return promptly, I fled before I could be swept up in the regime change."

"Why lie to us?" I interjected.

"Let's see," he replied with faux contemplation, "I was on my own against…hmm, a high lord older than me, two wizards, and whatever the fuck your other friends are. I'd already managed to antagonize your party once that morning, and as you seemed somewhat distressed when I explained what I'd done for Artur, I modified the other details to make the story more palatable to your sensibilities. A safety measure, you understand."

"That's not the only thing you changed," I pointed out. "Ros told us about what you did to Artur's mother."

He regarded me quizzically. "I told you that I bedded her."

"You didn't say that it was under false pretenses. Or that you did so repeatedly."

"Tell me," said Artur, her voice half an octave lower than before, "how many nights did you rape my mother?"

"Rape?" he echoed. "I assure you, she was most satisfied. She enjoyed every minute of your getting."

"Because she thought she was making love to her husband," I rejoined. "Seriously, you can't stand there and tell me she *consented* if she only had sex with you under false pretenses."

He swigged his beer. "Agree to disagree. And again,"

he said to Artur, "you're welcome. However unpleasant you may find your conception, the fact remains that it's the only reason you exist." With a final sip, he sent what remained of his drink back into the ether. "I created you," he said, smirking in the face of her anger. "Gave you life. Molded you into the stuff of legend. And now...well," he said, flipping his hand at her, "just look at you. The slightest loss, and you crumble. *Pathetic*. I thought I taught you better than that."

"You would speak to me of loss?" she whispered, her arms tense and shaking. "You don't *know* loss."

"Poor child. So dramatic," said Myrddin, rolling his eyes. "Mortals die, Artur. It's their defining trait. They come and go, and if you're not a sentimental idiot, you barely miss them. That was my problem," he continued, and shook his head. "I got attached to you. If I'd been reasonable, I'd have left you on the field, but Morgen offered, and I wasn't thinking clearly. Well, no matter. You're here now, you have your life, your...new look," he said with distaste, "for whatever that's worth. Really, you should be on your knees thanking me."

In that instant, the rage that had been building inside Artur boiled over. With a furious scream, she pulled Caledfwlch free of its scabbard and charged at Myrddin, raising the blade to strike.

He barely flinched, and she went sailing backward across the tower. When she slammed into the stone wall, the sword clattered on the floor, out of her reach, and she gasped to draw breath. "This is the thanks I get?" said Myrddin, storming across the room as she struggled to focus. "I *made* you, and this is how you repay me?"

Artur tried to rise, but before she could find her feet, Myrddin's enchantment yanked her from the floor and threw her into the wall a second time.

"Pathetic," he said again as she moaned, and then he squatted before her and watched as she blearily blinked. "Did you really think you could attack me and win?"

Again, Artur was lifted and flung into the stone, and when she fell, her eyes barely fluttered.

As my panic rose, I wasn't aware that I was calling Caledfwlch to me until I felt the hilt in my hand. "*Stop!*" I shouted at Myrddin. "Get away from her!"

Focused as he was on his target, he almost jumped at the sound of my voice. When he turned to see me a few yards away, holding the sword in my best amateur stance, he laughed in disbelief. "Careful, mongrel, you'll cut yourself with that."

I ignored the jibe. "You're both upset, I get it, but what are you *doing*? That's Artur, you've been waiting for her all this time…"

My protestation faded as he shook his head. "You liked that part, didn't you? I thought you would. Grieving father keeps watch for a millennium and a half, hoping his child will miraculously reappear—has a certain pathos, doesn't it? Women love a good sob story."

The tip of the sword dropped as I tried to make sense of what he was saying. "I don't…wait, I don't understand—"

"Simple." He took a few steps away from Artur, who was twitching as if her body were trying to stand irrespective of any concussion she'd suffered. "I missed Artur at first, I admit that. Had Morgen brought him back in, say, a week or two, before the kingdom went to hell, things might have been different. But then I left Afallon to fend for itself and came out here, and I carried on without worrying about child-minding a king. After a few years, I just assumed that Artur would never come back. No real loss, that," he added, spreading his arms. "I've done rather well for myself, I'd say."

"But you kept Artur's sword!" I protested, waving the blade. "Just in case—"

"Titania attacked," he finished. "It was a nice piece of work. Would have been a shame to obliterate it, so I kept it on hand as a weapon of last resort."

I heard what he was saying, but my heart rebelled against my head. "You gave it to me. You told me to take care of it…"

The look on Myrddin's face, though cold, was almost pitying. "I thought I was solving a problem," he replied, staring back at me through an ancient version of my own eyes. "You seemed spunky. Eager. I assumed that if I handed you a magic sword, you'd feel obligated to go questing—and what better sword for the occasion than Caledfwlch? You heard my sad history, you had Artur's blade—it was only a matter of time before you tried to return it to its original owner."

"You knew I'd go after Artur," I murmured.

"Yeah. I just hadn't planned on you returning."

His words should have been devastating—this was my father, calmly relating how he'd nudged me off on a suicidal fool's errand—but my mother had already done a fair job of scarring and deadening the place in my soul where they struck. "Tough talk," I said, "but I saw your reaction when I told you I'd brought Artur out. Whether you admit it or not, you care."

Myrddin shrugged. "A moment of sentiment, nothing more. The human side of me does flare on occasion. You want the truth? I was shocked," he said, slowly closing the distance between us. "I had a brief delusion that it would be a good thing to bring Artur here, and then I saw what a weeping mess he'd become. *And* he had the temerity to lash out at me when I revealed myself as his father. In all honesty, you should have left him in the Gray Lands. There's no place for Artur in this world…nor is there one for you."

I anticipated the bolt a fraction of a second before it left Myrddin's hand, but that was all I needed. Though the shield I called forth nearly cracked under the strain, it held, and I stared through the haze with faint satisfaction as he tried to puzzle out why the lethal strike had rebounded. "When you're raised a witch," I said, retreating a few paces, "you learn every focusing technique you come across. Some of those translate pretty well to enchantment. And then some asshole goes and gives you a magic fucking sword, and voila, shield."

He sighed impatiently. "Would you just shut up and die already?" he said, and fired again.

The second bolt was stronger than the first, and I felt it in the bones of my shield arm, thrumming from my splayed fingers to my shoulder like an electric shock. "I'll leave you be," I promised as I braced myself for the next attack, dancing away for distance. "We don't have to do this."

"You're right, we don't. Drop the shield, and I'll make this quick."

His next shots came as a volley, and I started to sweat with the effort of maintaining my defenses. "I've done nothing to you!"

"You exist."

A massive bolt sent me to my knees. Arcanum training aside, I was still only twenty-four, while Myrddin had nearly two thousand years of experience under his belt. True, he didn't seem to be half the fighter Val was, but his years alone conferred a massive advantage.

And I was trapped. Creating a gate would necessitate pulling resources away from the shield—and if I ran, I'd be leaving Artur at Myrddin's mercy. Distantly, my brain reminded me of the techniques Mina had shown me, like translocating out of harm's way, but I had no time to experiment. Every ounce of my strength and focus was devoted to the sole enchantment keeping me alive.

"If you kill me," I managed through the pain, "Marcus will hunt you down. And if he doesn't find you, Val will. You thought Titania was bad?" I said, then cried out at another powerful blast.

He chuckled as he drew closer. "Why would a king give a damn about you?"

"Because," I said, struggling to my feet, "family isn't

just about blood."

Myrddin's next shot was thin and focused, and it pierced my shield like a crossbow bolt through paper. I moved my hand away in time, but Caledfwlch took the full impact, and the force ripped the sword from my grasp. It flew halfway across the room and banged against the wall, glowing with absorbed energy, and I scrambled to shore up my suddenly weakened shield.

"Please," I begged, throwing everything I had into the insufficient barrier between us, "let us go. I'll take Artur away, we won't be back. Don't do this." Trying one last, desperate tactic, I said, "We're your *children*! You made us!"

"And now I'm cleaning up my messes," he replied, and raised his hand. "Starting with the drunken mistake."

Time slowed as I stared at him, waiting for the inevitable and praying for a change of heart that would never come. In the space between breaths, I saw a flash of light in my peripheral vision, but I knew it wasn't a gate. Help wasn't coming from Glastonbury, and I was going to die there in that tower on the hidden island. My mind flashed to Marcus, to Maria, to Beth…

At least she finally got my letters was my last thought before I saw the background magic activate around Myrddin's fingertips.

And then, like an enraged Fury, Artur appeared at Myrddin's side with Caledfwlch in her hand. She raised the sword, and Myrddin, caught unawares, only had time to turn his head before it sliced into his shoulder, cleaving the bones in one clean slice. His right arm dropped to the floor, and he stared at the gushing stump in shock for a second before he began to scream.

Shaking with the sudden reprieve, I realized that the flash of light I'd seen had been Caledfwlch returning to its true master. Artur was swaying on her feet like an inebriate on a pitching ship, but her grip on the sword was firm, and her kick sent Myrddin's severed arm skittering into the empty bolder at the center of the room.

"Gate," she ordered, putting him in a headlock.

A peek at her mind made her wishes clear, and I was only too happy to oblige.

I'd been in Coileán's office exactly once before, back in my first year at Arc 2, when Magus Leighton attacked me. Pain and fear are fantastic for impressing details upon one's memory, however, and so I probably could have sketched the pattern on that office's rug, had I been asked. Calling the room to mind, I ripped open a gate, then followed after as Artur dragged Myrddin through.

The king, who was deep in a stack of paperwork when we arrived, raised his head and gaped. "Moon and—"

"Hello again, Coileán," Artur interrupted, gesturing the gate closed. "This is one of yours. Do as you will—I want no part of him."

She threw Myrddin to the floor in front of his desk, then turned aside, vomited, and slumped to the ground.

By then, Coileán was up and moving. I saw twin blasts of enchantment flare over Artur and Myrddin, and suddenly, both were still and deeply asleep. An instant later, a panting aide ran into the room, and Coileán pointed to Myrddin. "Stop the bleeding, if you will, then see to her," he said, then took me by the wrist and pulled me to one of his leather couches. "*Sit*, kid."

Only after I sank onto the cushion did I realize I was trembling.

Coileán crossed to his bar and returned with a crystal tumbler halfway filled with an amber liquid. "Drink this slowly," he instructed, taking the couch opposite mine.

I'd never had a taste for whisky, but the double he'd given me tasted like the distillation of smoke and salt, and it warmed my throat without the burn I knew all too well from uni. "A pet project," said Coileán, watching me drink. "Passable?"

"Fantastic." The whisky sloshed up the sides of my glass with the tremor in my hand.

He gave me a moment to breathe and the alcohol a

moment to wash over me, then said, "What the hell, Kitty? And keep drinking, girl—you're white as a sheet."

As concisely as I could, I relayed what had transpired on Afallon between sips. "Artur's got to be concussed," I concluded, cocking my head toward her as Coileán's aide wove a healing enchantment around her body. "And Myrddin was going to kill us both, hence the amputation. If you want to reattach the arm, it's back in the tower," I added, trying and failing to suppress a short burst of hysterical laughter.

"You know," a familiar voice interrupted, "I wouldn't be overly concerned."

We turned to find Ros perched on the corner of Coileán's desk. "No?" he asked.

"Nah. He's had payback coming for a *long* time."

Though it was getting harder for me to focus—the alcohol was exacerbating my fatigue as the adrenaline ran its course—something seemed amiss with her declaration. "He insulted Titania's dress and ran away. That shouldn't cost him an arm."

She tilted her head and smirked. "Agreed. It's what he did later that night that makes me less than sympathetic." As I frowned in confusion, she said, "Titania was petty, but she wasn't *that* awful. She'd have forgiven a crack about a stupid dress. The reason that Myrddin fled for his life is because he killed one of her sons."

Coileán's eyebrows rose. "*Who?*"

"Brucon. He was only twenty, but he was one of her pets. *Beautiful* specimen. And since Myrddin's father was also Brucon's father, you understand why there was a tiny bit of jealousy there. Big brother's a half-fae lord of minor consequence, little brother's a full-blooded favorite of the queen. Setup for disaster."

"What happened?" I asked.

Ros stared into space, seeing the realm's collective memory. "Brucon danced with a girl Myrddin liked, Myrddin confronted him in the hall, and Brucon told him off. When he was walking away, Myrddin threw a bolt at his head. Killed him almost instantly. To no one's surprise, Titania was enraged, but she gave up the hunt pretty quickly. Thought that forcing him to skulk around the mortal realm for the rest of his life, always looking over his shoulder, was punishment enough. I mean, it's not like she didn't have other kids."

"Well, that's just dandy," I muttered into my rapidly draining glass. "My mother's a murderous traitor, my father's a murderous rapist, and I'm—"

I never finished that thought.

Later, I learned that Coileán had knocked me out to let me sleep off my shock and whisky. It might not have been what Wanda would have recommended, but at least I woke without a hangover.

When I opened my eyes again, night had fallen in Faerie, but Coileán had lit lamps in his office. I was still on the couch, albeit with a plaid afghan tucked around me, and Artur sat where I'd last seen Coileán, watching as I eased myself upright. "Hey," I mumbled, still tasting that last dram, "how're you feeling?"

"Better. I've been told that I may have dizzy moments for the next few days, but I'm intact." She rapped her knuckles against her head as proof. "And my ribs have almost healed."

"Didn't know you'd broken any."

"Five, as it turns out. Stone tends to be unforgiving." She waited until I'd pulled the afghan around my shoulders, then said, "Coileán locked him away. With everything else going on, he thought it best to deal with Myrddin later—'put him on ice,' that's what he said."

"Sounds wise." When Artur made no reply, I added, "Thanks for saving my ass."

"You froze," she chided.

"I was doing the best I could—"

"By standing there, letting him hit you?" Her voice rose in agitation. "Didn't Mina teach you anything?"

"I don't have the power you do," I protested. "Shielding took everything, and that was with the sword helping me."

"You could have run."

"And you might be dead, so all in all, I think I made the right decision."

She silently conceded the point but refused to end the reprimand. "And what were you doing with the sword? It's no use if you hold it still—your opponent isn't going to throw himself onto it if you stand there long enough."

"I was drawing from it, not fighting with it."

"Well, *that's* obvious," she replied, and huffed. "Do you even know how to wield a blade?"

"I know which is the pointy end," I retorted.

"Any idiot knows that." She stood, wincing as she caught a sore muscle in her chest. "Assuming we don't die in the next few days, you might ask Mina for lessons. But for now, Coileán said we're free to leave. Eat and go back to bed," she ordered as she opened a gate to my flat.

"Bossy, aren't we?" I muttered, following her through.

"Decisive. And—"

"Where have you *been*?" Marcus demanded, emerging from his bedroom as Artur closed the gate. "I've been calling all afternoon…did you get anything useful from Myrddin?"

Artur and I looked at each other, but her face was a careful blank. "I don't you want you to freak out, okay?" I said, running my hands over Marcus's tense shoulders. "Myrddin tried to kill us, but he's in Coileán's custody now. I napped over there while Artur—"

"*What?*"

"There's no lasting damage—"

The rest was lost in a grunt as Marcus pulled me close and squeezed. Opening my mind just slightly, I could sense the comingled fear and fury in his. "Coileán's got him locked away," I managed once Marcus let me breathe. "We're fine. Everything's fine. Besides the impending Gray

Lands invasion, I mean. Oh—turns out the gate Artur dealt with *wasn't* natural, so Glastonbury may not be as weak as we'd thought."

He said nothing as he continued to hold me, but before I could try again to reassure him, I heard my little sister's voice from across the den: "Hey, where were you?"

"*Beth*?" I yelped, extricating myself from Marcus's arms. "What are you doing here?"

She crossed her arms over her T-shirt self-consciously. "The Games are next week, and we're not in school, so, I mean, I thought I'd come over early and, uh…acclimate. To the time change, you know? Piper said it was okay. And *he's* in my room," she added, pointing to Marcus.

"I've got a new one waiting for you—"

"Yeah, and how the heck does it have a *window*? It's got rooms on all sides!"

I shrugged. "Magic. But, um…Beth, sweetie," I said, hurrying across the room, "this isn't a great time."

"Oh."

"It's not that I don't want you here, but—"

"No, I get it," she interrupted, turning to go. "I didn't unpack much. Let me call Piper—"

"You can stay if you—"

"If you don't want me, just say so, okay? I get it."

"Child," Artur snapped, "this isn't about you. The Gray Lands has promised war on the morrow, so unless you're a better fighter than our sister—"

Beth finally noticed her, then did a double-take. "Wait, who—"

"That's Artur," I explained. "Minus a transformation bind. She's staying in the bedroom next to yours."

"And I'll see you in the morning," Artur muttered, marching past us and locking her door.

While Beth, beside herself, began to squeal, Marcus quietly told me, "You know, if you wanted her to return to Montana, that might have been the wrong information to share."

CHAPTER 18

When Maria knocked shortly after dawn, I was putting the finishing touches on a coffee cake. The pan of brownies had long since cooled and been stuffed into Tupperware for safekeeping, and the egg casserole wanted only its final layer of shredded cheese and brief broiling. She took my messy kitchen in stride, tidied the dishes in the sink with a moment's concentration, and set about making tea without a word.

After all, there are friends, and then there are the friends who know how you take your tea and where you hide the vanilla syrup you keep around just for them.

When the oven timer beeped, I extracted the bubbling casserole and looked up to find Beth groggily shuffling out of her room. "Whassat?" she mumbled, squinting at the loaded baking dish in my hands.

"I stress-bake," I explained, putting it aside to cool. "Please tell me you're hungry."

She was, as it turned out, as were Maria and Marcus. I picked at mine until Artur emerged, fully dressed and armed but sporting an impressive set of dark circles beneath her eyes. Loading a plate for her, I asked, "Get any sleep?"

"Little." She tucked in robotically, sucking bits of egg and sausage from her fingertips as she worked, then glanced up when the weight of Beth's stare grew too heavy. "Yes?"

"You want a fork or something?" Beth asked, frowning at Artur's table manners.

She popped a piece of crisped cheese into her mouth. "No. Why?"

"Just, uh…wondering."

Before breakfast could devolve into a lecture on the historical use of personal utensils, Maria gave us the update from the Council side. "We met until one this morning," she said, nursing her third cup of strong tea. "Naturally, no one is thrilled at the prospect of hostilities with the Gray Lands."

"But they're not going to buck Toula, are they?" I asked.

"Not as of yet. I'm ruling nothing out," she muttered into her mug. "Arc 1 is, of course, being Arc 1, and Arc 7 is right behind them. They want to send Hope back."

"That's not unreasonable," said Artur. "She's not your responsibility. The Arcanum is taking an unnecessary risk by sheltering her."

"Because it's the right thing to do," I interjected.

She raised her empty palms. "I didn't say otherwise. But ethics aside, it's a great risk with little reward."

"And if it were against anyone other than Nath, I'd agree with you," said Maria. "But she's been making plans to come over for forty years. Now, she has a legitimate grievance."

"Oh, *right*," I interrupted, "because kidnapping—"

"Legitimate *from her perspective*. She's been slighted— maybe she thinks Faerie will stay out of it because her cause is not baseless and her actions are reasonable. Or maybe she just thinks she can take us. Who knows?" Maria sipped her tea and slowly exhaled. "The castle's going on lockdown at eight. If you left something in town, get it now. And you should probably go home," she told Beth. "If Nath mounts a direct attack, she'll hit us first."

Beth folded her arms and scowled. "I can help. I brought my wand."

"You're…a fourth-year?"

"I've read ahead! And I'm in the combat competition

next week—"

"She wants to be useful," said Artur before Maria could protest. "Let her."

Beth shot Maria a look of triumph, but Maria shook her head. "Solo combat against other teenagers isn't the same as fighting well-trained tennuwaya."

"I'll stay out of the way," Beth wheedled. "*Please*, Magus. I could, like, squire for someone. Keep up with spare gear and stuff."

Before Maria could respond, her phone rang. "I'm at Kitty's," she told the caller—Toula, I deduced. "What's...ah. On my way."

Ending the call, she glanced around the table and stood. "Val's troops have arrived. Who wants to help me keep the peace?"

Val had opened a gate just beyond the castle walls but well within the ward bubble, and armed faeries were still pouring through by the time we arrived. Toula, dressed in black sweats and a tactical vest, stood near the ceremonial door, gawking as the arriving forces made camp. "How many?" Maria asked as we jogged up to join her.

"I've lost count," she said, watching a pennant-topped pavilion bloom from the lawn. The flags flapped in the stiff morning breeze, ribbons of cloth signifying nothing but the owner's preferred color scheme. "I was hoping for, like, a few dozen of them."

Val approached with Kiet, the captain of his guard, and gestured toward the gate. "I've asked them to hurry. It shouldn't take much longer."

"You didn't have to schlepp the entire court over," she replied. "I...honestly, I wasn't planning on so many..."

He chuckled. "This isn't the entire court, little sister. You should get out more often."

"If I may?" Kiet interrupted. "Lady Fotoula, there is little love between much of the court and Nath. She *did* banish us upon taking power."

"So, you're telling me—"

"We had *volunteers*. I rejected some—I tried to keep the balance tilted toward the half-blooded in an effort to limit unnecessary infighting, but there were many who were adamant that they be allowed to participate. About three hundred in all, I believe."

"Thank you," she told Val, then nodded to Kiet. "And it's Toula, Captain. Grand Magus if you're feeling formal."

He glanced at the stone wall of the Arcanum stronghold and faintly smirked. "Of course. Is this an acceptable location to camp? We could…"

Kiet fell silent as a second gate opened and Mina strolled through at the head of Coileán's guard. "Good morning!" she said, raising a hand in greeting. "Who's ready for battle?"

The king emerged after the advance guard, took one look at the encamped army, and glared at Val. "*Really?*"

"It's a glorified grudge match," Val replied, grinning at Coileán's exasperation.

He grabbed Mina's arm and asked, "How many did you enlist?"

"A hundred and fifty," she replied, scanning the tents. "There are another hundred or so I could call upon if necessary, but for the moment—"

"Boys," Toula interrupted, looking between the two kings, "I love you both. This isn't a competition—"

A third gate appeared near the second, disgorging the dozen Stowe brothers, most of whom dragged carts of computer equipment. "Fringe delivery," said Aiden, closing the hole behind him, and waved to his surprised brother, who still seemed peeved at being outdone by his girlfriend's brother. "Amy and Vivi sent me over to set up the command center. Toula, do you have a clean room in here? Somewhere with limited magical interference?"

"Subbasement would be safest," she said, going into command mode. "Maria, take them down to the Away

Team's suite and try to set up blocking wards for the electronics. That conference room is decently large, yeah?"

"On it," she said, and pulled out her phone as the Stowes approached. "Mal? Hi, tell Ted the office is being appropriated. And your dad's here, so—"

"Ask him to put the coffee on," Rufus Stowe called from the head of the pack. "And we're going to need power strips, surge protectors, plug converters—"

"Is Antony there yet?" Maria asked Mal. "Oh, *good*. On our way down."

As she opened one intra-realm gate into our office, another appeared just beyond Coileán, from which came Carey, Tanner, and a score each of their people. "Caught a ride with the Minor Arcanum," said Tanner, strolling across the lawn in a seersucker suit and white bucks. "Any word from Nath?"

"Still waiting," said Toula, and gestured a pair of large tents into existence near their gate. "Thanks for coming. It's, uh...a little chaotic here right now, as you can probably see..."

"Understood," said Carey, and beckoned forward a stylishly dressed woman with bright pink hair and a computer bag. "Hua, I think I see the Fringe equipment. Why don't you go with them?"

As she passed me, I could see the signs of Hua's age—sixties at least, I estimated—but she was trim and spry, and Rufus waved and waited for her to catch up. Noticing me watching her depart, Carey murmured, "One of our Beijing-based wizards. She's worked with Badger and Seamus, so I trust her to play nicely with a mixed group."

"Okay," Toula muttered, rubbing her neck as she watched Coileán's forces make themselves at home, "I think we should have enough room within the wards..."

Another gate ripped open, and out marched Eleanor, already sporting camouflage-printed cargo pants, brown combat boots, and a pair of pistols—iron-free, naturally—on belts crossed at her hips. "Sorry I'm late," she said to

Toula, then nodded to the kings and stepped aside as her army spilled forth.

Val and Coileán seemed as surprised as Toula by the crowd from her court. "Uh," Toula ventured, scanning the rapidly filling lawn, "how many—"

"Oh, about five hundred," the queen breezily replied. "Don't worry, dear, they'll see to themselves."

"Five hundred?" Val echoed. "Where did you find so many?"

Eleanor regarded him as if he were slow. "Mine is the largest court, boys, and Gondor called for aid. Voila."

"Right," Toula said slowly, staring about her at the growing encampment. "So, it looks like I've got somewhere around a thousand faeries, shifters, and Minor Arcanum here, and…" She paused, then whistled low. "I was planning to put your folks in the dorms, since they're set up for the Games, but…"

Eleanor clapped her on the back. "The hospitality is appreciated but unnecessary. If you'd be so kind as to warn your people that our people are out here, that would be enough." Noticing Artur, Marcus, and me, she smiled grimly and gestured toward the impromptu tent city. "Are you three here as security or just gawking?"

"Maria's entourage, my lady," I replied. "Looks like y'all are, um…set…but if—"

"Kids, subbasement," Toula ordered before we could explore. "Whatever the Fringe needs, get it."

Val nodded vehemently, Coileán motioned us along, and seeing no sign of help from Eleanor, we retreated into the castle.

I could tell that Artur wasn't thrilled with the dismissal—she wasn't wearing her sword for nothing—and though I wanted to take her aside and ask how she was coping with Myrddin, there was no time. We found the suite in a state of barely controlled chaos, with Ted and several of the Stowes setting up Fringe equipment, Hua connecting hers to their grid, Aiden running down a checklist at each machine to bring it online, and Antony sending Mal and Daphne, two of the more tech-savvy Team members, on errands to retrieve power cords and spare generators. Frank had been unceremoniously kicked out as soon as Maria announced her intention to protect the machines by warding the area against magic—letting his bind break down there in a low-magic environment would have been disastrous to everyone's safety and the continued structural integrity of the tower. Lakshmi, the Team's organizational maven, had been drafted by Arc 2's main logistics crew to assist with the incoming forces from the other installations. As for Bob, he tended the coffee and tea and talked scones with Luce Stowe, who, though employed as Eleanor's chef and clueless about the Fringe's network, had proven game to go along with his brothers.

Soon enough, Aiden and Rufus had established a connection to the main network in Faerie, and Hua brought the Minor Arcanum's special array into the mix. "We have turned on the detectors again," she said to the monitor dedicated to the video feed from the Fringe's windowless war room in City Hall. She spoke with a strong accent I assumed was Chinese, but more specific than that was beyond my expertise.

Kip, who was watching the feed from the settlement side, nodded. "Amy's old detectors? How many are still operational?"

"All, as far as I know. She continued to build and repair them until she left this realm, so unless something has broken in the last twenty years…"

"Understood. How many?"

Aiden, who had paused to look at Hua's computer, muttered, "Whoa."

"Three hundred sixty-four," Hua told Kip. "Most in major cities, a few in more remote locations. All are being watched now. The range on each is sixteen hundred kilometers, approximately, but this program is built to triangulate and account for dark magic concentration."

I sneaked a look and found a slowly spinning globe on Hua's monitor, pocked with white diamonds—the locations of the detectors, I surmised.

"If an attack begins anywhere beyond Glastonbury," Hua continued, "then we will know."

Kip tapped a button, and the screen split to link in Yolanda, her hair braided back and covered with a black bandana. "You've got more eyes than you realize," she said, adjusting her headset for optimal microphone placement. "Amy's been making them for us, too. More sensitive models. We've been hiding them in remote locations over here for the last decade."

Hua smiled. "Good, good. How many?"

"Only about a hundred—we've lost some to floods and one *spectacular* volcano, but"—her microphone picked up the click of computer keys—"Carey shared your app, Amy patched us in, and our set should be coming online...now."

Hua's globe suddenly gained a set of yellow dots. "They'll alarm in the same way," Yolanda explained, "and they'll triangulate with yours. Of course, this is all probably overkill," she said with a soft laugh. "Given that Nath knows the way to Glastonbury, I don't see how she'd get lost..."

Yolanda fell silent as Hua's computer began to blatt. The border of the screen flashed red, the globe stopped spinning, and three of the indicators in Siberia strobed in time with the siren, sending out red lines that converged on a new red circle on the map.

"Probably a fluke," said Aiden. "That's the middle of nowhere. Could just be a new natural gate—"

The alarm restarted, and as the snapshot of the Siberia gate moved into the upper-left quadrant of the screen, the picture rotated to reveal another triangulation in process over southern Chile. That shot moved to the bottom-left of the monitor as a third location was detected, then a fourth.

By the time the seventh gate opened, Ted was on the phone to Toula. "Get down here *now*," he said, staring at the monitor as it populated with smaller and smaller alert maps. "She's not coming for Glastonbury. By the looks of it, she's going everywhere *but*."

There was no time to strategize—some of the gates were dangerously close to civilization, and closing them had to be the first priority.

The subbasement suddenly got a lot more crowded as Toula's aides and top magi swarmed in and out of the command room. The grand magus set up a laptop at the end of the table, linked into the Fringe's network, to monitor the updating spreadsheet of gates. Closure teams were dispatched through a steady stream of intra-realm gates with every dark magic detector that installation security could find on the premises. Though less magically adept than many, the Team were happy to tap into the Fringe's extensive records of location photographs and feed the data to the magi running the gates, while the Fringe hive back in Faerie fielded phone calls for updates on gate locations. Even with triangulation, the detectors could only offer a range of where the targets might be, and narrowing that range took time. A hastily configured central phone line into City Hall connected the deployed to three dozen Fringers, who worked with the calm patience of emergency services operators—and thanks to the collective linguistic skills of the Fringe, there were substitutes on hand who could relay information in languages from Afrikaans to Zulu.

At first, the four-member closure teams were segregated into bands pulled from the Arcanum and from each of the courts. As the morning wore on and the Gray Lands gates showed no sign of stopping, however, the teams began to mix. The returning rested together in the castle's dining hall—the overwhelmed staff, who hadn't been warned of the influx, did the best they could by tossing sandwich fixings onto a buffet line and promising a better spread that evening—and as closers traded reports and impromptu coordinators rotated the exhausted out of the lineup, a few names began to rise to the top of everyone's lists. I learned later that Ned Stowe was the first to swipe a pair of Council aides for his party, and when they returned quickly, others followed suit. Gray Lands gates were notoriously tricky things, and while enchantment *could* seal them, the Arcanum had far more experience in that arena. Thus, since no one knew exactly what would be waiting at a gate site, the teams got smarter. Faeries could quickly seal small gates. Wizards were better at the complicated craft needed for larger gates, leaving the faeries free to handle the other half of the equation: whatever had come through the gate in the time it had been open. And when the gates were big enough, there was no telling how many teeth the intruders would have.

There was no obvious pattern to the gates. A car-sized one opened in northern Japan and was closed in a matter of minutes. A hole as wide as my den opened over the Grand Canyon and released a swarm of creatures that could have been mistaken for bats, had they not been dark green and thirsty for human blood. At least a dozen gates opened over the Pacific alone, and there was no way to know what had been released into the ocean. The gates never disgorged tennuwaya or cynaeli, but nearly always there was something unpleasant waiting.

I volunteered for the closure teams, but Toula held me back, just as she did Artur. "Neither of you has much practice with your talent," she explained. "We have the manpower right now without resorting to anyone untested."

"I held it together in the Gray Lands, you know," I pointed out, miffed at once again being consigned to the sidelines for my safety. "And we both worked with Mina—"

"Who recommended that I not put you in."

Artur planted her palms on the desk and waited until Toula met her frustrated gaze. "I don't need magic to kill," she said, her voice low. "I'm more than competent with a blade."

"Understood and appreciated," Toula replied, "but sending you would be taking an unnecessary risk. You're untested yet."

"So test me!"

Despite her apparent youth, Toula was old and experienced enough to have mastered the art of the silent stare. Artur blinked first, and when she did, Toula quietly told her, "This bruises your pride, I get it, but your pride is the least of my concerns, kid. Do you want to be useful?"

"I wouldn't be here otherwise."

"Good. Go to the dining hall. Tell Neil Singh to give you a computer and show you the list. I need comprehensive updates on the situation out there and the condition of our closers, and we're understaffed. Ah—*stay*, Kitty," she ordered as Artur turned to go. "You're more useful to me down here."

There was no sense in appealing her decision, especially if Mina wanted me benched. And so I kept jumping in with information as needed, pulling from the Arcanum's and the Fringe's files as the situation dictated. Maria divided her time between the subbasement and the closure teams—since she knew our software, Toula preferred to keep her close, too—while Marcus had thrown himself into the chaos, partnering with his cousin, Seamus, who had come across with Val's contingent. Badger was understandably worried about her husband, and I did my best to give her updates as to his whereabouts, just as I did for Helen, who had both a husband and a brother to fret about from Faerie. With the computers stable, Aiden had joined the closure teams, and Joey slotted himself in as necessary. I felt for Helen and Badger—both were highly accomplished wizards, forced to remain in Faerie to keep from aging decades the second they crossed the border—but my updates that day were sporadic. We simply had too many fires to extinguish.

And having noticed Ros's boyfriend, Sam, among Eleanor's forces, I didn't even want to think about dealing with *her*.

By nightfall in Glastonbury, the B-string had rotated out, and the C-string took their turn, leaving in teams of six to eight to make up for their lesser talent. Still, it was barely enough to keep pace with the constant gates. Casualties had been reported among the Arcanum roster and the courts' ranks alike, and the castle's healers joined forces with the best of the fae talent to bind up the wounded. There was no official truce, no arrangement guaranteeing either side's safety, but exhaustion and a common enemy forged a temporary alliance. The kitchen made a point of having enough food on hand for the full complement of closure teams that night, and as a silent show of thanks, a few of Eleanor's guards whipped up a bar on one of the side tables.

Down in the subbasement, we did all we could to keep the gate monitors comfortable, bringing in food from upstairs and surrendering our office couches for power naps. The group in the conference room was not only keeping tabs of the closure teams but was also liaising with a squad of Fringers in both realms tasked with covering up the whole mess. All around the world, security cameras mysteriously failed, traffic lights went off-cycle, and even a few satellites suffered glitches. If it was connected to a computer, odds were good that someone within the Fringe knew a back door, but the work was never-ending, and scattered reports began to surface of bizarre incidents that the Fringe had been unable to fully suppress.

Shortly after midnight, as I downed another cup of coffee—my ninth of the day—Toula's phone went off in the conference room. "Yes?" she said, tapping the line open without looking away from the latest field reports.

"We've got a gate!" came the reply over the speaker—Australian and male, but otherwise a stranger to me.

"Hi, Connor," said Toula as she wearily rubbed her forehead. "Can you not handle it?"

"Magus Norleigh," Maria muttered, seeing my bemusement.

That explained why he had Toula's private number. Magus Norleigh was the recently appointed head of Arc 7—almost forty and quite talented, but given to bouts of panic as he felt his way through his new job. Maria had shared with me stories of his flustered speeches at the full Council meetings, and for an Italian raised in Faerie, her impression of his accent was pretty good.

"I wouldn't be calling if we could! You've got our best over there!"

"All right," she said, sounding far more understanding than she looked, "I'll get you on the list and have a team out ASAP—"

"For Christ's sake, woman, there's a fucking dragon in Alice!"

"Shit," she whispered, then said, "Got it. Team deploys momentarily. Be ready for them." Hanging up, she noticed Maria and me in the corner and pointed to the ceiling. "Gate's going to be big. I'm sending Arnold and Bert to do the closure. Meet them in the dining hall."

Maria straightened. "We're in?"

"I'm not talking to the wall. And get Frank!" she added as we hustled out of there.

From outside its wards, Arc 7 looked much like any other small ranching operation outside of Alice Springs: a few low buildings, long fences, and a hundred or so cows picking at the patchy scrub growing from the red dust. As far as cattle stations went, it barely deserved mention. But if you followed the dirt road past the camouflage—and good luck with that, as the outermost wards were designed to drain unshielded car batteries—the true scope of the complex became clear. Its residential towers were three stories tall and went twice as deep, offering ample space for the few wizards who chose to leave the convenience of Sydney or Melbourne for the middle of the Outback, while its main office complex had been designed inside a double-walled geodesic dome, magically insulated against the desert conditions.

Magus Norleigh, a fair-haired man with a peeling sunburn, met us outside the dome as we emerged from the gate. He'd eschewed a robe that morning—even in the Australian midwinter, the day was clear and pleasant—but quite honestly, with his state of fluttering panic, I was surprised that he'd remembered trousers. Relief washed over his face when he saw the two former grand magi in our party. Arnold Lowe, a contemporary of Toula's, had earned his reputation, while Bert Wold, though Magus Norleigh's age, had been a prodigy. Magus Norleigh seemed slightly less enthused to see Maria, and he regarded Frank and me with brief befuddlement before turning his attention back to the main players. "It's in the north pasture," he said, flapping one arm in that general direction. "*Huge.* I've got the place on lockdown, but if it gets a mind to wander—"

Bert stopped him with a raised hand. "I was under the impression that there was a dragon actively circling town."

"Not yet. That's why you're here," he replied, clapping Bert on the shoulder. "This way."

Bert, Maria, and Arnold traded looks as they followed their colleague—it spoke poorly of the installation head's abilities for him to call in reinforcements—but they held their tongues until we rounded the dome, and Magus Norleigh pointed to the problem. "You see? Bloody great dragon, yeah?"

To be fair, there *was* a dragon, but it was the smallest I'd ever seen, bluish-green and coiled around a downed cow. Scenting us on the light breeze, it raised its head and hissed in warning, and I looked up at Frank, who studied it with his arms folded. "Juvenile?" I asked.

"No," he murmured. "She's no dragonet, just...petite. Odd."

"*Petite?*" echoed Magus Norleigh with a bark of incredulous laughter. "That thing's a killer!"

"Assuredly so, but not a large one."

"Oh, well, the Archives sent their dragon expert, did they?" he snapped. "Got any advice on killing it?"

Frank looked down at him, then slowly removed his dark glasses, revealingly his inhumanly red eyes. "Why don't you wait there and keep your fucking mouth shut while I try to work this out, hmm?"

Twitchy already, the magus jumped back at the sight. "What the hell are—"

"Arnold," Frank interrupted, kicking off his shoes and flinging his T-shirt away, "bust it."

"With pleasure," he said, and waited until Frank had stripped and moved clear of the building to do as he bid.

Magus Norleigh let out a particularly undignified squeak once the flash of the breaking bind had faded. "That's—"

I'm small, too, Frank thought, flashed just enough teeth to make his point, and lumbered off across the pasture.

The blue dragon hissed again when she saw Frank, then growled and hunkered down over her cow. He stopped twenty yards away and went to his belly, keeping his head low and his wings tucked. I was no expert in draconic body language, but Frank's posture was apparently a sign of reassurance. After a moment, she resumed eating, and Frank raised his head. When she stopped and looked at him again, I assumed they were speaking, but neither broadcast to us, and I didn't want to interrupt by prying.

Five minutes later, Frank rose and inspected a small hole hanging in midair over the pasture, a gate barely larger than my couch and closing even as we watched. *Kitty, Maria, over here,* he called, and we jogged out to meet him under the blue dragon's wary gaze.

As I neared, I could make out the gashes on the blue dragon's neck and side, some dried black but a few still weeping fresh blood. "What's the situation?" I asked.

He nodded to the gate. *She says she found it and went through, but it started to shrink almost at once. She can't fit now, obviously.*

Maria frowned at the gate and rubbed her chin. "I suppose we could widen it…"

No. She's agreed to go to Faerie. Seeing our quizzical expressions, Frank explained, *She was nesting. A couple of males attacked to cannibalize the nest, and when she tried to fight back, they gave chase. She got through the gate just in time. And she's starving, hence the depleted herd.* There were no bones left to mark the dragon's mealtime progress, but the rest of the cattle were keeping well away from her. *I told her she could stay in the barn for now,* Frank continued. *Plenty of food, plenty of space, and my brothers will be around if she feels the urge to mate again. Seeing as she just lost a clutch, though, that could be a while in coming.*

The blue dragon watched as we spoke—I knew she couldn't understand what we were saying. "What's her name?" I asked Frank.

Amusement colored his reply. *She has none. Her clutchmates called her Runt.*

"Sounds familiar."

Maria opened a gate to the barn, and Frank stood at the edge and called for Ros, who manifested immediately. After a quick explanation, she in turn called for Georgie, who emerged from the barn so that Frank could plead his case. Seeing the injured blue dragon for herself, however, Georgie didn't take much convincing. She rubbed her head against her son's and rumbled, then turned her attention to the other female, who snapped up what little remained of the cow and tentatively crossed the border.

"Be *careful,*" Ros admonished us in parting, and Maria sealed the hole.

When we rejoined the magi, Bert and Arnold had finished patching the Gray Lands gate, while Magus Norleigh still seemed poised to soil himself. *Problem solved*, Frank told them. *And maybe a trip through the Archives would help you along*, he added to Magus Norleigh. *I've left a few notes.*

Arnold handled our gate home—a massive one, considering Frank was at full size—and once Australia was sealed off behind us, he sighed and muttered, "Stupid little wanker. Sorry about that, Frank. I'll put the bind back together—"

Don't.

"Come again?"

I'm of more use like this than I am compressed. You don't really think that's going to be the last large visitor from the Gray Lands, do you? He sank down in the courtyard and coiled himself into a tight circle. *Going to nap. Wake me when you need me.*

A knot of passing wizards emerged from one of the towers, screamed at the sight, and slammed the door.

"I'll try to see that you aren't disturbed, but I make no guarantees," Arnold replied, and shepherded the rest of us back to the dining hall. "Bert, lad, get some rest," he said, pushing open the inner doors. "And ladies, I don't know how long you've been at this, but you're probably due to rotate off for a few hours…"

His voice died as we caught sight of a bloodied body laid out on one of the wooden dining tables. The crowd kept back a few feet as Dr. Powell and Val worked on the patient's wounds, but as we watched, they shared a long glance, and then the doctor's wand tip sparked as a sheet appeared over the corpse.

A troll just outside of Lisbon had given the Arcanum its first fatality of the campaign. By sunrise in Glastonbury, three more would join that body in the castle's morgue. Only two of that group were wizards, but that day, no one seemed to care about the technicalities.

CHAPTER 19

In times of chaos, some panic, others freeze, and a tiny minority calmly assume leadership. Though equipped with computers and live access to Toula's main chart of closure teams, the hastily drafted coordinators in the dining hall were in over their heads and doing all they could just to stay on top of the constant updates in gate locations, wounded closers, and field data. By midnight that first night, most had dropped from exhaustion, and there was no B-string to replace them—there was only Artur, who quietly convinced a member of Arc 2's IT department to construct a basic command center along the wall near the bar. With three synchronized monitors showing her the full chart at a glance, she put her nascent computer skills to use but largely depended on a pencil and a stack of notepads to keep the teams flowing.

As efficient as Artur was, even she might have foundered had Beth not sneaked out of our flat in the wee hours to have a look at the goings-on. Maria and I had warned her to stay away and out of everyone's hair, but Beth had a mind of her own, a rebellious streak far wider than mine had ever been, and fortunately, proficiency with spreadsheets. She said hello to Artur, brought her a cup of coffee, then noticed the mess of notepads and pulled up a chair. As it so happened, Artur took notes in a bastardized form of Latin, courtesy of Myrddin's instruction, and with four years of Arcanum education under her belt, Beth was able to decipher most of her scratchings. While Beth updated the master list, Artur was free to debrief the returning teams and pry information from the few available magi. By morning, the list was tidied and sorted, the injured were properly tagged, and Artur had assigned a preliminary proficiency rating to every wizard in the chart on a five-point scale. She and Beth lumped the closers into three equally strong shifts, and then Artur sent aides to wake the ones who'd gone missing overnight. She didn't yet have the faeries properly catalogued, and the shifters were a class unto themselves, but the teams were beginning to deploy without such a confused frenzy.

It shouldn't have worked. The wizards assumed that Artur was fae, the faeries assumed the opposite, and neither had any idea why her technological aide-de-camp was a fourteen-year-old with pigtails and smudged eyeliner. But Artur remained cool and collected, a constant presence in the dining hall throughout the night, and that longevity somehow equaled authority in the bizarre calculus of disaster. She might have been a stranger, but by God, she could answer questions and issue orders, and people who had no reason to give her the time of day were suddenly dancing to her tune.

By midmorning, Artur had convinced Toula to assign a mixed team of medics to the dining hall as first responders for the returning wounded. Leaving Beth to manage the list—the two had worked out a balanced roster with a backup string of wizards to slot in as injuries occurred—she sought out Mina, Kiet, and Nico, Eleanor's captain, to catalogue the relative strength of the fae forces. Complicating her assignments was the linguistic matter: many of those born in Faerie spoke only Fae, which few of the Arcanum or Minor Arcanum had bothered to master. Consequently, as Artur and Beth produced team assignments throughout the day, the captains stood by to facilitate, directing their people to take languages as needed. To no one's surprise, the teams worked better when their members could communicate with more than gestures and grunts.

Boosted by the stamina of her actual age, Artur never took a break during the second day, eating on her feet and drinking whatever beverage was put into her hand. Beth was a different story, however, and once Artur realized she'd passed the twenty-four-hour mark, she ordered Beth to sleep. The kid protested that she was fine, but the caffeine tremors in her hands gave her away. Maria and I half-dragged her back to the flat and coaxed her into bed, and then Maria hit her with enchantment to knock her out before she could complain about the injustices heaped upon the young.

With Beth down for a few hours, I took her place in the dining hall around one on Friday morning, and not a moment too soon. The next four teams to return had fatalities, two who'd died in the field and two who expired on dining tables as the medical team worked in vain to save them. Artur watched in tight-lipped silence as the bodies were carried away, then directed me to change the roster. There was simply no time for mourning. I drank black coffee, kept a bowl of M&Ms by my left hand, and continued to input the latest developments.

The gates hadn't increased in frequency, but the creatures traversing them had skewed toward the large and hungry end of the spectrum. Trolls began to pop up with alarming regularity, followed by cyclopes armed with the Gray Lander version of the Dud Defender, a hair-trigger rod preloaded with bolts. Any gate that opened over water was apt to disgorge a pair of hydra—*always* a mated pair, never just a lone snake to kill—and those unfortunates who were tasked with dispatching them had to trick the hydras into biting themselves. Beheading them only made them angrier and multi-headed, but they were susceptible to their own venom…which proved equally effective on wizards and faeries. Two from Val's court had been nicked on one excursion, and their screams echoed off the dining hall's high ceiling until the venom stopped their hearts.

I worried that the Three would withdraw their forces—

it wasn't their realm at stake—but the tents remained outside the castle walls. Catching Mina in a rare slow moment that morning, I broached the subject and received an emphatic denial. "It's become personal," she said, pouring coffee from a ceramic urn. "At first, Mab's old followers had a grudge, and the rest of us saw the wisdom in assisting Toula in preventing Nath from conquering this realm, but now?" She sipped, winced at the heat, and added honey. "Remember how many of us are half fae. We have blood here, too. And now that we've lost people…" She smiled grimly and sipped. "I understand that we have a reputation here as somewhat vindictive."

"There's no 'somewhat' about it."

"Then you understand why we aren't leaving."

While Arc 2 coordinated the closure teams, the Fringe continued to orchestrate the cover-up, pulling in anyone with even minimal proficiency to close electronic eyes and draft official-sounding stories of weapons testing, rogue filmmakers, terrorist attacks with psychotropic inhalants, and the ever-popular atmospheric disturbance. Red flags were hoisted along perfectly calm coastlines. The major media outlets made passing reference to unusual occurrences, but thanks to the Fringe's toil and the closure teams' quick work, no mundane authority had yet sounded a doomsday alarm. We knew it was a matter of time—all it would take would be one botched closure or watching camera—but no one had the energy to spend on catastrophizing. *I* certainly didn't. By midmorning Friday, Beth emerged from her forced slumber, and I returned to the flat to take my dreamless shift in bed.

I woke in the late afternoon, having slept so deeply that I'd barely moved the blankets, and went down to the courtyard to check in on Frank. Joey was working on one of his hind feet when I arrived, and as Frank was preoccupied with the dozen dead sheep in a pile near his nose, Joey quietly explained, "Raiders." He pointed to Frank's flank, which was wrapped with the telltale glow of enchantment above a bedsheet-sized bandage.

"Shit. *Where*?" I muttered.

"South of Cairo, out in the desert, but rapidly heading north. We stopped them about fifty miles from the city."

"How many?"

"Probably three dozen." He finished his work on Frank's foot, which bore red-spotted bandages in two places. "Archers among them. A few of them were able to shoot before Frank brought out the flames, but we got them all. The sheep are a consolation prize," he added, nodding toward the carcasses. "He wanted to eat his kill, but we're on a schedule."

You could have brought them back here, Frank thought, snapping up a fresh sheep.

"Yeah, because raider barbeque is exactly what this madhouse needs right now," Joey retorted. "And it doesn't give off the best vibes for you, bud."

They're not human.

"They're bipedal, and that's close enough to freak folks out. Trust me, okay?" he said, giving Frank's side a quick pat. "And you're out of commission until morning. Let those heal."

Frank snorted and continued to eat. *I don't need that foot to fly.*

"True, but I assume you'd prefer to walk without a limp. Don't be stupid."

I headed inside to relieve Beth, whose drawn face told me that the raiders weren't the end of our problems. Pulling up a free computer, I reviewed what had come in while I'd slept: giant wolves in the south of France, more of Nath's cyclopean mercenaries in Thailand, and...

"*Minotaur*?" I asked.

My sister shrugged. "Two legs, head kind of like a buffalo, and pissed. No one's really studying anything right now, you know?"

She had a point. Between the confused yeti-like creatures in Central Park (which would have been killed had Seamus not taken one look at them and insisted that they be escorted to the Everglades for safekeeping) and the male dragon over Lapland (who refused to abandon his hunt of a family of reindeer herders and was reluctantly brought down by Frank and Joey), the closure teams' resources were stretched thin, and documentation of unknown species was low on the list of priorities.

By Saturday morning, we'd lost fifteen percent of our available forces to injury or worse, and Artur, who had been running the dining hall since Wednesday night, was nearing her limit. Glassy-eyed, taciturn, and with a slight tremor in her hands, she'd pushed herself to a dangerous place, but she refused to accept relief. While Val and Eleanor tried to talk her into a nap, Coileán sneaked up behind her and hit her with the necessary enchantment before she had sufficient presence of mind to shield. She collapsed, spilling lukewarm coffee all over the wooden floor, and Val absently willed it clean as he levitated Artur onto a table. A pillow and blanket appeared, but even after she was tucked in, she didn't budge.

"How long were you planning to keep her down?" Eleanor asked Coileán, who was lacing his coffee with a little something from the bar.

"I'm not." Recapping the whisky, he raised his mug in brief salute to my unconscious sister. "I just knocked her out. She's sleeping on her own." He *tsk*ed before he drank. "Kid crashed and burned."

"I know the feeling," Val muttered, and created a tent of blackout curtains around the table, plus a noise-muffling enchantment. "Leave her be," he cautioned the knot of concerned aides and gofers drafted into Artur's makeshift scheduling unit. "And stand clear when she wakes. I'm sure she'll be unhappy."

Val was experienced enough on that count to accurately prognosticate. Artur woke around ten that night in a dark mood, refreshed and once again thinking clearly but peeved at the ambush. Having filled in for her, I relinquished my command and sent Beth to bed, then moved into her slot and gave Artur a summary of events while she sipped a fresh cup of coffee and glowered at the world.

Artur had a realm to defend, or at least one upon which to impose order, but around midnight, Toula dragged her away from her post to the Council's primary meeting chamber. When she returned, her face was grim. "We've lost a full quarter of our forces," she said as she directed me to edit the table. "Some may have fled. Not the faeries, but half the Company is gone, and some of the teams never returned from the field. Dead or deserted, no one can say."

I input the changes, painfully conscious that the teams went missing on my watch and I had been too overwhelmed to notice. At least Artur didn't rub it in.

"The magi are haggard at best," she continued, sinking into the chair beside me. "Toula has ordered a few out of the field for their safety. One called Arnold was supposed to be in the morning group—"

"Magus Lowe?" I replied, tagging his name.

"Perhaps—she just called him Arnold. Ask Maria, I suppose. And Frank's been hit again, so he'll be of no use until tonight at the earliest. Perhaps I'm mistaken, but I think it would be best not to send him against any more dragons. Seems unduly cruel to me."

"I think you're right." Making a note in his slot, I pulled him into the list of the temporarily inactive. "Anything else?"

Artur hesitated before she spoke. "Your Council is restless. Some pointed out that these losses could have been avoided had Toula returned Hope as asked."

My shoulders tightened. "What'd she say?"

"That all capitulation would have accomplished would be a delay of the inevitable. This attack is too well planned to be the work of a moment's fancy. And it's brilliant," she said, rubbing her closed eyes. "These things we've fought—none of them are Nath's people, are they? They're just unpleasant creatures she could coax through gates to trouble us."

I nodded. "Yeah, no sign yet of any tennuwaya or cynaeli."

"She has suffered no losses. Her people are safe and rested, while ours are tired and dropping. We'll lose some to fatigue alone in the next days, and I expect to see more injuries—exhaustion leads to carelessness. It's brilliant," she repeated. "She wears us down, then engages at her leisure. As long as she can find trolls and wolves, all she need do is wait."

"Is there a plan to draw her over, then?"

Artur could only shrug. "If Toula has one, she's keeping it from me. And since I have a better idea of where her people have been deployed than she does, that would be a mistake." She watched as I made the last changes to the table, then said, "Rest, Kitty. I can manage through the night."

"You can barely type," I countered.

"Only because the letters are jumbled. Sleep. Beth will be back soon." Her smile, though weary, held actual warmth. "The girl's been helpful. Quick, anticipates needs…understands *this*." She patted the top of the closest monitor. "She's clever, your sister. Eager to please."

"Just a mild case of hero worship."

She grunted. "Then let us hope this invasion ends before Beth gets to know me."

I pushed myself from my chair and yawned. "Thank you."

"Certainly. You're far more useful when you can think clearly—"

"Not that. I mean, this isn't even your fight. Thanks for trying."

Artur looked me dead in the eye. "This land was mine long before it was yours, and I won't allow it to be lost again. Beyond that, Hope risked herself for me—the least I can do is return the favor."

"And then some."

"Perhaps," she said with a slight smile. "Then again, for some strange reason, your people think me a hero. I have a reputation to uphold."

"*Artur—*"

"Either you go to bed willingly or I'll attempt on you what Coileán did to me. Your choice."

I sighed and started for the door, but I turned back long enough to call, "You're not actually the boss of me, remember."

"Goodnight, Kitty."

"This is me leaving because I'm tired."

"*Goodnight*, Kitty."

Muttering under my breath all the way to my flat, I fell onto my unmade bed and was asleep before I could bother to remove my shoes. I stirred only once, when I woke to feel Marcus slipping them off for me, and then I mumbled and rolled over to make room. He spooned behind me, smelling of sweat and something else's blood, but I was too tired to care.

I hadn't set a clock before crashing, and I might have slept all throughout Sunday had Beth not shaken me awake that evening. As I groaned and tried to remember where I was and why, she ripped away my blankets and turned on the lights. "Get up," she ordered, shaking my shoulder for emphasis. "Nath sent someone to talk."

Once again, Nath's envoy stood before the gates of Arc 2, but that time, he was admitted no further into the castle. Instead, Eleanor threw together a private tent, where the Council and the respective heads of every other group present on the property could meet. The curious waited outside, our eavesdropping prevented by magic, until the flaps lifted again and the envoy departed through a gate he waved open.

The fact that said gate was within our wards was lost on no one.

Not content to wait for the official, sanitized version of events, I pulled Maria aside as soon as I saw her and led her to the corner of the courtyard where Marcus, Artur, and Beth were camped out in the darkness by Frank's head. The rest of him had coiled around the area, giving us relative privacy—though really, few in the castle had any desire to get that close to a dragon in the first place.

"She offered a cessation of hostilities," Maria reported, leaning against Frank's warm side with her arms folded. "All we need do is return Hope—"

"No," Artur interrupted.

"—and cede territory," she finished. "Nath will decide how much and where, but apparently, she's found some appealing spots."

I laughed incredulously. "That's not a serious offer."

"Her envoy seemed to think it was. Nath wants a holiday home in this realm."

More like a hunting lodge, thought Frank.

"Exactly. Toula was disinclined to accept her terms. So was the rest of the Council, fortunately," she added with a sigh, "but if we keep losing people at this rate, there might be some waffling."

"Forty-five percent down," Marcus told me as I started to ask.

"It was a difficult day," said Artur. "Eleven fatalities, maybe more to come from the infirmary. The medics are overwhelmed."

"Shit," I whispered, trying to digest that information. "What about the Three?"

"They told the envoy that incursions into this realm are being taken as threats to their own security and suggested that Nath back off," said Maria, "but I can't see that serving as a real deterrent. Anyway, Nath has generously given us a ceasefire until sunrise here to decide. Her mouthpiece promised that she has much worse in store if we reject her terms."

We stood in glum silence for a moment until Beth piped up with, "Has anyone considered the nuclear option?"

"Nuclear?" Artur echoed, perplexed.

"Big, and not necessarily good for us. Why don't we go public? The Fringe could figure out how to interrupt broadcasts, couldn't they? Put the Grand Magus on, explain that we're being attacked by a hostile magical force, and ask for mundane assistance. How big is her army, anyway?"

"No one knows," Maria replied. "And can you imagine the panic if the general population learned of our existence?"

"Can you imagine the panic if, like, a pack of dragons went on a rampage in New York?" she countered, then seemed to remember Frank. "Uh…no offense."

Hell, I'd panic.

"Maybe it would work in the short term," I told Beth. "But think about the ramifications. What's more likely, they offer Toula a seat at the UN or they try to eradicate us?"

"A literal worldwide witch hunt would be best avoided," said Maria. "Which means we're on our own."

Beth planted her hands on her hips. "So what's the plan, then?"

I couldn't see Maria's face well in the darkness, but the fatigue in her voice was evident. "Suppose we'll find out in the morning."

It was hard to say exactly when dawn broke over Glastonbury that day. A storm had rolled in overnight from the Atlantic, bringing leaden skies and lightning on the dark southwestern horizon. From my viewing spot on the crenellated battlements atop my flat's tower, the wind whipped my hair and snatched at my clothing, and I could detect the strengthening odors of ozone and petrichor as the rain neared.

"You're going to get electrocuted if you keep standing there," Beth chided, poking her head out from the trapdoor to the stairwell.

"Storm's not here yet," I said, hugging myself against the wind-chilled morning. "Did Mom never teach you to count between the lightning and the thunder?"

"There is *lightning*. You are on a *roof*. Don't be dumb."

I was reluctant to leave—part of me expected to see Nath marching from town at the head of an army at any moment—but I ducked back down the stairs with Beth. The kid had a point. "Thought you'd be with Artur."

"She's gone to the subbasement to talk to Toula. I, um…I made muffins," she offered awkwardly. "Blueberry. Just a pack of mix you had at the back of the pantry, nothing fancy, but if you're hungry…"

"Sounds perfect," I told her, and gave her ponytail a light tug. "I could teach you to make them from scratch sometime, if you want. I've got a recipe for chocolate-raspberry muffins that calls for Chambord—"

That was as far as I got before my phone trilled—and, to my surprise, so did Beth's. The message from Maria was brief: *GATES BACK, DINING HALL ASAP.*

"Muffins later," I said, and opened a gate on the nearest landing. Beth jumped through from three steps above and ran straight to the computer table. A second gate appeared in the dining hall, and Artur hurried to join her. I let myself in and closed both gates, then set about bringing coffee to the command center while Artur scrambled to line up magi and closure teams. Even with our diminished numbers, she sent them out in groups of six, banking on safety in numbers.

And gates were *everywhere*. The map was a constellation of blinking red dots and diamonds, and the Fringers struggled to keep up at their phone bank. By nine, forty-six teams had been dispatched, and more were lining up to depart as the first of the closers straggled back, some whole, some with casualties. With the flow of people and the constant updates, the dining hall was barely organized chaos. Artur and Beth did their best, but with such a glut of gates, the carefully tended shift rosters were tossed in the shredder. Any available wizard with average talent was drafted into play, and if the faeries at hand could understand him, so much the better.

I tried to stay out of the way, running messages to and from the subbasement and reassuring myself that I wasn't an irresponsible big sister for topping up Beth's coffee. As the dining hall's grandfather clock chimed the hour, I remembered that this was supposed to be the beginning of Games week. The other installation teams should have been starting the trip over, some coming earlier than others to acclimate to the time zone. The dining hall should have been filling with students of all nations and languages, most apprehensive about the week ahead and sizing each other up. There should have been chaos in the dorms and under-slept chaperones, not a faerie army at the gate and a convalescing dragon in the courtyard.

But Toula had agreed to shelter Hope. Hope had agreed to help me find Artur. I'd gone into the Gray Lands at Myrddin's prodding. Ted had dragged us to Port Warren to begin with, but I was the one who'd forgone the pub to explore on a rainy morning that seemed a lifetime ago, though it'd been barely a month and a half. At least that day we hadn't had to deal with lightning like the storm bearing down on Glastonbury—the booms rattled the castle's windows, while the bright bolts left afterimages if you looked out the window at the wrong second.

I'd just seen Marcus and Seamus off with a quartet of battle-weary wizards when Beth jumped to her feet, overturning her chair and sending it sliding into the wall. "*Artur!*" she shouted, her voice echoing across the dining hall. "We've got one!"

Artur ran back to her side, her eyes growing wide as

she looked at the map screen, and then she snatched her phone from the table and dialed. "Toula," I heard her say as I neared, "I need to see the land around the castle. This one is close."

She waited for a moment as Beth pulled up the requested feeds from our heavily shielded security array, but all that came through was pounding rain and the occasional lightning flash. "Man the teams," Artur said to Beth, then ripped open a fresh gate. I recognized our roof from the rusty grill another tenant had dragged up one summer, and I ran after my sister.

"Anything?" I asked, creating an umbrella, then fashioned a second one for her as she stood at the wall and squinted at the murky horizon.

"No."

Slowly, she made a circuit of the tower until she was staring off toward Shapwick Heath, and then she paused. "What is…"

I pulled binoculars from the ether and passed them to her. "Look through the small end, they magnify."

She did as I suggested, studied the heath for a few seconds, then whispered. I couldn't understand what she was saying, but her blanching face confirmed my fear.

I peered into the distance, but all I could see was mist. "What is it?"

"Death," she murmured, and passed me the binoculars.

At first, I didn't know what I was seeing—it looked like dark fog rising from the direction of the heath, unremarkable but for its sooty color—but then I saw flashes of bright red at its heart. "That's—"

"What killed my men. At least two of them, I'd say—too far yet to be certain."

Hearing a gate open, I dropped the binoculars and turned to find Artur retreating to our flat. "What are you—"

"They're not invincible," she said, one foot in the den. "I can stall them. Tell Toula to either find a weapon or evacuate."

"Wait—"

"*Now*, Kitty. Do you think they'll hunt the wilds forever, or do you suppose they'll come in search of larger prey?"

"Just...don't do anything hasty, okay? Give me a few minutes," I begged, then made my own gate into the subbasement.

Toula, who looked tired and grungy that morning if one was of a mind to be charitable, turned her weary gaze my way as I slammed open the conference room door. "Do we have visual confirmation on the gate?" she asked.

"Not the gate, but it's probably at Shapwick Heath. We've got company."

"Gray Landers?"

I shook my head. "Smoke monsters."

"Huh?"

"The things that almost killed Artur—there's at least two of them coming this way. She said she can buy us some time, but if we can't destroy them, we'll need to run."

Toula closed her eyes and muttered, and a calm, reassuring version of her voice began to echo from nowhere: *The barrier ward will be activated in three minutes. Stand clear of the barrier ward. I repeat, the barrier ward will be activated in three—*

A twitch of her finger silenced the announcement in the conference room, though I could still hear it through the walls. "Make contact with every team," she told the magi and aides around the table. "Loop the Fringe in to help you. Once the ward goes up, the landing zone will be outside the main doors, near the faerie encampment. Send the word out. We'll need an escort waiting at the barrier to admit them." She waited for the space of a breath while phones and fingers flew, then said to me, "Get Frank in the air. See if we can't kill them from above."

I sped to the courtyard, where Joey was removing

Frank's soggy bandages, and relayed the message from underground. Though I was ready to clamber up Frank's side, however, Joey held me back. Instead, he grabbed Aiden, who'd only returned from the field ten minutes before, and Frank launched with them just before the ward solidified over the castle, a magical shield like a translucent concrete bubble. Umbrella in hand, I returned to my roof to watch—the barrier ward was designed to let rain through, unfortunately—and followed Frank's path, hoping that the mundanes of greater Glastonbury weren't looking too closely at the sky from their office windows.

Frank slowed and banked as he approached the nearing smoke-like creatures, then let loose a brilliant jet of orange flame. From the magic flaring around the area, I assumed that Frank's passengers were firing as well, and I held my breath and hoped. But when they headed back toward the castle, I could still see the monsters in the distance—closer now, and seemingly unharmed.

I met Frank as he landed outside the ward, which the escort opened with a brief spell focused through his wand like a key. "No luck?" I asked him.

None. Impervious to fire, unaffected by magic. Everything went right through them, and when Joey and Aiden tried to trap the damn things, the traps failed. I think we just made them angry.

"And led them this way," said Aiden, sliding down. "What's Plan B? How do you kill smoke?" He raised his voice as Toula ran through the ward. "Struck out. Nothing we shot at them seemed to faze them—and there's three, incidentally. What do we do?"

She rubbed her face in agitation. "I...I suppose we could try something stronger, maybe we could knock them out, or...where are you going?"

Having opened a gate into the main courtyard of Val's villa, I paused only long enough to say, "Idea," then zipped through, not bothering to close the hole.

I heard Ros in my head almost immediately as she clued in on what I was about. *Left...down that passageway, nope, too far…okay, through that room and outside…*

Pushing open the door, I found myself alone in one of the villa's many walled gardens. "Uh…"

Oops. My bad.

A door appeared in the ivy-draped privacy wall separating the garden from its neighbor, and I let myself through, startling Hope and Hayleigh, who were playing cards at a sunny patio table. "Sorry to interrupt, no time," I said before they could ask me where the door had come from. "Hope, can you raise the dead?"

Hayleigh's eyebrows leapt. "Say *what?*"

Her daughter thought briefly as she parsed the question, comparing my English to the terms to which she was accustomed. "I can't restore people to life, no," she said, almost drawling the last word. "I can heal, to an extent—not here, obviously," she continued, pointing to her purple face, "but with sufficient magic—"

"No, no, I mean…" I paused as I sought the right phrasing, then managed, "You told me once that you can talk to dead people."

Though Hayleigh said nothing, she seemed unsurprised.

"Yes. That I *can* do," Hope replied. "Is there someone you want to speak with?"

"Not so much *speak*. Uh…" I leaned over the back of a free chair at their four-top and tried to calm my racing mind. "There are these things that have just come through from the Gray Lands. Like living smoke, a bunch of red eyes—"

"Scintol," she muttered, and dropped her cards on the table. "How many?"

"Three."

"Sorry," said Hayleigh, looking back and forth between us, "what's a…a skin…"

"Scintol," Hope repeated in a monotone. "They are…*unnatural*. The tennuwaya can create them, but they haven't done so in years, it's dangerous…"

"How so?"

She seemed to hug herself as she contemplated the question. "Scintol are dead things. They seem alive, but they aren't, not truly. A tennuwaya who's exceptionally talented can create them by calling forth their dead—scintol are amalgamations of spirit, I suppose you could say. Or what's left of it. They have a unified mind—you can't appeal to a component spirit and expect to have any luck—and they're destructive. The tennuwaya used them against us in the long-ago, but not anymore."

"Why not?"

"Because they're nearly impossible to destroy, and once they're released, there is little one can do to control them. Enough scintol turned on the tennuwaya to make them abandon the practice of using those things."

"But you *can* destroy them, right?" I pressed. "Myrddin said that when they attacked Artur's people, Morgen was able to call upon the dead to fight them off."

"Morgen was old and powerful. I'm twenty and half-blooded," Hope protested.

I grabbed her hands and stared her in the eye. "Three scintol are heading for the castle as we speak. We're wasting time. Can you help us, yes or no?"

"Wait just a minute," said Hayleigh. "If these things are around, then Nath has to be close behind. You're not going to risk Hope like that. *No*, ma'am."

Before I could reply, Hope took the reins. "If I can't help them, they'll die," she said simply. "You have no power with the dead, correct?" she asked me. When I shook my head, she looked back at her worried mother and said, "See? Only the dead can kill the dead. I have to try."

"*Hope*—"

"It's all right, Mama." She pulled free of my grasp and stood. "I make no guarantees, but if you truly have scintol, then I'll try."

"Thank you," I murmured, and opened a gate—not a

minute too soon, as it turned out.

Artur was standing in the pounding rain just outside the wards with Toula, dressed in leather armor, her sword belted on and her crown pulled low. From our distance, I couldn't hear what they were saying, but Artur's frustrated gesticulations toward the nearing clouds of smoke were easy to read.

"I told you to give me a few minutes!" I yelled, running through the gate to intercept her. "What are you trying to do, get yourself killed?" I fumbled my umbrella open, but by then, it did little to help.

"My point exactly," said Toula, glaring at Artur. "Going out there is suicide. Magic doesn't hurt them."

"And I assure you that *this* does," Artur snapped, drawing Caledfwlch. "I've faced these. I wasn't fast enough last time—"

"You almost died!"

"*I should have!*"

"Which is why you aren't going to fight them," she replied, calm in the face of Artur's temper. "I'm not about to stand here and watch you kill yourself for nothing."

"And I brought help," I cut in, beckoning Hope closer. "She's going to do what Morgen did last time."

"I said I would *try*," Hope corrected. "This is difficult magic, and I can't just order the dead about. They must be persuaded."

"What dead, and what do you mean, *persuaded*?" asked Toula, glancing toward the nearing creatures.

Hope sighed. "The only way to destroy scintol is with other dead. I'll try to draw upon enough energies to allow them to manifest, but whether any choose to rise and fight isn't something I can control. Do you have any dead here? Anyone you know who might be convinced to help?"

"Me?" Toula asked. "No. There are wizards buried on the grounds of Arc 2, but no one who's fond enough of me to take on a monster."

Kiet, who had been several yards away with his army,

suddenly appeared at Toula's side. "We are prepared. The others as well, I believe, but there are still some of us missing on closure missions."

"My people are mustering in the courtyard," she replied. "Maybe someone in there has a dead grandparent or two who'd take up the cause—"

"Let me try."

We turned to Artur, who closed her eyes and focused until her male glamour returned. "I know them by name. Kitty, come with me."

Toula hastily arranged a knot of armed faeries to protect Hope, who sat on the sodden ground, closed her eyes, and began to softly moan on each long exhalation as she channeled power from the dark magic around us. I heard emergency sirens through the rain and saw smoke to the northeast—a diversion from the Fringe, I hoped. There weren't many main roads between Shapwick Heath and the castle—plenty of fields and peat, but few people—and with any luck, the police wouldn't stumble onto the scene. Still, I suspected that someone in the subbasement was working up a way to close down the roads. By then, the scintol were visible from the castle, even with the steady rain, and if I squinted, I could just make out the figures marching behind them. There was no way to tell from my position how many soldiers Nath had sent, but if the scintol leading the pack were as destructive as we feared, then whatever force arrived in their wake would have little to do but clean up.

While the fae army began to get into formation inside the barrier ward, Artur brushed her fingers against my temple and muttered, "I hope this doesn't hurt."

I recognized the painless blast of language insertion and looked at her, perplexed, once my head had cleared. "What did you—"

"I may need backup. That's you," she replied, her words intelligible yet unfamiliar. Glancing at the wizards who were emerging from the castle to join their temporary allies, she sighed, then straightened her shoulders and said, "It's time. Come, we'll—"

"*Whoa*, now," said a voice behind us, and we turned to find Sam running up, with Seamus on his heels. "Where do you think you're going?"

Artur pointed to the fields between us and the scintol. "We haven't got much time—"

"And you're mad if you think you're going out there dressed like that," said Seamus, gesturing toward Artur's armor. "Seriously? That's the best you can do?"

"It's served me well—"

"Not well enough, if I've heard correctly." He frowned and gestured, and I felt the sudden weight of a heavy vest slung over my shoulders. Tough black fabric rippled down my arms and legs, and Seamus offered me a matching helmet. "Kevlar," he said, rapping his knuckles against my chest. "If it'll stop a bullet, maybe it'll stop…well, whatever the hell those things are."

Artur briefly studied her modified armor, then willed it back to the original brown leather. "Thank you," she told him, "but I'll use what I trust."

"This is better," Sam protested. "Seamus was a cop, he knows—"

"*Thank you*," Artur repeated, and Sam backed off, hands raised.

And so, with Artur in her pre-medieval best and me decked out to withstand small arms fire, we set off across the squelching green fields, both of us soaked and dripping, the rain percussive against my helmet. When we were perhaps fifty yards from the castle, Artur stopped, pulled out her sword, then plunged the blade into the muck and knelt behind it, one hand on the pommel.

"Men of Afallon," she called over the thunder and wind, "if there are any yet who know my voice, I ask you now to hear me."

There was no sign that anyone had come to listen, no movement but the waving grasses and the ever-nearing gray mass of the scintol trio.

"I failed you," said Artur, her head bowed. "You followed me and fell. Our lands were lost. And by all rights, I should have fallen with you. But I've returned, and I ask you to follow me once again." She paused as lightning flashed far too close for comfort, waiting until the rattling boom faded. "Afallon is no more, but if any of your children's children yet endure, they are here, in this realm, and invaders are at the gates. Creatures from beyond this world. They can't be stopped with ordinary swords. I will fight them once again," she said, rising and pulling Caledfwlch free. "For Afallon that was. For the world born from its ashes. But I cannot defeat them alone. Is there any man who will join me now?"

At first, I thought the pale mist I saw rising above the field was just another product of the storm, but it quickly turned into a fog and began to separate and solidify. Artur held her ground as shapes coalesced and darkened into recognizably human forms. Within a minute, I could pick out the details of faces, the straps of their armor, the unearthly glint of the naked swords some had already drawn. And as I watched, four stepped from the pack and approached, two dark-haired, two blond, all wielding long blades. One, I noted, had a deformed arm tucked close to his chest.

They paused a few feet from us, and not even the rain could mask the tears in Artur's eyes. "I'm sorry," she said, staring each in the face. "I'm so very sorry. I failed..."

A shade with a dark ponytail almost twin to Artur's closed the gap between them, and he paused for barely a second before placing his translucent hand atop her shoulder. "My king," he murmured, "you did what you could." She shook her head, and his mouth moved into a sad smile. "None fought more bravely," he said. "And it is my honor to fight for the Pendragon again."

"The honor is mine," Artur whispered, and roughly wiped her wet hand across her face. "Kitty, return to the castle. This isn't your fight."

"Nor is it yours," the man told Artur before I could object.

She started to protest, but by then, the other three had joined us. "You cannot win," said the blond with the withered arm. "We've seen this before, Artur."

The other blond nodded vehemently, and the fourth man pointed his sword toward the castle. "*Live*, cousin," he insisted. "Live and fight again."

Artur raised her sword, which glittered in a lightning flash. "This thing is made of pure magic. I can—"

"Live," the first man told her, then cut his eyes to me and smiled. I dipped my head in acknowledgement, and he stepped back from Artur, who, though visibly agitated, made no move to pursue him. Turning, he raised his blade high and wordlessly yelled, and the horde around him bellowed a reply.

I stood in the field with Artur, not quite believing my eyes as I watched an army of dead Britons bear down on the scintol. With a cry, they descended on the first of the three, which gave a screech like a panther from hell and exploded into dark vapor. I crossed my fingers, hoping they'd make similarly quick work of the other two, but instead, they stopped and waited, a line between the castle and the scintol.

And I realized what they had done.

The two remaining scintol were trapped between two armies, Nath's and the dead, but only one had any power over them. Even from that distance, I could hear the screams of the Gray Landers as the scintol turned on the center of their line, retreating for the safety of the heath.

"Think that's our cue," I said to Artur, who nodded and raised her sword.

Calling forth a shield, I ran with her through the puddles and lightning toward the scattering army, barely conscious that I was screaming until my throat began to ache. I heard the sound of gates opening behind us, and before we'd crossed the field, there was an army of wizards and faeries at our back—and one pissed-off grizzly shifter, who ran ahead on four legs and bit through the nearest tennuwaya's arm. With the dead in pursuit of the scintol, Nath's people had lost their secret weapon, and the few hundred soldiers who had come with their queen, anticipating an easy victory, were no match for the combined forces of the Arcanum and the courts. Bolts flew, shields firmed and shattered, and the air between us turned hazy with the active magic and dark magic. Some of the Gray Landers held the line, racking up a few casualties before they were cut down, while others turned tail and ran before the scintol toward the gate they'd left in the heath.

I learned later that there was no gate left for them. With Coileán overseeing the forward charge, Val, Eleanor, and Toula had made their own gate into Shapwick Heath behind the enemy line, portable dark magic detectors in hand as they sought the escape route. By the time the retreating scintol arrived, the original gate was long closed, and the dead were able to complete their work while the grand magus and the king and queen squared off against the fastest runners of Nath's fleeing army.

It wasn't a long battle—maybe an hour all told, including the later passes through the fields to incinerate the overlooked dead, though Frank had done a fine job of that already—but it was the end of Nath's campaign. The Arcanum lost five in the fighting that day, the courts another twelve, and the Company and Minor Arcanum suffered two losses apiece, but those of Nath's forces who couldn't escape through their own gates were slaughtered.

We found their queen trampled in a drainage ditch, her body soaked and bloody, the deep gashes across her torso suggestive of a scintol attack. Toula nudged Nath with her toe to be sure she was dead, then nodded. "Killed by her own weapon. Serves that bitch right," she muttered, then opened a gate into the Gray Lands, tossed the corpse across, and sealed the hole behind her.

As I joined Artur in stabbing the last of the bodies for good measure, the four shades appeared before us again. Seeing them, she dropped to one knee and bowed her head. "You have my gratitude. I don't know what I can do to repay you..."

Their leader extended a hand to help her rise, and Artur attempted to take it before they both remembered that such contact was impossible. She stood, her clothes filthy and sodden, and he quietly said, "There is one thing I ask."

"Name it."

"I would look upon my king's true face."

Artur stiffened and stared at him. "You...you know about—"

"Few secrets remain beyond death," he replied. "And we can see through the illusion around you. More than that, I cannot tell you."

"Forbidden," the man with the withered arm concurred.

The first man nodded. "But...yes, Artur," he said gently. "Yes. I know. You need not hide the truth."

She hesitated for a moment, then closed her eyes as if bracing for a blow and let the glamour fall away—still drenched and dirty, but my blonde sister once more. When she looked at him again, he rested his palm against her cheek, cupping it as well as he could, and smiled. "I wish I had known sooner."

"Kei," she whispered, reaching for his face in turn. "I'm sorry."

"You had little choice," he said, and, to my surprise, laughed nervously. "But if you had told me..."

"You would have chosen a new king?"

"No. Your feelings would have been reciprocated. They *are* reciprocated," he amended, a cast of sadness falling over his expression. "You...were not alone in those troubling thoughts, Artur."

Her eyes closed again, and she scrunched up her face as

she tried in vain not to cry. "Let me come with you," she murmured. "Please. Afallon is dead—"

"It's not dead while you live," said the one-armed man.

That had to be Bedwyr, I realized, and the dark-haired man who'd called Artur his cousin must be Madoc...meaning that the other blond was Medraut, who certainly didn't seem like he was ready to run Artur through. "You were the first of us," he said. "And now you are the last of us. Live, my king. Remember us, but *live*."

"Should the time come," said Kei, "I'll be waiting. We all will. But until then..." He glanced at me and smiled again. "You have another to fight with you in our stead, do you not? Perhaps a better companion for this world. You're not alone."

Artur turned my way then, seemed to realize what she'd said, and reached for me. I took her hand and squeezed as hard as I could, and when we looked back, the others had vanished—all but one, a fifth man who stood at a distance, middle-aged and armor-clad, a gold band like Artur's resting over his gray hair. He raised a hand in greeting, and she fell to her knees and cried, "*Father!*"

But he had already begun to fade. "Be well, my dearest," he said, and disappeared.

I knelt with her in that trampled field, holding on to her as she sobbed and the storm around us slowed. The rain dried to a drizzle, the thunder moved to the east, and while the cleanup crew finished their macabre work, Artur mourned her dead.

CHAPTER 20

The mundanes of greater Glastonbury knew *something* had happened, but no one had an explanation, much less anything approaching the truth. The Fringers may not have been exceptional magical talents, but they were pros at manipulation. Official accounts of the day included reference to heavy storms, floods, and powerful winds that ripped gashes through fields. The electrical storm had wreaked havoc on the traffic signals, and roads leading to the southwest had been blocked by downed trees (some, strangely, where no one had heretofore seen any trees, but storms are odd things). The biggest story of the day was a fire in an empty house in the northern part of town. There were no mentions of blue or purple people, and only one old man who swore he'd seen a dragon on the horizon—though with all the rain and clouds, who could say, really? Glastonbury had always been a funny sort of place.

As soon as the monitoring crews were confident that no further gates would be forthcoming, the faeries packed up and left, and the Council let out a collective sigh of relief. The Minor Arcanum, the Company, and the Fringe representatives departed shortly thereafter, leaving Arc 2 to tend to its wounded in peace.

Among their number was Hope, who had poured everything she had into the army that came for Artur. Exhausted, she'd finally fainted outside the wards and was taken to the castle's infirmary, where her worried mother sat by her bed and watched the systemic projection of her body for signs of trouble. But Dr. Powell had been confident that Hope just needed rest and time, and four days later, she was proven correct. Hope opened her eyes, ate a massive steak dinner, and only then remembered that she was unglamoured and changed her face. Considering that Hope was much of the reason that Arc 2 hadn't fallen to Nath, the infirmary staff didn't care what she looked like, but Hope wanted to go home, and one couldn't very well walk around Pauline, Oklahoma, with a violet complexion. Mother and daughter departed the next day, the shopkeeper and the amateur necromancer, but not before Toula gave Hope her private number, just in case.

The Games were delayed a week that summer. I'd assumed they wouldn't be held—we still had people going through physical therapy from their injuries, not to mention families in mourning—but Bert, of all magi, had insisted, explaining that the Arcanum needed normalcy, and that meant the Games. The weary kitchen staff did their best, the cleaning crew worked overtime to sweep away the previous week's leavings, and one week after Nath's invasion, the first of the other installations' children began to arrive with their chaperones. Soon, the dining hall was at noisy capacity once again, but that time, the shouts were excited—friends from previous years' Games happy to be reunited, rivals yelling taunts to each other across the room, and overworked teachers calling for decorum.

I asked Beth if she wanted to stay in the dorms with the rest of her class, but she declined. She had a comfortable bed in my flat, a stocked refrigerator, and a TV with more satellite channels than she knew what to do with. As for the rest of our flatmates, Beth and Artur had developed a rapport from their work with the closure teams, and Beth seemed to have silently decided that Marcus's presence, if not exactly wanted, was tolerable.

I needed him. Though grateful that my strange little family had made it through unharmed, I was plagued with nightmares of monsters in the rain, and Marcus held me when I woke screaming. At least there were people around to eat the results of my insomnia baking, as I couldn't very well take my cakes to the office. By Ted's edict, the Away Team was on holiday for the rest of the month. *I think we've all had enough Grail questing for one summer*, his message concluded. *I'm going to a family reunion at Arc 1. Spend time with your loved ones.*

We obeyed. Lakshmi and Rodney took their sons and their soon-to-be daughter-in-law on a Caribbean cruise. Bob and Sylvester rented a flat in Normandy. Daphne joined her brother, his wife, and their two young daughters on a trip to visit cousins in Jamaica. Mal went home to Faerie to see his parents and his father's doting family. Maria couldn't leave—as a magus, she had referee duties during the Games—and Antony and Madison, of course, stayed at Arc 2 while Allie competed, but Frank returned to Faerie for a full two weeks. Though he insisted he was making the trip to see his sister's clutch of wobbly hatchlings, I suspected that the little blue dragon was in his thoughts. I said nothing to him on the subject, but when he returned, he told me, "She's decided that she wants to be called Ione. Don't pry," and that was that. I had half a mind to point out to Frank that he did nothing *but* pry, but prudence dictated that it was a bad idea to antagonize a dragon, no matter what form he took.

When the Games had ended, I took Beth back to the Audleys' home to retrieve her belongings. "Thank you for everything," I told Piper as Beth shoved her winter clothing into suitcases and took down her posters.

She clasped my hands and smiled. "I'm just glad she's back where she's meant to be. Orson would approve," she added, giving me a quick squeeze.

I wasn't sure about that, but Beth seemed to settle in well, enjoying her last days before the short British summer holiday came to an end in late August. She lounged around her new room with a stack of books from the library, played her music too loudly, and was always up for takeaway. By contrast, Artur said little to anyone, spending most of her days at the table with her computer as she continued to study the history she'd missed and the world in which she'd awakened. I knew she was hurting, but I didn't know what to do besides make her tea and keep her fed. Even Marcus counseled me to give her space.

In the end, it was Beth who broke through Artur's funk. She plopped down at the kitchen table one morning in early August, folded her arms on the placemat, and said, "Hey, question for you."

Artur looked up from her early reading—which may very well have been her late reading, considering how little I saw her sleep—and waited.

"You're pretty good with a sword, right?"

"More than competent, yes."

"Teach me?"

She frowned and slid the computer aside. "Why? It's of no use to you. Forget magic—you have guns."

"But it's *awesome*," said Beth, "and around here, you never know. *Please?*"

Artur hesitated, considering her open computer and untouched breakfast, then looked back at Beth, who had mastered puppy eyes. "Dress," she said, snatching up her toast. "You'll want full sleeves and trousers, not...that."

Beth, still sporting the tank top and shorts in which she'd slept, replied, "It's going to be warmish soon enough."

"Agreed. By all means, wear that," said Artur between bites, "but if you dress properly, then the bruises I give you won't be as bad."

Ten minutes later, Marcus and I watched from the top of the tower as Beth clumsily swung a wooden practice sword in the courtyard while Artur, similarly armed, barked correction. As Beth yelped below, I felt Marcus's fingers entwine with mine and smiled.

By September, Beth's shoulders had started to tone, and her early grades were excellent. Artur had threatened that she would only continue training her if Beth did well in school and didn't make trouble—a stipulation I had strongly suggested—and Beth kept up her end of the bargain. She'd had a rough few days, first as the new kid, and then once someone realized she was related to Mom, but Beth managed not to punch anyone. When the taunting increased, however, word got around—her teachers compared notes, then pulled Maria aside—and one day at lunch, Artur calmly walked up to the girl who'd been giving Beth the hardest time and flung her into the rafters. She folded her arms and stared up at her screaming, struggling victim, then said, "If you upset my sister's sister again, I will throw you off a goddamned tower and make it look like an accident. Understood?" The girl whimpered in the affirmative, and Artur, leaving her clinging to a support beam, returned to the table where the Team had been eating. Nodding to Maria, she sat and picked up her chicken breast, then smiled faintly as one of the teachers tried to coax the terrified girl down.

Beth had no further trouble, and rumors of a different sort began to fly. No one was quite sure what to make of the stranger who seemed to have been drafted onto the Away Team, but then again, there was no telling what sort of people Ted Girard would hire. Those who'd been in the front lines during the invasion spoke in hushed tones, whispering reports that she could command the dead to do her bidding, and anyone who went for an early morning walk in the courtyard knew that she was a gifted swordsman, but Artur didn't go public with her past. "I've become little more than legend," she told me one evening as we sat alone in the den, Beth's forgotten copy of the *Morte* lying on the coffee table. "Were I to come forward now and tell the truth, I'd be taken for a madwoman."

Artur had no plans, no responsibilities, and no clue what to do with herself in the long term, but Ted was more than happy to help fill the gap. Sure, her computer literacy was lacking, but Artur's raw talent was almost comparable to Marcus's, a bonus to anyone going into potentially dangerous territory. She proved to be teachable—indeed, eager to learn—and by Christmas, Ted had given her an office of her own. "AP" began popping up on the travel calendar, and little by little, she emerged from her shell. When she showed up at a Monday meeting with a plastic gem-studded chalice full of orange juice just to mess with Ted, I knew she'd begun to heal.

And then Coileán came to call.

Beth opened the door on a snowy night in January to find one of the Three standing in the corridor with a navy hoodie partially obscuring his features. "Uh...hi?" she managed, which was far better than the standard wizard response of "run screaming in terror to get a wand."

Coileán shoved his hands into his sweatshirt's front pouch. "Hi. Is your sister home?"

"Uh-huh," she mumbled, stepping aside, and I rose from the couch to greet him.

"Lord Coileán? Is something wrong?" I asked, muting the television. Artur, who'd been reading in a recliner, stood as well, her hand darting of its own mind to the sword that wasn't there.

"Could we speak privately?" he replied.

Marcus, who had poked his head out of his room at the knock, beckoned to Beth and headed for the main door. "Come on, girl. Gelato?"

She huffed but followed him. "I'm not *six*. You can't bribe me with ice cream."

"I know a gelateria in Rome that makes it with wine."

"Okay, that'll work."

The door slammed behind them, and Coileán gestured toward the couch. "Sit, please. I have...possibly difficult news."

Trading glances, Artur and I took our seats, and Coileán pushed back his hood and joined us. "I wish there were a delicate way to say this, but I don't know of one. Myrddin is dead."

"How?" asked Artur, her voice almost perfectly neutral.

"By his own hand. I made it clear that I considered him a danger and wasn't inclined to release him from my custody in the near future, and he couldn't cope with incarceration. The cells are warded, you see—there's virtually no magic that leaks in. He kept a bone from a dinner, sharpened it against the wall, and stabbed himself in the neck."

"Jesus," I whispered.

"Yeah. I asked Ros why she didn't warn me, but it seems she really didn't care. Can't imagine why," he said dryly. "Anyway, I wanted to tell you in person, and I'm sorry for your loss."

"It's no loss to me," said Artur. "Nor much to Kitty, I imagine. He *did* try to kill us."

"Believe me, I understand," Coileán replied. "Still, you two are the next of kin, and I have a couple of matters to discuss with you. First thing, what do you want done with the body? Burn it, bury it?"

"Throw it to the wolves, for all I care," my sister muttered.

"Or just make it go away," I said. "I don't plan to set up a memorial for him."

The king nodded. "As you like. Second item: there's the little matter of Afallon."

"What, the island?" asked Artur.

"Exactly. I can't imagine there being anyone with legal title to the place, and while I'm fairly sure that it should belong to the British Crown, what the UK doesn't know won't hurt it. Again, you're the next of kin. As far as I'm concerned, the place is yours."

Artur chuckled softly. "Ah, yes, I can be king of a tiny rock. This would be the 'rex futuris' bit, correct?"

"You may as well. I mean, it's got a tower already—what more do you need?"

She smiled at his sarcasm. "As thrilling as it sounds to defend Afallon against invading Saxons once again, I want nothing of Myrddin's."

"While I appreciate that sentiment, don't be so hasty." Turning to me, Coileán asked, "Don't you people do team-building exercises and such? You could have your own little well-warded summer retreat, ancestral pile and all. I'm sure Toula wouldn't mind helping you redo the wards as needed."

I considered that, then glanced at Artur. "He *did* have a nice yacht."

"Can you see Ted on a yacht?"

"Oh, honey, I have *seen* it."

"Think about it, then do with it as you like," said Coileán. "Raze the tower, start over. I know it's not the same," he told Artur, "but technically, it's the last piece of the Britons' territory that's as yet unconquered. Consolation prize, sure, but seeing as how an all-out war for the British throne would be highly inadvisable, it's the best I can do for you."

She nodded. "Thank you."

"Of course." He rose to go but paused before opening a gate. "One more thing. This may sound stupid, but I've read quite a bit of the Arthurian canon over the years. I, uh…I'm glad you exist."

Her smile that time was genuine.

While Marcus and Beth were away on their dessert run, I took Artur back to the island, where we started a roaring fire on the patio and sat together beneath the arbor trellis—still somehow fruiting, despite the snow—and the shimmering dome of Myrddin's incredible wards. "He would be so pissed to see us here right now," I told her, lifting a glass of champagne in salute.

Artur clinked hers against mine, and we drank. "Seriously," she said once she'd drained her flute, "what are we to do with Afallon?"

"No 'we' about this. The place is yours."

"Kitty—"

"Primogeniture, babe. I suppose you have no choice now but to be the overlord of this lovely little rock. Might even call yourself king. Up to you—there are smaller micronations out there."

She sighed and exchanged her empty glass for a mug of ale. "Then I suppose that I, in my generosity, might permit the Team to visit as schedules dictate."

"Royal favors are always appreciated."

"Naturally. And in exchange, I get continued use of your flat."

"Well, *I'm* not going to be the one to kick King Artur out of my house."

"Mm. Marcus?"

"As I said, my house," I replied. "And we both know how Beth feels, so I guess your bedroom is safe."

Artur mulled that over as she drank. "We could split the island, you know. Haven't you ever wanted to be queen of half a rock?"

"Nope. Just let me visit, okay?"

She put her mug on the flagstones and linked her hands behind her head. "If you don't, little sister, I will be extremely cross."

I smiled to myself and topped up my champagne. "You do know we're about the same age, right? I think you have a year on me."

"Plus fifteen centuries."

"Which you slept through."

"They count," she protested, but grinned. "So...what do we do with this damn island, anyway?"

"I don't know," I said, "but let's keep this patio."

"Done."

"Royal decree?"

"You're damn right it is," said Artur, and toasted the heavens. "Here's to you, Myrddin, you devious old shit.

Like it or not, your king has returned."

"Long may she reign," I added, and drank deeply.

Over the next few months, between field trips with the Team, Artur slipped off to Afallon and gradually reshaped it to her liking. By the time I visited again in April, Myrddin's tower was long gone, replaced by what appeared to be an overgrown hunting lodge straight from an architectural showcase...outside, at least. Artur gave me the tour of the dozen empty bedrooms and the other chambers, explaining their purpose, but admitted that she wasn't sure where to begin with the job. "I've never been one for decoration," she admitted, and so I promised to return over a long weekend and help her finish up the lodge. There was no rush—the wards performed beautifully, and Afallon remained a truly private island, a tiny kingdom unto itself with a largely absentee king. She'd given me free rein of the place, however, which was why it leapt to mind when Hope called out of the blue one afternoon.

We'd barely exchanged pleasantries before she got to the point. "Your dead are very persistent."

"What do you mean?" I asked, frowning at my office couch.

"Ours generally don't bother us. There aren't so many, I suppose, and they can talk to whomever they like, so no big deal. But seeing as most of you don't have talent, they've all started coming to me." She paused, then said, "Your father would like to speak with you and Beth. Would that be possible?"

The next evening, my heart in my throat, I brought our foursome out to Afallon so that we wouldn't be interrupted: Hope, of course, and Beth as requested, but also Artur, who had taken one look at my face once I got off the phone and demanded to know everything. Eschewing the comfortable patio, Hope led us around the unfinished house to a flat patch with a sea view, then sat in the grass and pressed her palms against the ground. "Not so hard as last time, I hope," she murmured as she closed her eyes.

I felt her power begin to flow, like the charge in the air before a thunderstorm, and my sisters and I waited while a shimmering mist appeared and took form. As its features became clear, I had to choke back a sob.

My dad was standing a few feet away, translucent but unmistakable in his favorite overalls, just as I'd last seen him before finding him on the kitchen floor.

It took every ounce of my willpower not to start bawling, but I managed to whisper, "Daddy?"

He beamed. "Hey, princess," he drawled, "how're you doing? Oh, now, don't cry, baby, there's no reason for that," he said hastily, reaching for me, then seemed to remember that he wasn't solid and stayed his hand. "Please don't cry, Kitty, I'm so happy to talk to you."

I smiled tightly, trying to hold the tears at bay. "Me, too. Are you…uh…okay?" I asked lamely.

Daddy nodded. "And that's all I can say on the subject, hon. Some things are forbidden, but…" He paused, mulling over his words. "Don't you worry about me."

Seeing him again, my cocktail of emotions—grief, joy, a few others that didn't fit neatly into boxes—was so overwhelming that I almost forgot about Beth, who stood a touch behind me, uncharacteristically shy. Catching her out of the corner of my eye, I wrapped my arm around hers and tugged her forward. "Daddy, this is Beth—"

"I know," he replied before I could start to ramble, and gave her a big smile. "Hey, sweetheart. That was a really nice job you did at the Games last summer."

Beth coughed to clear her throat. "I…but I didn't win—"

"So? You did well! That girl from Arc 6 is a freak of nature, don't worry about her." His expression turned wistful. "I hate that I've missed everything. You'd have liked the farm. Kitty knew all the good hiding places, and I bet she'd have shown you. Well, maybe *most* of them," he teased, cutting his eyes to me. "But you're growing up so fast, and…and I want you to know I'm proud of you, Beth. You had one hell of a year, but things are bound to get better now, right? Put Montana behind you."

By then, Beth's eyes—Daddy's eyes transposed and fringed with clumpy mascara—were brimming. "I'm not a very good wizard yet," she said, her voice simultaneously apologetic and pleading.

Daddy shook his head. "You are *plenty* good, and even if you weren't, I don't give a damn. I'm just happy to see my girls together and kind of getting along." He extended a hand toward Artur and amended, "My girls, plus. I wish I could claim you, too, but in any case, it's good that you three are together."

My chest clenched at his words, and even though there was so much I wanted to say to him after almost fifteen years apart, I knew I had to broach the topic I was dreading. "Daddy," I said, drawing his attention from Artur, "there's something you need to know—"

"What, that your mama cheated on me?"

I paused, my speech aborted, and swiped at my leaking eyes. "You know about that?"

"There aren't too many secrets on this side."

"So…" I swallowed hard. "You, uh…you know that I—"

"Baby," he said with all tenderness, "I've known since you were three months old. Ran a paternity test on you because the dates didn't work out."

My eyes flew open wide. "You *knew*? All along?"

"Not about the faerie thing, but I knew what I needed to know."

"But you…you kept…"

"Of course I kept you," he said, sounding hurt at the enquiry. "You're my little girl, no matter *what* Eva slept with. I'd never give you up, sweetie. Not for anything."

I couldn't help it. I started to cry in earnest, and Daddy drew closer and tried in vain to stroke my hair. All I felt was a sensation like cold wind along the side of my head, and he soon accepted that the exercise was futile. "You listen to me, young lady," he murmured once I'd brought my tears under control. "I will love you until the end of time, you got that?"

Somehow, I nodded.

"Good. And I can't tell you how proud I am—*my* kid went to friggin' Oxford! You've worked so hard, baby girl. Really, I couldn't be prouder." He reached for me again, swore when he couldn't get a grip, then waited until I looked him in the eye. "Go be amazing," he murmured. "Wow them all, Kitty. I know you can do it. And, uh…that boyfriend of yours is all right."

I laughed through my tears. "Glad you think so. I'm keeping him."

"Atta girl." He stepped back, then blew me a kiss, which I caught and pocketed like I had as a child. "And I mean it, don't let me cause you grief," he said. "You were the greatest joy of my life, Kitty. I hate to see you hurting because of me."

"I miss you, Daddy," I replied, sniffling.

"And I miss you. But sweetie, I'm never far." He smiled again at Beth. "I love you both so much. Be good to each other."

I pulled Beth close and watched until my father disappeared, then plopped into the grass and cried afresh while Hope picked herself up. "I can bring him forth again another day, but I need to train more first," she said, and waited until I calmed sufficiently to take her home.

When I got back to my flat, Marcus was waiting in my bedroom, and I assumed Artur had filled him in. "Do you want company?" he asked as I kicked off my shoes.

Wordlessly, I fell into his arms, and we lay together in bed, both of us still dressed. "I love you, Kitty," he mumbled after a time.

"I love you, too."

We weren't whole, Marcus and me. Honestly, I don't think anyone who's lost someone is ever completely whole again. But that night, we had each other.

I lay there and listened through the door to my sisters' muted voices in the den, then let myself drift, secure in Marcus's arms.

Maybe, I thought, *this is what home feels like.*

And if it wasn't...well, it was close enough.

ACKNOWLEDGEMENTS

And now we meet again here, at the back of the book. Thank you for reading! If you have thoughts, please feel free to reach out—and reviews are always most appreciated.

To the Novel Chicks, here's to surviving the madness of 2020! My continued gratitude goes to Adam Domby for his excellent feedback.

And yes, here's to you, Mom and Dad.

ABOUT THE AUTHOR

When not writing fiction, Ash Fitzsimmons is an appellate attorney and an unrepentant car singer.

Find her online:
www.ashfitzsimmons.com

www.ingramcontent.com/pod-product-compliance
Lightning Source LLC
Chambersburg PA
CBHW020250030726
47499CB00001B/137